The
GIRLS OF
LAKE
EVELYN

Averil Kenny grew up on a dairy farm and began work in the tourism industry at a young age. She studied Education at James Cook University, before completing a Bachelor of Journalism at the University of Queensland. She currently lives in Far North Queensland with her husband and four children. When not dreaming up stories, she can be found nestled in her favourite yellow wingback chair reading and sipping tea, in her library overlooking the rainforest. *The Girls of Lake Evelyn* is her second novel.

Also by Averil Kenny
Those Hamilton Sisters

AVERIL KENNY

The
GIRLS OF
LAKE
EVELYN

Echo Publishing
An imprint of Bonnier Books UK
4th Floor, Victoria House, Bloomsbury Square
London WC1B 4DA
echopublishing.com.au
bonnierbooks.co.uk

Copyright © Averil Kenny, 2022
Cover design by Louisa Maggio Design

Echo Publishing acknowledges the traditional custodians of country throughout Australia. We recognise their continuing connection to land, sea and waters. We pay our respects to elders past and present.

First published in 2022

Printed and bound in Australia by Griffin Press, part of Ovato.

MIX
Paper from
responsible sources
FSC® C009448

The paper this book is printed on is certified against the Forest Stewardship Council® Standards. Griffin Press holds FSC® chain of custody certification SGS-COC-005088. FSC® promotes environmentally responsible, socially beneficial and economically viable management of the world's forests.

n by M   Design, instagram.com/midnight_purple_design
                                                    illion Images

For my dad – dairy farmer, storyteller, heart's guide.
And my mum – businesswoman, singer, best friend.

PART ONE

'Exit, pursued by a bear.'
William Shakespeare

CHAPTER ONE

THERE GOES THE BRIDE

June 1958

The Range Road, Far North Queensland

The lonely headlights of a white Jaguar roadster arced up the darkening range like a fallen star struggling back to the heavens.

Between mountain's sheer face and its breathtaking edge, the roadster slewed, gravel spitting under wheel, engine straining. Six hundred and thirteen bends comprised that Range Road – an ascent so narrow, so vertiginous, only a single direction of traffic was permitted, at allotted times, through manned gates.

Cycads and towering rose gums clung to the rocky ravine, but there were no safety rails. At a plummeting distance below, rippled an endless counterpane of peaks and vales.

A young woman hunched over the steering wheel, squinting through tears, bracing hard against each hairpin turn. The sheath skirt of her going-away suit was rumpled and travel-worn, her butter blonde waves, so carefully set three days earlier, long since flattened by sultry air and cheap hotel pillows. Her ears protested this climb, her stomach revolted, but on she went, sliding and bracing. lashed by an internal chant: *keep going, keep going, keep going.*

There was no turning back for Vivienne George. She had ruined everything.

Balled up in the passenger seat footwell were umpteen unfinished epistles, penned during rest stops. All variations on the same plea . . .

Dear Mother, forgive me—
I must unmake my bed; I will not lie in it.
You cannot force me to marry him, and I will not compel myself.
I need to be free, to figure out what I want.
For once, please let me choose . . .

On the passenger seat, her honeymoon trousseau perched beside a single wedding present – the last left to unwrap. At least she'd saved her mother returning this one gift.

Vivienne skimmed a breathless glance over the rearview mirror, and those dark corners in her wake. She drew up the collar of her jacket, unable to shake the sense that matrimony itself had become a dark beast roaring up the range after her.

But no one could be possibly tailing her up this mountain. Her car had been the very last one through the Bottom Gate before it closed to up-traffic for several hours. And her plan, once so preposterous sounding, had almost reached its zenith.

She'd put half a continent, and a guarded mountain pass, between herself and jilted groom, Howard Woollcott III, heir apparent of the Woollcott winemaking dynasty. Yet, how would she ever outrun the ignominy she'd wrought?

Vivienne saw again the crisp white, gold-embossed wedding invitations sent out to the Who's Who of Australian business, politics and academia . . .

Mrs P. M. George requests the honour of your presence at the wedding of her only daughter, Vivienne Aster . . .

She groaned; the guttural quality of it shocking her. The Society Wedding of 1958, a year in the planning since Howie's dashing, and oh-so-public proposal at the Woollcott Winter Ball, left in tatters on its very eve.

All her life, Vivienne had been reprimanded against scene-making, impropriety, social downfall – admonitions she had dutifully heeded until the eleventh hour of her maiden years, at last discovering she could not obey one more day, not a single hour longer . . .

CHAPTER TWO

PROPRIETY LOST

Three Days Earlier

Centennial Park, Sydney

On the last night of her unmarried life, Vivienne George was willing herself to vanish into the ether.

After a late dinner of thin soup and strained conversation, her mother, Geraldine, had gone directly to her dressing room, to begin her long and elegant toilette for the big day tomorrow.

The *Mother of the Bride's* big day, Vivienne bristled, as she tiptoed by Geraldine's door, firmly shut. In truth, Mother's door was never much open to her. She pictured Mother within: slathering on various unguents and potions, hair in magnetic rollers, carefully wetting her Frownies patches to paste over whatever disobedient wrinkles dared show themselves this momentous evening. So many hours of life traded for the appearance of one shorter lived.

Vivienne scurried on into the formal parlour, where long tables stood bedecked with wedding gifts, all unwrapped and itemised, with gracious notes of thanks already signed from Mrs Howard Woollcott.

Not yet married, and already surrendering her own identity.

She wandered slowly down the middle aisle, hands tracing lightly over silver and gold, lead crystal, Venetian glass, gleaming pearl handles and gilt-edged bone china. From an ornate, pressed metal ceiling, the grand chandelier cast a glittering light over this treasure. She might have been standing amidst a pirate's stolen bounty.

So why did it feel *her* life was about to be robbed of all value?

Panic swelled in Vivienne's throat; a rolling wave of vertigo nearly swept her from her slippers. She gripped the table, setting the glassware atremble, praying for the dizziness to abate.

These attacks – her 'turns' – had been coming ever more frequently, lasting longer each time. Her mother had already chastised her roundly for the spectacle Vivienne made of herself when she took a turn. Not, *suffered* through a turn, or somehow survived it – no, *took* it.

It was unbecoming, Mother said.

But that was just it! Vivienne's mind and body both baulked at *becoming* Mrs Howard Woollcott. Couldn't they delay the wedding, Vivienne had pleaded, until she was sure it was what she really, truly wanted?

Mother had turned her slim back, and set her iron will forthwith against this anguished entreaty. In lieu of mercy, Geraldine proffered a bottle of Dr William's Pink Pills. *For your nervous headache*, she said.

It wasn't *Vivienne's* headache that Mother wanted to quash.

This turn was worse than any before – she thought she might crash through the table entirely. She reached blindly for a chair, lowered herself into it, gripping forehead in hands.

'It's all right,' she soothed herself between short, hard breaths. 'You're all right. It will be over soon.'

But it wouldn't be. Tomorrow was only just the beginning. Then it would never be over, not until death itself released her.

She was recalled from her own whispered comfort, by a susurration far less soothing: the rustle of her mother's nightgown.

Slowly she raised her face, already knowing the hardness she'd find in her mother's pale, blue eyes, nevertheless hoping for something resembling, if not compassion, at least kindness.

Perhaps it was only fitting her worst turn thus far would draw her mother's coldest fury. The lines at Geraldine's pressed lips blanched white.

'*Get up.*' A harsh, sibilant command issued from between closed teeth. 'I will not have any more of this. You're a polished young lady, marrying into one of the finest families in the nation. *Act* like it.'

Vivienne's breath became a pant.

'*Get. Up.*'

She pushed to stand. Behind her back, slim fingers gripped the table.

Geraldine crossed the room, hair rollers bobbing imperiously. Mother's Arpège fragrance enveloped Vivienne; the closest she would ever come to a touch. She blinked rapidly.

Up close, Geraldine's great beauty – begrudgingly bequeathed to her daughter – was marred only by fine lines and silver threads among glossy blonde waves. None of these inevitabilities, had Geraldine consented to.

Wretchedly Vivienne stared at her mother.

Geraldine's cheeks pinched tightener. 'I told you to stop this.'

Help me to stop it! I need more time to think this all through properly, before I sign my life away.

Vivienne's hand flew to her throat, where her voice should reside, were it not for ballooning panic.

Speak, she compelled herself.

'I'm . . . not happy.'

'Stop mumbling.' But Geraldine wasn't really requesting volume, or clarity; rather, cessation.

'Mother, I'm not happy.'

Geraldine's eyes darted around the parlour, scanning reflexively for eavesdroppers. 'Not *happy*?' An incredulous puff of air.

Vivienne gave a tiny headshake. 'I'm most unhappy.'

'Ungrateful, you mean, to possess *everything* a woman could aspire to, and all you've been so finely educated for.'

'Not – everything.'

Geraldine's gaze swept the display of gifts. 'What *more* could you possibly want?'

Her voice dropped to a whisper. 'I . . . hardly know.'

I only know I've never had it. Not from you, not from the man I'm set to marry, not from life itself.

'I've never heard such nonsense and lack of class.' Geraldine's look was pitiless. 'Howard is a good man.'

He probably was, too. Vivienne had no valid dispute with Howie – nor, any longer, a whit of tender feeling for him.

'He will afford you every privilege you could dream of. Secure your future, and your children's too. Make a woman of you.'

'But I don't love Howie.'

'You green, green girl! *Anyone* can fall in love – but very few people may marry within the upper echelons. Marriage is a tactical choice, made in accordance with your cleverness, and aspiration. And *you* have chosen a future surpassing all. You'll simply grow to love Howard, as *I* did your father.'

No, my father died before you ever had to stir such feelings in yourself. And is that all I have to look forward to – outliving a man, beauty preserved?

As if intuiting these thoughts, Geraldine's face twisted into ugliness. Vivienne's eyes dropped to her feet, unable to stand this cruelty revealed.

But she must try, one more time. 'I can't go through with it, Mother. You can't make—'

'Hold your tongue!' A hiss. 'These are last-minute nerves, and nothing more. You *will* stand up there tomorrow, say your vows, smile for the photographers, and be the envy of every woman in this city. And *that* is my final word on the matter. The beautician arrives at six o'clock – get yourself to bed.'

Vivienne watched the hem of her mother's nightgown swirl away.

She choked back an anguished cry, and fled for the roof terrace.

The lights of Sydney were many splendoured from this vantage point, but no stars glimmered above. The day had been full of drizzle, the next would be even drearier. Rain on a wedding day heralded good luck, Mother said. But what did a deluge of tears foretoken?

Where her lungs should have been, was only a wood barrel, wool packed. She kept a hand to her chest, so that she might be reassured her body was, in fact, still breathing for her.

Vivienne's thoughts, habitually given to vacillation, had become a maelstrom. Her hope of a last-minute reprieve utterly dashed. How foolish and cowardly she had been not to try for a breakoff earlier. She had spent so long overthinking her misgivings, she had missed her chance to change course. They were past even the eleventh hour. How *cruel* to drag Howie into this abysmal mess, their marriage would be a misery, a sham. She would spend the rest of her life playing a part she already despised. The thought filled Vivienne with staggering dread.

She wasn't going through with it! No matter what, she would not walk down the church aisle tomorrow, could not sit at that Wedding Breakfast. She must telephone Howie, right now, and tell him it was over! Beg *him* to tell her mother, while Vivienne hid, trembling, in her room.

Geraldine would drag her right out again. Not by the hair – never such a scene – the mere rime of maternal rage would be sufficient. Vivienne never had been able to withstand it.

There was *no way out*.

On the street below, tyres spattered through the gutter as a Jaguar roadster came to a crooked stop. The driver, bounding out somewhat unsteadily with a winking cigarette in hand, had been expected at dinner and was abominably late, as usual.

Vivienne flew from the terrace.

She tumbled down the staircase, frantic to see him again after so many months. There he was, doffing his jacket at the door, turning to her with the doting grin she'd cherished throughout her childhood.

Uncle Felix. Her mother's inveterate bachelor brother. The nearest thing to a father she'd known in her life.

Unfortunately, he wasn't much *in* her life, travelling abroad many months a year, dealing art and dazzling women. But whenever Felix did return, his first call-in was to his only niece. His solicitousness was a blessed relief in a home otherwise devoid of it. Indeed, if not for the fine, fair looks they shared, it was hard to believe Geraldine and Felix were siblings at all. Their natures could not be more different. Nobody had ever spoiled or indulged Vivienne as her beloved uncle did, and she did not care to grow out of it.

The gift he carried this evening, however, pulled Vivienne up short. A wedding present, elegantly wrapped in red and gold brocade. She guessed immediately what it was: the bridal portrait Felix had himself taken, months ago, at his art studio. From now on, would all her beloved uncle's gifts be so unexciting?

Felix, unused to such dismay from his niece, faltered in his cheerful expectation. 'My girl – what *is it*?'

Oh his tone! She broke into a silent, slack-mouthed cry. With a look of horror, Felix ushered her out into the dark courtyard, glancing back for sight of Geraldine. He eased her down at the bistro setting, kneeling before her.

On and on she went crying, and there was nothing quiet or pretty about it. Her face had split apart, and she could not seem to bring it back together.

Felix tutted gently, taking her hand. 'Please tell me.'

Vivienne averted her face, unable to bear the reverse of her mother's implacability.

'Let me guess, then,' Felix said. 'You're worried about your wedding night? You've heard some things, and it doesn't sound your cup of tea at all.'

Vivienne pulled her hand away, face burning. 'Uncle Felix!'

He winked. 'You needn't worry. Howard has more than enough experience to carry you through.'

She began to rise, Felix pushed her firmly back down. 'Come on now, don't be all coy and virginal with your favourite uncle.'

'It's not . . . that. I just don't want to be Howie's wife. I don't think I ever did.'

'Well, you picked a time to announce that. Bit late now.'

'No one's allowed me to speak of my doubts at any time. Not even the man I'm marrying, he won't hear of my feelings. Howie keeps telling me these are normal "maidenly nerves" – but it isn't that! Howie . . . repulses me, Felix. I've fallen completely out of love with him. I don't think I had any sincere feelings to begin with – merely accepted him as the best option for my life.'

'He is your best option.'

'That doesn't mean I *want* him.'

'You don't have to want him, just the appearance of him. You should certainly want his name and wealth, and the freedom it will afford you.'

'Freedom? I'll be *immured* in marriage.'

Felix ventured to take her hand again. 'It's freedom to possess such means and respectability that you can have whatever pretty trinket you like, be esteemed wherever you go, travel abroad for half of every year, and hardly ever have to see the man. Perhaps you might even come along with me, on my next jaunt?'

The barrel round her chest compressed. She gripped the white filigree of the chair, drawing shuddering breaths.

Felix took her shoulders in his hands. 'My poor girl – look at you!' He stroked her cheek. 'Christ, you really are petrified.'

For many long minutes she sucked at the air like this, while Felix stared at her, consternation deepening.

After a time, he muttered, with the finality of a gavel: 'That's it then, you can't marry him.'

'I *told* you I can't.'

'Yes, all right.' He glanced up at the second storey, streaming light. 'We'll go tell Geraldine now, together.'

'I tried, only an hour ago. She won't have it, won't even hear of it! I never can stand up to her!'

Felix gave a bitter laugh. 'Neither can I, my girl. Your mother's a harridan of the highest order. But if you want out, you're just going to have to. Come on, let's do it right away; catch her while she's plucking her chin whiskers. Courage in numbers, and all that.'

'I can't! I'd rather go and tell Howie myself.'

'You can't see him the night before your wedding.'

'There won't *be* a wedding.'

Felix chortled. 'Guess you can see him all you please, then.'

But Vivienne was growing more serious by the second. Could *she* really carry out such an unflinching thing?

'I will go, this instant, to Howie's.' To the Rose Bay mansion that was meant to be hers, too, after their return from honeymooning in the Blue Mountains.

'And then come back here and break it to Geraldine?'

'No! I need to get away from Mother. I can't . . . *I can't* be here when she discovers the wedding is off, much less live with her through the fallout. She'll disown me, or worse; carry me hogtied to the church!'

'I don't see you have another choice. Wasn't that one of the advantages of marrying Howard – escaping to your own house?'

She could admit it: getting out of Mother's house had been the first thought to cross her mind when Howie dropped to one knee in that opulent ballroom, to thunderous applause.

Panic pulled tighter. 'I have nowhere I can go.'

Felix tapped his lips with an index finger. 'We must be able to think of somewhere you can stay for a few days, until things simmer down. What about with your maid of honour?'

'*Deirdre?*' She made a choking noise. Geraldine had chosen her own goddaughter for the honour, over the few acquaintances Vivienne had offered from her boarding school days. 'Every time I've tried to influence, much less change, any part of the wedding plans that snitch runs straight to Mother.'

'Don't you have any friends of your own?'

'None that I can count on for this! Who will want to be associated with the scandal?' The wedding of Vivienne George and Howard Woollcott III would fall from the Society Event of 1958 to Society Shock of the Century. Think of it: a Woollcott *jilted*!

'I need to get away, to a place where no one can persuade me into anything. Put a buffer between myself and Mother.'

'I'd take you in myself, but you know Geraldine will be over like a shot. I'd have to barricade my front door, and then we'd live under siege! Besides, I've got another trip coming up, I can't be there to look after you.'

A sob burst forth. 'I won't stay *anywhere*, then! I'll jump in my car, and drive and drive until I run out of fuel, and wherever that is, I'll camp out on the side of the road!'

'Not entirely a bad idea. I knew I taught you to drive for some purpose. Listen, though: if you refuelled instead of running out, you might actually find a hotel.'

'That's exactly what I'll do! I'll drive south—'

'Go north, towards Brisbane.'

'North, then, and I'll find somewhere I can settle for a while – and really think my life through.'

Felix chuckled. 'I don't recommend that business. Best to leave all the thinking for after the living is done.'

Her whole life, Vivienne had prized cautious restraint above all else; every decision preceded by second-guessing, and followed up by rumination. How different might her existence, her happiness, have been if she'd acted impetuously?

'I am going to run away.'

'Sounds like you are.'

'I might not ever come back.'

'You'll get tired of shoddy hotels and the hoi polloi soon enough.'

'I'll find somewhere private to stay, then!'

Felix's hand, nursing hers, gave a little jump. He cocked his head, as though hearing a far off cry. 'I'll be damned. Listen, I don't want to get your hopes up, but I *might* know a place that fits the bill . . .'

This time, her hand leapt.

'It's far enough away from your mother, and the bomb crater you're about to leave. A place where you might do all that "thinking" of yours.' He hammed up an expression of distaste.

'*Where?*' She couldn't keep the breathlessness from her voice.

'Now, hang on a bit – I don't want to disappoint you, if it turns out to be impossible. I'd have to make some calls first, arrange some things . . .'

Her uncle might not have meant to get her hopes up, but there they were; slowly inflating.

Felix considered her – really considered her – as though weighing up her courage and capability. He seemed to see something in Vivienne she didn't herself feel. 'All right,' he said, decisive now. 'Let's give it a shot. I'll head up and keep Geraldine distracted. See if I can't loosen the old girl up with some special Felix nightcaps. You go pack some things–'

'My wedding trousseau has been packed for weeks.'

'Grab that.' He looked her up and down in her silk pyjamas. 'That's very cute, but have you got something else you can wear for the road?'

'My going-away suit is laid out next to my wedding gown.' *Oh, the irony.*

'Jolly good. And my car has a full tank, so you'll take that.'

Felix's cherished roadster? She couldn't possibly! Felix had pressed many extravagant gifts upon her in his time, but this was beyond anything.

'You will so take it,' he said, answering her look. 'What, were you planning to steal Geraldine's car?'

She flushed. Mother was right: she was as green as they came.

'You'll borrow my car – for once she will be sedately driven – and that way both my girls are taken care of.'

The more Felix assumed direction of her escape, the bolder Vivienne felt her nerve to be.

'You get straight on the road now – go directly to Howard's, break the poor fellow's heart – then on you mosey, to Brisbane. I'll try and give you an hour's head start before your mother finds out.' Felix mimed a full body shudder. 'Once you're over the border tomorrow, I want you to call me. I'll have the next step organised for you.'

Felix stood, pulling her up by the hands. He drew close, squeezing her cold hands. 'Are you really sure you want to do this, my girl?'

She'd never been surer of anything.

CHAPTER THREE

LATE CHECK-IN

June 1958

Atherton Tablelands

Darkness had overtaken the roadster. Vivienne was climbing now into a mist-swathed lushness, where crisp mountain air carried the call of whipbirds.

At the top of this interminable mountain road, she would pass through the Top Gate – then press her foot down, and roar towards sanctuary. A place wherein to wait while her mother's rage subsided, and her shame abated. Surely one of these things would come to pass?

She swerved around a last wall of rock, and clear ahead spied the Top Gate, with a line of cars awaiting their descent; headlights aglow.

Vivienne slowed to a putter as she neared the man at the gate, directing her through. She straightened in her seat, set her face in trained pleasantness, powering forward.

Nearly past.

The gatekeeper, however, stepped out in front of her bonnet. He opened his notebook, and began copying her numberplate. Her heart flailed beneath her ribs as he gestured for her to wind down the window.

Oh goodness, what did he want?

Vivienne tugged her skirt to her knees, straightened her shoulders. The gatekeeper leaned down to peer under the convertible roof. In the gatehouse behind, a radio was playing Perry Como's 'Catch a Falling Star'.

She drew back into the shadowed interior, swallowing compulsively.

'Evenin',' he said.

'Good evening, sir.'

'You're the last car up the range.'

Had he *really* pulled her over just to state the obvious?

Politeness forbids any display of resentment. 'It would appear so.'

'Have some problems on the way up?'

'None at all, thank you.'

'Took your time, but. Got all these people waiting on you. I was about to send the young fella down to rescue you from overheating. You lady drivers!'

The polished surface throws back the arrow. 'Yes, I am sorry.'

The gatekeeper bounced back and forward on his heels. 'Never seen you pass through before, I'd remember.'

'I'm just journeying up to family.' A lie. Where she was headed, there wasn't a familiar soul waiting.

He let out a low whistle. 'Well, we don't get many glamour pusses like you on the range.'

Affronted, Vivienne reached to wind up the window – only to realise the man was patting her car, and not meaning her at all.

The gatekeeper called over-shoulder, 'Bob! You've got to come see this roadster—'

A hulking shape emerged from beyond the gate.

She blinked tears away, breath shortening. 'You really *must* excuse me. I am due for supper.'

The man stared at her, chewing his lip. 'Where'd you say you're from?'

She sank deeper, shoulders hunching into a shrug.

The gatekeeper went on staring.

Just let me go – please!

A single car horn from the waiting line of down-traffic punctured his musing. The gatekeeper harrumphed and straightened, patting the roof of her car one last time.

'You watch out for wildlife, ma'am, wouldn't want a big roo dent in the front of a Hollywood car like this.'

He stood aside, allowing the roadster to purr on. Vivienne looked straight ahead; chin raised, hands trembling on the wheel.

In her rearview mirror, she watched the stream of tail lights slowly disappear around the first of those myriad corners. The direction had reversed; no one could catch her for at least several hours.

And nobody on Earth but Felix knew where she would be hidden.

She hadn't, as it worked out, spoken to Howie before fleeing. At least, not directly. For when she'd arrived in Rose Bay, her fiancé had not even been at home. 'Out celebrating,' his housekeeper, Wilma, had answered with a purse of pure disapproval. Not at Howie, no fear, but rather Vivienne's impudence for thus appearing: after dinner, on her wedding eve.

Vivienne had not been permitted entry to wait for him, and she would have been risking her escape anyway to do so. From Wilma, she had accepted a pad of Woollcott monogrammed writing paper – and written Howard, instead. The briefest note, with which to break a betrothal . . .

Howie, I cannot go through with it. I know you've sensed the change in me these last months – though you've been in staunch denial. I am not the wife for you. I would make us both miserable, and tarnish the Woollcott name doing it. Disgraceful and cowardly as my actions are, they will save us both from future disaster. Tell them all that I am recovering, privately, from a bad case of nerves. And please, say you will forgive me . . .

She wondered if Wilma had even waited until the roadster roared out of the drive before opening the folded note.

There had been hounds, it felt, on her heels ever since. The prickling sense of relentless pursuit remained unabated even after three days, and fifteen hundred miles.

Vivienne roared up and down an undulating dirt road, across tiny creek bridges, past distant farmhouse lights; ever braced for a kangaroo to spring through her sweeping headlights.

Where was this 'Barrington Downs' Felix had sent her to? Was she lost? *Perhaps* he'd meant Barrington Tops near Sydney, and she'd been too stupid to understand him on the telephone.

Hadn't that been the hardest phone call she'd ever made? Ringing from a roadside hotel in Brisbane, hours after her wedding breakfast had failed to take place, to ask her uncle what she should do next. Felix had been at his own home, awaiting her call – *thank heavens* – still; her heart nearly stopped when he picked up.

Felix endured her sobbing remorse for a time, before silencing her with a phlegmatic chuckle. 'You don't really regret this – do you?'

No, she didn't. She was deeply ashamed, but she wanted to keep on doing it. The proof: she did not verbalise one word of concern about either her mother, or Howard, much less how the aborted ceremony and festivities were being handled. Her mind, however, ran flat out with questions . . .

Is everyone terribly angry with me? Shall I ever be forgiven? Will they come and drag me home again?

She voiced only one query. 'What place have you found?'

His answer shocked her into aghast silence: *The Atherton Tablelands!* Agricultural mountain land in the far tropical north of the country, known only for tin mining, logging, and cows. How might Vivienne George – city girl, born and raised – fit into such a place?

'Be thankful I can even offer you this,' Felix said. 'I had to pull some strings.'

'I'm more grateful than you could possibly know ... but how can how I *ever* repay you?'

'No, don't you worry yourself about that right now, my girl. Uncle Felix will look after you. Listen; I'm sending you up the mountain to Barrington Downs – a small dairy village, right out of the way. I've secured a private lodge, tucked away in rainforest, right on a lake. It's not marked on any map, no neighbours, only a narrow dirt road into the place.'

'Sounds charming,' she lied. But it was just a place to *think*, while she figured out a future of her own choosing.

'You'll find the keys in Barrington proper,' Felix said. 'They'll be left at the front of Niall Jeffries' Corner Shop, on the main street. He's the lodge caretaker.'

'This chap will just *leave* the keys lying on the footpath for me?'

'People are trusting out in the sticks. I'll also organise with Niall for a basket of supplies to be waiting for you, enough to keep you going a few days. In fact, to save you going back into town, I'll sort out a weekly delivery of groceries. You won't have to see a soul.'

Felix seemed to have thought of everything. But her biggest concern remained unuttered, unanswered: how long, exactly, would Felix let her stay hidden there before she would be marched home to face the music?

'Who else knows I'll be hiding there?'

'Apart from me, only Niall. But the fellow has taken care of this lodge for years, he understands our need for discretion very well. No one will find you; I promise.'

'What a stroke of luck. How did you *find* this place?'

'Ah, that's a long story. The lodge was built before the war by my old friend, now living overseas. Rudy Meyer is his name—'

'Not *the* Rudy Meyer of musical theatre fame?'

'*The*, indeed. With your love of singing, you would be familiar with his work.'

'But how are you acquainted?' She shouldn't be surprised; no connection was too far-fetched for Felix Brinsley.

'Good old Rudy and I go back a long way. He invited me up to his lodge for a time, during the war. In those days, Rudy was entertaining the Australian and American troops based in the region, with some theatre productions.'

Vaguely she recalled something of this. 'But is the lodge well known? I don't want to stay in a property that will attract sightseers.'

'Sightseers! It's in the middle of nowhere. The place has hardly had a guest this last decade. There's a bit of history with it, the dopey locals won't go near the spot.'

'*What* history?'

'No, don't set your mind against it, Vivienne. It will suffice for your needs.'

'So I am reduced to a deserted forest hovel.'

'Just the ticket,' Felix laughed, 'for a woman disappearing off the face of the Earth.'

The small town of Barrington Downs was exactly where Felix had promised, and every bit the backwoods Vivienne anticipated. Apart from a thrumming country pub, and a milk bar spilling jazz music, the streets were empty. The Corner Shop was closed, but her basket of essentials was sitting out on the veranda, tied with a gift bow. She encountered no one as she slipped to and from the car, gratified that another of Felix's assurances was proving true: she wouldn't have to see a soul here.

Safely back in her car again, she was out of the township in minutes, already dusting her hands of the place.

Now, where's this lodge? It was meant to be hidden in rainforest, but all she saw was barbed-wire fencing, and never-ending hill country. Had they razed the rainforest to the ground for pastureland? As she rocketed up over another hillock, the bulky white shape of a cow moving in its paddock made her cry out.

Finally, thick rainforest appeared on her right-hand side, running parallel to the interminable fencing.

She nearly missed the turn-off. There was no marking, no signage; only a brief slit in the trees, and a narrow, rocky road, channelling deep into the forest.

Vivienne entered, holding her breath as the car rocked and bounced. Branches slapped at the car; potholes sought to sink her wheels completely. Moonlight did not breach the canopy.

'Oh, this is hideous.'

The lodge took her by surprise, looming up suddenly in the dark forest, blacker than the night. She sensed, rather than saw, a heavy wood structure three storeys high, with a steeply pitched roof aspiring for the towering canopy itself.

The roadster rolled to a stop. Vivienne remained in her seat, peering up through her windscreen at the balconies jutting high above. There was no light to guide her, no welcoming bellhops to carry her few bags, no concierge to trust she would enjoy her stay.

She opened her car door to an ambush of noise. Strident night calls and understorey scurries; the distant, lumbering passage of a nocturnal mammal. Somewhere, close by, water ran on and on.

Up the stairs she tottered, dragging her trunk. An unknown creature – oversized rat, or diminutive kangaroo – jumped across the porch as her feet touched the landing. She yelped, then stood stock-still, listening to the inordinate crackle and crash of its flight across the underbrush; infinitely magnified in this clearing of forest giants.

Above the door, a carved wood sign named the lodge as, simply, 'Sylvan Mist'. The key had to be wrenched around hard before the door gave up its stubborn guard. Inside, acrid mustiness engulfed her. She fumbled for the nearby wall switch, and held her breath waiting for the sconces to burst into light.

Weak, yellow light seeped into the lodge, leaving many shadowed corners. She stood in a large, lobby-style room, with a grand staircase to the next floor. The exotic tropical timber seemed to suck light from the room, the gloom only magnified by the dark forest peering through the many louvred windows.

She spied the kitchen through a passage off to the right, and heaved her basket over to a central island with pots and pans hung above. She ought to unpack it, but couldn't find the will even for something so simple. All she wanted was a place to lay her weary head.

Vivienne wandered about the lower level looking for a bedroom, unable to evade the putrid mildew and unnerving gaze of the undressed windows. Even glimpsed in peripheral vision, her pale, slim reflection was more spectral than she could take.

She began now to notice an abundance of torchs placed around the lodge. In this grand room alone, there were torches atop the Ascherberg piano, another leaning against a voluptuous vase of peacock feathers; and two more set upon the oak gramophone cabinet. She'd never seen so many torches. And for what purpose – did they routinely lose electricity here? Why would occupants be so concerned with having light at hand? What could be *out* here?

Worry clamped around her forehead.

She drifted up the grand staircase, deeper into the lodge. On the fingers trailing the balustrade, her engagement ring scraped wood. Vivienne whipped her hand back.

She found a library occupying most of the upper floor, full of odorous, ponderous books. On any normal day, the sight of so many books at her disposal might have touched her spirit. But this was no normal day.

The forest gaped in here, too, and the ornate fireplace and Turkish rug seemed out of place in the humid fug. Vivienne left the library sighing. There were no curtains on *any* of the windows. She was wholly exposed to the forest; a small, distressed creature in a windowed box. The watched.

Perhaps she'd begun to see the point of those torches, after all.

She found the master bedroom on the top floor, and here she stood for a thankful moment before a four-poster bed with closable curtains. One place, at least, in this lodge where she might escape the gawking forest.

Vivienne washed and changed, leaving her going-away suit to lie in a crumpled heap. There was no need to carefully spot-clean and bathroom-steam her travelling outfit this night: her marathon journey was accomplished, and she would not be going back.

Too weary now to perform her face-care routine, she left her beauty case unopened on the dressing table, and stole back to the kitchen for food. Taking a cloth-wrapped parcel at random from the top of her basket, she retreated to the safety of the canopy bed. Tomorrow she would sort the rest out.

She'd hoped the bag might contain a simple sandwich, but inside found handmade cheeses instead. Hardly a dinner for Vivienne George, who'd been taught early to eschew pudding with feigned indifference. *Slim and trim, that's what a woman should be.*

Oh, but they were scrumptious cheeses! Delicately flavoured, dissolving on her tongue like a dream. She sat in the darkness, shivering, and scoffed the lot.

CHAPTER FOUR

STAR LIGHT, STAR BRIGHT

June 1958

Barrington Downs

In a crooked little farmhouse, hidden by rolling hills of green, a young woman woke to a dream of stars.

Josephine Monash had been waiting all the painfully drawn-out weekend for Monday morning. On this day, dawning more slowly than any before, the theatre reviews would be out in the *Tablelands Sun*. Josie Monash's local theatre production of *A Doll's House* would be reviewed by none other than esteemed theatre critic, Hugo Bernard, who had recently toured the regional theatre offerings from faraway Sydney. All Josie's vivid hopes and dreams had come to rest on one man, one day, and one hopefully well-starred review.

She wanted to be in Barrington outside the Newsagency the very instant it opened. Had her father agreed, Josie would happily have camped out the front of the storefront overnight. Taking no for an answer had never been her strong suit, and Josie was proud of herself for having made it through the whole weekend, with as much patience as she could muster. That is to say: a little.

Before tearing into town, Josie had first to clean the farmhouse, serve honeyed porridge to her father on his return from milking the cows, and make waxed paper-wrapped lunches for her three older brothers:

26

Reg, Ernest and Owen. Stroppy at having to delay her quest, she wasted no time buttering the bread or cutting triangles. The corned beef was shoved in without the relish they all adored.

She might have left the whole task to Reg's new wife, Daphne, now living in the crowded farmhouse too, but, as a rule, Josie did not cede any ground to her sister-in-law. Daphne needed no encouragement to martyr herself resentfully on a domestic hearth Josie had never invited her to. Let it be known, and Josie frequently did, the sooner Reg finished building – correction, *started* building – his own farmhouse, and took Daphne off to live in it, the better. Indeed, Josie frequently wondered why Reg couldn't build the farmhouse just for Daphne – and send her off to live in it alone.

Josie had always intended her brothers to stay, if not boys, bachelors. Just because she sometimes found it overwhelming caring for four men in her long-lost mother's place, it did not mean she would assent to her replacement by any other woman. Especially not by Daphne West, who was a limpet. Fetching, sure, and sporting an enormous belly impossibly soon after the wedding to boot, but a blight on Josie's halcyon realm.

Josie knew her place in the world: the very centre of it. *Too big for her britches*, her brothers often laughed. But it was with cheerful control she ran her family of men, her merry band of amateur actors, and, seemingly, most of Barrington itself.

Made mindful once more of the blessings she did not care to share, Josie made sure to slip a home-baked shortbread into each of her brothers' lunch bags, along with a scribbled wisecrack. Daphne might be capable of cutting buttered sandwiches with put-upon sighs, but she didn't have a sense of humour to save herself. Josie added her name to each of the lunch bag notes – lest her brothers forget who brightened this place up, and always had.

Rightful order thus maintained; she hurried off to bathe. Whistling excitedly, she dressed up for town in her favourite boat-neck fuchsia dress – indeed her only dress fit for town. Hidden beneath her bodice, hung her mother's ornate gold heart locket.

The locket had lived on her father's bedside bureau for as long as Josie could remember, and as soon as her sticky little fingers could reach it, she began to steal away with it to play, while her father's back was turned. In recent years, flagrant ownership had become her game – though, out of respect for her father's grief, Josie returned the necklace to his bedside at the end of each day's wearing.

Taking the Ford coupé utility, she bumped her way down the long farm drive lined with pines. She passed the old Monash farmhouse ruins, nothing more now than a rusting corrugated iron pyramid fallen to the earth, with the old stone chimney alongside, and tall grass enclosing it. Here, Josie always tapped her necklace to ward off spirits. One, in particular.

When her brothers were still young, before the old roof finally collapsed, they had teased Josie it was haunted by a long-haired wraith. Though her brothers swore they still occasionally glimpsed this ghost on their dawn pilgrimage to the dairy, Josie had long since grown into understanding. Those young Monash boys had been traumatised more by the death of their mother than any ghoul haunting cow paddocks.

Nevertheless, she could never pass that felled roof without double-checking for stockinged legs, with ruby slippers upon them. Was she conflating her brothers' farm ghost with her favourite girlhood movie, *The Wizard of Oz*? You bet. There wasn't much Josie couldn't make more theatrical.

Over the stock grid she rattled, and on to Barrington through rolling pleats of bucolic green, presided over by volcanic cinder cones. It was God's Country, set so close to the heavens, they frequently seemed to live in a cloudland. And though it was officially winter, the sublime days had not yet asked more than the odd cardigan.

Josie parked on Main Street, which sloped around a wide, central island and was lined with brightly hued cottage storefronts, all verandaed and hung with baskets of perennial flowers. Tropical plants, large leafed, in flamboyant reds and pinks and oranges flourished in every garden bed. Pastel bunting lined the street.

Outside the Newsagency, magazine and newspaper posters lined the veranda. Princess Grace featured prominently this week, holding her baby, Albert, beaming maternal serenity and unassailable beauty.

Josie stood a moment, studying the princess's platinum flawlessness – so different from her own shiny, mahogany ponytail and heavy fringe. Beside the princess, Josie was a countrywoman's Audrey Hepburn. Her brown eyes, already bold before lining, had never fluttered serenely; were always flashing, ever frank. There was no point holding the princess's alabaster skin against her own, since Josie bore a generous splash of freckles across her nose and cheeks. The effect, combined with hypermobile brows, nose-crinkling smile and petite height, sometimes gave Josie a doll-like appearance. Josie made sure no one dared such condescension in describing her.

She hadn't come to moon over royalty, rather her own big moment in the spotlight. She marched inside for her papers, anticipation inflating her chest.

At the mere sight of her, chronically nervous Clarence Reece, behind the counter, was already mopping at the shiny dome of his bald head with a handkerchief, and beginning his infernal dithering. As dear as Clarence was, there was only so much hemming and blathering a person could tolerate. Nevertheless, Josie was proud of Clarence for working on the front counter, when he could have replaced his wife Elsie out back.

'Have you read it, yet?' Josie said, hurrying coins out of her pouch.

'Read it . . . first thing,' Clarence finally got out between sputters. His white hanky went from temple to top lip.

'Don't tell me anything,' Josie cried. 'I want to read it for *myself*.' She heaved her pile of newspapers off the counter – wishing she had the funds to purchase even more copies.

'Your latest novel came in too,' Clarence said, producing a Mary Stewart book from under his counter. She swiped it up, beginning to turn away. Only the hurt crease of Clarence's brow reminded Josie she had shown none of her usual excitement.

'Thank you, Clarence,' she said, patting his hand. 'I've been hanging out for *months*.' She leaned in close so that shrewish Elsie Reece, no doubt loitering just out of sight, might be deprived of her next hushed words. 'By the way, your front window needs a clean. There are grubby handprints all over it.'

Clarence shot a swift look towards the back room. 'Will do, thanks, Josie.'

Elsie Reece materialised at the back-room door as though called by name, her lips already puckered into a fierce purse for the day. *Yellsie*, Josie called her privately – poor Clarence. Outside the Newsagency, she tapped the offending windowpane for Clarence's benefit, and departed with a cheeky wave.

Excitement coursed through her veins, but Josie fought the urge to plonk down on the pavement, spreading newspaper everywhere. Triumph, delayed by just a few more minutes, would be *all* the sweeter.

Up Main Street she went, at a clipping pace. Short she might be, but Josie could outpace the tallest of women – she had twice the energy of most, and took three times as many steps. Into each shop she'd bustle now, her convivial laughter rushing ahead to announce her: warm as sunshine, gusty as a breeze.

First, into Niall Jeffries' Corner Shop for sugar and flour. Niall, still the town show pony well into middle age, had scored the major role of Torvald Helmer in Josie's latest production. The very least he owed her then this Monday morning was a vote of thanks. Niall wasn't in, though. No doubt swaggering around town somewhere garnering his own accolades. He did that, even without a play.

Josie was forced to leave her grocery list with his beautiful shop girl, Laura, who confounded Josie with her unwillingness to hold eye contact or conversation – no matter how thickly Josie piled on the charm.

Laura was a frustrating mystery. The young woman had accepted Niall's job and lodgings after her good-for-nothing father gambled away their family home, then drank himself to death in short order. It was a sensible move on Laura's part, cinching a job and accommodation securely in one, but she was too shy for front counter work. Laura had joined Josie's theatre group in recent months, seemingly at her employer's insistence. Perhaps Niall hoped Josie would bring Laura out of herself? Josie was good, but not a miracle worker.

After a largely one-sided conversation, Josie swept out again, seething that Laura did not even *ask* about their theatre review.

Next, she popped her head in at Peggy West's Flower Shop for a quick bite of gossip from its most glamorous purveyor. Sometimes, when Josie listened especially avidly, Peggy would gift her a full-lipped, pink-tipped rose to wear – but not today. Josie dashed away when she spied Peggy, bright auburn head bent over the newspaper, running her long, red nails down the page. The review was *Josie's* to savour in full, she would not have it summed up for her, even in Peggy's outrageous style.

Midway down Main Street, Josie scowled to see a familiar Bedford OB Bus double parked in front of the Butter Factory, decanting its passengers.

'How many times,' she muttered, striding towards the driver's window, 'have I *told* Athol not to hog car parks?'

Athol Harford was only the tour operator still coming to Barrington, and had been doing so since the thirties. His bus was known colloquially as the Chook Chaser – though that was more about Athol than his vehicle.

Sitting behind the driver's seat was a middle-aged man in a safari uniform, replete with epaulettes and long socks. At the sight of Josie, Athol leaned out of his window to flap his newspaper at her. 'Can you believe it, Josie? What do you have to say to *this*?'

Josie swerved away in a hasty arc. 'Want to read it for myself. Go park properly!'

Crossing Main Street over the central island, she sang out good morning to a volunteer just unlocking Barrington's rather unique community library. It had been Josie's brainchild, to convert the rectangular concrete air raid shelter left over from the war for use as an unstaffed library comprised entirely of donated books. The town had voted to convert the shelter to a library, instead of a public amenities block, with an overwhelming majority. Josie suspected the naysayers of illiteracy, and weak bladders.

The shelter, once stark and ugly, had magenta bougainvillea climbing its sides, pink cordylines abounding at the front entrance, plenteous books within. Josie had been Member 001, as proudly typed on her borrowing card. She was also the town's biggest donor of romantic suspense fiction.

Lastly, she scooted by Rita Caracella's Old Curiosity Shop to check the front window display for treasures, and to reassure herself Rita hadn't sold *her* long-coveted typewriter to some other ungrateful sod. For many months, Josie had been pinching pennies for one of Rita's modern plunders: a coral pink, Smith-Corona Silent Super typewriter.

One day, Josie would fulfil her playwriting dreams upon that very typewriter.

Frustratingly, almost as soon as Josie thought she had saved enough coin from her farm wages to afford the typewriter, up would come some necessary expense for the family. Continued novel buying, justified to herself by subsequent donation, wasn't helping her savings, either. Josie couldn't make such a decadent purchase, when so many dear people depended on her. Still, every week she came to this window, held her breath and hoped to spy her Silent Super.

She breathed out. There was her pink darling, patiently waiting to be claimed.

Like the good omen it was, the sight of her Smith-Corona sent Josie scooting up the road to the teahouse, radiating joy. It wasn't enough just to receive a good review, one must also be *seen* to receive it – and Josie knew the teahouse would be full of farm wives, and other such useful news-spreaders, on a Monday morning.

As she weaved through the busy teahouse, Josie admired her dress and perky figure, in the ornate wall mirrors. Her nose-crinkling smile was in full scrunch as the greetings came thick and fast. Nobody had missed her arrival. She nabbed a table by the front window, in a flood of morning sunshine, and spread her newspaper out eagerly.

Now Josie could digest the review she'd been waiting all weekend to feast her eyes upon. Her hands trembled as she cast aside the hard news and social pages, and reached for the arts section. Her eyes ran carefully down each column, searching out Hugo Bernard's byline.

Midway down the page, Josie came to a screeching stop.

LOCAL TALENT ON NATIONAL STAGE, read the article headline – and beneath it, from a small headshot, a sandy-haired young man smiled confidently back. A handsome and familiar face, well loved in Barrington.

Miles Henry.

Josie glanced around quickly, then allowed her fingers to lightly touch his portrait. *Damn*, he'd only improved his best features since they'd graduated Barrington High School together some five years earlier. That roguish, smiling downturn at the corner of his tawny eyes more pronounced, and the expressive dark brows better groomed; all the better for conveying incorrigible wit. That was why audiences, particularly the fairer sex, purportedly so loved Miles: his country boy charm, glimmering with wicked humour. Greatly it diverted Josie to see Miles lauded for the mischievousness that had landed him in so much trouble from their school master back then.

At the jangle of the teahouse door, her fingers jerked away from the photo, to twitch guiltily in her lap. She read the accompanying article with a heart aching on two counts of longing.

The first, for the rascally friend who'd grown up two farms over, had shared her ride to school on the back of Mr Henry's milk truck – the 'milk bus', they'd dubbed it – along with top billing on several Barrington High drama productions, but had never considered, much less approached Josie as anything more than a farm paddock chum.

The second pang was one of envy, for a life and opportunities that could never be hers. After senior year, Miles had gone away to a prestigious drama school in Sydney – proudly funded by his family – and had enjoyed several years' success on the stage, culminating in this latest: a lead role just finished in *Gumtree Gully*, which had run in an old baroque theatre, to sell out shows and stellar reviews.

Josie and Miles had collaborated – *competed* was a better word – on many theatre club productions. While they'd both lived for the stage, Miles alone had gone on to make a life *of* it, while Josie was still here in lowly Barrington – correction, *lowing* Barrington – milking cows, and her aptitude for amateur theatre both. Imagine how ridiculous Miles

Henry would think Josie Monash, clamouring for a meagre newspaper review in their local rag, when everyone knew Rosa Henry clipped articles about her son from the national broadsheet.

Miles would think no such thing. He was kind and affable, and he loved the theatre too much to begrudge *anyone* a slice of it. He had a head start on Josie, that was all. He was a man, for starters, unencumbered, hailing from a well-off family, not to mention the good looks bestowed upon him through no conspiring of his own. It wasn't Miles's fault he'd had all the luck, and she wouldn't resent him for it.

Besides, when Rosa Henry clipped today's article from the *Tablelands Sun*, she might accidentally include Josie's review too and pin it to her feature wall. Then, one day, when Miles might visit home, he'd read about her astounding local success and finally see in Josie what she'd always seen in herself. Then he'd ask, no, *implore* her to come to Sydney, and share her gifts with the world . . .

There was nothing Josie enjoyed so much as letting her imagination run off with her. But it was time to rein it in, she was here for something far more important. Josie moved past Miles's article with a decisive nod. Her fingers went to touch her gold locket talisman, hidden beneath pink fabric.

And there it was. A DIRE HOUSE, read the title of Hugo Bernard's review.

Clever, Josie thought, though she didn't know how it was going to be clever, only that every review Hugo Bernard penned was *clever* – everyone with taste said so.

Her eyes began to scan Hugo's review, but for a few moments her brain baulked at interpreting the words for her heart jumping up and down, asking to hear the good news.

No, Heart, you don't want to hear this. It's harsh and mean-spirited, and even if some of it is true, you shouldn't have to hear it.

Very reluctantly did her brain begin to make sense of the words.

'One always must make allowance for amateur theatre,' Hugo Bernard wrote, 'but Josephine Monash's provincial production begs for more allowance than any theatregoer should have to give, sinks under the weight of its own earnestness; is not so much callow as cack-handed.'

Josie's hand moved from heart of gold, to protect her very human organ. Twang came the arrows . . .

'Miss Monash completely misinterprets Ibsen's masterful work . . .'

'Her actors are lacklustre at best, torpid on the whole.'

'. . . one must wonder whatever emboldened a theatre director of so little talent to attempt a piece of such majesty.'

Twang, twang, twang!

Josie gaped up at the tables surrounding her in the busy teahouse, gentle chatter and clink of china and tap of spoon suddenly intolerable.

Mr Bernard cared nothing for full teahouses, though. On he went: 'Miss Monash's production is rivalled in its dreadfulness only by the town's "theatre" itself, a decrepit World War II hangar called, unimaginatively: the Igloo.'

Decrepit?! Barrington was darned proud of its Igloo! The hangar, clad in corrugated iron, was originally used as an army military store depot, when a hundred thousand Australian and American servicemen had been based on the Tablelands for jungle training. The Igloo had been reappropriated as a community hall after the war ended, and was now used for everything from the annual Dairy Queen Ball, Saturday night dances, wedding receptions, and the always eventful town meetings. And she'd have him know: their Igloo, humble though it might be, was the *only* venue in town fit for a theatre production!

Not quite *true . . . but beside the point.*

Mr Bernard had saved the cruellest arrow – though it was hard to award it over all the others – for his summation . . .

'They *say* Barrington's local lake is cursed, pulling the town's young beauties into her depths, and the townsfolk live in fear of it. But if there's one thing to sink in that town it will be the Barrington Theatre Company, while ever under the inept captainship of Miss Monash.'

Josie leapt to her feet on a cry of outrage, crumpling newspaper pages up, spilling the milk jug, and fled the teahouse.

CHAPTER FIVE

LAKE EVELYN

'This is the forest primeval'
Longfellow

Vivienne woke at first seeping light, with a stiff neck and aching hips. The mountain air had proven cool during the night, and her bed sheet inadequate. There was a fat, false eyelash crawling across her pillow. She eased herself from the bed carefully, as though not to disturb a fellow bedmate.

Though daylight had stolen in, the forest had not given up its shadows. She was relieved, nonetheless, to sight dense greenery instead of gaping blackness, and her own haunted reflection. She pressed close to the window, scanning the forest. Not a soul. Something almost like relief breathed, fogged up the glass.

She reached for her beauty case. First, to freshen up! But her hand wavered. On a crystal plate atop the dresser, precisely laid out, was an elegant, brass-filigreed vanity set. The kind a stylish woman would treasure; incongruous with the masculine styling of this lodge. Vivienne turned the brush over to find long, raven hair thickly caught in the bristles.

A hairbrush well used, and waiting.

Vivienne's lips drew back on a repelled grimace. To have trespassed in another woman's bedroom like this! Hurriedly she removed her case and trunk. Best find somewhere else to unpack for the duration of her stay.

She'd left every light on, and she tiptoed quietly downstairs now, extinguishing each one in turn. The lodge was a little less imposing in the subdued glow of morning, but she could not bear to tarry in any room too long.

New details began to leap out – chiefly, the photographs on every wall of the same woman, or an iteration of her. She was impossibly beautiful, raven-haired and long-legged, and posed seductively in 1940s swimwear against multiple fake backdrops. A sultry pin-up girl. Vivienne supposed her to be Rudy Meyer's wife or daughter – although she did not recognise her.

She'd reached the grand central staircase, and paused a moment here to survey the ground floor. It could easily have rivalled a hotel lobby. Certainly, at any moment she felt she might disturb another paying guest.

Vivienne craned her neck to absorb a large painting at the head of the staircase, featuring a glamorous coterie of bathing beauties, frill-skirted and floral-capped, diving into a lake cloaked in mist. Below the painting, a monstrous grandfather clock presided, still and silent; a hulking, antiquated shape. Vivienne looked at it with distaste. Next, would she find a knight's coat of armour? Perhaps an exotic beast's head, mounted to a wall? Ah yes, *that* was the notion nudging all along: Sylvan Mist felt like a hunting lodge.

Her basket of supplies was still sitting on the kitchen island bench. In her bone weariness last night, she hadn't thought to check the basket for products needing refrigeration and saw with horror it had contained several slabs of raw meat. Juices ran through the bottom of the basket, pooling over the bench.

Vivienne fought a gag. She didn't eat red meat – or really anything that bled – and these juices had leached through the rest of her supplies. When was her next delivery of food due?

She turned to the butler's pantry, finding a sack of flour, a jar of sugar, a pot filled with potatoes, herbs unlabelled. In the refrigerator, there was a generous pat of butter, pickled onions, and a bottle of unidentifiable claret in a crystal decanter. There were apples too, and eggs. She let the door thump closed with satisfaction. She had enough basics to survive a week in isolation, if she used her culinary skills creatively.

But she was neither creative, nor hungry right now.

Prompted by the staircase painting, Vivienne recalled Felix's mention of a nearby lake and wondered if it were visible now in daylight. She unbolted the front door and went to stand on the front balcony in the cool, pressing damp.

Elaborate and peculiar birdsong greeted her from hidden chambers; an incongruous orchestra. Colossal boughs stretched above the lodge, crushingly close.

Already, leaves were gathering on the roadster's dew-wet windscreen. She stepped down to the car, gently stroking off the leaf litter.

A giant rainforest mantis, camouflaged among those leaves, moved away from her hand to continue praying. 'Hope you're interceding for me,' Vivienne muttered. She should really count it as a good omen: female mantises knew males were better cannibalised than kept around.

In daylight, Sylvan Mist was a gloomy, presiding thing, with a garish overgrowth of red caladiums around the front stoop. Vivienne put her back to the lodge, unnerved by the sight of the many windows through which she might be seen inside. She stared at the driveway winding out of sight, then began to scout for a path to the lake.

A little way behind the lodge, she located the source of the water song. A dainty waterfall flowed over a jagged rock face into a pool ringed by mossy rocks, growing lithophytes. King ferns dwarfed the falls, and a Coalbrookdale cast iron garden seat sat losing its seat to mould and rot. 'Chimera Falls' read the wooden sign, half askew.

Vivienne turned away, unimpressed.

She couldn't bear to stay here any longer with the lodge glowering at her back, and that maddening rush of water. Where was the lake?

She might never have found it, if not for a single yellow ribbon tied around a marking stake. The lake path was almost invisible among trees heavily hung with vines and climbers.

She entered the trail among trees white-lichened. The path was dark and narrow, at times seemed to run out altogether, and there wasn't any lake in sight for a long time. Soon she came to a natural tunnel leading through the tentacles of a hulking fig tree. Spiders scurried in the shadows of the passageway and the smell of putrefaction was thick. Vivienne gritted her teeth and hurried through.

As though she'd passed into another realm, the lake revealed itself through the forest wall. Her heart and pace quickened alike. The path diverted to a lookout on the very edge of the water, with no shoreline to speak of. The lake was a perfect circle of swirling mist, seven hundred yards wide, densely rimmed by jungle. Behind the forest wall, a flotilla of dawn pink clouds sailed by.

It was magnificent, but inhospitable too; offering no entrance.

And yet, squinting, she thought she could just distinguish a clearing, further round the lake circle. Onward then!

The track stayed close to the lake, and her curiosity was magnified with every step closer. Vivienne was almost at the clearing, she was quite sure of it, when she came up against a large gate, locked, and overgrown by rainforest vine. A faded sign, etched wood, read simply: ACHTUNG.

Danger, she interpreted, utilising one of three languages she'd acquired at school. But *what* was dangerous?

She gnawed at her lower lip, wanting to see what was further around the lake. But what if someone *caught her* going past the warning sign?

Mother's voice sliced in: *Careless, reckless girl!*

Well, Mother could transmit thoughts into Vivienne's head all she pleased, but she wasn't here to stop her. Vivienne released lip from teeth, mind made up. She *was* going to look!

The gate proved easy enough to scale. On the opposite side, she found the same sign, which begged the question: which should she be more concerned about – lake or lodge?

She was off down the path again, with a defiant spring in her step. The track continued on in much the fashion as it had begun, until she arrived at a large clearing overlooking a terraced slope to the waterfront. It appeared to be a public day use area, but the entire place was overrun by towering weeds and wild grasses.

Still, it wasn't too bad. Hardly *Achtung*.

And what about that view? Rising rays speared the mist brazenly, lit the water with a gold sheen. *Ah, she's a grand lady, this lake.*

From her position above, Vivienne could just discern the shape of what looked like an old, semicircular stone amphitheatre built into the slope, enclosing a masonry stage at the water's reedy edge. A diving platform beside the stage had nearly rotted through.

An open-air theatre? How marvellous!

It was a derelict, neglected thing now; but once upon a time, this venue must have boasted of its naturalistic design and magnificent lake backdrop.

Vivienne descended the grass jungle to peruse a sign, falling off its poles. She tipped her head to the side, scratching lichen from the tourist information. It was an Aboriginal creation story of the lake, describing a deafening roar, red cloud and great rupturing. A scientific panel below illustrated this massive volcanic eruption which had formed the crater ten thousand years ago – now filled with rainwater; and unfathomably deep.

She straightened to admire the water. 'A volcanic lake,' she pronounced, pleased.

With sun lifting, and mist rising, the ancient lake's true colour was revealed: an almost lurid emerald. But was it truly bottomless? An audacious thought was forming. What if she went for a paddle? Just a little way out, just to have a better look? No, she couldn't! She wasn't even wearing a swimsuit. Did it matter? The place was deserted. She could be in and out, in a trice . . .

Don't you dare disgrace us!

'No, I won't,' Vivienne muttered. Her gut wrenched. Half a continent between them – yet Mother's excoriating tongue stayed as close as her own conscience. And how would she ever escape her there?

Vivienne was quite famished by the time she reached Sylvan Mist, and acutely conscious of her malodour. *I smell worse than this lodge.*

First, to bathe – and then cook herself a hot breakfast.

She ascended the grand staircase, humming to mask the ghastly silence. But *good heavens*, her adventure had taken a while, look at the time on the grandfather clock – about to strike nine o'clock this very moment! As she passed, right on cue, the clock began its sonorous Westminster chimes.

She hurried a few steps on, before coming to a sudden halt, hand clenching the balustrade; all colour draining from her face. Unwillingly she turned, and took three faltering steps back to stand before the clock once more.

On the clock resonated, stirring her bones. She stared at it, stupidly. This clock shouldn't be ringing out at all. When she had passed it by, only two hours earlier, the hands had been at rest, the pendulum still. Vivienne peered closer, breathing hard . . .

There, on the glass face, right in the centre, where she could never have missed it before, was a single large fingerprint – blood red, as though dipped in the juices that even now dribbled across the kitchen floor.

CHAPTER SIX

CHARADES

Josie drove home from Barrington with her head, if not dignity, held high. Her plans for the remainder of the day, chiefly: to swan around town, visiting all of her theatre group members, basking in praise and accolades, had been abandoned. She cast an apologetic grimace at their 'decrepit' Igloo as she passed it by.

Only after she'd entered the comforting green blanket of farmland, thrown as far as the eye could see, did Josie dip her chin and allow anguish to drip down upon it.

Hugo Bernard had made a mockery of her in front of every member of her theatre company, every resident of Barrington, every person who read the paper across the whole of the Tablelands – and, for that matter, wherever else his reviews were distributed, too.

Though Josie knew this dirt road, and its rainforest verge, like the back of her small hand, she couldn't push through such blinding tears. She pulled the utility over to the side of the road, and laid her head against the wheel, clutching her locket in a shaking fist.

After three minutes' indulgence – but no more – Josie wiped her face with the back of her arm, sniffing fiercely. She put the utility into gear with an angry thrust, and bumped on again, becoming more furious with every sniff.

What would *Hugo Bernard* know anyway?

Not flaming much if he couldn't appreciate the history and significance of their Igloo! That very information had been printed on the back of his program on Friday evening. Yet *Hugo Bernard* had the hide to tell everyone Barrington was afraid of its own lake! Like they were all a bunch of ignorant scaredy-cats. It wasn't fear, *thank you very much*, rather prudence and care for one another, especially their young ladies. Hugo Bernard should try living with a curse over *his* damned head and see how he liked it!

Josie didn't even blink when her hands turned the steering wheel at the unmarked forest turn off to Lake Evelyn. The sign was long missing, purposely removed to deter any on the tourist trail. Locals had proved harder to keep out – at least, until the ban was put in place.

There was a twist in Josie's gut as she cut through the rainforest, recognising old forest giants she hadn't set eyes on for yonks, surprised at how they'd lost some of their imposing size in the intervening years. She rattled into the potholed car park and pulled up by the collapsing amenities shed, to swing her legs out into a grass jungle. A hot blaze of indignant pride carried her from the safety of her car. She marched to the terraced shoreline, hands on hips.

See, Mr High and Mighty Bernard? Do I look scared to you?

It was true that she hadn't stepped foot near Lake Evelyn for years, despite living only a few miles away. Indeed, the Monash dairy farm was the closest property to Lake Evelyn – putting aside that deserted lodge. In her school years, Josie had been strictly warned off Lake Evelyn, as had most Barrington girls after the war. And, like those same girls, Josie had snuck out to the lake at least once or twice, just to spite the superstitious old folk. Secretly; to test her own mettle.

But she'd always loathed it here, the whole place was *eerie*. From the unplumbed depths of the lake, to the legendary underwater chute, and the monster rumoured to live within it. And that was before you even got to the Curse causing so many of the town's young women to drown. Who *would* want to linger round here for long?

No one did, anymore.

Yet, this morning, under glitzy mid-morning light, with the lake glittering and pinked by water lilies, the amphitheatre wasn't nearly as shabby as Josie remembered. Neither did the lake look like a graveyard for sunken army vehicles. Standing here, Josie could *almost* imagine what the place must have been in her golden age . . .

Only twenty years ago, Lake Evelyn's granite amphitheatre, the Obsidian, was the jewel in Barrington's verdant crown. The Obsidian had proudly hosted waterfront musicals to provide entertainment for the Australian and US servicemen during World War II. The creative mind behind Barrington's amphitheatre had been a wealthy, eccentric European, Rudy Meyer, who had arrived between the two great wars and constructed his rainforest lodge nearby. He'd brought several young actresses to the region to entertain the troops, paramount amongst them: Celeste Starr, a songstress. With her raven locks, va-va-voom figure, and winsome smile, Celeste had been a particular favourite of the American troops.

How lucky Barrington had thought itself then to boast two of the biggest drawcards on the Tablelands: a volcanic lake amphitheatre, and the region's most promising actress: Celeste Starr.

That was a name not often uttered around Barrington, though she hung over all their lives as a cautionary tale. It was because of her death they had lost their amphitheatre – and gained a curse. Celeste didn't just hang over their heads, she actively haunted.

Some said, *lured* . . .

'But as for me,' Josie muttered, tramping down onto the first amphitheatre row, '*I* don't believe in ghosts. Much less haunted theatres!'

It wasn't much of a theatre, anyway. To begin with, the whole clearing required a good tractor slashing, then each terrace level salvaged from weed, and inspected for damage. There were signs overdue for replacement, the old amenities shed needed replacing, and the diving platform, originally built by US servicemen, could be repaired . . .

What on earth am I thinking?

She couldn't possibly be thinking *that*. Hugo Big-headed Bernard was making Josie consider ridiculous things. She'd seen enough, had well and truly proved her point here; it was time to go home.

She stalked away from the lake amphitheatre, scratching grass itches at her knees – equal parts proud of her boldness, and unnerved by her audacity. At the door of the Ford, Josie turned back for a final, defiant glare at the crater. Her head reared back on a harsh intake of breath . . .

Dead centre of the lake, floated a woman with arms and legs splayed. Hair streamed about her; ripples rolled out from her figure.

Josie tried to shake this horrible apparition away and, when it refused to disappear, drove her knuckles into her eye sockets instead. It was impossible! *No one* swam the lake anymore. *No one, except* . . .

Nuh-uh. Nope. No way!

Josie threw herself behind the wheel, twisting the keys savagely. 'I don't believe in you, Celeste!' she hollered over the engine's growl.

Josie gunned it from the clearing without a backward gaze.

There was no regard so guileless and understanding as the large, slowly blinking eyes of a calf.

Josie had taken comfort and refuge in the calves' shed for the afternoon, redolent of manure and hay. Though she was in charge of the evening feed – in truth, the shed provided the only private spot in which to prepare her splenetic rebuttal to all that great and esteemed critic had to say. Round and round the shed she stomped, newspaper clenched in her hand, composing her soliloquy for an audience of gentle-eyed babes.

Mr Bigshot Bernard deserved every word of it – she could be just as pitiless as he! It was hardly fair to inflict such peppery language upon so tender ears, but her beloved calves were, it must be said, accustomed to it. By dusk, Josie was satisfied with her spiel, and quite prepared to deliver it to her family.

Home she stalked across the hillcrest, past the blue-shadowed dairy, backlit against a sky afire. Like a church set in the heart of a village square, this dairy tolled out the rhythm of each day for the Monash clan. Each one begun and finished with the milking. There were never days off, and no holidays.

Josie had learned this tempo at little more than a baby. From eighteen months of age, she would climb out of her cot at first light, cloth nappy drooping right down to her knees, and waddle up the hill to join her father and small brothers at the dairy. She would return each morning on her father's shoulders, with arms outstretched for the slim, aproned mother waiting at the farmhouse door.

Until there was no mother waiting, anymore.

In the years that followed, Josie's morning pilgrimage to the dairy would come to be considered yet another example of neglect in the midst of their father's grief. Eventually, the farmhouse was emptied of children entirely, and no longer did any small figures scamper up that hill, in the birdsong and gold-lit mist, to their father's side.

In the bleak wartime period, the four young Monash siblings had been spirited away from their still-grieving father to live with their maternal grandmother in town. It was the 'done thing' in those days, for the orphaned baby or the one too many; taken off to live a better life with grandparents. Many children had been sent away from the Tablelands altogether.

And perhaps they might have been as happy, raised in relative prosperity and luxury in town by their grandmother Beryl Frances. Certainly Grandy had put up the fight of a lifetime saying so. But Josie never stopped thanking her lucky stars that their father had come a few short years later, just as the war was ending, to demand them home again. It had caused no small rift between her father and maternal grandmother. A breach that existed still, and seemed to widen in animosity with every passing year.

Throat aching at these meditations, Josie set her eyes upon the farmhouse, a dilapidated cosiness beneath the fire-rippled sky. She smiled, holding gratitude for the full and rowdy evening ahead in the bosom of her kinfolk. The Monash family might have been separated once, but nothing could divide them now.

Not even Daphne.

Josie's eldest brother, Reginald, shucking off his boots at the farmhouse door, was first to sight the youngest Monash sibling. He swung down from the front step to kiss Josie's cheek. 'I know it's your night,' he said, 'but Daph has done oxtail stew. Wants us seated in two minutes. She's stroppy, mind.'

'Thanks, Reg.' Josie gave his cheek a grateful pat.

Stroppy. Of course she was. And Daphne was never content until she had dragged everyone down into the mood along with her.

Josie kicked her sandshoes off into the pile of boots at the front door and entered the warm fug of the kitchen. Daphne was at the wood stove, ash-blonde braid hanging down her back, calling stridently for her errant brothers and father-in-law.

'Why do you all take off as soon as I call you?' Daphne huffed, piling bowls into Josie's arms before she'd even had a chance to wash her hands.

Josie pretended not to hear this, knowing it was exactly what her brothers did. Even the rocks on Monash land scurried away at the sight of Daphne. The woman belonged in a web, not on a farm.

Ernest, the second eldest Monash child and self-proclaimed title holder of 'best-looking' and 'black sheep', sauntered into the kitchen holding his book open in baiting objection. Likely Daphne would threaten, for the hundredth time, to throw it in the stewpot. Her lack of follow-through only encouraged Ernest, who'd never met a person he couldn't needle.

The last brother, only two years older than she – a broad-shouldered, brown-bearded man – came to relieve Josie of the bowls so that she might wash her hands.

'Josie-posie,' he said; stooping to kiss her forehead.

'Owen,' she answered, tipping her head into his shoulder. She would have traded both her other brothers, just for this one. Luckily, she'd never been forced to choose.

Owen had recently moved out into his own house – no more than a tin shed, without even electricity, hastily erected after Daphne's arrival. Josie missed him desperately; though he was only a two-minute tractor ride up to the top paddock.

Around the kitchen table the Monash clan clamoured for seats. This table, crafted from prized red cedar timber, had been made large enough to seat all four growing Monash children and, one day, their descendants. Daphne's belly bumped over it, as she flung out spoons.

'My kitchen *stinks* of bovine! How many times do I need to ask for you all to shower before you come to tea?'

Glances were exchanged between siblings. *Her* kitchen now? As ever, it begged the question: with such a stated anathema for dairying, what had she ever seen – rather, smelt – in Reg? The chatter went

51

louder to compensate for this gaffe. A single chair, the sturdiest, with no cushions to soften its hard lines, remained empty at the head of the table.

The commotion around the table was peaking as a tall man – straight-backed and unsmiling – appeared in the kitchen doorway, and paused, eyes roving around the table, needing a moment, before he was ready join the fray.

Josie's eyes were first to break from the hubbub and settle on her father's handsome, dignified face. He looked weary. Not only the bone weariness of a dairy farmer's drawn-out day, but the soul-weariness of a widower's grief, long grappled with. As always, when their father came upon their unruliness, Josie was struck by the desire to leap forward with an apology on behalf of the four . . .

Sorry, there's so many of us, Pa. Sorry we take up so much space, energy, money.

Josie's father was her favourite person in all the world, in her book the very best of fathers. To think she'd nearly missed out on growing up with him at all.

Noise receded at the farmhouse table. Every face turned to Gabriel Monash. He came to sit at the head of the table without a word. The hush deepened as Gabe bowed his head and gave thanks.

Josie, sitting at his right-hand side, eyes open and head unbowed, watched her father's eyebrows moving expressively as he prayed. Affection jostled for position with nerves. As soon as everyone had a spoonful in their gob, she'd tell them about her review.

But the moment Gabe lifted his head, the table erupted. Had to be quick, and convincing, to get a single word in edgewise, much less an entire soliloquy on dastardly theatre critics.

Gabe reached to pat her hand. 'You look like you're sitting on some news, chickadee. How was your day?'

Josie's terrible review so publicly received, her trip out to Lake Evelyn, the ghastly spectre she had seen floating there with her own eyes: she couldn't seem to get any of it out. Josie had been incensed the whole day, but now that she sat in the circle of her family, the review felt over-analysed; her floating ghost, silly. She realised, too, that Hugo Bernard was going to take a pummelling from her protective older brothers. Perhaps this time she didn't need to call in the cavalry.

'Fine,' she answered, digging busily into her bowl.

Gabe considered her. '*Fine?* That doesn't sound like our Josephine.'

'Stew's delicious,' she told Daphne, avoiding her father's eyes.

'You just tell us when you're ready then,' Gabe said, turning to pat Owen's hand on his other side, with a similar enquiry.

No moments presented themselves during the main meal. Soon they were at tea and sweets, and still Josie was avoiding the sight of her newspapers, set high atop the china cabinet.

Josie watched her father begin his nightly tea ritual, mesmerised as ever. Having added the farm's own honey to his tea, Gabe poured the contents of his delicate teacup out into its saucer to fully cool. He sat back with an upper body stretch, waiting for the saucer to do its work. Josie's favourite part of this routine had always been the pouring back in, and how Gabe never spilled a drop. Few things calmed her busy mind as watching this ritual.

Josie decided she was glad to have kept the review to herself. She didn't need to go running to her father, to dob on a man as small and nasty as Hugo Bernard. He was beneath her, wasn't even a topic fit for this table.

And yet, there he was this instant – laid in the middle of it.

Daphne, clattering out dessert bowls, had plonked Josie's newspapers in the centre of the table. 'Check out the most outrageous news in town today,' she declared.

Gabe was reaching for the top paper, already so helpfully opened to the review. 'What's this, then? Our Josephine in the paper? Chickadee, what an achievement!'

Josie spun on Daphne with a scowl. What was *wrong* with her?

Daphne returned a mulish shrug. 'Peggy rang up about the article this afternoon, all of Barrington's talking about it. You might want to reconvene your theatre group soon, sounds like they're *not happy*.'

Owen had come to read over their father's shoulder. Ernest had taken the other copy, and was reading it aloud in a rapid-fire murmur for Reg.

Her throat sought to choke her as she watched Owen and Gabe's faces fall from wide-eyed pride to shock, dismay, and finally – pity.

Pity!

Josie had never been pitied by her brothers, much less her beloved father; had never known anything but their indulgent pride. She jerked to her feet on a furious growl.

Daphne, placing the crystal bowl of flummery on the table, looked genuinely confused – innocent even, like she hadn't meant to upset Josie in front of her family. Around the table, brothers traded worried looks.

'Well, does anyone want flummery or not?' Daphne asked, scanning rapidly between a ferocious Josie and her Reg, firing-off frantic warning looks. Daphne failed, spectacularly, to grasp the subtext. 'I'm sorry if I wasn't supposed to use Mother Monash's good crystal bowl. It just sits in my china cabinet all the time, and I worked very hard on this dessert, even though my feet have been aching all day, and no one ever thanks me for the sweets I make—'

Owen dropped his hands to grip the table, intuiting Josie's next move, for when, as she tried to shove the table in disgust, it didn't shift an inch.

She stormed from the kitchen to take refuge in the grubbiest and most comfortable couch in the lounge room.

Even from the next room, she could hear them slurping flummery in deference to Daphne's effort and complaining. Fixed sightlessly on her new Mary Stewart novel, Josie listened to their low tones discussing the review, tearing apart Hugo Bernard's words, talent and reputation, indeed his impudence to critique their Josephine.

As Josie had rightly anticipated, their loyal defence made her feel worse; magnified her shame and inadequacy. Josie was thankful they knew her well enough to understand she needed to punish them, for a time, with silence.

Later, the rest of the family drifted into the lounge for a game of charades. Reg led the way, assuring Josie the review wasn't so bad as she thought.

'No,' added Owen, in his honest way, 'it's even worse. But *you* can handle it.' Owen's sincerity had the desired effect, perking her up faster than any sympathy might have.

Gabe ruffled Josie's hair in passing, saying nothing, then spread himself out on the floor with an exhausted sigh, laying his face against the carpet. Gabe didn't participate in the rowdy after-dinner games but he never missed a front row seat – or sprawl, as it were. Josie had vague memories of her father regaling the Monash kids nightly with his mouth organ. But that instrument had sat on top of the tallest china cabinet for years, and never came down.

These nightly games had become more stilted in the months since Daphne joined the clan – the numbers were now uneven, and the Monash siblings had invented most of their parlour games, obscure to outsiders. Most nights Owen hurried home to his shed, as soon as dinner was done. Josie treasured the evenings he stayed.

Owen had taken to the centre of the lounge for his turn at charades. At his back were hand-hewn red cedar bookshelves, boasting the Britannica set, and all their father's favourites: *On Our Selection*, Henry Lawson and Banjo Patterson, volumes of Wilde and Dickens and Wodehouse. Josie had cut her teeth on her father's tomes, before she'd started to earn her own farm wage.

As soon as Owen's large hands went up to indicate the 'movie' category, the siblings groaned. Ernest threw a cushion for good measure. Owen was a walking compendium of movie titles – none of which anyone else seemed able to guess.

Owen shrugged. 'It's not my fault you lot are as uncultured as you are uncouth.'

'Can't you at least pick a film we've heard of?' complained Ernest.

'Exactly my point,' Owen muttered.

Reg, with Daphne seated caressingly on his lap, interjected: 'Something that's actually played at The Regent during the last decade, then?'

They might have a chance that way. The film offerings changed slowly at their small country cinema. Owen often drove all the way down the mountain just to catch a better selection – sometimes with a pretty date, but more often alone. His older brothers agreed: Owen was weirdly obsessive with his movies.

Owen eyes lit up. 'OK, got it, this one's easy.'

No one could guess it. As usual, Owen had to spell it out like they were children. 'It's *The Man Who Knew Too Much*,' he sighed finally.

Ernest was on his feet, red-faced, by the time the title was revealed. 'That's not what you were miming!' he roared. 'You're cheating again.'

'Knock it off,' Josie said, taking to the front of the room. 'It's my turn.'

But which category? She jiggled on the spot, thinking, until it seemed like she was in danger of receiving a barrage of cushions herself. Ernest was just raising his cushion when it came to her. *Place*. A brilliant idea rushing to her, fully formed, and making such thunderously perfect sense, she began to wonder how her subconscious mind had got away with the formulating of it . . .

Nimbly she mimed putting on a swim cap, pegging her nose, lining up to dive. The group got 'swimmer' and they'd reached 'lake' with no problems. Next to recreate the amphitheatre. She mimed out the steps and stage, then added back in her bather, readying to dive.

The chorus of guesses ceased abruptly. Josie, having completed her dive, paused from her acting, to take in the circle of worried faces.

'What?' she demanded; slightly puffed, already indignant.

Daphne spoke up. She sounded embarrassed for Josie: 'But you can't possibly mean . . . *actress*?'

A lone, awkward cough punctuated this guess.

Josie scowled. 'Owen's right, you do all suck hind teat.'

'Not quite the words I used,' Owen said.

She stamped a foot. 'It's *place*.'

'So it's not that *actress* then,' Daphne said, a hand fluttering at her chest.

'Geez! I'm showing you an amphitheatre. I'm not miming "Celeste Starr", so you can stop looking so horrified. The answer is: "The Obsidian"!'

Ernest sent a cushion sailing.

Josie ducked, but refused to vacate the stage. '*Actually*, while I've got you all, the Obsidian is something I want to talk to you all about tonight.'

'Oh, here we go,' griped Daphne, 'only Josephine could turn a game of miming into a speech.'

'I want to broach an idea with you all.'

'About the Obsidian?' asked Reg doubtfully, shifting Daphne on his lap.

There was no point testing the waters any further, in she plunged: 'I've had this idea—' Josie did not qualify for how long '—of reopening the Obsidian for my theatre group's next performance . . .'

At least they didn't outright laugh. This stricken silence she could deal with. Gabe was no longer attempting to doze; he'd lifted up onto his forearms, and was watching her very carefully.

'But it's closed,' Ernest said.

'Hence why I should *reopen* it.'

'I wouldn't put it past you, Jose. But – why *would* you?'

Somehow, Josie didn't think 'proving Hugo Bernard wrong' was going to suffice with her family. 'It's *our* amphitheatre, and it's just sitting there, going to waste.'

'So?'

'So, I want to redeem Barrington's reputation as a stellar theatre town.'

Reg was frowning. 'And you think an amateur theatre group playing in a shabby, cursed amphitheatre is going to do it?'

'It won't be shabby once I'm through – it will be the most unique and picturesque theatre in the whole country! And we're not an amateur group, it's *community theatre*. We have great performers in Barrington.'

'Who?' asked Ernest.

'Nobody in this room,' Josie snapped. 'But I'm proud of my troupe, no matter what certain out-of-towners may say. We're ready to take back the Obsidian from the annals of history.'

'It's *history* for a reason,' Reg muttered.

Ernest shook his head. 'You won't get this past the old fossils in town.'

'Of course *I* will.'

Ernest was, if Josie dared hope, looking less dubious. 'But how are you going to counteract the Curse?'

She tried for a look of scorn, though her heart had jolted at 'the Curse' uttered aloud. 'Doubt it will even come up.'

'The Curse will be the first thing anyone mentions,' Ernest said. 'That's if they even let you finish talking.'

'Then I'll cast my best look of condescension upon them.'

'You're good at those,' Ernest returned.

'But *you* believe in the Curse too,' Reg interjected. Daph was no longer stroking his arm – her fingernails were under attack by her teeth.

'I reckon I outgrew that silly tale years ago.'

'That's strange,' said Reg, 'because I seem to remember you declaring even the road itself into Lake Evelyn should be blocked off after Denise Lapham drowned.'

'That wasn't any stinking old curse,' Josie said. 'That was Denise Lapham being a drunk, who never learned to swim.'

'That right?' Reg said. 'Then how come you haven't set foot in Lake Evelyn yourself for years?'

'I'll have you know, I stepped foot there today.'

'Did not.'

'Did so! And I'm going back tomorrow to draw up my plans!'

Daphne could bear it no longer. She lurched up from Reg's lap to stand, arms akimbo. 'Josephine Monash, this is dangerous, reckless talk! You're just steaming mad about that theatre critic, and looking for a way to shock us. But you can't reopen the Obsidian. *Nobody* will agree to it, and you know it!'

The hysterical edge to Daphne's voice seemed to charge the room. No one spoke. Josie cast a nervous look at her father.

Gabe Monash had indeed reached his limit. 'That's enough,' he said quietly, pulling himself to his feet. He turned to his only daughter. 'You drop this whole idea. I won't have it. That's far enough.'

Far enough? She was only getting started!

Gabe swung a stern look around the gathering. 'I'd have you all off to bed now. It's late, and the milking waits for no man.'

59

Heads nodded; eyes skirted away. Josie fiddled with her fringe as her father stepped over reclining bodies, and out of the room. Silence reigned until their father's bedroom door dragged closed.

It was Owen, thus far refraining from the barrage, who broke the silence. He turned to Reg in appeal. 'She'd only have to get an enthusiastic minority on her side. Even the four of us would be enough. It's not like she's talking about reopening the lake itself. And if the Monash clan was backing her from the outset . . .'

Josie saw where Owen was going with this. She turned to Reg. 'More importantly, if I had the support of a brother like you, Reg, the eldest and most respected Monash son . . .'

Reg nodded, turning to his wife. 'What do you reckon, Daph? If I put the word out that I don't *mind* this idea, and I can see some good could come out of it, might give Josie the initial momentum she needs—'

Daphne threw her hands up. 'Absolutely not. You'll make us look like *fools!*'

Josie drew near to Daphne, nose crinkling into a beseeching smile. 'Please, Daph. You could let people know – just quietly – that you don't *really* approve. But if I had the backing of my brothers, more people might listen to me.'

'No! You don't have my permission to open that ghastly amphitheatre.'

'I don't *need* your permission, or any of my brothers', I *am* reopening it. But I'd appreciate your support, since we're—' she thought she might choke on the word '—*sisters*, and all.'

Daphne's voice shook. 'You won't get my support! You might think you have sway over your brothers, but no one in town will agree to your ridiculous idea. The people of Barrington want to keep their daughters *safe.*'

'But I'm not trying endanger *anyone's* daughter,' Josie said.

60

'Then don't lure them back down to that godforsaken lake! This town has lost six of its daughters to its cursed waters. *Six!* You've obviously been so wrapped up in yourself over the last fourteen years you haven't noticed or cared, but as for the rest of us in Barrington – those girls mattered! *We* will never be so selfish as to forget them.'

Haven't noticed or cared?

The next words were out of Josie's mouth in a furious torrent: 'Valerie. Barbara. Martha. Glenda. Loreen. Denise!' A terrible roll call, indelibly imprinted on her young heart. '*Those* were their names,' Josie rushed on, 'and *that* was the order in which we lost them! Each one of them was aged between sixteen and twenty when they drowned. Valerie was the first floater in 1946, only two years after the actress, Celeste Starr took her own life—'

'*Don't!*' Daphne screeched, clapping her hands over her ears. 'I don't want to hear about that woman – it's all her fault! *She* started the Curse.' Daphne fixed Josie with a deadly look. 'And it will be all *your* fault, if you reopen that lake.'

There was a long, fraught silence as the two women stared at each other, both breathing fast.

Daphne's hands went to cover her belly. 'I'm going to tell *my* daughter the same thing Mother Monash would have told you, if she were still here: Lake Evelyn is cursed, and it's out of bounds. When young women swim there, they drown. That lake, and its flaming amphitheatre, *stays* closed.'

Daphne swept her long plait over her shoulder, gesturing hard at her husband. 'Come on, Reg.'

Josie walked Owen partway home, to the top of the hillcrest. Neither Owen nor Josie spoke until they were nearer the dairy than the farmhouse.

Silken moonlight cast a muted glow on the camp of cows nearby, and drew a Willie Wagtail's nocturnal ode. The farmhouse lights shone in the distance; from this vantage point, the only light on earth.

'Do you think it's a stupid plan?' Josie blurted. She didn't think she could bear it if Owen disapproved. The idea had utterly seized her.

Owen took his time formulating a reply.

'I'm doing it anyway,' she said, hurrying him along.

Owen, still thinking, cracked his knuckles. A horrible habit – but she missed the sound of those knuckles cracking at four o'clock every morning.

'I love the idea,' he said. 'I think you knew I would. In fact, I'd like to be part of it, if I can. I'll slash the amphitheatre for you.'

'Good,' Josie said, giving a joyous clap.

Owen hadn't finished. 'I am worried you might be biting off more than you can chew. You're going to find a lot more resistance from some in town.'

'But they'll get over it.'

It was hard to discern the expression on Owen's face in the dark. She thought it might be concern.

'If anyone can make them get over it, you can, Josie.'

She nodded vigorously.

'But I hope you're truly doing this because you're passionate about theatre, and smashing superstitions, not because you're determined to prove some arrogant theatre critic wrong.'

She didn't trust herself to reply. In her mind's eye, she was dancing down the middle of Main Street, waving Hugo Bernard's next grovelling review above her head.

'I see,' Owen said.

Only Josie didn't know how he could see her blushing in the darkness at all.

'Well, if you're that set on it, you're going to need all the support you can get. I think your next stop is to visit Grandy.'

Grandy! Oh fudge, here comes trouble...

CHAPTER SEVEN

HELL'S BELLS

Morning arrived before Vivienne was ready to face it. She had slept the night on the floor of the library between dark wood shelves, cloistered away from the forest's dark glare, and her own haunted reflection. Even with her head under a pillow, she had been unable to evade the call of some strange owl; like the whistle of a bomb that never seemed to land, only fell down and down, over and over again.

She was going *mad*.

What other conclusion could she draw from yesterday's fingerprint discovery? She must have restarted the clock herself, after touching the meat spillage, and she'd done it without even being aware.

She was losing her mind – but gaining a demon. Shame was its name. Even now it crouched on her chest, talons deep in her ribs, snarling: *You've ruined your life. You've made a terrible mistake.* Beneath its weight, she could only draw in oxygen in quick, shallow breaths.

'All right, Vivienne,' she murmured. 'Time to rally.'

She pushed to sitting, but the fiend didn't shift an inch. She stood up, and it only gripped harder round her torso. Concentrating so hard thus on simply breathing, she failed to mark the remnants of her night's dinner. The yolk-stained plate clattered and split beneath her feet, and the empty crystal decanter rolled away. It had been a dusty-tasting bitter claret, and her head suffered for it.

I have to get out of this blasted lodge!

Vivienne was going down to paddle at the lake. That dreadful claret might have given her this woozy headache, but it was deadening her inhibitions yet.

She dug her honeymoon swimsuit out of her trunk – a red, polka dot halter-neck, with a tiny, belted waist – changed, and only then unbarred the library door. The furniture she dragged away felt infinitely heavier than the evening before.

Unsteadily she descended the grand staircase, careful not to look at the grandfather clock she had covered with a white sheet.

She stepped out into a cloudland; a forest submerged. A bird call, like splintering glass in the swathing fog, raised the hair on the back of her neck.

I've got to get away from here!

The beribboned trail marker took some time to locate in the mist gloom, and her growing panic. Having finally stumbled upon it, Vivienne set off determinedly. She *was* going to paddle. Fog be damned, sign be damned, headache be damned, and Mother *especially* be damned. Indeed, the closer she came to the lake, the more resolute she felt herself to be.

Reaching the grass-choked amphitheatre, Vivienne shed her chiffon peignoir on a granite step, leaving it to lie safely hidden by the grass. She stepped ankle deep into the reed-edged lake.

A sharply indrawn breath at the water's coolness showed Vivienne that her lungs could in fact still breathe around the beast squatting on her chest. She had not managed to throw off that constriction on her long walk, but perhaps she could *drown* it instead?

She waded deeper in between parting reeds, water lilies moving around her. Unlike the previous day, it wasn't possible to sight the far bank through the fog. She couldn't see more than twenty feet in front of her, which, she decided, was a blessing.

Vivienne stroked a little way out before pausing to reach, tentatively, for the bottom. Her toes made anchor. She could still stand; for now.

Keep going, a little further.

The shelf of shallow water dropped off precipitously. One minute she could touch, the next she was treading water above unknowable depths. Hastily she back-pedalled, reaching with her toes to dig into the sandy floor.

She gulped air, contemplating the bottomless expanse.

'*Don't you dare disgrace us,*' she warned herself obediently.

But it was not Mother's refrain that drove her off the safety of that ledge; rather the sudden ripple of an eel by her calves. Vivienne did not flail or shriek; she simply dived out then, over the deep.

Swimming across an untold abyss was, as it turned out, the easy part.

She'd been a strong swimmer since girlhood – forced into lessons by Mother, who had cared less about the skills conferred, than swimming's position on a checklist of accomplishments, between elocution and deportment classes; singing, tennis and piano lessons. Only the singing lessons had ever been truly valuable to Vivienne, and might even have inspired her vocation – in another life.

Instead, she'd been sent to a finishing school meant to make of her an impeccable and gracious wife. Nothing offered there had taught her how to bear Mother's tongue, rather how to bide her own.

Vivienne's breaststroke was beautiful, if slightly modified to keep her head above water, as she waited for the opposite bank to emerge from fog. Swimming was easy; it was the thinking that was hard . . .

Had she crossed the point of no return? What lurked beneath her? If she sank, how long would it take for her body to settle on the nethermost depths of this crater? Vertigo was no less powerful for the plummeting height concealed.

Vivienne soon found herself swimming among water lilies once more, then rising reeds. She'd done it, she'd actually forded the lake! A glow of triumph lit her from within; like striding across a stage, to rapturous applause.

But the lake, as she turned again, was silent. Only the slap and splash of her own limbs accompanied her second crossing. The fog was dissipating. With increased visibility, Vivienne found herself in the middlemost of a wide turquoise expanse, bounded by thick rainforest.

Movement on the shoreline caught her eye – the briefest flash amongst the dense greenery. Someone on the far shore, watching. A man, most likely, perhaps a countrified woman. It was impossible to distinguish individual features. Whomever it was, they were standing so still, Vivienne began to wonder if she was simply making people shapes out of trees.

What should she do now? If the stranger was waiting for her to come back to shore, there wasn't a chance she was obliging. And why did the mere thought of that figure stepping into the water fill her with such panic? She had the intolerable sensation of being a sitting duck.

Vivienne flipped onto her back, sinking into the water so that only her nose and mouth cleared the surface. It was no hiding place, but felt like a refuge. It seemed a barely breathing eternity, floating dead centre of the lake expecting something she had no words or image for, only the sheer dread of it.

But when Vivienne turned to upright position again, the watcher was gone.

Slowly, she began to stroke towards the shore, head above water. Her eyes darted everywhere, blinking hard. If she saw so much as a flash, she would take off in the other direction.

She reached the shallows without a further glimpse. Ducks came to greet her with a familiarity to humans incongruous with the wildness of this place. Perhaps the person on the shoreline was simply a watcher of birds, and not of women at all. She was letting paranoia rule over rationality, and that was enough of that.

Vivienne rose from the lake, lighter than she had been. Somehow in her exertions across that vast expanse of freshwater, she had managed to cast off the demon. It might drag itself from the waters yet, but for now, she could breathe again.

Unfortunately, she could not find where she'd hidden her peignoir. It was not on the step where she *thought* she remembered its gossamer spill, and though she walked carefully around, peering into the thick grass, she could not turn it up.

Vivienne was shivering now, the morning sun failing to dry out her swimsuit quickly enough. The loss of her peignoir soured the morning's triumph. It was one of her most treasured accoutrements. Cranky at her claret-addled carelessness, Vivienne headed back towards the lodge.

As she came out into the clearing, Vivienne heard a telephone ringing, deep inside the bowels of the lodge. Her first instinct was to laugh, she'd had no clue there *was* a telephone hidden within.

Vivienne tore up the steps, desperate not to miss the call.

She pursued the sound into the library, where the bell came from inside a closed roll top desk. Vivienne pressed her ear against the wood, ran her hands over the roll top for a lever or groove.

'Open, damn you; *open!*' she cried, nails digging beneath the bottom.

At last, a little give, and then movement: the roll top began to slide. Slowly, with a noisy drag, the desk opened. Inside the hidden compartment, shrilled a Bakelite telephone.

Vivienne swooped on the handset. 'Yes, hello?'

A crackling silence, a telephonist's impartial tones, and finally, a familiar throat clearing.

'You made it.'

'Uncle Felix!' she cried, relief soaring. 'Yes, I'm here!'

'Where have you been? I was calling and calling.'

Vivienne opened her mouth to tell him about her triumphant lake crossing, before biting down on it with inexplicable guilt. 'Oh, I couldn't find the telephone, it was hidden. I searched everywhere, and the desk wouldn't budge.'

'And how's my girl?'

'I'm fine.'

'I meant my car, but I was coming to you next. How are you – really?'

'Not really fine. Frankly, this lodge gives me the heebie-jeebies.'

'You already had the heebie-jeebies in Sydney, that's why you left your fiancé standing at the altar like a chump.'

Vivienne absorbed this comment as a physical blow. 'What do you *mean*?'

'You didn't tell poor Howard.'

'I did so – I went straight over there! He wasn't home, so I left a note. The housekeeper was to give it to him.'

'Howard, it seems, stayed elsewhere that night – bachelor celebrations I am to understand – and was not handed the note, until after the appointed hour of your nuptials.'

The telephone handset could have exploded under the force of Vivienne's clenching. 'But did Mother not telephone him to discuss the . . . cancellation?'

'Did you ask her to?'

'I didn't *talk* to Mother! That was your – you said *you* would tell her the marriage was called off!'

'Did I? Isn't that silly, I thought my job was just to keep her distracted until you could get away.'

Vivienne's voice continued its climb to higher pitches. 'Yes, but then you were to *tell* her I had left!'

'Oh, I had it quite the other way around.'

'But didn't she ask where your car was? Where *I* was?'

'When she finally kicked me out at half twelve and staggered off to bed, she wasn't in a fit state to ask about either of my girls. I told you I'd take her out with some Felix Special nightcaps, gave you plenty of time to escape, didn't I?'

The *absurdity* of this news! Vivienne's heart knocked frantically, sweat flooded from her brow. '*Wait*—' she gasped '—are you telling me the marriage went ahead?'

'Not *without* you, Howard isn't that daft. But the *ceremony* wasn't cancelled until the bride was found to be missing on the morning of.'

'Uncle *Felix*!' It was a shriek without volume.

'Now, now, don't lose your head. It's over and done with. Be thankful you weren't here to deal with it.'

'But this is absolutely ghastly! You mean to tell me, I stood him up before all of Sydney society? It's unimaginable!'

'What makes it less imaginable than fleeing the night before?' His teasing tone only incensed.

'It's unpardonable! I can never come back from this. People must think I've lost my mind!'

'You have made quite a mess of it, my girl.'

Don't you mean we *made a mess of it?*

'It's been all over those social pages you so love.'

Vivienne writhed. How could she have *done* such a thing – to Howie, to Mother? They didn't deserve it, no matter how desperately she'd wanted to escape a life with either of them. What Mother must have gone through that day, what she must be dealing with, still! She hadn't ruined just her own reputation, but Geraldine's too.

'Why didn't you *tell* me this, when I called you from Brisbane that . . . first day?' She couldn't bring herself to say: wedding day.

'But you didn't ask.'

She hadn't, that was true.

'And I knew it would be too much for you, when you needed the courage and conviction to keep driving north. I was trying to protected you. Besides, what could you have done about it?'

'I might have rung to apologise.' It was a childish whimper.

'Trust me, if you think you've caught the sharp end of Geraldine's temper before, its nothing on what she's whipping out now.' She heard the wince in her uncle's voice.

'I'm sorry that you have to bear the brunt of that.'

'Never mind, at least I'm saving *you* from it. You got away, you're free! We should be shouting *hurrah*!'

A heavy stone seemed to fall in her gut, sinking deep. How could she ever face any of them again?

'Please, Uncle Felix – how long will Rudy Meyer let me stay here?'

'No, don't worry yourself about that for a minute, I'm taking care of everything. You just enjoy your peace and quiet. Once things have settled, I'll come and get you. Then you won't have to front them all alone.'

'Does Mother know where I am?'

'She knows you're safe. I told her you'd called me.'

'You mustn't tell her where I am.'

'I won't give you away, I swear.'

CHAPTER EIGHT

UNSINKABLE

Josie put off seeing Grandy Beryl for several days, knowing the discussion could only go one of two ways: a squabble, with Josie invariably declared the loser; or a takeover of the whole shebang by that feisty octogenarian.

First, Josie would have to butter her up. Their last visit had ended in petulant tears – Josie's. Treats and flowers might just do the trick, though. The former was easy enough to acquire: gourmet cheese, made by her dearest of brothers. Beryl had an abominable sweet tooth, even if she had none of her own left. Josie wrapped up Beryl's favourite flavours – chilli mango, passionfruit spice – and headed for the Flower Shop as soon as the day's trade began.

This part would require some diplomacy. Peggy West had banned Beryl from her Flower Shop months ago for publicly criticising the quality of her blooms. Beryl still coveted Peggy's orchids for her collection, however, and Peggy still needed Beryl Frances as her biggest buyer. Neither woman was going to be the first to give in. The compromise saw Josie traipsing regularly into the Flower Shop, pretending to purchase orchids for herself, while Peggy nipped off insults to send home for the real collector.

Peggy had spied Josie coming down the street, and was already smiling like a sun-warmed cat, as she opened the door. 'Running low on orchids for your witch's garden?'

That's a good one, Grandy will like that.

A long curlicue of smoke rose from between Peggy's scarlet painted nails. Peggy's non-stop smoking, Beryl said, turned all her white flowers a dingy shade.

Josie smiled as she placed her purse down on Peggy's counter. She decided to tell the truth today. 'I need your best orchid for Grandy Beryl. I've got to sweeten her up for an idea I'm running past her today.'

Peggy drew on her cigarette, painted lips twisting. 'That would be your outrageous amphitheatre plan, I reckon.'

So Daphne had already dobbed to her cousin. And there were few gossips in town so committed to their craft as Peggy West – which guaranteed the news was already exploding up and down Main Street. Josie should have been miffed, but it was something of a relief to know the shock wave ran ahead of her. Besides, it was hard to begrudge Peggy this news – she was a founding member of the Barrington Theatre Company, and one of its most talented. Peggy West fancied herself the next Bridget Bardot.

'Yep. I'm going to put Barrington back in lights as a Drama Town,' Josie said proudly.

Peggy blew a long whorl of smoke, eyes narrow. 'Uh-huh. Instead of a Dairy Town?'

Josie grew sunnier under Peggy's scrutiny. 'Much less a Drowning Town.'

Peggy snorted. 'Right then, you'd better follow me. You're going to need my showiest *Phalaenopsis*.'

Josie clipped out of the Flower Shop minutes later, with a yellow and scarlet moth orchid in hand and, under her belt, an avowed supporter of her bold plan.

Reg Monash had married the wrong West girl, of that there could be no doubt.

Despite nerves, Josie smiled as she approached Beryl's homestead on the corner of Main Street and Frances Street, gaudily painted to match her favourite orchid, the Vanda. Everyone knew it as the Purple House.

She entered through the orchid house; a semi-detached glasshouse reserved for Beryl's overriding obsession. As always, the miniature winding pathways and peering orchid faces sent her meandering back into girlhood whimsy.

Josie emerged into the formal lounge, calling out. *'Yoo-hoo?'* She had timed her arrival to make sure she would be in and out before Grandy's beloved 'stories' started, the radio soap serial *Blue Hills*. Nothing irked Grandy so much as having her stories interrupted by callers.

A voice came from the rear of the house. 'Entertain yourself, child – I won't be long.'

She knew better than to go looking for Beryl, who did not care to receive visitors until after she'd donned her various corsetry and finished setting her hair.

Josie wandered around the lounge, dusted to within an inch of its life, inspecting the photos and ornaments she'd looked at countless times before.

Most of the photos were of distant relatives long passed – including the grandfather she'd never met – or Beryl's trophy-winning orchids. Grandy had one photo of Josie's mother, her only child, sitting in pride of place on top of the large pianola.

She reached for the picture: Maureen Monash holding Owen, just two years old, on her thin hip. Owen's chubby legs almost covered the jutting protrusion of her belly; and, Josie within. A wind was blowing and Maureen's long dark hair streamed over her face and Owen's. They were both laughing, with wide open mouths; one a small replica of the other.

It was how Josie always thought of her mother: an effervescent laugh, and flowing hair.

But another wind had been blowing the day Grandy's picture was taken; a squall of dark fate, which had swept Maureen Monash less than three years later.

Leukaemia. A slow, pallid shrivelling – or so the story went. For in Josie's memories, hotly disputed by her brothers, their mother was never sickly pale and weak, or bedridden at all. She was vibrant and blithe, chasing Josie round the farmhouse; always play-acting, ever laughing. All the brothers jibed her for it, deploring Josie's runaway imagination. Her father, when she insisted on her recollections, would only look at her with infinite sadness.

Josie owned one photograph of her mother, kept in her sleepout bedroom. She could recall every detail, for it hung above her rickety bed: a black and white image of Maureen Monash, shot at a distance. She was standing at the farm gate, thin limbed and dark tressed, with face half turned away towards the far distant cinder cones, as though considering the journey she must take alone. Even in monochrome, Josie could read the sorrow and regret in her mother's figure, that trailing hand on the farmhouse gate, the great heaviness in such small shoulders. It ought to have been a depressing image, but on the contrary Josie derived immense comfort from it. That photo was the last thing Josie looked upon before sleep each night. *Goodnight, Mum*, she would whisper: *You mightn't have been mine for long, but how I loved you.* Josie had stared at her photograph so many hours, she had appropriated it as a last memory of her mother: watching her walk to that gate, crying after her; begging her to stay.

I saw her leave.

Yet Josie had been assured a hundred times; she and her siblings were happily playing in the other room when Maureen Monash slipped silently away, in her own bed. In darkly imaginative moods, however, Josie sometimes questioned if she'd been told the truth. Maybe Maureen Monash hadn't died of a blood cancer at all. Perhaps, like so many young women of Barrington, she too had followed the Curse's hypnotic pull to Lake Evelyn and . . .

No. Josie shook away an image as macabre as it was impossible. Maureen Monash *had* died of leukaemia, years before the lake took the first and most famous of its victims, and no amount of morbid fantasising could make her mother's story more tragic. Josie gave Maureen and Owen a kiss, wiped the smudge off the glass, and put it back down on the pianola's polished top.

A mood change was necessary.

Beside the pianola stood a tall cupboard, filled with rolls of music. Josie flicked open the door and perused the titles on the ends of each roll, searching for an upbeat favourite. Ah yes, here was one she had loved playing since she was a small girl: 'It Had To Be You' by Frank Banta.

Josie sat down on the piano stool and slid open the hidden panel for the rolls. She slotted in the music, hooked it on, and settled her feet onto the large pedals. Slowly she began to pedal, watching the roll rotate. The first inscriptions appeared and, like magic, the piano keys began to play. Josie pedalled enthusiastically, hands dancing in the air above the keys; quickly falling into the spell of imagined genius which had not abated since childhood. Only the pedalling had become easier as the years had gone by.

From behind her, a voice cut through. 'To what do I owe the pleasure of this unfortunate concert?'

Josie's feet fell from the pedals. She swung around on the stool.

Beryl Frances stood in the doorway. She was a short barrel of a woman, with a back ramrod straight, and a regal carriage of neck and chin. Her lilac housedress was neatly belted over a midsection firmly held in check by whalebone corset, her still naturally dark hair – her gloat at over eighty years old – was permed, neatly rolled and pinned into a hairnet that would brook no breeze.

Josie smiled, crossing the room to embrace her. 'Grandy,' she said lovingly.

Scent of lavender talcum powder enveloped Josie, as she kissed the creped petal softness of Beryl's cheek.

Beryl drew back to inspect Josie's strong, bare legs below her skirt. She clucked in disapproval. 'No stockings *or* petticoat, Josephine.'

'Why else do you think I'm so popular with the boys?'

Beryl held Josie's eyes for a long second. 'That shelf you're sitting on is beginning to look quite empty, isn't it?'

Josie hoisted up her handbag impatiently. 'There's no one right for me in Barrington.'

That Beryl thought she'd scored the first point was evident in her Cheshire grin. She went for the second. 'Last time you were here, you swore you weren't speaking to me for as long you lived.'

That's right! I really ought to write these things down. 'You took Daphne's side, then refused to apologise for your meddling.'

'A married couple deserves at least a brief honeymoon.'

'You funded their fancy holiday to Brisbane, too late to be called a "honeymoon", when they should have used that money towards their build!'

'It was the inheritance always promised to Reginald on his marriage, it's not up to me what they choose to do with it.'

'That's funny,' Josie steamed, 'because most of our decisions aren't up to you, and yet that's never prevented you sticking your big nose in!

You could at least have held back some of it, with the stipulation it was to be used on their home.'

'Oh, I see: "Don't interfere, Grandy, unless it suits me, then have at it."'

'But they're *never* going to move out,' Josie cried, face hot. 'I'm fed up with it. I want my house back! If she doesn't move out soon, I bloody well will!'

Beryl grinned wider.

Dammit. That was exactly what Beryl was hoping for: a knock on the door, and her only granddaughter standing beyond it, begging for sanctuary. It was no secret Beryl had been awaiting that very thing for fourteen years – ever since Gabe had come to reclaim his children from the grandmother who had no intention of giving them back.

'So.' Beryl eased herself into a lounge chair, straightening the opal brooch on her collar, below the soft drape of skin at her décolletage. 'Why *have* you come?'

Standing before her, Josie readied to deliver her spiel with bold pizazz. Grandy hated a tepid performance.

'First things first,' she declared. 'I bought you a new orchid.'

'Obviously,' Beryl said – although Josie hadn't seen her take any notice of the plant. 'And what did the puffing chimney have to say for herself?'

'She said it will make the perfect addition to my witch's garden.'

Mirth rattled Beryl's wide bosom.

'I also brought you some more of Owen's cheese.'

'Whatever you're here for *must* be good.'

Josie crinkled her most winning smile. 'My latest production,' she began, in majestic tones, 'has been reviewed by one of the country's leading theatre critics.'

She paused for impact.

'A *review*? Is that what you call his pontificating drivel?'

'It's true, he did have some significant issues with my directorial style, and venue, and casting, and choice of play, but I'm confident that next time—'

Beryl snorted. 'Get to the real reason you've come to me. You know I don't give two hoots how you plan to genuflect before that bumptious fool.'

'Oh, you'll be hooting all right,' Josie said. 'Because I've come to let you know I'm reopening the Obsidian.'

Only the barest flicker of an eyelid hinted at Beryl's surprise. '*Let you know*, she says . . . not ask my permission.'

'Why should I ask your permission?'

'*I* closed the theatre and recreation area.'

'That's overstating it,' Josie said. 'You didn't personally close it; it was a unanimous town vote to "deter public use of the area".'

'*I* agitated for the public area to be closed so loudly and for so long, the rest of Barrington had no choice but to fall in line.'

'I don't think so,' Josie said casually. 'Rudy Meyer abandoned his theatre for his own good reasons. And most of the World War II sites were razed to the ground after it ended. They would have done it eventually anyway – with or without your petitioning.'

'You impertinent little minx,' Beryl said; admiringly.

Everyone knew the story of Beryl Frances hurtling into that town Igloo meeting in 1951, resolved to force her way. A 'loose cannon', attendees had described her at the time. But when she took her mind to a thing, Beryl Frances was more a fully armed warship than single cannon. *Unsinkable*, Josie often thought. She wanted to be like no other woman so much as Grandy Beryl.

'All right, fine: Beryl Frances made them close it. But I'm reopening it.'

Beryl moved the cloth-wrapped cheese that she had placed on her lap to doily-topped side table.

'You have a callous disregard for the number of lives already lost in that godforsaken lake.'

'I just happen to think the *amphitheatre* has nothing to do with it.'

'And you're willing to risk more young girls on your theory.'

'No one's swum in Lake Evelyn for years!'

'Because of our ban – they had to be *made* to stay away.'

'Closing the area didn't put a stop to them dying. By my count, there were still another two girls after that.' *Loreen, Denise.*

'Two more senseless deaths until the message finally sunk in: *keep away* from the lake.'

'A theatre won't change that.' Josie felt herself growing petulant.

'This is just about the theatre? Why don't you just smarten up the Igloo, if you're really going to take the opinion of Mr Kafoops as gospel?'

'I'll continue to use the Igloo for practices, but we want to reclaim the amphitheatre.'

'We?'

'Still me, at this stage. But Owen's offered his support.'

'So. You haven't run this by your father.'

'I told the whole family last week.'

Beryl smirked, triumphant. 'And *he* said no way.'

She rushed to soften her father's knockback. 'Actually, he just said: that's far enough . . .'

'Put his foot right down, didn't he?'

'Only because conversation was getting heated.'

'I *bet* it was getting too heated for Gabriel Monash,' Beryl said. An obscure statement, more to herself than her granddaughter.

Enmity ran thick between Gabe and Beryl, and had for so long as Josie could remember. Maureen and Gabe's wedding photos, with grandmother and bridegroom beaming side by side, proved it had not always been so. But Josie had only ever known a father and grand-mother at war. Both parties upheld their own explanation of the rift. After Maureen's death, *Gabe* said, a scheming and possessive Beryl had muscled in while he was laid low with grief, and hustled the children off to live with her. Three years she'd kept them from him – the better part of the war – while Gabe had been co-opted in the massively increased local production of dairy, for those American servicemen being so fond of their milk. Josie was almost six by the time Gabe had reclaimed his children.

Beryl had fought furiously, *she* said, to raise Maureen's children as her own, and, especially, to save her only granddaughter from a hard farming life. But Gabe was too selfish, short-sighted and stubborn to give his children up to a better life. Gabe Monash, she alluded ever darkly, had made himself undeserving of his children, and should have been *ashamed* to ask for them back.

Neither party would elucidate, much less recant their invectives, and everyone else in the Monash clan had learned to tiptoe around the animosity. Even as a woman come of age, with her own strong views, Josie couldn't choose who to believe. She knew her father was neither selfish nor short-sighted – though he *was* stubborn – just as she knew Beryl was possessive, and certainly a schemer.

Indeed, Beryl was scheming right now. She could hear the telltale tongue clucking, behind closed lips.

The sound stopped. 'You broached it with your father,' Beryl said, 'and he tried to shut you down. But you won't stand for that, so you've come to me for courage. Not permission, mind; you just want *me* to put the wind up your sails.'

Josie shrugged. It was an accurate summary.

Beryl pushed out of the lounge, and walked out into her orchid house, carrying her new plant.

Josie waited to hear if she'd just been dismissed, or was expected to follow. The sharp sound of her name, a minute later, confirmed the latter.

She rejoined Beryl at the pond. Her grandmother contemplated her with narrow eyes, clucking. Josie endured this scrutiny, po-faced, recognising a plot under development; praying it was to her benefit.

The clucking stopped. Josie braced.

Grandy's tone was carefully neutral. 'And what does your theatre company think of this idea?'

Josie brows quivered in the effort not to reveal flaring hope. She matched Grandy's light tone. 'I haven't discussed it with all of them yet. But I've got members on-board already.'

'Who?'

'Peggy, for one.'

'Well, don't despair; with good lighting and a lot of face powder, she might pass for something other than a leather boot.'

Josie tutted.

Beryl tipped her head. 'You're worried half your troupe will up and quit when they hear, and you're right to be. This town is full of cowards and bad actors.'

Josie recognised the crafty edge to Grandy's words – though she couldn't grasp the meaning.

'What play are you planning on using for your audacious reopening?'

'I'm thinking a playful piece this time, a classic everyone knows – *A Midsummer Night's Dream*.'

'No.'

'What's wrong with Shakespeare?'

'Nothing's wrong with the man, but he doesn't belong in that amphitheatre.'

'What then?'

Josie watched her grandmother draw in breath, seeming to inflate the barrel shape of her torso. Here it came. She was about to find out exactly how Grandy planned to take over . . .

'*You*,' Beryl said, jabbing her finger towards Josie, 'are going to retell the story of Celeste Starr.'

'The actress? Like heck I am!'

'Like heck you are.'

This was Grandy's grand scheme? For Josie to dramatise the very event which had set off the Curse in the first place? A complete and preposterous turnabout. She, who had closed the lake, now proposing they dredge up the whole story again! What the dickens was Grandy up to now?

Josie served her an incredulous glare. 'I don't know what you're up to, but my answer is *no way!* I'm not touching that story.'

'You are the perfect person to tell it.'

Josie threw up her hands. '*Me?* I don't know the story of Celeste Starr well enough; no one ever likes to speak of it.'

'It's well past time you started working it out for yourself. Make sure you ask the right people; some have got more stake in it than others. Once you've got the story right, you sit down and write your own debut production for the Obsidian's grand reopening.'

'I can't produce *that* play!'

'Can't you now?'

'Am I allowed to write something so controversial?'

Beryl swung a scornful look her way. If Josie didn't shrivel under it, the orchids might. 'Of all the things you suddenly decide to ask my permission for – it's *writing*?'

'No,' Josie answered, her mind already taking the first running strides off ahead of her. 'I don't need *permission* to write Celeste's story. Her legend hangs over all of us. It should be told, properly, once and for all . . .'

Beryl raised her brows, nudging Josie on.

'. . . to put an end to all the frightened whispers, half-truths, and ghoulish details meted out to manipulate young girls.' She meant herself, and she knew it.

Beryl was nodding hard. Josie found herself mirroring the action. 'Yes,' she said. 'I see it now.'

Beryl grinned.

'But first,' Josie said, 'I have to cobble together some kind of community consensus on reopening the Obsidian. Josie tugged up her handbag, ready to take flight. 'And the news is already seeping out, so that's something I'd better get started on, quick smart!'

Her grandmother raised a liver-spotted hand to pat Josie's cheek firmly. 'Be on your way then. And you tell them – Beryl Frances has got your back.'

CHAPTER NINE

BACKWOODSMAN

Every morning, Vivienne woke with that demon on her chest. It went, she'd discovered, by many names. Not just Shame – but Remorse, Self-loathing; Rage. Each day she rose again, carried it briskly through the dew-spangled mist to Lake Evelyn, and drowned it there. After her swim, she could breathe easier, the whole day.

For the first time in her twenty-three years, the hours were *hers* to do with as she pleased. Mostly, she stayed in the library, making a dint in the endless books now at her disposal. She hadn't read so freely in years. *Reading is a lazy and unfashionable habit for a woman*, Mother had maintained, and too much of it would drive unattractive wrinkles between her brows.

Vivienne furrowed harder with every volume cracked open. If she were lucky enough to earn wrinkles, let it be for reading, then.

Her only egress, for both exercise and leisure, was to the lake. Vivienne's arms and shoulders were growing strong with all her swimming, a pleasing new definition emerging. Throughout the day, she would run her hands over her own body, relishing the rapid evolution, such a contrast to the slow strengthening of her spirit.

Vivienne had become fond of lounging by a lakeside jungle gap, where a submerged forest of fallen trees branched out, climbed by turtles. Vivienne loved the mellow paddling play of those turtles, wished she could steal one back to the lodge to keep in a large vase. She recognised this desire as loneliness.

Days, thus, were survivable. But the unquiet nights never seemed to end.

As the sun sank low, the record track for a nightmare began to spin. A bird screaming like a cat; the owl's whistling bombs; ceaseless snaps and cracks and scurries on the forest floor; scampering movement over the ceiling. Cicadas, katydids and crickets were legion. Most maddening, was the mammoth tree that groaned all night with a sound precisely like a heavy foot on the staircase . . .

Creeaaaak.

She was being driven out of her wits by this outlandish symphony. If she had the nerve, she might have sent a torch slicing into the dark forest, to identify her tormentors – be they possum, snake, or wallaby. But it was all Vivienne could do to hold the pillow tight over her head, until morning arrived. No wonder she woke with such terror on her chest.

The days, with their dichotomy of light and dark, ran one into the other, but Vivienne knew she'd been camped out in the lodge for a full week, when groceries appeared on her front porch.

She found the basket at dawn when she emerged, with swimsuit on, towel around her waist, ready for her morning swim. Vivienne cast an uneasy look around. Someone had been here while she was sleeping, and she hadn't heard a thing.

Vivienne hastened to unpack her basket. Mustn't waste these supplies, she'd never been so sick of egg and potato in all her days. Frustration was an unexpected way to feel about this bounty, nevertheless, as she put her goods away, there it was. Felix hadn't asked Vivienne what she might actually want ordered, and she was in dire need of tea or coffee, and milk for either. She must remember to make her requests for the following week.

From the basket, she took three large onions, sliced them neatly into halves and laid them out around the lodge, to try and absorb some of the noxious damp odour. A nifty homemaking trick she'd learned at finishing school. Not that she was making herself at *home* here, no fear!

Outside, a brush-turkey was scraping its giant nest up against the porch. Seeing her, the turkey flapped boldly onto the front balcony, claws clacking on wood.

'You can have this damned place, it's *all* yours,' Vivienne muttered, trotting off for the lake.

She was so busy resenting territorial turkeys and grocery deliverers who slunk about in the dark, that she failed to notice the locked, vine-strangled gate was gaping open, until she had sailed right through it. She stopped, turned around, and stared at it. Perhaps the delivery man had come this way instead of using the driveway?

Vivienne continued on warily, emerging into the benched clearing, to find it profoundly altered. All the long grass and weeds had been slashed back so that the granite steps stood out starkly in the morning rays. Construction rope around the rotting dive platform showed it was under repair. The stage area had been prepared for the laying of new concrete. There even looked to be a new floating walkway and stage, held up by drums.

'I'll be *deuced.*' It *was* an amphitheatre, and it wasn't abandoned at all.

She heard the approaching rumble of a large vehicle. There was little time to take this in, much less retreat from sight, before a tractor trundled into the clearing. Vivienne raised a hand to shield her eyes from the slanting sun, as the tractor belched to a halt not twenty feet away from her.

A towering man, with a dark beard and broad shoulders, leapt down from the cab. If he was shocked to come upon a strange woman standing in this deserted clearing in naught but a swimsuit, he was hiding it most chivalrously.

Neither seemed willing to speak first.

Vivienne waved a hand around at the mowed area; an imperious gesture, it felt. 'Did you do all this?'

'Most of it,' he said. 'What do you think? Not exactly The Globe is it?'

'It's frightfully bare now. I didn't mind it overgrown; it was somehow . . . charming.'

The man chuckled. '*Charming?* You're not from round here, then.'

Time to move on, before an encounter became conversation. Vivienne's feet were apparently mired in concrete, though. She tightened her towel.

He nodded towards the forest. 'You staying in Sylvan Mist?'

'No,' she answered hurriedly, 'somewhere else.'

'Well, I just opened the old gate to somewhere else, didn't know anyone was up there. Feel free to close it again. I'm Owen Monash.' He extended a large hand. 'My property's not far from here.'

Vivienne placed her cool fingers in his palm – shocked by the human touch, after so many days.

'Charlotte Vale,' she replied – taking the alias on impulse from one of her favourite movies: *Now, Voyager.*

Inexplicably, her name caused him to grin.

She withdrew her fingers from his warm palm before they were tempted to curl up and stay there.

'Are you finding it OK in that place?' he asked, with another nod towards Sylvan Mist.

It was none of his business. She shouldn't be countenancing this conversation, and yet . . .

'I'm getting by,' she said. 'Days are fine. The nights are . . . something else.'

He nodded, not looking the least surprised. 'You hang in there, Voyager.'

She didn't trust herself to reply to this perceptiveness without crying. Something in his kindness was quite unbearable.

'Well, I'd better get back to it,' he said. 'Josie will have my hide if I don't get done today.'

Vivienne nodded, forcing her feet to turn away.

She'd traversed several of Owen's freshly hewn steps, before the tractor grumbled back to life. He idled there then, watching, while Vivienne dropped her towel, and waded into the lake.

She might have been offended at being so blatantly ogled in her swimsuit, but the strangest thing was, she didn't think he was admiring her fine figure, or looking at her, at all.

His eyes were set on the lake, and there was no appreciation in them.

Vivienne's path to the lake was closed again the following morning. This time, by a monstrosity.

'What fresh hell is *this*?'

The strangled tree passage was blocked by spider web, the biggest she'd ever seen. A little scarlet honeyeater had been caught in the web, and in its thrashing struggle for freedom, had only managed to make a parcel of itself, before dying. At least, Vivienne hoped it was deceased, since a giant, golden orb spider was at work on its prize.

A bird-eating spider? This place is nightmare upon nightmare.

Vivienne scanned around for a branch to smash it away. She located something suitable – but didn't have the heart to strike either spider or bird. The bird was already lost, and the spider was just making the best of its dumb luck.

She dropped the branch, and turned away.

Perhaps she could take the open road around to the lake clearing?

'*Don't you dare disgrace*—' began Mother's voice in her conscience.

'Will you be quiet,' Vivienne snapped. 'I need to get to my lake.'

Vivienne passed out of the rainforest onto a narrow lane of richest volcanic red, bordering a rippling topography of fertile green. After more than a week alternating between frigid lake and damp forest prison, where little sunshine intruded, the morning rays burning off mist in the many pockets and hillocks of farmland, warmed more than just Vivienne's form. Crisp country air rushed to clear the miasma of mildew that seemed to live permanently in her nostrils. The trees here were not strung with spiders, but heavily hung with white cockatoos, their wings flashing off brilliant light.

There was a new jig in Vivienne's step as she headed on down the lane.

The first Friesian cow appearing on the road ahead stopped Vivienne dead in her tracks. It was quickly joined by a whole herd, lumbering unstoppably for her.

Vivienne yelped. *Good grief*, she was going to die in a stampede. She'd have to hightail it into the nearest paddock, where the fencing would protect her until the herd passed. She had not reckoned, however, on barbed wire. There was no going over this fence – she'd have to squeeze beneath.

A loud bellow from the cattle mob, coming inexorably closer, decided it. Vivienne flung herself to her knees, pressed flat to the ground and began to wriggle beneath the rusty barbs. An inelegant endeavour, if ever there was one.

She squirmed beneath the fence and lay prostrate among cowpats, panting from the adventure of it. The herd plodded slowly past, three or four abreast, lowing.

'That was close,' she huffed – though it wasn't, really.

Vivienne might have laughed at the ridiculousness of hiding, neck deep in cow excrement, without having to suffer the humiliation too, had it not been for the tuneful whistle of an approaching farmer, following his herd.

She had a few seconds to entertain the prayer he would miss her here, partially hidden by brambles, and nature's stinking camouflage.

But, no; the whistling halted, and so did he.

Vivienne pushed up and turned to face the bearded farmer leaning against the fence post, with a single grass weed in the corner of his mouth.

Who does he think he is – Montgomery Clift?

She told him so.

The grass jumped at the corner of Owen Monash's mouth. His brown eyes danced. Vivienne promptly regretted her rudeness.

Owen tossed the weed aside. 'I think you're swimming in the wrong place.'

'Your cows frightened me.'

'If you think my girls are frightening, wait until you meet Sam the Bull.'

'I'd rather not,' Vivienne replied; picking her way back through the cowpats.

'Might want to hop out of his paddock, then.'

'Naturally I would be in the bull's pen,' Vivienne muttered, moving more rapidly. 'And what else would I be wearing but red?'

'Actually, the "hating red" thing's a myth,' he said.

Vivienne was about to crawl under the fence. 'Would you please turn around?'

'Sure. Or you could use my gate.'

Vivienne glanced along the fence. Yes, there was the gate; less than twelve feet away.

'I'd prefer this way,' Vivienne said, miming a spinning motion.

Owen turned quickly away.

Under and out again, Vivienne cleared her throat.

He looked back at her with frank admiration. 'Is this some kind of newfangled beauty bath?'

Vivienne knew she had a lovely physique, but surely nobody, even Vivienne George, looked good in manure. Then again, maybe manure was a 'thing' for farmers?

She told him that, too.

Owen had a laugh as broad as his shoulders. 'Not since I was a kid, no. Josie and I used to love stomping on cowpats. But the trick is to land on a dry one.'

Vivienne grimaced.

'It's a bit like life,' he said. 'A cowpat looks solid; you take a leap, land yourself in the middle of a steaming pile.'

'Oh look, he's a philosopher,' Vivienne sniped, starting to walk.

Owen joined her. 'Not following you,' he said. 'Just got to get my girls up to the north paddock.'

'Why do you keep calling them your "girls"?'

Owen smiled. 'They're my favourites.'

'You can tell one black and white cow from another?' Vivienne asked, disbelievingly.

They'd reached the tail end of his herd.

Owen moved in amongst the cows, stopping to stroke the ears and temples of one with a pirate's eye mask encircling long lashes. 'This is Cowsette.'

If such a thing were possible, it almost looked like the cow enjoyed the petting; eyes nearly rolling back in her head.

'This one,' he said, patting the speckled rump of another, 'is Udder Gabler. She's my best producer.'

He weaved over to a cow spotted not unlike a Dalmatian. 'This beauty is Madame Bovine. No fence is a match for her.'

The two cows alongside received a touch each. 'This girl is Lies and Dolittle. And this one, Anna Cowenina.'

'They're names for actresses,' Vivienne said, surprised by the cleverness. He grinned.

'I get it,' she said 'You're *mocking* my alias from yesterday.'

Her tone did not seem to disturb his tranquillity. 'These are my cows, and those are their names. Josie feeds the calves, and has naming privileges. But if you want to talk about mocking, you're the one who accused me of having a "thing" for manure.'

That was fair. Vivienne walked on, with Owen continuing wordlessly alongside.

After a time, he said, in aside: 'Please don't tell the rest, but Madame Bovine is my favourite girl.'

Vivienne hid her smile behind closed lips.

At the turn off to Sylvan Mist, she departed with a shrug, and not a further word. Vivienne had the feeling she'd be seeing Owen Monash again, and the very thought was the first to make her feel optimistic in many dispirited days.

No . . . *months.*

CHAPTER TEN

THE PLAY'S THE THING

Josie was in the Igloo, moving the last few seats into rows, as towns-folk rattled through the door for a hastily convened meeting of the Barrington Theatre Company.

Being here in the Igloo again only brought back all Hugo Bernard's criticisms of their beloved war relic. Her heart hurt. What was *dingy* about the fairy lights strung through the trussed arches? What was *decrepit* about the potted lipstick palms lining the red cedar stage sawn and built by Barrington's prized woodworkers? Sure, the concrete floor was unassuming, the corrugated iron walls unglamourous, and there were only four, plain casement windows, but when the lights dimmed and that first hush fell over the audi-ence, the same ageless magic flowed in this auditorium as the finest in the country.

'How dare he,' Josie incanted, through clenched teeth.

She had penned a speech, only penned was too soft a word; she had *poured* herself into this passionate spiel. Might even garner Josie a standing ovation; if her audience was so inclined.

All four brothers had come to Josie's meeting in support – Reg, in defiance of his new wife. Her father had declined entirely, and the image of Gabe Monash sitting at the kitchen table with only Daphne for company was more than Josie could think about.

Reg and Ernest had grabbed seats up front. Josie expected Owen to do the same, but he was unaccountably standoffish, taking a seat at the back, with only the briefest greeting kiss.

The Igloo was richly fragrant with baked goods and cigarette smoke. Josie's theatre group had convened a potluck for supper. Stomach cramping, Josie swung past the trestle table to snatch a plate for a long evening ahead.

She hurried the last Devon rolls onto her plate so greedily that mashed clouds of potato squeezed out of their meat wraps and over her fingers.

'You always were a fiend for my Devon rolls,' laughed the elegant brunette coming to stand beside her.

Josie gave a startled chuckle. 'Mrs Henry!'

Miles's mum. Never before had she come to any of Josie's meetings, and she had to choose *this one* for her first? Her pulse fluttered.

The women leaned forward to kiss cheeks. Rosa Henry patted her arm. 'You look worried, dear girl.'

'Do I?' Josie licked mashed potato off her finger, as casually as one might do in front of a long-coveted mother-in-law.

'Positively vexed.' Rosa winked. 'The exact expression your mother wore when she was about to get the cane.'

Josie nodded over her shoulder at a corpulent elderly man in horn-rimmed glasses. 'Can you blame me? Headmaster Beauman has seen fit to turn up here tonight.'

'We're all terribly curious. There have been such rumours floating around town, you wouldn't believe some of the schemes they're accusing you of.'

'You might be surprised.' Josie grinned. 'I'd better go settle the troops.'

Coming to the front of the auditorium, Josie had to admit: her company looked peeved, and they'd brought reinforcements. There was a reckoning planned for this meeting, and Josie just hoped she could hold them off long enough to explain her brilliant plan in full.

Josie's eyes swept the room, seeking out her allies on Main Street.

Clarence Reece was perched on the edge of his seat, already blotting his shiny head at the prospect of Josie's calling on him. Purse-lipped Elsie Reece had camped out with her noisily chittering friends, far from her husband.

Rita Caracella had carried her own plush chair and teacup all the way down from her Old Curiosity Shop, without disturbing a single hair in her silver bouffant. She was studying Josie right back, her pince-nez spectacles attached by a chain to an ornate Victorian hairpin.

Niall from the Corner Shop was in his usual prime position, Brylcreemed high-quiff tragically at odds with his age, which was the same as her own father's. Niall had brought his shop girl, Laura, along as his date. She sat limply by his side, like a ventriloquist's dummy awaiting animation.

There was a familiar clack of court shoes through the door, as Beryl Frances made an entrance.

'Grandy?!' Josie cried. 'But you can't drive!'

'No, I just can't get caught doing it,' Beryl replied, taking stock of the attendees.

Josie tried for sternness. 'Constable Jacobs took your licence for very good reason.'

Beryl stood pointedly in front of a young man, tapping her walking stick until he jumped up from his seat, muttering apologies, and scuttled away.

Beryl sat with a pleased huff. 'I was wiping Constable Jacobs' fat little bottom not too long ago.'

Constable Jacobs, returning with a plate, emitted a Beryl-weary sigh. 'Really, Mrs Frances.' He held out his hand for her keys.

Josie left the pair to squabble over female independence in advanced years versus the recent prevalence of fender benders on Main Street.

Josie had a full Igloo now. She cleared her throat with dramatic licence. Babble eased to murmuring, then fell to silence. Faces lifted to hers. Like a trilling prelude, the rapt attention triggered familiar upsurge of exhilaration.

Josie was born for centre stage. Her hand lifted to pat the locket heart at her clavicle, then she launched . . .

'Ladies and gentleman, there's lots of new faces here this evening, so I'd like to welcome you all to this meeting of the Barrington Theatre Company. I hope to see more of you on a regular basis. We meet every Friday evening, with a performance at the end of each season. Straight up: let's address the recent review . . .'

Josie unfolded her notepaper, and began to orate. 'We have been too meanly criticised. Let me remind you: Barrington has a long, proud history of supporting the theatre. *Barrington* was the place Rudy Meyer chose to build his rainforest lodge, to accommodate such rising talent as Celeste Starr.'

There was a shifting, throats cleared. Josie dropped in a wide smile to reassure the audience she wasn't heading in that direction.

At least not *yet*, she appended silently.

'Our proud record has continued right through to today – even with an allegedly dilapidated Igloo, we still play to sell-out shows. Wally Mosely, from the *Tablelands Sun* has described our plays as, "a rollicking good time", "the best theatre on the Tablelands", and "insipid"—' Josie blanched. 'I mean, "*inspired*"!'

A current of laughter gathered charge.

'*So*, we are not going to let one out-of-towner's *opinion* sour the pride we take in our town's theatre company.'

A voice came from the back: 'What about the trust we have in this town's theatre *director*!'

Josie's hand went to her hip. 'All right, what about it? Let's put it to a motion. If you agree with a town *outsider* that I should step aside as director, let's have a show of hands . . .'

Josie counted the rising hands, poker faced. Her eye twitched as she tallied Niall's hand among them. Niall had taken every lead role for five seasons running, and *this* was how he repaid her?

Josie gritted her teeth. 'Next, we'll have a show of hands for those who think . . .' She amended the proposition in her head: *that uppity city folk, far removed from the realities of rural life, shouldn't have the right to judge any of us for what we hold most dear, or the hopes we aspire to!*

But, finished thus: '. . . that I should be given another chance to prove myself. Those in favour?'

She stared at her speech notes, waiting for the votes to hike up into the air. Finally, she looked up.

It was a veritable sapling forest.

Josie gave a decisive nod, not bothering to count. 'Righty-ho, you're stuck with me. And now, I'd like to discuss our end-of-winter production.'

'What's the next play?' called Rita.

'Please not Ibsen again,' said Peggy. 'Anything but that old fool.'

'Knowing the kind of stuff our Josie reads,' piped up Clarence, 'it'll be romantic suspense.' Josie was surprised by this betrayal by Clarence, proud of his boldness too.

Ernest raised his hand. 'I have it on good authority we're doing Wilde. *The Importance of Being Me*!'

The group groaned widely.

Across the group, Beryl Frances issued a small, firm nod. Josie took a deep breath, not letting her smile slip, and launched into her next speech point.

'Before I get to the play, I want to talk about the *venue* we'll use.'

Their befuddlement was plain to see. *Venue?*

'I think you've forgotten, we have a choice of theatres in Barrington. We're not limited to the Igloo, *lovely* though it is.'

The rabble had fallen into a strained silence. No time like the present. 'I am planning to reopen the Obsidian for our next show.'

There was a shot of laughter, followed by a mortified hush.

'But you *can't*!' Rita said, flicking spilled tea off her lap.

'She certainly cannot,' Elsie sniffed; settling it.

Peggy laughed. 'She already *has*.'

There was a thunderclap of collective shock.

Josie raised her voice. 'It's true. I've already taken steps towards reopening . . .'

Elsie stood up, cheeks like a puffer fish. 'You don't have approval!'

Josie's smile was apologetic. 'I certainly do. I've already talked to the Lake Evelyn Trust, and got it. It's a public use area, we're a non-profit group, and there's no law against it. There's nothing, other than superstition, to stop me.'

'But it's not *safe*!'

'Look,' Josie said, placatingly, 'I'm not doing this to encourage *swimming* in the lake again. We're simply going to reclaim a magnificent amphitheatre currently going to waste.'

Elsie spun on Constable Jacobs, shaking with rage. 'You tell her! She can't reopen a crime scene!'

Thanks, Yellsie – now everyone's going home with a headache.

Constable Jacobs looked anxiously between Elsie and Josie. 'Else, no crimes, despite proper investigation, were found to have occurred at Lake Evelyn. They were drownings, nothing more.'

'*Six girls!*' Elsie cried – a screech, really. 'Seven, if you count the flaming actress who set off the Curse. Don't you *dare* tell me no crime has been committed! *That* lake has seen more police searches than any other place on the Tablelands. Constable, you cannot allow it to be reopened – for the sake of our girls!'

Elsie plonked down, quaking, to a female cheer.

Constable Jacobs stood now, hands making a quelling motion. 'Folks, police will not be preventing Barrington from enjoying its lake.'

A loud rumble of shock circled the room.

Beryl rapped her walking stick on the floor. 'Now let Josephine *finish*!'

Constable Jacobs sat with a relieved plumping of cushions.

'All right,' Josie said, reining in her crowd. 'It's true, our lake has seen some appalling tragedies. And they have affected our town terribly. *However*, that doesn't mean we should allow these tragedies to keep us superstitious for ever.'

Clarence raised a hand. 'Josie, I think we all appreciate what you're trying to achieve . . .'

'Speak for *yourself*,' Elsie shot out.

Clarence's neck gave a spasm. 'But – *why* does it have to be that amphitheatre?'

Josie was prepared for this one. 'To quote Eleanora Duse: "To save the theatre, the theatre must be destroyed, the actors and actresses must all die of the plague—"'

There was a rumble of disgust. A snipe came from the mid-section: 'You're really not selling this, Josephine!'

Josie held up a hand. '"They poison the air, they make art impossible. It is not drama that they play, but pieces for the theatre. We should return to the Greeks, play in the open air; the drama dies of stalls and boxes and evening dress, and people who come to digest their dinner."'

She swung her big brown eyes around the group, nodding significantly. 'Don't you see? No fancy sets or fusty old theatres. Just a play in open air.'

'Why are you doing this now?' Rita demanded. 'Why can't you just wait to see if the Curse settles on its own?'

Beryl tsked. 'Curses don't "settle", they get broken, Rita.'

'It's not our job to break curses,' Elsie snapped. 'We just want our daughters kept safe.'

'You *still* haven't told us what play you're working with,' put in Headmaster Beauman.

'Already told you,' interjected Ernest. 'It's all about Me.'

Headmaster Beauman reached to flick the back of Ernest's ear.

But the group had caught on this tangent. 'Tell us the play!'

This brought Josie to the most heavily underlined, sweated over, crossed out, and rewritten portion of her notes. Josie's eyes darted to Owen's. His head was cocked, a groove forming between his brows. To Beryl's eyes she fled next. She imagined she could hear Grandy clucking her tongue. Finally, Josie's gaze tiptoed along the row, to rest, ever so fleetingly, on Miles's mother. Mrs Henry was not echoing the throng's vocal cry, rather twisting a pearl at her ear lobe, the beginnings of a smile working at her lips.

'I have in mind, an Australian tragedy.'

Several townsfolk were sitting straighter in their seats – Owen among them. Josie skimmed quickly back to her paper. 'A story with deep emotional resonance.'

Nobody drop a pin, you'll ruin this glorious silence.

'I want to dramatise the story of Celeste Starr.'

101

There was a collective breath indrawn; its exhalation like a thunderclap.

'I won't stand for this,' Elsie cried, leaping to her feet. Josie might have snorted at this irony, but Elsie was motioning for Clarence. 'And none of you should humour this lunacy, either. This meeting is *over*!'

The Reeces were quickly followed in departure, with townspeople scraping back chairs across the room. An outraged buzz had overtaken.

'Wait, please!' Josie cried. "If you'll just hear me out—'

But the Igloo was in uproar. Those not skedaddling for the exit, were forming loudly dissenting clusters around the supper table.

'That Josephine,' Rita groused to a set of similarly coiffed heads, as they removed their offerings from the trestle table. 'She's Beryl all over again.'

The flock gathered momentum. Through the door they flowed, in a procession of grumbles and objections and re-covered platters, clutched tight.

Josie trailed behind, corralling chairs; refusing to let defeat show. 'See you next week, everyone. Same time, same place!'

Josie stepped aside at the front door, allowing the headmaster to exit, balancing a plate – not his own – stacked high with leftover food.

'Washed and returned, Mr Beauman' Josie snapped, turning back to the waiting circle of ever-loyal brothers.

CHAPTER ELEVEN
LEAF EATER

Neither pillows nor fingers sunk in ears while humming; not even the metronome of Vivienne's feet against the floorboards, was working to cover this night's dreadful, thronging sounds. A fretful wind had come to harangue the forestland. The squall had quieted the owl-bombs and bird-yowls, but only amplified the assault of rasping branches and falling limbs on her strained nerves. Always she was waiting for the next crack and groan.

In the barricaded library, Vivienne lay in her swag of blankets, right beside the roll top desk housing its black telephone. If Felix really cared for her, surely, he would sense, even from so far away, that she needed a kind word. No, his *permission* to run for the roadster, buried deep in leaf fall. Every moment longer that Felix didn't ring, her resentment grew.

To distract herself, Vivienne had resorted to soothing repetitions of her old singing scales. She hadn't practised for years, and her first attempts were strangled and reedy; ridiculous. But it was all she had right now: treading up and down those scales, major and minor, like a ladder ascended out of mental anguish. Slowly, her voice began to warm; her courage, to grow.

There was movement on the porch below. Her singing cut off abruptly.

Vivienne sat up, hugging her knees. She was grateful the lights were already off as she slid stealthily to the window, pressed her forehead against it, and peered into the darkness astir. She saw naught but her pale face and hair; a wraith transposed over the shifting forest.

Clumping came again.

Something was out there. And all she had for protection was a barred library door, and a telephone.

Vivienne squinted hard, lashes brushing the windowpane. Whoever or *whatever* was down there – her noisy visitor would show itself the moment it stepped out from beneath the porch awning. Unless it was not leaving, only just arriving.

She held her breath, straining.

There! A loping movement towards the trees. Yet another creature – but what *kind*?

Vivienne took a torch, and eased open the library balcony door to the tempestuous night air. Branches whisked along the balustrade, wind licked her hair across her eyes; spitting cold raindrops, whipping up her negligee. Bitterly, she counted the loss of her peignoir once more.

Eyes adjusting, Vivienne beheld a luminescent, bluish-green light gathering round tree bases and climbing the trunks in great glowing clusters. *Foxfire?* Vivienne illuminated her torch. Lightly, she touched the shaft of light upon that eerie glow, transforming it, instantly, back to mere greyish fungi. *How astonishing!*

Even more astonishing, however, was the unearthly crash of branches nearby. Her torch beam circled skittishly for a glimpse of the interloper – not really wanting to find it at all.

'*Courage,* Vivienne,' she hissed. 'Where's your mettle?'

More boldly, her light beam moved now, following a moving shadow. Finally coming to rest on a branch where sat a peculiar, red-brown furred creature unlike anything she'd seen or imagined before: muscular forearms; long tail snaking down; black gloved hands grasping the tree; and, in a dark face, were eyes shining like red discs, and staring directly at her.

Vivienne yelped. Her torch flew from her hand, and dropped to the ground with an extinguishing *thwack*.

She would never sleep again.

Morning came, all the same. She must have dozed, though there was no rest in it. The memory of bioluminescent fungi lent the peculiar quality of a dream – or nightmare – to the creature she had seen.

Vivienne trudged to the lake for her lap, barely able to keep her feet on the path. Remnant drops of the night's rainfall plucked at the leaves, making them leap and dance, so that the forest seemed to be shivering, glossily, around her. Earthstar fungi proliferated on the water-logged trail. Just beyond the strangler fig portal, an improbably lurid blue snake crossed her path.

This goddamned, otherworldly place!

By the time she'd swum her lap and returned to the lodge, Vivienne was flat out fuming. *She* was the guest here; she should be left to sojourn in privacy and isolation. Whatever was out there, it had no *right* to disturb her. Vivienne refused to put up with another night like that. She'd investigate the trees in the safety of daylight, and chase the creature off.

Vivienne found a ladder, propped indolently against the lodge, library side, and hauled it over to the trees, refusing to entertain nagging new questions. *What was the ladder doing there? Who put it there?*

Fat lot of good the ladder was anyway. Though she hauled it from tree to tree, stretching and straining to see, there was nothing to be found; not a clue remaining. Maybe she could frighten it out with noise? After another search, Vivienne returned with metal buckets to smash together.

'Come out!' she cried from atop her ladder, smashing her cymbals. 'Show yourself! Where are you?'

'Where's who, Nancy Drew?' enquired a familiar voice, on her right flank.

Vivienne cast a look of aspersion over shoulder at her bearded tres-passer. 'What are *you* doing creeping around here like a peeping Tom?'

Owen grinned, holding up a milk pail. 'I brought you some milk, fresh from our dairy – but now I'm afraid you're just going to toss the milk and use my pail instead.'

'Give the pail to me,' Vivienne said, hand outstretched.

Owen stopped smiling. 'Seriously?'

The corner of Vivienne's mouth hitched up, amusedly.

Owen came to stand beside her, pail hanging safely by his side, and stared up into the trees. 'Looking for inspiration?'

Vivienne sighed. She really didn't want to stay here, balanced above the dairy farmer's head in nothing but her bathers. Come to think of it – why did the backwoodsman turn up every time she was scantily clad?

She put this to him.

He gave her a dry look. 'It is starting to cast me in a bad light.'

Vivienne indicated he should help her down. She took the large hand offered, and dropped lightly to the ground.

She dusted her hands and faced Owen, hands on hips.

'I'm looking for a freakish creature that was terrorising me last night. I'll be damned if I have to suffer through that again!'

Owen had been smiling, but quickly ceased. 'What *kind* of creature?' he asked carefully. A little too carefully, Vivienne thought.

'For your information, a hideous one.'

'Hideous, like a . . . ?'

'Like a hideous, hairy thing,' she replied. 'Not quite so hairy as you, though.'

She'd expected to elicit a smile, but he did not break from seriousness. 'Was it tiger striped? We've had some thylacine sightings locally.'

Vivienne rolled her eyes. 'No, I didn't see an extinct animal.'

'Describe it then.'

'Large. Long tail. Bigger than a possum, or any other mammal that could conceivably be in a tree. Also, it was very . . . *staring*.'

Owen mused over this. 'Would you say it looked like a – bunyip?'

'Now a *bunyip*? You must think me the greatest idiot to have ever ascended this mountain.'

'No, I don't,' he said. 'I'm asking you quite seriously.'

'No one believes in bunyips anymore, they're just a tale for children.'

Owen shot her a sardonic look. 'You'd be surprised.'

'Actually, I expect people believe in all manner of things up here. I saw a *blue* snake this morning, bright as a jewel.'

'Ah, a tree snake.'

'No, it was on the ground,' she retorted, beginning to take down her ladder.

Owen moved to carry the opposite side.

Across the ladder, she shot him an accusing look. 'Why did you say the creature was a bunyip? I was already bothered by it, and now *you've* quite terrified me.'

'Thought you didn't believe in bunyips,' he said.

'I certainly don't. But I don't believe in freakish hairy things in trees in the dead of night, either. And yet here it was.' Vivienne cast a simmering look at the lodge.

Owen followed her eyeline. 'Are you still handling it all right in there?'

'I will be fine, once I take a heavy torch to my bunyip.'

'Wouldn't do that.'

'Why ever not?' she said, hand rising to polka dotted hips.

'Well,' he said slowly, 'it could be a bunyip, if you believe the legend of the Lake Evelyn Monster . . .'

Vivienne stayed an eye roll.

'Then again, might also be one of Barrington's fabled tree kangaroos.'

'Tree-what-nows?' Vivienne said.

'Tree kangaroos.' He pointed to the canopy. 'They live up there.'

'What utter nonsense,' Vivienne replied.

Inside, the Bakelite begin to ring.

Felix!

Owen appeared not to have logged the telephone, or her disparagement. 'I've never seen one myself, but the red gold loggers, back in the twenties, used to talk about the strangest creatures in these trees. Did it look a bit like a wallaby?'

'Oh, I—' Vivienne was having difficulty following Owen's conversation. The telephone shrilled incessantly – how was Owen not hearing it? – and the urgent trilling pushed Vivienne's shoulders to her ears, ran her heartbeat into her throat. She was unsure if she wanted the telephone to stop, or for a chance to break from Owen.

The telephone cut out.

Vivienne sighed, shoulders shaking loose. 'It *was* dreadful, though. And I won't stand for it another night.'

The telephone shrieked again.

Vivienne's eyes went wide. 'I'm so sorry,' she cried, 'I have to—'

She abandoned Owen and the ladder, banging through the front door into the lodge, up past the grandfather clock, taking the stairs two at a time, panting out his name: *Felix! Wait!*

She slammed into the roll top desk with her hip, scooping up the handset, clutching it to her ear.

'Felix, here I am!'

'Why did you not pick up? You must answer when I call, or I'll think something terrible has befallen you.'

'Yes, I'm sorry. I didn't mean to worry you.'

There was a catch in her voice, and Felix seized on it. 'What's the matter?'

'No, it's nothing.'

'You're fibbing, I can hear it in your voice.'

'I just . . . I don't like this place.'

'Never mind; it's a roof over your head, for now.'

'There's all kinds of noises and disturbances. My nerves are frayed to bits. Then last night, there was a . . . creature. And this is going to sound ridiculous, I know it is, but the locals say it might be a bunyip—'

'The locals! Have you been meeting people, my girl?'

'No.' Vivienne's lie surprised her. But Owen wasn't 'people', he was just . . . Owen.

'Remember, I did warn you about the dopey locals there.'

'That's right, you did.'

'What have you been doing to amuse yourself?'

'Oh, I've . . . been reading a tremendous amount lately.' Vivienne flicked a glance at her toppling pile. 'At the moment I'm engrossed in *The Enchanted April.*'

'And what else?'

What *else*? Vivienne thought she might be close enough to the window to see below. She tugged the cord along with her, stretching to peer through the glass.

Owen was standing beneath the trees, his back to the lodge, scrutinising the branches above.

The sight touched something small and most fragile within her.

She snapped away from the window. 'I'm sorry, but do you have an update for me, or are you just—'

'And what kind of update would you like?'

Vivienne blinked hard at the uncharacteristic barb in Felix's tone. She hadn't meant to sound brattish. 'I'm sorry. Only, it's killing me not knowing how angry they all must be. I thought perhaps you might have some news?'

Felix was silent for a long time.

Vivienne realised how hard she was grimacing in expectation of his reply, when her lips began to burn. 'Please,' she said.

'Here's something: Howard called me over to see him.'

Vivienne threw her free arm around her belly, wrenching in her ribs. 'Oh God, is he furious?'

'On the contrary, he's very worried about you.'

'About *me*? He was the one made to look a fool.'

Felix gave a dry chortle. 'Howard has been consoling his hurt pride very well.'

She frowned. 'What does that mean?'

'Howard has also been expressing concerns about your . . . disturbed state.'

'*Disturbed?*' Tighter went Vivienne's gripping arm, nails digging in where the talons of terror left their daily imprint.

'He's worried you've broken from reality. And he's certainly letting everyone know it.' Vivienne shrank from the serious way Felix was speaking, so unlike his normal playful manner. 'He doesn't want you to suffer alone so unnecessarily, when there are professionals able help you.'

Recovery, professionals – these were the words Howie used?

'I'd better call him, and set some things straight.' The thought hadn't even occurred to her until now, that this phone line went both ways. How witless she had been! It was a lifeline at her command.

'If you think you're up to that? Just remember: I can't protect you from the things Howard will say to you directly, nor the influence he might have over you . . .'

No, she *couldn't* call Howard! 'I should ring and apologise to Mother, though. I think I can do a better job of standing up for myself, now that I've put some distance between us.'

'I'm surprised you're feeling strong enough to handle Geraldine – all that thinking of yours must be working wonders!'

Vivienne pressed her thumb to the painful furrow between her eyes. Perhaps Felix was right. She wasn't ready for that, either. Her mother had not abided Vivienne's unhappiness even gingerly hinted at, imagine how she'd react in the wake of such public disgrace; the George name dragged through mud.

'It's probably best,' Felix said, 'to let Howard and Geraldine be, for the time being. Out of sight, out of mind, and all that. Wait until this nastiness simmers down, before you think about coming back. You'll be all right, tucked away there for a while longer – won't you, my girl?'

'Yes, I'll be all right,' Vivienne repeated dully.

'Good girl. Keep up your reading, and don't let your mind be too troubled about what they're all saying down here. You're safe from it there. I'll let you know when all this nonsense has passed. Hear me?'

Cold dismalness came crawling up her spine. 'I do.'

The connection clicked out.

By the time Vivienne had neatly dabbed her tears away and returned downstairs, Owen had finished his own inspection of the trees, and sat waiting on the front stoop, forearms resting on large thighs. Beside him was the milk can.

'You didn't have to wait,' she said.

Something in her voice must have struck him, for he looked up at her searchingly.

'Really,' she said, unable to bear his expression. 'You should go.'

Owen cracked his knuckles then stood up, pail in hand. 'Would you have a jug?'

The broad size of his chest, so close, made her eyes hot with tears inadequately shed.

She turned abruptly into the lodge.

Heavy footfalls, moments later, indicated he had followed her in. In the kitchen they said nothing as she banged around looking for a pitcher. Both were still wordless as he poured the milk carefully into her enamel jug, not spilling a drop.

Only after he'd finished, and she'd followed him back out onto the porch, did Vivienne speak – hopeful now of controlling the lachrymose quaver that had caught his notice earlier.

'I'm not irrational, and I'm certainly not ... disturbed. I know my own mind."

Owen's simple nod, spurred her on.

'I'm no liar, either. I *saw* that creature.'

For some reason, this made Owen grin widely.

'What are *you* smiling at?' she demanded.

Owen's brown eyes were gentle, though he hadn't stopped grinning. 'You reminded me of my sister Josie, just now. You know when I told you about the thylacine sightings locally?'

Vivienne frowned.

'Those were my sister's. She swears, and I really do mean *swears* . . .' Owen chuckled, 'there's a Tablelands tiger living in the scrubland up behind our dairy.'

'A *Tablelands* Tiger?'

'It wouldn't be called a Tasmanian one, would it?'

Vivienne thought she might laugh, but none came. She stared at Owen, until his smile disappeared, and his eyes grew serious.

He hoisted up his pail, readying to leave. 'Don't let this place get to you.'

'It's not really *this* place,' Vivienne said, hearing the quaver back in her voice.

His searching look was back. 'The place you've come from, then.'

'More . . . people there.'

He nodded. 'Your husband.'

Vivienne glanced at her hand, discovering she had been wrenching her engagement ring around. 'The man I left standing at the altar on our wedding day,' she corrected. 'And, for that matter, the mother who wouldn't let me break off the engagement in the first place.'

'So this is your hiding spot.'

None of these were questions, she realised; rather statements of insights.

'You might say I'm on my . . . hidingmoon.' She saw his appreciation for this droll line, held in check. 'I don't know how I'll ever recover from the shame of it, and I don't want to see anyone, ever again.'

'Not even an excessively diverting sister of mine, who believes in thylacines?'

'Not even her.'

'Probably for the best,' he said. 'Josie would talk your ear off, embroil you in all kinds of schemes. We send her up to the calves' shed just to have a *minute's* peace. You shouldn't have to put up with that kind of company when you're feeling fragile.'

Vivienne smiled – the very feeling of it bringing fresh tears. 'I'll think about it.'

CHAPTER TWELVE

RETURN TO MAGIC

After Josie had served up breakfast for brothers and bovines alike, she sought escape from watching eyes. Chiefly, those of her increasingly pensive father, and exponentially aggravating sister-in-law. Josie also needed privacy to open the mysterious letter that had arrived for her that morning. For hopes so impossible to utter aloud as hers today, only her true childhood refuge would do.

She skirted successfully by the dairy, without being spotted by Reg and Owen, who were hosing out the milking floor. Then, over the hillcrest and down the other side she glissaded in her manure-splattered gumboots, ankles taut against the steep descent. Her right hand roved between her heart locket and the letter concealed in her overalls' top pocket.

The billabong nestled in the gully below, within a grove of paper-bark gums, was fed by a seasonal creek during the Wet. Its summer fill depleted, the billabong had withdrawn from sight, leaving only secret pockets of water beneath the large boulders strewn around.

The Hiding Billabong, Josie called it.

In this place, she felt closest to those precious years after the war, when Gabe had brought the Monash siblings home again. They had been wonderful years for Josie: *all together once more*. And though there was surely no danger of being sent away again, Josie had striven, just in case, to be the most captivating daughter a bereaved father might ask for: always bright and scintillating; provoking his laughter every chance she got. Her father's happiness – or the hope of it – had been always at the forefront of her mind.

Shortly after reclaiming his children from Grandy's, Gabe had brought young Josie down here, to show her how the billabong never fully disappeared, rather hid away in secret until the next Wet drew it all back together again. Gabe lifted a large rock and invited Josie to peer into the hollow with him. She expected mere dirt, perhaps worms springing up or giant centipedes scurrying away, but beneath that rock lay a tiny pool of water – deepest, dusky blue – becoming luminous as the sun lit once more upon it.

'It's *magic*—' Josie cried, peering in.

Her father looked at her with ineffable sorrow, but the words he spoke over her, were not mournful at all. 'Don't you ever stop believing in magic, chickadee. Life has robbed us both enough already, but there is *still* magic, waiting to be found.'

Josie considered her father in wide-eyed wonderment. Was *this* the serious man who baulked at fanciful children's stories, reading to the Monash children each night from his own bookshelves? Could this be the same man who believed in only one unseen world – a Heaven, which to Josie's mind sounded suspiciously like sombre Sunday services running without end, and certainly no compensatory morning tea.

Yet; believe in *magic*, he said. In fact, 'Promise me,' he said next.

'I promise,' she replied, scrunching up her nose into a smile. If Josie's father insisted, well she would do just that.

She had, too.

116

First pursuing magic through both literature and theatre, later creating her *own* magic as scriptwriter, and theatre director. Josie held on to that girlish vow after her father had stopped coming down with her to find the Hiding Billabong, when his mouth organ went away for good, even once Josie matured enough to understand: she could disobey her father, disappoint him, drop her beguiling best self, even raise his gentle ire, without losing his love for a moment.

She would never be sent away again.

And she hoped *that* understanding would sustain her in the months ahead, as her father's countenance would certainly grow more sombre. Gabe didn't know it yet, but Josie Monash was going to write the most shocking story that *could* be told in these parts. *That's far enough*, Gabe had told her that first night, before he had an inkling how far she really planned to go. *I won't have it.*

It had to be done. If the mere mention of Celeste emptied the Igloo in minutes, then the dramatisation of her death would fill amphitheatre seats faster still. No play by a long dead Englishman would sell as many tickets as the beautiful, controversial actress could.

Josie discarded her boots to sink her feet deep in the drift of paperbark leaves, forming whorls and shapes, savouring the texture and crunch. Around the grove, quartz stones sparkled in the brilliant light. A Willie Wagtail darted along the creek bed, on the hunt. The rock-ringed outline of the sandpit her father had built for her one dry season was still visible, too – though the sand had long ago been washed away. Now to find the Hiding Billabong . . .

Josie scouted for the right rock. She was frequently wrong, but that was part of the game's wonder. Except when she might pick a boulder hiding a huge red belly black snake, coiled up asleep. Silently though Josie backed away, she was always sorry to have outed a serpent. Reg considered it his duty, both as eldest brother and the childhood survivor of a snakebite – likely dry, but nevertheless cut and sucked out by Gabe – to eradicate all snakes from the Monash farm. Reg seemed to go everywhere armed with a shovel.

Josie chose her boulder, applied her nails to the underside, and began to lift. The boulder peeled out of the earth, and the cloudy, sapphire pool was revealed, already beginning to glow.

See? Magic.

Josie sat back; nostalgia a delightful ache. She was not sorry she'd failed to outgrow this. Wind was funnelling down the gully, a rolling wave through the treetops – one of her favourite sounds. Josie tipped back her head, smiling.

Time for my letter.

Josie tapped her heart locket for good luck, drew out the letter and stared at it. Luckily, she had spied the envelope on top of the pile Ernest collected from the mail barrel, and swiped it hurriedly away before Daphne sighted it. Josie had learned that lesson: until Daphne moved out, nothing was private, much less sacred.

The front of the envelope was addressed, in a slanting hand, to Miss Josephine Monash. There was no return sender on the rear of the envelope, just a hand-drawn rendition of the Barrington High logo, which featured a tree kangaroo. It was an unskilled drawing of that fabled creature, but it made her grin. The sender had also included their old school motto – 'Together We Climb' – and from that alone, Josie had no doubt who had written to her.

Still, the potential for disappointment was paralysing.

Josie took a thin twig for a makeshift letter opener, and slid it into the side of the envelope, sawing carefully. She extracted a single, folded sheet of writing paper and smoothed the page out, eyes flying to the name and address at the top of the page . . .

Mr Miles Henry, Sydney.

Josie's breath puffed out of her. No contact, not a word between them in years, and yet here was a letter! Josie blinked away a tilting moment of déjà vu: the strangest sense that she had been expecting this unlikely letter all along; had, somehow, conjured it into existence.

There was a brief sting of frustration, for here was not more than a few sentences. But how familiar his penmanship was! She'd studied Miles's handwriting obsessively in her autograph book, which he had signed in senior year: *I'll look for you upstage, Daydreaming Milkmaid.* A single, teasing sentence that had infuriated and delighted her in equal measure, for years.

Dear Miss Josephine, his letter began, and Josie beamed to think Miles had taken time to check her marital status before beginning . . .

I write to congratulate you on receiving your first review by none other than Mr Hugo Bernard.

I remember very well the first time that esteemed man reviewed my stagecraft. (I promise you won't forget it quickly, or easily, either.)

Please give my best regards to your family.

Keep climbing,

Miles

Josie crumpled the letter closed, and threw her exasperation to the heavens above. '*Flaming hell*, he had to read it! Couldn't have missed it, could he?! Look at him: writing to gloat, letting me know I've humiliated myself *and* Barrington!'

Only that didn't sound right.

Josie reopened the letter and read it over, repeatedly, so that she might divine its true intention. A splinter of disbelieving wonder emerged.

She closed the letter, stood up, and walked around and around the gully, rousing herself anew. 'Miles didn't write this letter to gloat, he would never! He's commiserating. He's saying he *knows* how I feel!'

Josie wondered if she'd ever read Miles's bad review, if Mrs Henry had brought it into the teahouse to show off, as she did with the rest. For one audacious second, Josie imagined asking Mrs Henry for a copy of it. Not to gloat, no way – to commiserate right back with Miles. Because that was exactly what Josie must do: write Miles, and thank him.

Wait. Unless . . .

Josie checked the date at the top of the letter. *Damn.* Miles had written her after Hugo Bernard's review came out but before the theatre company meeting, with her outrageous announcements about the Obsidian's reopening, *and* dredging up the old Celeste Starr story. Mrs Henry would surely have passed on that news since.

What must he think of her? That pint-sized upstart from back home who had not only earned herself the bile of Hugo Bernard but then, in short order, that of their whole town, too. Bet he was regretting the spontaneous kindness of this letter.

Too bad for him, though. If Miles didn't want a reply, he shouldn't have written to the queen of last words.

Josie charged back up the gully, already composing her return serve.

At the kitchen table, with balled-up letter drafts around her ankles, Josie was perusing her reply one final time before folding it into a waiting envelope. Then to clear up before Daphne returned from her trip into town.

Josie had settled on a cheerful, plucky missive. If Miles remembered the girl he'd riffed with at high school, he should recognise she had changed very little . . .

120

Dear Miles,

Thank you for your congratulations on my first syndicated review. Are you feeling threatened now that someone else from Barry is garnering attention from the likes of Hugo Bernard? You should be. Wait until you hear what else I've got planned for our poor town. Frankly, Mr Bernard might have a conniption.

Best be off to pin up my review. I'm starting a glory wall, like the one your mother shows off to callers. In time, mine will be bigger – and far more daring.

Climbing fast, and coming for your fame,
Daydreaming Milkmaid

Josie finished her perusal with a satisfied smirk. It was a good reply, and would not fail in its objective: proving Josie Monash was not cowed, and would not be condescended to by anyone.

The rattle of the Ford over the stock grid sent Josie to her knees on the kitchen floor. Frantically she gathered up the discarded paper, swearing about the predictable ill-timing of her sister-in-law.

Daphne arrived on the kitchen step with the air of one bearing triumphant news. Probably she'd heard something *else* to repeat about the now-legendary theatre company meeting. Josie struggled to summon forth a smile. She really *had* to check her negative attitude, which was growing worse with every passing day. Alternatively, perhaps Josie should offer to build Reg and Daphne a house herself? (A lean-to, using odd sheets of corrugated iron. She could have it done by this evening.)

'Guess what?' Daphne crowed.

You've annulled the marriage! You're going home to your own people! At last Josie located a genuine smile.

'The licence inspector is in the district checking radio licences! He's already given out a ton of fines. Kids are running all over town warning people.'

'Heck!' Josie jumped to her feet. 'Did you get to Grandy's house before the inspector?'

Daphne gave Josie a daft look. 'Grandmother Frances?'

'Oh Daphne, *surely* you went by Grandy's?'

'Why would I do that?'

'She never has a licence! She refuses to buy one on principle. That fine's going to cost her *fifty* pounds!'

Daphne sniffed. 'I guess she'll learn the principle of it now. If she wants to listen to her soapie, she should have the receiver's licence for it. Why doesn't she just buy one? If Reg and I had *that* kind of money, we certainly wouldn't be hoarding it, when so many others could use it.'

Josie's fist clenched hard around a ball of paper. *Never* did the Monash children talk about Grandy Beryl's wealth, much less entitlement to it. Neither had any of the Monash children taken a cent from Grandy – until, that is, Daphne West got her hooks into one of them.

Josie spoke with deadly quiet. 'Tell me you went to the post office and got *us* a licence for the farm . . . ?'

'Oh, I couldn't,' Daphne said, caressing her belly. 'I was having dreadful back pain, and everyone told me I needed to hurry home for a lie-down. My friends all agree that I work way too much for a woman in my condition. It's just been so hard for me looking after a big family, when I'm in such a delicate way.'

Josie's eyes went from Daphne's woebegone face, to the large paper bag at her side, emblazoned with milliner's logo, and stuffed full. She nodded. 'Uh-huh. I *bet* your back's sore – what with all that preening in front of mirrors today. I'm glad you're spending Reg's inheritance well. Wouldn't want to have wasted it on a home! When are you going to get it into your head that none of us even *want* you to—'

'*Josephine.*' Her father, at the kitchen door.

Josie clamped her mouth down on the cruellest, and most honest, thing she had to say yet.

Gabe moved to stand between the women, smelling of milk and grass, wiping sweat from his forehead. Josie scrunched up the last of her draft paper into her overalls pocket.

'Daphne,' Gabe said, 'I'm about to have a cup of tea, may I make you one?'

Daphne simpered her way to the kitchen table, holding her back, easing herself down.

Josie turned hastily away, hiding a scowl. The only thing Daphne knew how to milk was sympathy.

'Chickadee,' Gabe said, 'do you think you might help Daphne's load today by preparing lunch for your brothers?'

Help *Daphne*, who played the martyr every chance she got, pushing in on all Josie's responsibilities despite the firmest refusals, only to turn around and claim domestic slavery? Help *her*?

Tears prickled hotly beneath her cheeks. Gabe had always empathised with every indignation and injustice of Josie's young life. Never had he solved them *for* her – expecting Josie to fight for herself, think for herself, speak for herself – but always he'd understood her heart and hurts. For the first time she could count, it was not her side but another woman's he was taking. Jealousy stuck in her throat like a peach pit; unswallowable.

'No,' Josie told her father. 'I can't cook luncheon today. I want to go and help Grandy with her radio licence, and then I have some business to attend to regarding the Obsidian.' She watched the shadow pass over her father's face with some satisfaction. 'Help yourselves to anything you want from the larder. And try not to disturb Daphne – she's tired from hat modelling this morning, and needs to rest.'

Josie stomped out of the farmhouse without even removing her gumboots. She'd go into town, manure and all.

It would sum up her mood entirely.

CHAPTER THIRTEEN
WOMAN, ERASED.

Vivienne had been hemmed in by a grey, miserable drizzle. The precipitation was soft, but the forest greedy with the receiving of it; leaves quivering and gulping noisily. Though she'd made her morning pilgrimage from lodge to lake, leaving the relative warmth of the water again for the return had chilled her to the bone. There seemed no way to escape damp's cloying drape, and she had not packed enough soft, comforting things to soothe herself within her own goose-fleshed skin.

Thus sequestered, Vivienne wandered up and down each level, shoulders hung with an old wool blanket smelling of mould spores; lonelier than any cloud. She might as well have been hiding out in a mausoleum – the raven-haired ghost of Sylvan Mist followed her every step.

After yet another tedious luncheon of cheese and toast, Vivienne's mind was made up. She would not suffer through another day under the constant scrutiny of that morbid femme fatale who hung on every level and in every room.

The woman *was* dead – that much seemed clear. She did not age or change her hair in a single photograph, did not appear in a wedding gown alongside Rudy Meyer, nor acquire children; remaining in black and white pin-up glamour and 1940s costumery for perpetuity. Had she been an actress here? What part had this woman played in the life of Rudy Meyer that he should keep her memory so ghoulishly preserved, far from his glamourous life in Europe?

Vivienne had come to this decision: she might be powerless to prevent the watching creature eyes outside the lodge, but she certainly could thwart the dead ones inside it. Every picture would be turned to politely face the wall.

Vivienne began on the top floor, where she had spent only one night, with the brass framed picture beside the four-poster bed.

In this image, the woman sat in the pool of Chimera Falls, surrounded by king ferns, with her bare back and the top of her buttocks exposed to the photographer. She wore only a heavy gold necklace and a diaphanous wrap, tucked low around her hips. Her arms were crossed over her breasts, her head thrown back over shoulder; raven locks tumbling long as the waterfall behind. Hers was a look of pure allure.

And why should a dead woman have to suffer any longer such gratuitous ogling? *Rest in peace, I say.*

Vivienne opened the frame and checked the back of the photograph for a pencilled name or date. Nothing. She turned the photograph to face the rear, relatched the back, and returned the frame to the bedside. One photo down, oodles to go.

Methodically, Vivienne moved through the lodge, turning photographs over in their picture frames. Room by room, the pin-up actress was freed from her sylvan limbo. Vivienne was thwarted in her expunging only when she came to the ginormous painting on the staircase. There was no way she could take *that* down, far too heavy. But at least the dark-haired woman wasn't alone in the painting, she was surrounded by playmates. Vivienne would just have to pretend she was a carefree young lady holidaying with friends – rather than, well, *whatever* she was.

Vivienne finished her erasure on the ground floor, boldly singing scales to cover an internal monologue devoid of self-compassion . . .

Mother has turned every portrait of me to face the wall, too. She'll never forgive me. There's no coming back from this.

Exhausted after so many hours clambering to the top of shelves and bureaus, Vivienne prepared for a deep, restorative sleep. The endless drizzle was at least conducive to bedtime comfort. After a long, warm bath, she heated a cup of cinnamon milk on the stove as a nightcap, and carried it carefully up the stairs. Tonight, she planned to lose herself in Kate Chopin's *Awakening*.

She had nearly reached the library level, when she heard the creature on her front stoop again.

Tree Kangaroo, she reassured herself. It was the fourth time she had marked its visitation; each time following its scurrying return to the trees with a torch. Even now she was reaching for the closest torch, looking for the nearest window.

Except, then; the creature tried the doorknob.

Vivienne's stomach seemed to drop several storeys. She pushed hard back against the wall, hot milk splashing over her hand, torch bumping against her teeth to stopper a cry. No tree kangaroo could possibly make such a sound!

The doorknob jiggled again; with firm purposefulness. Terror came, flooding down her veins. She had to get back behind the library barricade, and get her hands on that telephone! Why had she ever left the safety of her blockade at all?

Once more came a sound from the door, this time the distinct stroke of metal against the knob, and the jangle of keys.

Go, go, go—!

Vivienne dropped her cup and thundered up the stairs, throwing doors closed, heaving furniture; heedless of the noise she was making, knowing only that she needed fortification before she could telephone – *screaming* – for help.

With the last cabinet pulled across the door, Vivienne sunk to the floor of the dark library, panting like a rabbit, a lamp base brandished high, ready to defend herself.

She listened.

All was silent.

The front door did not fling open, no footsteps crossed the lobby, there was no one charging up the stairs after her. Vivienne gripped the lamp harder, twisting her neck to hear something, *anything* other than silence. She did not pick up the phone; too petrified to speak aloud, or miss any further sounds.

Long, long minutes passed.

The forest had gone eerily silent.

Gradually, Vivienne's wheezing pant began to space out.

It was probably just a local hooligan, trying to sneak into the lodge for whatever lawlessness they got up to in the country. Definitely wasn't Owen's bunyip, the thought hadn't crossed her mind for a second, not even this one. It might be any creature, really. A possum's claws *could* sound like a key on metal. A winding python might accidentally jiggle a door handle. None of those things were surely *unthinkable*. In fact, she was thinking them this minute.

Vivienne placed the lamp base down. The front door was locked, and she had the key. She was safely barricaded in the library. There was a telephone at her disposal. There now, see? Her heart and breathing alike were both coming, slowly but surely, back to more regular rhythm.

Outside, Vivienne heard the familiar loping noises of the kangaroo returning to the trees. *Silly Vivienne*. She hauled herself up. *Making such a scene over nothing.*

She pushed her torch through a louvre gap, tracing her beam along the trunks, hunting her arboreal interloper. Usually, he preferred the giant fig tree, though she had watched him leap, rather seeming to fly impossible distances from tree to tree.

He was not in the fig, nor the heavily vine-choked tree alongside. Her torch scanned methodically, back and forward, and up and town each trunk. Tiny rain droplets shimmered in the sweeping beam. Once she'd sighted his red-brown fur and creepy eyes, she would feel much better.

Back and forward, up and down, back and forward, up and—

Oh God! Vivienne shrieked, stumbling back from the window, light beam bouncing wildly around the library. Breath and heartbeat bolted away.

For it had not been the devilish, red eye shine of a tree kangaroo she had lighted upon, or even – wishful thinking – Owen's bunyip.

It was a very human face, concealing itself a second too late amongst the glowing fungi.

'Geez! *Then* what did you do?'

Owen's countenance was a contortion of horror – though he could see for himself Vivienne was not lying murdered on the library floor.

She was standing before him on the porch with slim arms folded, alive and well, albeit about to refuse his pail of milk.

She wouldn't be needing it today – or ever again. Vivienne had packed her bag before sunrise and she was driving the hell out of here, as soon as she'd thanked Owen for his previous kindnesses.

But right now, Owen was still waiting to hear how Vivienne had survived the Stranger.

'I just did what anyone would do next, and tried to scare the fellow off. I stormed onto the balcony swinging my torch wildly, yelling about having called the police, and throwing . . .' she paused for a beat '. . . books.'

Owen looked as though he didn't dare laugh. 'You and I have very different ideas of what anyone would do next.'

'Don't worry, I didn't damage any of the books. I picked them all up this morning, and put them right back again.'

It had taken Vivienne so long to retrieve all those tomes from the forest floor and roof of the roadster that she had missed her last lake swim before her departure. There was a peculiar sorrow at the thought of never swimming her lake again.

'I'm impressed by your quick thinking. Most people surely would have died of fright in the first instance.'

'Oh, there was no need for that.' She felt her face crimson.

Owen's brow furrowed.

'Look, I'm fine,' she told him. 'Not a hair on my head out of place.' It pained her to see this man who scarcely knew her so obviously worried about her. 'Only reason I told you was so you know what kind of weirdo you have in your district – prowling around, watching women at night.'

'I already have my suspicions who it might be,' he replied, darkly. 'I hope you don't think I've told anyone else about your being here.'

'I do not.'

'What did the man's face look like?'

But *had* it been a face? In morning light, several Bumpy Satinash trees had shown white lichened protrusions which could so easily have been mistaken, in a grove of foxfire, with a fit of midnight madness, for a peering face.

'What are you going to do,' she asked, 'drag him back to apologise for interrupting my beauty sleep?' The droll tone belied her sense that Owen Monash might do exactly that. Vivienne's eyes skimmed from Owen's dark eyes, over his strong shoulders, to the large, tanned hands holding the pail, and quickly away again.

'In any case,' she said lightly, 'he won't be bothering me again. I'm leaving.'

'I don't blame you,' Owen said. 'Today?'

'In a trice,' she said, making her voice sound more determined than she felt. She should have left before Owen turned up. His calming proximity might prove a problem for her resolve.

'So, where to now, Voyager?'

Vivienne shrugged, unable to speak.

Owen seemed unwilling, or unable to speak himself. He looked away from Vivienne, to stare at the roadster, thoughts tugging at his brow. In this silence they lingered for some time, until Vivienne felt her voice might sustain her.

'So, I won't be needing your milk anymore. Thank you, though.'

'Glad to hear it,' Owen said. 'I was getting really sick of coming over here.'

Vivienne smiled. Owen answered it with a grin, and the wide sincerity of his expression snapped the last vestige of resolve. She wanted to leave this God-awful lodge, but she didn't want to be *alone*, any longer. Owen's compassion, and her lake swims, had been the only two things sustaining her.

And where *would* she go?

'The only problem is,' Vivienne ventured slowly, 'I *had* been meaning to set your sister straight on that thylacine theory of hers. I could have given her a genuine tree kangaroo sighting instead.'

'It's a shame someone won't get to set her straight,' Owen said, mirroring her faux musing tone. 'I guess I could always tell her myself.'

'You'll tell her some nonsense about bunyips.'

'What a good idea.'

Vivienne laughed – a mellifluous outpouring like the clear notes of a flute, betraying her trained musicality. At the sound, something soft and tender came into Owen's eyes. Vivienne looked away, tucking a platinum strand behind her ear.

But she'd heard it, too; had felt a rare ease and freedom in it.

'I think I'd better get to your sister before you do that,' Vivienne went on; exhilarated by finding herself doing the very opposite of what she'd determined to do. She had little desire, really, to meet Owen's sister, but desperate need of an anchor.

'Today?'

'Right now, in fact. I'm leaving momentarily.'

'I don't know if that will work,' Owen said. 'She'll be swanning around Barrington today. Got a project she's working on at the moment, she's interviewing everyone on Main Street. Unless you're willing to go into town and meet her?'

'I'll be passing through town, on my way out. Do you think we could meet her somewhere quiet, with not too many people?'

Owen rubbed his beard. 'I could ask her to meet us at the community library. It's in the old air raid shelter, in the middle of Main Street. Say, two o'clock?'

'I could hang around a few hours longer.'

'Then you've got yourself a date with my nosy, obnoxious sister.'

'And I assume she looks like you – big, with facial hair?'

Owen chuckled. 'Nope, she's tiny, and all her hair's up here.' He indicated his forehead. 'You'll know it's Josie: she'll be the woman in bold pink, fairly sprinting down the street, glaring at slow walkers in her way.'

'Chasing tigers?'

'You have no idea how right you are.'

CHAPTER FOURTEEN
THE NIGHTINGALE

Josie had come to Barrington this morning to get the legend of Celeste Starr straight. She was going to the town's best storytellers, bold as brass, for what they knew about the Curse's origins. Owen had asked her to meet him, afterwards, for afternoon tea at the library bunker. A rare treat, but she suspected Owen just wanted to be the first brother to hear her juicy research, and didn't blame him one bit.

Josie's first stop was at the Newsagency. Elsie Reece might have been spitting chips at Josie's theatre group meeting, but she was not so vocal without an audience today. The back-room door slid hastily closed as Josie entered.

'Morning, Else,' Josie sang out; pleased by the loud thumping out back in response to this. Stirring was one of Josie's favourite pastimes.

Clarence, spluttering a greeting, had evidently weighed up the cost of offending his wife versus Josie, and had chosen in favour of the brunette beaming before him.

'Thought I'd come and have a chat with you about our upcoming play,' Josie said, sympathetic to, but unmoved by, Clarence's squirming and forehead blotting.

'Got a ... a new book in I think you might like,' he deflected, heading for his wall of novels.

'You didn't keep it aside for me?' she said, shamming injury.

'I didn't know if you'd be ... in again, any time soon,' Clarence dithered. 'I worried maybe my ... comment about your favourite books the other night might have ... hurt your feelings.'

Josie laughed. 'I'm not so embarrassed by my reading tastes, as you suppose.' She reached for the novel, tapping the cover. 'Yep, it's got a woman running from gothic house, just my type. All right, I'll take it, thanks, Clarrie.'

He was breathing a sigh of relief. The perfect moment to spring ...

'*Anyway*, about Lake Evelyn.'

'I ... can't!' Clarence choked. 'You heard Elsie; she won't allow the amphitheatre reopening.'

'Don't worry,' Josie said. 'I don't want to talk about the Obsidian.'

'Oh good,' Clarence said.

'I'm here to find out what you know about the Curse.'

Poor Clarence; he was pale at the best of times. He retreated behind the counter. 'I don't know *anything*.'

Out back, the banging of stock stopped.

Josie spoke up, to save Elsie straining her ears. 'What rot. *Everyone* in town knows about the Curse! But if I'm going to dramatise Celeste Starr's story, I want a town accord first on what, exactly, the Curse is. How does a long dead actress manage to make so many girls drown? What say you, Clarence?' Josie flashed her crinkliest of smiles, knowing full well how desperate Clarence was for a lightning bolt to take him out right now.

'But ... why ... why are you asking ... *me*?'

'Why not? You were here, in your Newsagency, when Celeste was swanning around the streets of Barrington during the war. You saw her shows. You sold the very newspapers screaming of her death. Clarence, you're the perfect person to start me off on her story.'

'You're ... actually going forward with this, then?' It was more a groan then a question.

Josie nodded, brows springing high. She pulled out her notebook and pencil, and placed them on the counter.

Clarence glanced behind him. Josie waited. The door might fall off its roller with the force of Elsie pushing her ear against it, but Clarence seemed mollified by its closed aspect. His handkerchief was mopping high once more – as far as Josie was concerned: a white flag of surrender.

He sighed. 'I don't know what you want *me* to tell you about the Curse. Just believe me, it's there. It took Celeste. Poor girl, she didn't start the Curse, she was its first victim. And then ... it took six more daughters, and sweethearts and sisters.'

Yes, but what is *the Curse?!* Josie gritted her teeth. *You'll have to back him into it, then ...*

'All right. Tell me about Celeste.'

'I only ever saw her from a distance ... she spent most of her time holed up there in Sylvan Mist, with all those parties they used to have. I didn't know her, never talked to her.'

'What were your impressions of her?'

'*Beautiful!*' Clarence said, more quickly than she'd ever heard him answer a question before. His eyes went over Josie's head. 'She had long dark hair, right down to here ...' His hand indicated low on his back. 'She was an awful good actress, but her singing was heavenly. The soldiers called her The Nightingale of Lake Evelyn. Made to boost any man's morale, they said. I reckon her pin-up postcards went away in many soldiers' pockets. Niall made a pretty penny selling them from beneath his counter.'

Josie was scribbling manically. Hard to know how long you'd get before a nervous performer clammed up again.

'We'd never had anyone like Celeste in Barrington before. Never had anything like that amphitheatre and its bathing starlets, neither. Whole lot of them were out-of-town girls . . . living up there in Sylvan Mist with Rudy Meyer and his crew. But Celeste, she was . . . the star of every show. Not surprised, after she died, that Rudy just closed up the amphitheatre and left. Mustn't have seemed any point to keep going after that. Celeste *was* Lake Evelyn.'

Josie looked up from her scrawl. 'There! In your own words, Clarence: "Celeste *was* Lake Evelyn." Don't you see why I must start with Celeste's story to *reopen* the theatre?'

Clarence drew himself up, stony faced. 'Celeste was the last star of Lake Evelyn. There should be no more.'

Josie tapped her pencil against her lips, watching Clarence carefully.

'So, what was it like in Barrington – the day she died?'

Josie had only been a small child at the time; blissfully unaware of the finer points, until force-fed the ghoulish details by other girls once she started school. No adult ever wanted to deep dive the particulars.

Clarence grimaced. 'Was a day no one would want to remember. How all those cars came tearing down Main Street, heading for the lake – not far behind them, the newspaper men, preparing dramatic headlines for me to peddle.'

'Nightingale Drowns in Volcanic Lake,' Josie said in her best news-reel tones.

'She weaved herself a drowning suit of coiled grass and lawyer vines, weighted with rocks.'

'It was planned, then.'

'She told exactly how she was going to do it, in that note she left up at Sylvan Mist . . . described herself with a ghoulish line of poetry: "Some Maenad girl with vine-leaves on her breast".'

'Yes, that's right!' Josie was madly jotting. 'It was Oscar Wilde. And there was another line too – something about a bird?'

Clarence shrugged, words drying up.

'Yet her body was never found,' said Josie, nudging him along.

'They only found part of the suit . . . torn apart amongst the reeds.'

'Torn apart – from a drowning?'

Clarence looked once to the back room. 'Reckon maybe the croc got to her.'

Josie looked up sharply from her notebook. 'Croc! Surely you don't believe in that old myth.'

'Myth?' Clarence looked properly hurt. 'I'm telling you what I've seen with my own two eyes.'

'*You've* seen the crocodile,' Josie said, dubiously. When was Clarence last out at the lake? 'Probably just a lace monitor. At an absolute stretch: a freshwater crocodile.'

'Freshie nine feet long? Pah!'

Josie shook her head. 'As I live and breathe! Clarence Reece, you think there's a *saltie* in Lake Evelyn.'

'It's there all right.'

'A saltwater crocodile has got Buckley's chance of being two thousand feet above sea level.'

'Escaped from that croc farm north of the river, if you ask me. Not the first, neither. Farmers swear they've seen them in their dams.'

'And promptly shot them, no doubt. I am not too young to remember the croc shooting party that stayed in Sylvan Mist in fifty-three, and stalked Lake Evelyn for weeks. They went home empty handed. Declared it a waste of time!'

'Croc probably escaped through the underground tunnel the Aboriginals talk about.'

'What's it feeding on then?' Josie shot out.

'Aside from young girls never to be seen again?' Clarence returned, with sudden sourness. 'Saw-shelled turtles are a favourite for it, too.'

Josie was quite flummoxed, but saved by the back-room door thrown open. Elsie Reece was not going to stand mutely by while her husband played the fool.

This scenario was to be repeated at Josie's every call-in. First, resistance and refusal to play the part and then, after some cajoling inducement punctuated by nose-crinkling smiles, the story would come pouring out, as though they'd been just waiting for someone to ask the question.

Josie had been right to choose this play.

Fair dues, Beryl Frances had been the one right, but it was Josie breathing life into the story. Her notebook filled rapidly; her fingers itched to get writing.

In the warm, smoke and rose-fragranced heart of the Flower Shop, Peggy West stared at Josie's notebook trying to read, upside down, what other townsfolk had already offered.

'Look, if you ask *me*—' Peggy began, tapping her cigarette into a delicate lead crystal ashtray.

Why did they always start out like that? Josie told each and every interviewee: she was specifically asking *them*.

'—that lake is the most prolific serial killer on the Tablelands.'

Josie laughed. 'That's one way of putting the Curse. But this isn't an Agatha Christie play.'

'Maybe it should be,' Peggy said, her Cupid's bow pursing.

'I think Celeste did a pretty good job of taking herself out.'

139

'Sure – that's what a serial killer would *want* you to think.'

Josie set pencil to paper. If this was Peggy's impression of the Curse, then she'd take it down too.

'So, Lake Evelyn's been *killing* girls.'

'Not the lake, no . . .' Peggy left her cigarette to smoulder on crystal, reaching for a basket of dried flowers. 'The swagman.'

Josie arched an eyebrow. '*Swagman?*'

Peggy busied herself arranging a small posy. 'The *swagman* who comes through here every three or four years, and sets up camp at Lake Evelyn.'

'Old Bennett?'

'That's the one,' Peggy said. 'Comes here, not long after the Wet finishes. He's been doing it for decades – even the war didn't stop him. And every time he passes through town with that roll on his back, another girl is killed.'

'Drowns,' Josie corrected.

Peggy rotated the gilt bronze base of the tray, to take up her cigarette once more. 'So the police say.'

Josie stared at the next ruled line on her page. She wasn't really going to write this down, was she?

'Peg, some of those girls left notes.' *Barbara, for one.* She gave Peggy a stern look. 'You're hardly suggesting Old Bennett held his swag to their heads and made them write those – are you?'

Peggy nodded, as though this was the first time the idea had occurred to her, and yet made perfect sense.

Josie jotted quickly. *Swagman dictates suicide notes.*

Peggy was easily able to interpret that mockery, even upside down. 'Well how else, Miss Smarty-Pants, *do* you explain the lake lying dormant for the years between that swagman's visits?'

The 'lake lying dormant'? Geez, Josie liked that one. She'd have to think of a way to work it into her play.

'And why exactly does the swagman come killing our girls?'

'Haven't you noticed? They're always young stunners. Dark haired, the lot of them.'

'He wants to kill all the beautiful brunettes in Barrington?'

'Not all of them. I'm still here, aren't I?' Peggy pressed her carmine lips together with a loud smacking.

Josie laughed, pretending to read back what she had written. 'Swagman killing beautiful women – but hasn't got around to Peg West, yet.'

Peggy squashed her cigarette into the tray, gone serious. 'If it's not the swagman, it's some other pervert loitering in that creepy forest, taking our girls. And he hasn't got me yet, because I wouldn't dare go out there and swim in that old bitch of a lake.'

'You're excusing yourself from my play, then?'

'Not on your nelly.' Peggy smiled. 'You need a woman with her head screwed on properly, to keep an eye on you pretty, naive things.'

'Selfless of you, Peg. I greatly appreciate it.'

'But you mark my words, Josephine Monash: it's been three years since the serial killer struck, he's well overdue for his next. Don't you leave a single girl out there alone, hear me? Don't you *dare*!'

Josie pushed open the door of the Corner Shop, hoping for Niall, who possessed a braggart's loose tongue, instead of Laura, with the skirting eyes and locked lips.

Both Laura and Niall were behind the counter today, and leapt apart as Josie entered.

'Morning!' sang Josie – rather obnoxiously, she could admit, given the coughs and straightening going on, but there was no way Josie was letting their awkwardness delay her interview.

Laura skedaddled upstairs, with a hand covering the round circle of burst blood vessels on her neck, and Niall's eyes on her back.

Josie pulled her notebook from her handbag, placing it on the glass lolly counter in a declaration of intent.

Niall, overconfident in the way of a rapidly silvering fox reliant on long reputation, waggled his eyebrows at Josie. 'Looks like I'm in hot demand today.'

Josie had no weakness for Niall's vaunting. 'I shouldn't worry. We all have odd days.'

Miffed, Niall reached for a large wicker basket on top of the counter; settling in grocery items.

'Who's the basket for?'

There was a beat before he answered. 'None of your concern.'

So Niall's got someone staying in that lodge again.

She smiled. 'That's exactly what I've come to talk to you about: Sylvan Mist.'

Niall picked a leaf out of the basket, flicking it away with more force than was necessary. 'What about Sylvan Mist? It's my business, not yours.'

Josie tapped her notebook. 'That's right, you've been the caretaker since Rudy Meyer moved back overseas, so I know you're up on the history of the lodge and its most famous guest. I want to hear what you think.'

Niall closed the basket with a snap. 'For your little play.'

'My curse-breaking production, you mean.' Josie smiled at her own turn of phrase, wondered if she should put that on her show posters.

'I don't know anything about what happened to the actress.'

'That's not true. Everyone knows Celeste Starr drowned, but it seems some people differ on the how and why. I want to hear what you think.'

'What does it matter what *I* think?'

Josie laughed. 'I'm surprised, Niall. You normally seem quite sure it matters to us.'

'I had nothing to do with Celeste Starr.'

'You must have seen her around though. Watched her shows? Perhaps even talked to her down the street?'

'She was too hoity-toity for the likes of us in Barrington. Spent all her time with the rich people up at Sylvan, and all the big men with guns.'

This snide addendum nettled Josie. 'You mean the servicemen you sold her pin-up postcards to?'

'What if I did? They couldn't get enough of her, could they? Their pin-up fantasy made flesh. She surrounded herself with the soldiers – always laughing her head off, acting like she didn't give two hoots that half those sorry lovesick bastards would be dead in months, and glamour girls like her were half the reason they were going off to Hell.'

Josie watched Niall's face, thinking hard. 'But you didn't go to war, did you, Niall?'

Niall smiled. 'Neither did your father, girlie. But at least I *tried* to enlist – unlike Gabriel Monash.'

Josie's eyes stayed fixed on Niall's face, refusing to acknowledge Niall's bad leg, almost lost in adolescence to a bone infection. 'My father was a primary producer, making milk for legions of American servicemen, and was recently widowed, with four dependent children.'

'Excuses that any of those slaughtered bastards *wished* they had.'

Rage rushed up the back of Josie's gullet. She stared at her notebook, smoothing the page, blinking furiously. When she looked up again, it was with cold disdain. 'You think my father is a coward, Niall?'

Niall shrugged. 'I can't say *what's* been going through Gabriel's head these last twenty years.'

He turned his back against her, shifting items on his back wall. That might have been her cue to leave, but Josie refused to take it. She sent a flurry of hateful thoughts at his back, standing her ground.

When Niall turned again, she had her pencil primed. 'As we've established, you were here in Barrington during the war, selling your dirty pictures of Celeste. Why don't you start your story from there?'

Niall pushed his guest basket aside. 'Never talked to the woman. Can't tell you anything for your play. Not going to, either.'

Josie took back her notebook. 'Fine, I've other people to see.'

That Josie was done with him of her own volition seemed to rile Niall. His face twisted. 'I'll tell you this: a girl that full of herself doesn't jump in a lake and end her own grand show, does she? Where was the standing ovation in *that*?'

'She left a note,' Josie said, not taking her eyes off Niall.

'Oh, and those are so hard for anyone else to write.'

Josie strove for casual lightness. 'How did she die then?'

Niall fixed pale eyes hard upon her. 'The Lake Evelyn Monster took her.'

Josie gave him an incredulous look. 'The bunyip? There's no such thing!'

Laura had reappeared, love bite on her neck unsuccessfully covered by a curtain of dark hair. Her eyes were wide.

At her entrance, Niall smiled; sly as a fox. 'You just take a walk around Sylvan Mist one-night, girlie, and *then* come tell me there's no such thing . . .'

Josie wandered through Rita's Old Curiosity Shop touching this and that, stopping now and then to exhale delight. Vera Lynn's 'A Nightingale Sang in Berkeley Square' drifted from Rita's prize gramophone, infusing Josie's pleasure.

If Josie could, she'd buy everything in the shop, and she'd never farm another day, because she'd be happily polishing her treasures every hour. Rita's shop was a trove of museum-worthy wonders, and Rita reigned sternly over it all: director, curator, docent and security detail.

With gimlet-eyed Rita out of sight, Josie headed straight for *her* Smith-Corona. She ran her hands over the bright coral carriage, over the platen, stroking the keys; clacking out the full eight letters of her name.

'You break it, you buy it,' Rita called, from somewhere in the vast cluttered interior.

'It's just me, Rita.'

Rita popped up, polishing rag in hand, to deliver a dour look. 'You *especially* can't afford to break it, Josephine.'

Josie's fingers slid reluctantly from the typewriter.

Rita waded between narrow aisles to Josie, bending to protect her heavily sprayed bouffant from hanging spools of bric-a-brac. She adjusted her spectacles. 'I see you've come to beg for what I know about the Curse.'

'I don't need to beg,' Josie said. 'You've been watching me walk up and down Main Street all day, wondering when it was your turn.'

'You've wasted most of today giving ear to the wrong people.'

'This is a community play; I have to ask everyone.'

'How wrong you *are*,' Rita said, motioning Josie further into her cave of treasures. 'Come, *I'll* show you the Celeste Starr you won't glean from the nursery tales they've been feeding you.'

Josie trailed Rita obediently past the red brocade curtains, into her private office. The heavy cloud of Cedel hair spray and furniture polish within was somehow comforting. Josie curled up in a green velour art deco armchair and watched as Rita shifted items in a large baroque display case. So, Rita preserved her Celeste Starr artefacts behind glass doors? Josie gave her pencil a quick sharpen.

Rita came to sit before Josie with arms loaded. Right off, she passed a pile of yellowing newspaper articles. 'I started gathering these when

Rudy Meyer first arrived in Barrington and built his lodge and theatre. Then Celeste rocked into town, and I could tell right away she was a star in the making! Such a talent, and a real beauty. I scoured the papers for anything about her shows, snipped everything I could, pressed them into my albums. I counted myself her biggest fan. Then Celeste went and drowned herself, *fool girl*, and my albums grew too morbid. I put them out of sight.'

Josie took the clippings in hand, thumbing gently through the progression of Celeste's tale. First, the photos of a master stonemason on Lake Evelyn's shore, and debonair Rudy Meyer in dapper hat and suit, pointing across the water, for the benefit of the press. Next, the images of Rudy Meyer's actresses arriving, practising on the floating stage, lining up on the steps of Sylvan Mist in their glamorous swimsuits, with Celeste front and centre of each picture. Soon, came the images of uniformed troops assembled on the amphitheatre steps, constructing the diving platform, holding swimming carnivals on the lake – Australian vs American servicemen – with Rudy Meyer's actresses cheering alongside. Then, those histrionic headlines – 'Nightingale Drowns' – and the heartbreaking scenes of policemen scouring the edge of Lake Evelyn. Finally, there was Rudy Meyer, hat in hand and grief on stark display, pleading for privacy and, regrettably he said, closing his amphitheatre.

Rita had the full tale here, every tragic word and impression of it.

'*Rita*,' Josie breathed, 'how can I *thank you* enough – these are incredible!'

Josie thought Rita might offer a rare smile, as she sometimes did when she'd found just what a heart most desired. But Rita glared, instead, at those pages clutched in Josie's hand.

'They're just newspaper clippings, and no newsman ever did a woman's story justice.'

Josie clasped the pile to her chest. 'Maybe not, but I'll try to. I can't tell you how much this means to me. I'll have them back to you soon as I'm done.'

'Oh keep them,' Rita said. 'Mere background for the more exciting story.'

Josie's eyes twinkled. '*More* exciting?'

Rita was shuffling rapidly through photographs. 'Tell me some of the furphies and rumours you've heard today.'

Josie flicked back through her notebook. 'To explain the Curse of Lake Evelyn, so far I've got: a swagman murdering beautiful women, a saltwater crocodile in the lake, and a bunyip in the forest.' Josie cringed. There really was nothing she could use from that dross; she wasn't writing a pantomime.

'Shaping up as a bona fide horror story,' Rita said. 'You'd be telling the wrong story though.'

'How so?'

Rita stopped shuffling, having found the image sought. She gave her spectacles a careful polish, to better study it.

'The Curse of Lake Evelyn,' she said, handing the picture over to Josie, 'is a love story.'

Josie gazed at the black and white image of Celeste Starr at the lake's edge, with a long, diaphanous dressing gown around her bathers, spilling feathers at her wrists and ankles, and a crown shining like stardust upon her head. Surrounding her, were several men in army uniforms. Celeste's neck was tipped back on a draught of laughter.

Just as Niall had said then. Of all the people she'd spoken to this day, *he* had to be right!

'She was fond of the soldiers?'

Rita pshawed, tapping the photograph. 'No, she *loved* that one.'

Josie refocused, seeing the candid lean of Celeste's body towards one member of the group – a tall man, with a wide, movie-star grin of his own. He might have been the one to impart whatever witticism had tipped her into laughter, for her slender hand was laid gently upon his arm.

And the way he looked at her! Such love and longing; it vexed a cavernous sorrow in Josie's belly.

'Who is he?'

'His name was Zach Miller.'

'Was?'

'Died in New Guinea, not long after this photo was taken. Shot to bits.'

'Dreadful,' Josie said, tracing the man's wide smile. 'But why haven't I heard of Zach before?'

Rita nudged Josie's notebook. 'Everyone's too busy embellishing the Curse, to talk about the real tragedy.'

'Give it to me then,' Josie said, scratching a new heading.

'The Curse,' Rita said, 'isn't some prehistoric beast, or mythical creature. It's something older still; the tragedy of love!'

Josie wrote this down, buzzing at no-nonsense Rita's sudden turn to the dramatic.

'Celeste Starr drowned herself for love lost in a jungle slaughter,' Rita added, watching Josie's pencil fly across the page.

But something in this didn't quite ring true to Josie. She chewed the inside of her lip, thinking. 'She really loved him *that* much? They must have had precious little time together – and wasn't Celeste involved with Rudy Meyer himself?'

Rita tsked in disgust. 'Rudy Meyer thought he was keeping his own personal harem up there in Sylvan Mist.'

Oh yes, Josie was going to write *that* down.

'But no, she wasn't in love with Rudy Meyer. Indebted to him, perhaps, but her *heart* was for Zach Miller.'

This was all great stuff, but Josie had to ask the burning question.

'The Curse is a woman in love?'

Rita nodded, unsmilingly. 'Yes. She sings from the crater for her lost lover, luring our young women to her side.'

A shiver set Josie's neck spasming. She heard again the old childhood rhyme she and her peers had been raised on: "*Up she reaches from the deep . . .*"

Josie shook this childishness away. Nonsense then, and nonsense now. And Rita clearly spent too much time wading around her tomb of morbid history and antiquated relics. She might have expected an explanation like this from the painted lips of Peggy West, but serious, businesslike Rita?

'Where could I get more information about this love story angle?'

At last, a smile from Rita. She plopped a second pile of magazine cuttings atop the first. 'Their story was serialised in the *Worldly Woman*, in 1950.'

Josie flicked through the clippings, seeing Zach, devilishly handsome in army uniform, and Celeste as a glamourous pin-up girl, transposed over a brooding artistic rendition of Sylvan Mist, and the amphitheatre.

'Fiction?' Josie asked, skim-reading.

'Meant to be read as fiction – maudlin love story, wretched ending – but I'm telling you: it's all true. Wasn't a young lady in Barrington who didn't swoon over the story, it was smuggled from girl to girl, all over town.'

'No one let *me* read it.' Josie had her finger on the byline. 'Who was the author – Victoria Bird? How did she know all this?'

'Pseudonym, apparently,' Rita said. 'Caused a terrible stir, everyone trying to guess who'd written it. Had to be a local, we thought – a troublemaker. People said it would only heighten the Curse. And sure enough ...'

Josie was already calculating dates. 'Nineteen fifty, that means ...'

Rita sighed. 'Glenda, only a month later. Yet another one out of her depth, the fourth since Celeste. After that, we couldn't deny it. The spirit of Celeste Starr, whatever you believe it to be, was calling young women to their death.'

'As in, copycats?'

'Contagious hysteria.'

'What a horrendous term,' Josie said, nose wrinkling.

'Fine then: girls driven from all good sense by the glamourised death of a beautiful actress.'

Josie sat back. 'I really think the girls of Barrington deserve more credit than that.'

Josie charged back down Main Street towards the library bunker, in a reverie. Evocative scenes spun around her: the serviceman and the actress falling in love by the moonlit lake; the telegram arriving at Sylvan Mist with news of his death; Celeste Starr, in her vine corset, casting herself into the crater.

'Don't you see?' she told herself, 'It's a *love story* ...'

CHAPTER FIFTEEN
VIVIENNE COMES KNOCKING

Vivienne packed her possessions into the roadster and locked up the lodge, ready to leave as soon her get-together with Owen's sister was done. She pilfered some linen from the lodge too, in case she might need to sleep in her car overnight. She would ask Uncle Felix to fix Rudy up for it.

All of these preparations were merely for show, Vivienne suspected; and no less contrived than her meeting with a stranger's sister. For where else *could* she go after this?

Vivienne set off for Barrington in the roadster, though it was mostly her impoverished spirit driving her here. Rash as this plan seemed, ridiculous as it felt, *anything* was better than sitting alone in that forest mausoleum, waiting for the telephone to ring.

Vivienne did not want to draw attention in town. She hoped her black turtleneck and slim white pants would not stand out amongst the no doubt countrified fashion of the local women. Her butter blonde hair, in a low chignon, was carefully concealed by a Schiaparelli scarf. Oversized sunglasses covered much of her face.

Vivienne realised she was going to be the biggest news of the day, the moment she entered the town limits. Every face turned to goggle.

No wonder; Main Street was lined with nothing but Holdens. Vivienne parked, affecting polite indifference as her car was quickly surrounded by men. *Is one of them* my *prowler?* She slipped through this gathering without having to field any questions, the roadster proving a handy decoy.

The old air raid bunker was easy enough to find on the street's main island, the basic concrete rectangle charmingly bedecked in bougainvillea. The door was held open to the midwinter sunshine by a brass potted fern. A woman could be heard inside, talking animatedly to herself.

Vivienne inched past the door, peering. At a makeshift table – a slab of hardwood across two barrels – sat a petite, heavily fringed brunette, in a dress of outrageous fuchsia, with two pencils tucked into her pony-tail. She fitted Owen's description to a tee.

The young woman was too invested to note Vivienne's presence. Spread out before her were photographs of Sylvan Mist, maps of the lake, and a photo of a woman floating in the lake. Was that Vivienne herself? Had Owen's sister been *spying* on her? Was this some kind of sick family joke?

Turn! Leave! Go!

Backing away in quiet desperation, Vivienne nicked the potted fern with her foot, overturning it with a clatter.

Owen's sister looked up in glazed shock. Vivienne shovelled dirt back into the pot, apologising profusely.

The woman came to kneel beside her. 'I've never been a fan of this ugly maidenhair; you've done me a favour.' She put a small, square hand out in front of Vivienne's, waving her away. 'Stop, you're just spreading it around everywhere.'

Vivienne stood, brushing off her knees.

Owen's sister was a full head shorter than Vivienne, even with the overreach of that glossy ponytail. She peered up at Vivienne with nose-crinkling intensity. Pretty heart-shaped face and pert, freckle-splashed features gave her a doll-like appearance – though it was Vivienne who felt herself the oversized and useless doll.

'I'm Josie Monash,' she said, dusting soiled hands against her dress.

'Vivienne George. I'm here to meet Owen.'

'No, *I'm* meeting Owen,' Josie laughed, a gusty sound, seeming to carry sunshine itself.

Vivienne smoothed her scarf back from her forehead. 'We're both meeting Owen. Did he not mention me?'

Large, heavily kohled eyes scrutinised Vivienne. 'Are you sure you have the right Owen?'

'He's quite hirsute.' Vivienne swept her hand around her chin. 'Like a . . . bushranger.'

Owen's sister shot another warm draught of laughter into the air. 'That's marvellous, he'll never live that down!'

'Oh, please don't make fun of your brother on my behalf; he's been very kind to me.'

'Making fun of brothers is what I do best. Where did he find *you*? I'm guessing you're from down the hill. But I've never had to meet any of his girlfriends before, so I take it you're finally the keeper, which begs the question, why has he not mentioned you? Actually, no, the real matter of interest is the size of that diamond ring on your finger. I *know* my brother can't afford anything like that, unless he applied to Grandy, but he wouldn't dare, and if he did I'll never speak to him again—'

Josie talked faster than anyone Vivienne knew; it was a race to keep up. Her face must have shown disorientation, for Josie ceased. 'Come sit with me,' she said. 'I'll get you some tea.'

Vivienne followed her to the table and watched while Josie set out a Thermos and cups.

'Tell me,' Josie said, 'How long have you and Owen been . . . ?'

'We're not! I've been sojourning here a while. Owen was bringing my milk.'

Josie chivvied open the Thermos, not taking her eyes off Vivienne. 'I should have heard by now if a beautiful new blonde was staying in town. You're going to have to tell me what the devil this is really about.'

'I'm leaving today, and Owen thought I could meet you, to . . . tell you about the tree kangaroo which had been visiting my accommodation.'

Josie plonked the Thermos down. 'Pardon me?'

Vivienne coloured. It really was an absurd excuse to have come here. But what else could she say? *I'm lonely. I need a friend.* 'It's the most peculiar creature. Hops like a real kangaroo and all, but it lives way up high in the trees.'

Josie withdrew an envelope from her dress pocket and held it out for Vivienne to inspect a drawing on the rear. 'Like *this*?'

'Owen *wasn't* kidding when he said you'd be interested.'

'I've never seen a real one,' Josie said, gently tracing the drawing with a finger, before sliding it back in her dress pocket. 'They're elusive. You're very lucky.'

'Not at all lucky, the pesky thing comes every night to the lodge, making all kinds of noise on my front porch.'

Josie thumped the table. 'You're the guest! At Sylvan Mist – *you're* the guest!'

'That's *my* gothic hideaway all right.'

Josie tipped her head, eyes alight with intrigue. 'Hideaway?'

'Temporary respite.'

Josie's speculative gaze was flying up and down Vivienne's person. 'Respite from what, exactly?' Owen had already warned Vivienne his sister was nosy, but to find herself so quickly set upon and prised open was, apprehension aside, rather amusing to behold.

Vivienne glanced around the bookshelves, avoiding the piercing gaze of the small brunette before her. 'I . . . jilted my fiancé.'

Josie didn't miss a beat. 'A runaway bride!'

'It felt more like my wedding was the thing run away. I merely jumped off.'

'But you're still *wearing* that colossal engagement ring.'

'I haven't had a chance to give it back, and it's too expensive to leave lying around that lodge.'

Josie nodded, chewing hard at lip and thoughts alike. 'Where are you from?'

'Sydney.'

Josie's eyes went wide. '*That* far!'

'If I could run gone further, I would have.'

Josie pushed a teacup towards Vivienne. 'Drink that. Then you need to tell me what Owen thinks I can do to help.'

'I don't need your help. I'm on my way out of town.'

'Where to?'

'Wherever I end up.' Vivienne shrugged, knowing how childish and ill prepared she sounded.

Frustration was apparent on Josie's face, but her eyes had moved past Vivienne's face to the road beyond. 'Damnit, Athol!'

Vivienne followed her look. Across the street, a safari-suited man was leaping out of a very badly parked Bedford OB bus.

'Who?'

'Athol Harford,' Josie growled. 'Bringing down the tone of Barrington as usual.' Josie patted Vivienne's arm. 'Stay here, I'll be right back.'

No sooner had Josie swooped out, Athol's nasal twang could be heard, rushing to meet her. 'Hallo, Josie, been meaning to sit you down for a chat, what's this I've been told about a grand lakeside production?'

'We're not up to the "grand" part, yet,' Josie was heard to reply.

'Not the way folks are talking about it. Most audacious thing any-one's attempted in years, they say. You reckon it's smart to reopen that amphitheatre again?'

'Revive the most picturesque theatre on the Tablelands? You bet.'

'I want in.'

'Yes, when I was a girl, I remember you always did include the lake in your Saturday tour.'

Athol guffawed. 'No, I want in on the *play*, about the actress.'

'But you're not in my theatre group, you don't even live in Barrington.'

'No matter, I'll be here on Friday to liven up your company for you. No way we're getting another review like the one that southerner dealt you.'

'I had no clue you *were* a performer, Athol.' Josie's voice dripped irony; Vivienne couldn't help pitying the man.

'No clue? Josephine Monash, you've heard me play my lagerphone at the Dairy Queen Ball many a time.'

'I can't forget *that*,' Josie replied. 'Listen, as long as you leave any percussion instruments at home, you're welcome to attend our next theatre meeting. No promises we'll have a role for you, though.'

'Spiffing!' Athol cried. 'I'm going to be a *thespian*!'

Vivienne compressed her lips against a smile. What *was* this play Josie was writing? She tipped her head to study Josie's notes, reaching for the photograph of the lady floating in the lake. Not *Vivienne* – what a paranoid notion. It was the woman from the lodge; long dark hair streaming around her. She was on the magazine serial clippings, too. Vivienne skimmed quickly for a name: *Celeste Starr*, an actress, during the war. Dead, just as Vivienne had surmised – although it was shocking to learn the woman had drowned herself in the lake.

Vivienne sat back in her chair, absorbing this. Thank goodness she had turned those photographs around! How could she sleep another night there, knowing she had a drowned woman's eyes upon her in every room?

Because she *was* going back to the lodge, wasn't she? Vivienne was calling her own bluff: she had nowhere else to run. Who else, but these oddly intrusive Monash siblings, might show her any kindness?

Josie rejoined her inside the shelter. 'I never can say no to the ring-ins. Now I have to find a role for *that* joker, too.' Josie's annoyed huff-ing was contradicted by eyes flashing with gratification.

Vivienne stared at this young countrywoman so full of pluck. *Ill bred*, Geraldine would proclaim her; *vulgar, too*. How did a farm girl come by such supreme confidence bolstering her to boss brothers, and theatre groups alike?

Ask her, Vivienne ordered herself: *why are you making a play about my lodge's ghost?*

Josie plonked herself down opposite Vivienne. 'Right, listen here: I know Owen doesn't really care about my many fabulous creature sight-ings, but of all my brothers, I trust Owen's judgement implicitly, so you and I need to figure out why he really sent you here, and what I'm meant to do with you next.'

'Must be nice,' Vivienne mused.

'*What* must be?'

'Having a big, close-knit family.'

Josie snorted. '"Family is the theatre of the spiritual drama."'

Vivienne regarded her quizzically.

'My mother's dead, I never knew her. My father's *still* a grieving widower, twenty years later. Our grandmother tries to run all our lives – I'm never sure if I want her to or not – and my father and grandmother have been bitterly estranged all my life. I have too many brothers, and did I mention my new sister-in-law, Lady Muck? She moved in uninvited and won't leave, wants to rule us with an iron

fist, but that might break her nails, so she's settling for passive manip-
ulation instead.'

Vivienne hastened to apologise for assumptions made, but something in Josie's bright eyes made her hesitate. If Vivienne's instincts
were right, Josie prized honesty way above politesse . . .

'I'm an only child. I've always envied large families.'

'I'd envy my family too, if it weren't mine.' Josie considered
Vivienne. 'Why aren't you hiding out with your parents?'

'I'm hiding out *from* my mother.'

'Why?'

Vivienne felt her face rushing to fill the planes of well-mannered
indifference. 'Oh, when I tried to call off the wedding, my mother
made it expressly clear there was no respectable way out of it. Marrying
Howard was a tactical choice, and the best one a woman of my station
could make.'

'Have you always been rich?'

Vivienne suspected Josie Monash was rarely reprimanded on
what she should or shouldn't say. She shrugged. 'Born sucking on the
proverbial spoon.'

Josie nodded – pityingly, it seemed to Vivienne.

'So how did you come upon that old lodge?'

'My uncle took pity on me, and rented it for me. He's a friend of
Rudy Meyer's.'

Josie raised her brows, clearly impressed. 'And what happened to
your fiancé?'

'To save face, Howie has been telling people I've been sent to
Callan Park Mental Hospital.'

'My God.'

'To be fair, I alluded to my nerves in the note I left him. Thought he
might be gladly rid of me if he believed I was losing my mind.'

'Are you losing your mind?'

The effrontery of this woman! It was so oddly compelling...

'I might, if I have to stay too much longer in Sylvan Mist.'

Josie grimaced. 'I don't know how you *can* bear it; the place is full of ghosts.' Josie seemed to regret the cruelty of this statement. 'Not real ones.'

'Believe me, I try to be outdoors as much as I can. Luckily there's that lovely lake nearby, so I swim a lot.'

Josie's whole face and posture had slackened – *horribly* – her mouth dropping away with her shoulders. Vivienne's heart gave a double thump in response.

Josie reached to take Vivienne's finely boned fingers in her fervent grasp. 'The lake's closed. You mustn't swim in it.'

Vivienne laughed, removing her hands. 'Closed? It's a *lake*.'

'There's a ... *curse*,' Josie said, speaking carefully. 'Lots of young women have drowned in Lake Evelyn.'

'You mean it's a suicide spot?'

Josie blanched. 'It isn't clear why so many women have drowned there. But we're a small town – it's more than any community can take. We dissuade anyone from swimming it.'

'*Not* a curse then; propaganda to scare young people off. But surely a whole town isn't scared of one lake?'

Something in Vivienne's words seemed to have struck a nerve. Josie recoiled, frowning.

Vivienne studied her. 'If your town wants everyone to stay out of the lake, why are you setting up a theatre on the very edge of it, much less making a play about it?'

Josie looked pained. 'I'm only reopening the public use area *around* the lake, and my play will break the ... put an end to superstition.'

Vivienne tsked. 'You'd be better off offering swimming lessons.'

'The lake is closed for swimming.'

'I've already swum it, many a morning.'

'But you *won't* anymore. Say you won't.'

'I have every intention of swimming it again. I won't be here much longer; I'm going to figure out a new life for myself. But in the meantime, a silly story is the least of my worries.'

Josie was shaking her head; Vivienne's voice gained volume. 'My morning swim is one of my few pleasures. Otherwise, I'm just sitting around in that lodge like a . . . helpless princess in a tower. I need to wrest back some control over my own life and happiness, or I *will* go crazy! Can't you understand that?'

Vivienne stood, shocked by the rising passion of her petition to do as she liked, to have what she wanted – to live her own life. Her eyes threatened to overspill. She blinked rapidly.

Josie's face was anguished. 'I understand. I do. I just couldn't bear it if our stinking, cursed lake took another girl.'

Vivienne dabbed quickly at her cheeks with the back of her hand, blood cooling in her veins by sheer force of will. She looked Josie straight in the face, allowing haughtiness to elevate her tone and graceful neck alike.

'You can keep your curse! I'll take my own chances with that lake.'

She swept out.

CHAPTER SIXT1EEN

PIN-UP

Josie had eaten scarcely a bite of dinner this evening, though Reg's rissoles were usually her favourite. She offered none of her sunny conversation, spurned her father's gentle enquiries, chipped several of her mother's blue willow-patterned plates in her slamming rush through the washing-up, and had left Daphne to bemoan Josie's recklessness and rudeness without riposte. The concerned looks thrown after Josie, slid right off her back. She had more important objectives than familial harmony to fulfil.

In the hours since dinner, Josie's research notes had taken over her bedroom, in the farmhouse's annexed sleep-out. Sheets of paper lay over bed and floor and dresser; were stuck to windows and pinned to walls. She'd even emptied out her glory box, long forsaken, to store the overflow.

But though her room was covered with notes and images of Celeste Starr, Josie's mind was entirely on another woman. Still, she could hear Vivienne's precise enunciation and silvery cadence, see her soft grey eyes, recall her high-bred grace. Josie's heart ached for Vivienne's vulnerability, beneath the blinding sheen of finishing-school polish.

The woman obviously had a death wish. Hiding out in Sylvan Mist, *swimming* Lake Evelyn? Josie shuddered to think of the poor thing sitting all alone in that dark lodge this very moment, with her swimsuit laid out for the morning.

A fresh groan escaped Josie.

'What have you got wrong?' Ernest had come in to lounge against Josie's bed with great insouciance. He tapped his lucky cigar from hand to hand as he watched her work. It was the only one he'd ever owned – payment for helping a fellow in town – and though Ernest carried it everywhere, Josie *knew* he'd never smoke it.

Josie flung a filthy look his way. 'Would you give up on that cigar? It's terrible for you.'

Ernest shrugged, his pretty lips curling. 'Farming is terrible for me too, but they still make me do it.'

Josie smiled. 'Well, farming's how you earn your keep – but acting in my theatre group is about to become your new calling. I'm planning a lead role that's made for you in my new play.'

Ernest raised his cigar towards her. 'Cheers. I'll take it.'

Despite the privacy she'd planned to enjoy, and the work she'd wanted to get done, Josie was holding court for a revolving door of brothers this evening. The Monash men were clearly collaborating to overcome Josie's moody silence from earlier. Reg had already been in, juggling Daphne's dispatched grievances like hot rocks. Josie laughed every one of them away, and Reg sailed out again on an airstream of relief. Ernest had dropped in to nettle and sass, and drive her barmy with his infernal tapping cigar. Owen would be the next brother by, the call-in Josie looked forward to. She had twenty questions to put to *that* brother.

In the doorway, a throat was cleared. *Speak of the devil.*

Ernest pushed up. 'Right, I'm off.'

'Next,' Josie said, waving Owen in.

'Josie the Marvellous Playwright,' Owen declared, plumping onto her bed like a great oaf, so that notes spilled to the floor. 'I can't believe you're finally doing this.'

'I can't believe you're doing *that*,' she muttered, rescuing a sheaf of papers from under his backside.

On second thoughts, Josie wasn't going to ask him *any* questions. Owen should start off with an apology for setting her and Vivienne up, and then thoroughly explain himself.

'Fill me in,' Owen said, sans apology. The cad.

Josie feigned a loud yawn. 'Had such a busy day,' she said. 'After you stood me up, I had to help some weird blonde in town pick out the perfect, "Sorry I Jilted You, Take Me Back" card, and then give her directions back to Sydney.'

Owen watched her with unsmiling intensity. Josie put her back to him, sequestering a smile.

'You did not,' he said.

'Did too.'

'I'd never forgive you.'

'I'm already never forgiving *you*.'

'For?'

'Not enlisting my help sooner.'

'She doesn't *want* help.'

'Ha, she needs it! Would you believe she swims Lake Evelyn every day?'

'I've seen her do it.'

'She's clueless!'

'She's daring, and determined.'

'Such flattery. Meanwhile she called *you* hirsute. Like a bushranger, she said.'

Owen's laugh was heartier than she'd heard in ages. 'She's got a won-derfully sarcastic sense of humour.'

'No, she was being quite serious about your hairiness.'

'Nothing the barber can't fix.'

Josie snorted. 'I haven't seen your chin since you were sixteen. You've picked the wrong woman to finally clean your face up for. She's like a . . . wounded mouse, horribly entangled.'

To this, Owen did not respond. The seriousness of his expression made Josie wince. He might as well hear the hard truths straight up. 'She's not your type, Owen. Not a country girl. More like a foreign creature from some rarefied world – the way she speaks and gestures and carries herself, those giant jewels dripping off her, I mean, she doesn't even *dress* properly.'

For some reason, Owen seemed to find this last point privately entertaining.

Josie waited to be enlightened; scowling when he kept this amuse-ment to himself. 'By the way, I'm ready to accept your apology for not showing up.'

'Didn't need to be there.' Owen smiled. 'Vivienne obviously trusted you enough to tell you her troubles.'

Josie sighed. 'I didn't do as well as you might have hoped. When I told her not to swim in the lake – she *ran off*! Seems to be a pastime of hers . . .'

'Josie, she needs a friend.'

'What she needs is a whole new life. But she told me she's leaving as soon as tomorrow.'

'I don't think she knows anywhere else to go. She's stuck in limbo.'

'Purgatory, you mean.'

'Can you imagine hiding out in that place?'

'I can't fathom any of it, including *her*. She strikes me as the loneliest girl in the world.'

Disturbed by Owen's pained look, Josie sped into a wisecrack. 'I wouldn't mind having her holiday though: lounging around reading all day, with no brothers to irk me.'

'You jest, but the truth is you and I are not the only ones who know she's staying at Sylvan. Someone's been watching her from the forest at night. She caught them.'

Josie imagined this with a spasm of horror. She narrowed her eyes. 'A woman that beautiful, all alone? I bet Niall's been enjoying his job as caretaker with some . . . extra perks.'

Owen nodded. 'I thought so too, I'm going over to have a word with him.'

'No. I'll do it. I've been talking to Niall about my play, I'll see him again on the pretence of needing more information.'

At mention of Josie's play, Owen descended into pensiveness.

'Look, I'll try and help,' Josie said. 'I just don't know what use I'll be to her.'

Owen grappled with something he wanted to say. Josie waited. It was always worth waiting for Owen's sagacity.

He cracked his knuckles. 'Josie, none of this is coincidence. Think about it: we would never have found out Vivienne was there in the lodge, if you hadn't sent me to prepare the amphitheatre for your play about the damned lake that she just so happens to be brave enough to swim. I don't know how or why, but I believe *you're* meant to do something important with this. I think this is about *you* . . .'

As the house was creaking back on its old bones for the night, Josie's father came to her sleep-out.

Gabe walked slowly around the room, arms crossed, inspecting all the appended pages, brow fixed in a furrow. Finally, he stood looking up at Josie's photo of her mother. He reached to gently stroke Maureen's form.

There was an albatross about Gabe's neck as he sat down on her bed. This time Josie did not gripe at the disordering of paper. She blinked away a gritty rawness.

'Tell me what you're writing,' said Gabe.

She winced.

'I'm interested, Josephine.'

'As you can see,' she said quietly, 'I'm telling the story of Celeste Starr and Sylvan Mist, and how Lake Evelyn got its curse.'

Gabe stared at her. 'I thought you were only opening up the amphitheatre.'

'I was, but then I talked to Grandy and she said I should—'

Oh, her father's face!

She made a hasty correction. 'After a chat with Grandy, *I* decided I want to tell the *real* story of Celeste Starr.'

'And which story is that?'

'A love story,' Josie said.

'*Beryl* told you this.'

Ignoring the customary inflection on Grandy's name, Josie said: 'No, I've been talking to many people, and I've done my own research.' She passed Gabe her magazine clippings.

Gabe ran the briefest of glances over the clippings before pushing them back again.

'It's going to be a tragic love story,' Josie sped on. 'About an extraordinarily talented and promising actress and an Australian soldier, brought together by the war effort in Far North Queensland …' Emboldened by Gabe's silence, Josie rushed to lay out the skeleton plot of her play, growing increasingly animated. She finished with a flourish: 'So, after Rudy closes the amphitheatre and locks up Sylvan Mist,

166

I'll have this moving final scene, where Celeste is dancing along the shores of Lake Evelyn, under a single spotlight, on her joyful way to being reunited with her lover for eternity. And it's going to be beautiful and powerful, and ground-breaking for Barrington too, because I flip the script, see? So we don't end with Celeste drowned, and calling out for evermore from the depths for new victims, instead, we finish with the redemptive picture of Celeste getting her happy ending.'

Josie found herself on her feet, carried away. Her eyes shone as she perched down next to her father.

Gabe sat longer in silence. Josie watched worriedly for the slump of shoulders which alone would signal his unspoken disappointment. Why, Josie had never understood, couldn't her father yell and bully and beef himself around like so many other girls' fathers? At least then she might regard him with deserved contempt, and disregard his advice without regret. It was her father's dignified silence that had made flouting his wishes a painful experience since childhood.

To her incalculable surprise, there was no drop of shoulders. He spoke: 'Josephine, I'm only going to ask one time, and I wouldn't ask at all if I didn't think it my place to do so ...'

'You can ask,' Josie said. 'But you already know my answer.'

'Will you not turn back from this? Is there not any other play you can do, in any other place? The damage that ... curse has already done our town, the lives lost, I'll never forgive—' He cut off thickly.

'You'll never *forgive* me for my play?' Josie said, aghast.

Gabe covered her wringing palms with one hand, squeezing hard. 'Chickadee, there's no unpardonable thing you could ever do.'

Josie refused to be mollified by this – then *who* wouldn't he forgive?

She slid her hands out of Gabe's, giving him a stern look. 'Is this about Grandy again? Are you set against my play only because Grandy suggested it? Why must you two be ever at war?'

The wounded pinch of his brow made short work of her railing.

Gabe stood. Josie watched him go, concocting a last word to ease familiar guilt. 'Dad?' she called out, just as he reached the door. He turned slowly back.

Her handsome, gentle father. She *loved* him, never wanted to do *anything* to hurt or disappoint him. But she would not turn back from this.

'I'm going to make you proud, Pa. I promise. I believe in this play with all my heart. It's the right thing to do for Barrington.'

Gabe nodded, with a smile every bit as brave and sad as hers. 'You're the right person to do this, chickadee – for all of us.'

'When you deliver her milk,' Josie had told Owen at dawn, as they trooped up the hill, crunching over frost, to the dairy, 'tell her to come and see me in the air raid library. I'm going there to write after the milking.'

Anything to get away from Daphne, who was sewing her baby's elaborate layette at the kitchen table each day with long-suffering sighs. Josie couldn't even volunteer her services to hasten the process – shut her up – since Josie had bombed in sewing at school.

The moment breakfast was cleaned away and the veggies peeled for luncheon, Josie gathered up reams of paper, filled a Thermos, and high-tailed it for town. She had been hoping for privacy, and was elated when she arrived at the library to find it still locked up for the day.

Inside, Josie spread out her writing implements and picnic basket on the table, and set to work. Vivienne would come, she just knew it.

Josie started at every voice passing by, and ran to double-check she hadn't accidentally locked the door multiple times, but no Vivienne appeared. Just as Josie had finally given up on the ridiculous idea, she heard the quiet clip of kitten heels up the pavers towards the shelter.

Josie drew in a breath, laying her pencil on the table. The door opened and a pale face, concealed by scarf and cat's eye glasses peered round.

'Morning. How was your swim?' asked Josie.

'Bit chilly,' Vivienne replied.

The women stared at each other.

If she wants my help, she'll come in.

Vivienne stepped into the shelter. 'I have to tell you; this is such a marvellous use of space. I couldn't fathom it when Owen first said you'd made a library of a bomb shelter.'

'Air raid shelter,' Josie corrected.

Vivienne nodded, unruffled. It was so exhausting living with a perpetually affronted woman, Josie had forgotten not all women were like Daphne.

'Did you get raids here during the war?'

'Thankfully not. Though there was one farmhouse just north of the Tablelands bombed. A little girl about my age at the time was injured.' Josie held up her Thermos and mug. 'Want a cuppa?'

'I do, thank you' Vivienne said, closing the door behind her, fiddling with the delicate pearl buttons of her soft, Alice blue cardigan. 'But you're working, let me make it.'

'It was time to take a break, anyway.' Josie pushed haphazard paper piles even more askew. 'Sorry about all this.'

'I don't mind,' Vivienne said. 'You should see the slovenly state of Sylvan Messed.'

Josie laughed. *So, Owen was right about the droll humour.*

After serving the tea, Vivienne leafed through Josie's first draft. 'This is wonderful.'

Josie tried to look casual. 'Is it? What parts in particular?'

'It's an enthralling drama developing. You've got a great imagination.'

'It's all true.'

Vivienne looked up. 'Truly?'

'Substantiated by local sources.'

Vivienne skimmed a little further through Josie's notes, with a little frown. 'I think you're leaving the character of Rudy Meyer rather undeveloped, though. He hardly plays a role.'

'Rudy? He's supposed to remain a background character. This isn't a story about *his* grand plans and subsequent fame – it's about Celeste's heart and talent, and the tragedy of love and war in women's lives.'

Vivienne arched a brow. 'Aren't love and war the same thing? Strategic endeavours, mostly concerned with the accrual of wealth and power?'

Josie tossed this proposition around for herself. Love was, so far as Josie knew: an unquenchable ache, the lost and tender dream, a quiet yearning, unceasing – but *war*?

'Love and war,' Josie allowed, 'are two very different things in my tale.'

Vivienne shrugged. 'Well, it's your story. But I think if you took a walk around Sylvan Mist, you'd disagree that Rudy is a background character.'

Josie perched on the table, intrigued. 'What do you mean?'

'The man was obviously obsessed with her. His lodge is a giant memorial to Celeste Starr, and yet how many years has it been?'

'Fourteen, give or take – she drowned herself before peace was won.' Josie's thoughts whirred. 'I know Rudy was *said* to love Celeste, and her death affected him so much he shut down his shows out of respect for her. But he's since carved out a critically acclaimed career overseas, he's moved from one love affair to another, hasn't shown the slightest interest in this place. If that lodge is a "memorial" as you say – and I'll have to take your word for it, no locals are allowed inside – that's probably because he's simply never come back to dismantle it.'

'Nobody hangs that many pictures of a woman they weren't intimately involved with or otherwise fanatical about.' Vivienne observed Josie's resistance. 'I'm telling you: I've had a dead woman's eyes following my every move there.'

'She doesn't haunt the lodge,' Josie said. 'Only the lake.'

Vivienne shrugged. 'It's your play.'

'Does it frighten you, being in that lodge, all alone?'

Vivienne put the picture of Celeste away, face down. She stared at Josie – a direct, open look, needing no explanation.

Josie nodded. 'Don't envy you. I've never slept a night alone in my life, much less somewhere like that.'

'I sleep on the library floor, hidden from all the windows, behind a barricaded door, with a pillow over my head, and a torch in hand.'

'You want a gun?' Josie regretted blurting something so bald, even before she'd witnessed the effect of it on Vivienne's fine features. 'Don't take me the wrong way. I'm a farm girl . . .'

'I wouldn't have thought dairy farming required much shooting.'

'The guns are for the big snakes and wild dogs.'

'Good grief. I think I'll take my chances with the birds determined to bomb me out of the lodge.'

'Ah, that would be the lesser sooty owl. When the troops were training here during the war, they must have bemoaned the whistling bomb sound of that owl. It was like the forest was preparing them for the horror ahead.'

Vivienne tapped the image of Celeste's lover. 'So, this part of the story, with the handsome soldier, that's true too?'

'Mostly, with some romantic embellishment.'

'Zach is *very* fetching,' Vivienne mused. 'Who's going to play your lead?'

'I'm not exactly spoiled for choice of men in Barrington.'

'Better than being spoiled *by* your choice of man,' Vivienne said.

'Amen to that.'

'In a small town like this, you must be getting incessant commentary on your marital status.'

Josie laughed. Talk about nail hit on head. 'Most people here have come to accept I'm fulfilled by mothering my family of men.'

Vivienne inclined her head to evaluate Josie. 'But you're not, are you?'

'Thought I was. Then my insufferable sister-in-law moved in and started taking over, and I realised how replaceable I am to my father and brothers. If a woman like *Daphne* West can assume my role so quickly, then what was the point of my staying to look after them all in the first place?'

Vivienne was twisting her obscenely large diamond around. 'The way your brother looks when he talks about you, and how he brings you into every conversation – I doubt your family thinks *any* woman could fill your shoes.'

Josie smoothed her fringe, faking indifference.

'But if you had known, years ago,' Vivienne probed, 'that you didn't *have* to stay and take care of all those men, where might you have gone?'

'Nowhere else,' Josie replied – too quickly. 'I *love* Barrington. It's my own little kingdom.'

Both women looked around the library bunker. Josie was suddenly conscious of concrete cracks, the dust film on shelves she was too short to reach, the inadequacy of light and unfreshened air. Josie frowned, feeling accused. *She* wasn't the one running away, nor had she ever contemplated it. The hide of *Vivienne* to insinuate Josie had missed her chance to leave.

Josie's hand itched to touch the heart locket beneath her neckline. She settled, instead, with a squeeze of the well-creased envelope carried in her pocket.

'What about you?' Josie said, fixing her frank gaze on Vivienne's dove-soft eyes. 'What are you going to do with your new-found freedom?'

Vivienne sighed. 'I'll tell you when I find it.'

'You're not free yet?'

'I've spent my whole life being told how to act, and what to do and say. It's going to take me a while to find my own feet in the world.'

'You'll find them. A woman like you doesn't go long without.' Josie had intended no spite, and was glad to see Vivienne take no offence.

'I just hope I can reconcile my girlish expectations with my life's new outlook. I've thrown away the kind of opportunities you couldn't imagine. I was the envy of every debutante in Sydney.'

'You're right,' Josie said dryly, 'I can't imagine that.'

Vivienne's lips lifted with a wry lopsidedness, which transformed her beauty from cool to endearing in an instant.

'That's the first time I've seen you smile.'

'I am often accused of seriousness. Men, in particular, dislike that my personality does not match my bright, flaxen hair.'

'My brother described you as wonderfully sarcastic.'

Josie watched Vivienne's lips press closed, denying a smile.

Ah, now it is I *who sees, Owen.*

Josie propped her chin on her hands with an inviting nose crinkle. 'Please tell me the story of running away from your wedding ceremony. I'm beginning to think you'll never spill the beans, and it promises to be so thrilling and dramatic!'

Vivienne could easily have reacted indignantly, or issued cold refusal, but the marvel of it was: she didn't.

Instead, the silky blonde opened her mouth and freely poured out her story. Josie sat quite agog through all of it, her left hand pressing her writing hand hard against the table. *Don't take notes*, she warned herself. As Vivienne's story concluded, Josie couldn't help it – she clapped. 'I've been writing the wrong story! Sell me *your* splendid tale, so I can produce a play about a runaway bride, downtrodden by her socialite mother and pampered by her playboy uncle, and now trapped in a haunted house.'

Vivienne crimsoned. 'You must think I'm spoiled, privileged and weak.'

'Like heck you're weak. Obstinate, more like.'

'You're in a lonely club with that opinion.'

Josie placed a hand on Vivienne's arm. 'You *are* strong. Not only to flee, but to stand that spooky lodge and swim our cursed lake, and ward off mysterious faces in the forest.'

'Owen told you about that.' Vivienne looked guiltily around the library bunker. 'I am sorry about the books I threw outside.'

Josie adjoined her gusty laugh to this. 'I just hope they were heavy ones! Owen and I think we know who it was – Sylvan's caretaker, Niall. He can be obnoxious, about time he got a good doink on the head. He's always lorded it over everyone about Rudy Meyer's lodge being *his* to look after. He never lets anyone near it, or his guests. Keeps those gates locked, hunts bushwalkers away, acts like *he* owns the place! Used to have a horrid "trespassers will be shot" sign out on the main road, but someone accidentally drove a tractor over it – whoopsie-daisy. If Niall's been skulking around out there, I'd say he's checking you're not destroying the joint. Or, making sure none of us plebs are getting near you.'

Vivienne was visibly lightened by this. 'A caretaker does make more sense than . . . other thoughts I'd entertained. In fact, now I realise he must have come poking around inside, once, while I was out, and restarted the grandfather clock. I thought I was going quite mad, you see there was a . . . fingerprint left.'

'When?' Josie asked sharply.

'First day I arrived. I've slept behind a reinforced door ever since.'

Josie had no trouble imagining Niall being so sneaky. 'Listen here, if he bothers you again, in any way, I want you to come and see me. I'll sort him out quick smart . . .'

CHAPTER SEVENTEEN

INTREPID

Vivienne returned to Josie's bunker library each noonday for the next fortnight. On foot, to avoid the male attention. She told herself the exercise was essential now she was so full of cream, though her morning lap in increasingly wintry temperatures was exhausting enough without the additional cross-country walk. Mostly, she wanted to extend the time before she must return to the dim forest and dank lodge.

Vivienne was very much enjoying the progression of Josie's play, now titled: *Nightingale Lake*. Who'd have guessed a provincial play by an amateur writer scribbling messily away in a bomb shelter would be the most engrossing story Vivienne had read all year?

In truth, she craved Josie's friendship – and how free she felt *in* it – more than exercise or entertainment. Josie said 'chewing the cud' with Vivienne was the highlight of her busy days, and Vivienne awoke each morning already rehearsing the droll lines she might drop to elicit one of Josie's gusty laughs. She went all the way to that bunker in Barrington just for the laugh that lay beyond it, then carefully she brought the lively, musical feel of it back to her lonely lodge, to keep her company throughout the dark hours ahead.

Hope might be the thing with feathers, as the poetess professed, but *solace* was a warm breeze bearing birdsong.

In the last fortnight, Vivienne had stopped fixating on when she might be forced to leave Sylvan Mist and return to Sydney. Indeed, when Felix had called again this morning to check on her, she hadn't even raised the prospect. If he wondered why she was suddenly disinterested in the news from home, he did not ask. Felix's main concern had been how she would fare without his attentions over the rest of winter, for he was leaving her there – in fact, leaving the whole country.

'I'm sorry, my girl. I've got dealings in America scheduled, and I can't get out of it. I'll be abroad for a while.'

'How long?'

'Only a couple of months. But you'll be all right tucked away there, won't you? You just treat it like your own private health farm, and try not to let it all get to you while I'm gone.'

'A couple of *months*!'

'Yes, I know. You won't have to fend for yourself though, everything is organised. In fact, how about I phone up to Mr Jeffries and order some extra treats in your upcoming deliveries, to cheer you up. Your favourite lemon drops – doesn't that sound good? Won't be long at all, and I'll be back. I'm going to fly in up north, and come directly to you. You can manage alone until I get there, can't you? Then we'll go back to Sydney and face the music, together. It's all going to work out, you'll see . . .'

'But can I really stay on here that long? Rudy won't mind? I don't want to put anyone out.'

'Don't worry about a thing, I'm taking care of everything.'

'I feel so indebted to you, Uncle Felix.'

'Oh, Possum – *no*, don't be silly! Your happiness is the most important thing. Just let me look after you, and don't fret so much . . .'

For hours afterwards, Vivienne fought back a fit of weeping at being so left behind by her uncle. Until, that is, she forgot it entirely under the spell of Josie Monash and her play.

Sitting now in the airless warmth of the bunker library, Vivienne had just finished telling Josie about her latest evening torturer: a lost bat, which flew around the lodge for hours, pinging its cry into the black, creaking night. Vivienne suspected she was projecting her own emotional state onto the bat, but she did not say as much to her friend.

For we are friends now, aren't we?

'Bats don't get lost,' Josie said, dismissively. 'I'm pretty sure they've got some kind of homing system.' She countered Vivienne's brooding look. 'Listen, why don't you come for dinner at my house tonight? Get you out of that hellhole for a bit. In fact, why don't you stay over for a night? You're already sleeping on the floor anyway; you might as well be on the floor of my room.'

'That's really very kind, Josie. But I don't want to have to meet people here.'

'Unless I dreamed you up, you've been meeting me every day.'

And how could Vivienne answer that?

'Come over for dinner,' Josie pressed. 'You won't need to worry about *meeting* anyone else. It's Satdy night, all my brothers will be in Barrington for the dance. Daphne tags along too, just so she can complain about how late they kept her out. It would only be you and me, and my dad – but you'd love him.'

I'll be fine at the lodge, Vivienne prepared to say, *I'll just cook my lonely meal and eat it under a blanket fort, singing with my mouth full* . . .

It came out all wrong, though.

'Thank you. I will. Dinner would be lovely.'

Vivienne had been sent back to the lodge to shower and change, with instructions to be ready by six, when Josie would pick her up.

It was Owen, however, to whom Vivienne opened the door in her favourite figure-hugging cashmere sweater, the colour of cream. Her blonde hair was set in flowing waves to her shoulders, pearls gleamed at her ears and throat, there was baby pink colour at her lips, and Shalimar dabbed upon pulse points. She was the very epitome of softness, and she did not miss the admiring glow in Owen's eyes.

'Sorry I'm late,' he said, a flush at his temples.

'Sorry *you're* late? Where's Josie?'

'Josie is endeavouring to make dinner for you. She sent me to get you so she can finish cleaning the ceiling.'

'The *ceiling*?'

'Cooking under duress is a recipe for Josie-projectiles. Beats me why you invited yourself to a meal.'

'Seems like you've invited *yourself.*'

Owen laughed. 'Nope. You're on your own with that casserole. When Josie called, I was chasing Mooranda out of my veggie garden again.'

Vivienne ignored this cow namedropping. 'You've trimmed your beard.'

He smoothed his close-cropped beard, colouring. 'Even bushrangers have a clip occasionally.'

Vivienne turned away to lock the lodge door – her own blush hidden.

She followed Owen down the stairs, conscious of his spiced oakmoss aftershave scent, and the neat press of his shirt. Maybe it wasn't only Mooranda who had made him late. Vivienne smiled at Owen's back.

But in the clearing, there was no car waiting behind Vivienne's.

'Where's my cab?'

'Sorry, I had to bring the tractor, didn't have anything else.'

Vivienne stared at Owen. *Oh, did you just*, she thought; intuiting better.

'It's out on the road,' he said, straight faced.

'Dear me,' she said, indicating her kitten heels. 'I can't ruin my expensive shoes, walking up the mucky driveway. You'll have to carry me, then.'

Owen stared at Vivienne.

She fluttered her lashes, miming a spinning motion. 'Quick, give me a piggyback out to the road.'

After a beat, Owen knelt. Vivienne climbed on his back with as much confidence as if she'd worn her slim-fitting jeans for precisely this purpose. Her arms were slung around his neck, so that her hand-bag bounced against his chest as he set off up the heavily canopied road, saying nothing.

Vivienne compressed her lips against laughter.

The urge to laugh passed quickly, as she settled into the gentle rock-ing motion of being carried by this large, broad-shouldered man, who smelt divine, pressed so intimately against his warm back . . .

By the time they'd reached the road, Vivienne was working hard to avert her thoughts, so that Josie's brother would not hear – *feel* – her breathiness.

At the road, Owen tipped her off his back without ado.

'Your limousine, milady,' he said, with a bow towards a large red tractor, slasher attached at the rear.

Vivienne stared at Owen, noting this time it was he who was suppressing laugher.

'There's only one seat. Shall I go on the roof?' she said, hands on hips.

Please don't say I sit on your lap, Vivienne thought, a mutinous part of her wanting him to say just exactly that.

180

'You sit on the slasher,' Owen said, extending a hand so that she might climb onto the square, flat top of the machinery.

Vivienne settled herself down, crossing her legs elegantly: a beautifully acted model of nonchalance; one hand gripping hard at the chain.

'Don't fall off,' he said, climbing into the cab.

From the smile moving behind Owen's closed lips, Vivienne understood just how equally matched they were in this evening's game.

The tractor rattled into motion, belching fumes. Under this cover of sound, Vivienne allowed herself a giggle, her trepidation of meeting another Monash relative forgotten. Could Owen be persuaded to share their dinner? How bad a cook could Josie really be?

By the time they'd arrived at Josie's farm, Vivienne was beginning to think slasher-riding was an underrated form of transport. Not *quite* so enjoyable as Owen's back but it was a delightful, bouncing ride over rolling green hillocks and across dusk-shadowed fields as the sun, setting in pearlescent clouds, gilded the far-off mountain tops.

Josie's farmhouse was every bit the rustic affair Vivienne had anticipated, surrounded by farm machinery parts, lit welcomingly against sprawling paddocks. Josie herself came running to meet them, observably flustered.

She shot Owen an accusing look in the cab as she helped Vivienne from the slasher. Vivienne found herself apologising: 'Your brother said he didn't have anything else to bring me here in.'

Owen came to stand alongside Vivienne, looking equally guilty. 'Your friend made me piggyback her through the forest because she was wearing her best shoes.'

Josie looked between the pair, shaking her head. She settled first on Vivienne. 'Owen has recently refurbished a salvaged car – it is his pride and joy, polished inside and out.' She turned to Owen. 'And *Vivienne* wears those shoes every day on her farmland hike into town.'

Vivienne scuffed at the rich volcanic farm soil with the worn point of her shoe, hiding a smile.

'Anyway,' Josie huffed, 'you'll have to take her back.'

'Take me back?' *Expelled just for toying with Josie's brother?*

'I'm sorry,' Josie said, and truly she did seem to be. 'But it's all fallen apart – everyone's home! Daph has gone into labour – typical, never checks her plans with anyone else – and she's rushed off to Atherton Hospital. Reg is here pacing the floorboards, or should I say *staggering*, because useless Ernest went and got him terribly drunk this afternoon to celebrate his imminent fatherhood. So now I'm trying to stretch what little casserole I didn't burn to feed more mouths, and it's a *calamity*!'

Owen shortened this for Vivienne. 'Dinner's *off*.' He nodded towards a saucepan, lying upside down on the grass outside the kitchen window. 'Also cancelled.'

Vivienne could not help a snort of laughter. Josie served the pair a filthy look. 'Go on, take her back; in the *Ford* this time.'

Vivienne gazed over Josie's shoulder at the farmhouse, a wellspring of boisterous laughter and giddy expectation. She visualised another pitifully lonely and endlessly stretching night back at the lodge, under siege by eyeshine, scampers and shrieks – the latter, lately, her own.

Owen, somehow intuiting her sudden longing, leaned to catch her eyes. 'You've met the worst of my family already, I promise.'

A smile came to Vivienne. 'Josie, I think . . . I'd rather like to stay.'

All were silent around the farmhouse table after grace. The heat of the wood stove was at Vivienne's back, and every eye – even the bleary gaze of the expectant father – was on her. Only Gabriel Monash, stately and handsome at the table's head, was eating the meal with gusto, seemingly indifferent to her presence.

The strangest thing was, Vivienne had the distinct sense Gabriel was more acutely aware of her than any other person round this table.

Minutes earlier, Josie had introduced her to the circle of her family simply as Viv, no further explanation, and though Vivienne had gone around the group shaking hands, expertly memorising names, not one Monash had questioned her odd manifestation.

In the middle of the table, a Mateus Rosé bottle sat with a candle burning in its neck, and long lines of wax running down the bottle. This homespun decoration touched Vivienne's heart.

She took a mouthful of charred casserole, swallowing hard.

Josie leaned to whisper. 'You don't have to eat that. Stick with your cheese on bread.'

Vivienne cut herself another slice of cheese, scoffing gratefully. 'This is delicious,' she said, hoping to break the hush that had descended over the kitchen. 'I'm sure I enjoyed the same cheese at the lodge, I've never tasted anything like it.'

'Owen makes it, and sells it in town,' Josie said proudly.

Vivienne looked up at Owen in surprise, to find his eyes already on her. They shared a steady look. *I bet you hung Barrington's moon next.*

Ernest, the prettiest of Josie's tall brothers, tapped his unlit cigar in an impatient beat against the table. Apropos of nothing, the eldest brother, Reg, burst into laughter. Josie gave him a withering look, but the laugh went on, and on. Vivienne forgave his manners. He *was* drunk . . . *and* waiting for his first baby.

Ernest cut through the laughter. 'How'sh your play going, Jose?'

At this, Josie's father placed down his cutlery, giving Josie full attention.

'Excellent.' Josie beamed. 'Aiming to introduce my play and open up casting at the next meeting.'

Ernest replied in a tone of pure goading: 'Any new . . . *bombshells*?'

Gabe followed the combative look between Ernest and Josie, frowning.

'Nope, everything going according to plan,' Josie said airily. 'Although I'm still searching for the quote Celeste used in her suicide note. No one seems to remember *exactly* what it was, and I need something really goosepimply.'

To Vivienne's right, Gabe murmured something – a name, perhaps, or a snatch of prose? She inclined her ear, but the rest of the Monash clan had joined a rowdy debate on the ethics of making a death note *more* dramatic. Gabe returned to eating, head down. Vivienne kept her eyes on Josie's father, waiting for him to try again.

The talk grew more voluble as the serving bowls emptied, and plates were wiped clean with the last chunks of bread. Vivienne found herself beset by sudden sorrow. This table, with its vivacious banter and many participants, was nothing like her own growing up: finely set for two, tense and formal, with nothing to cover those cold, aching gaps that her mother's sincere interest might have filled.

Tears threatening, Vivienne excused herself for the bathroom.

It smelt, in that small out shed, like the dank towels of men, carbolic soap, boot polish. Even scrubbed clean, there were whisker remnants round the sink, an odd piece of farm machinery in the corner. How did Josie stand living with so many men in this humble abode? Was it only hankering for female company that had made her so kind to Vivienne? Perhaps they weren't really friends at all – only a charity case adopted by a woman in want of a sister.

Vivienne trudged back to the farmhouse. From the back door, she heard the two older brothers speaking, and her own name.

'She's a bit dull, don't you think, for a city dweller?'

'For a *woman*,' amended the other.

Josie's sunny laughter cut through. 'Listen to the cheap seats! She doesn't have to charm either of *you*. Go get onto the washing up.'

Eyes burning, Vivienne slipped back out, into the night.

Gabe found Vivienne in the yard, sitting on the large metal body of a go-kart under construction, and gazing up at the splendiferous throw of stars across a firmament unpolluted.

'May I sit?' Gabe asked.

'It is yours,' Vivienne said, scooting over.

She went on watching the sky a-swarm with stars, while he crossed his arms, and gazed across the dark farmland.

'Vivienne, is it?' he asked, after a time.

Vivienne turned to look at him. 'That's what my mother named me.'

'And now my daughter calls you Viv.'

Viv. Yes, she liked that.

'Your Josie is wonderful,' Vivienne said. 'She has a huge heart.'

Gabe did not reply. Well, Vivienne had just stated the obvious, hadn't she?

Josie's father was uncommonly handsome, unnecessarily so for a widower living the drudgery of farm life. Evidently Gabriel Monash was to credit for the good looks of all the Monash children. Vivienne realised it must be Gabe whom Owen took after in his placid economy with words and calm self-possession.

But where did Josie get *her* mile-a-minute manner of speaking and walking, her bold manner and temperament? Vivienne didn't think Josie had ever known her mother, but perhaps she embodied something of the woman.

'This is interesting,' Vivienne said, patting the go-kart beneath. 'Looks like a plane.'

'Yes, it's made from the belly tank of an aircraft, a relic from the war. I've been meaning to finish it for years. My children are probably too old.'

'You seem to have so many leftovers from the war around this region.'

'Indeed, many of us feel like leftovers.'

Vivienne could not think how she should reply.

'Young folk,' he said, sparing her the awkwardness, 'would modify the belly tanks to use for boating on Lake Evelyn . . . back in the day.'

'Before that actress ruined it for everyone. And now you're all afraid of your lake.'

She felt Gabe draw himself up very straight beside her. Her breath sounded overloud in the sombre, elongated silence that followed.

Finally, he turned to her. 'Do you believe in second chances, Vivienne?'

Her laugh was unnaturally harsh. 'I have to. I've got everything pinned on it.' Only in saying this did she realise Gabe was asking for himself.

'Do *you* believe in second chances?' she asked; lamely it felt.

'I believe in the God of Peter.'

What on earth does that *have to do with chances?* Vivienne thought of cocks crowing thrice, of a church perched awkwardly on a rock.

Gabe stood, his arms still folded. 'I believe God loves us enough to repeat the miracles we need.'

Vivienne absorbed this with a small frown.

'Please don't hurt Josephine,' Gabe said, very quietly, but with no scope for misinterpretation. 'She has a terrible fear of losing people, and she tries so hard to be *necessary* to everyone. You are her first true friend. Don't hurt her.'

Inside, a game of Wink Murder was underway in the lounge – a room apparently reserved for books and parlour games. Vivienne had heard

186

of Wink Murder but she had certainly never seen it played by a troupe of inebriated dairy farmers. Bemusedly, she watched this spectacle, until laughter rumbled silently in her middle. Her abdominal muscles aching from withholding it.

Having won yet another round, Josie came to sit beside her with a satisfied sigh. 'They're so easily defeated.'

'Only when they're several cows short of a herd?'

'All the time. Won't you play?'

'At murder? Perhaps something else.'

Josie grinned wickedly. 'I have just the thing.' She turned Owen's way. 'Oi, charades – you're up.'

Owen accepted this offer looking, Vivienne thought, nervous for the first time she'd seen. Swiftly, she deduced the reason for it. Owen Monash had both exceptional talent for charades, and confounding his siblings.

Vivienne looked around the room, shaking her head. Did they not have a picture theatre on this mountain? Was *no one* going to guess his mime?

Finally, she'd had enough. '*A Star is Born*!' she cried. 'How did you miss *born* – aren't you all waiting on the very thing?'

'Is *that* what he was miming,' Earnest said dryly, 'I was too scared to guess.'

'At least someone in this room is discerning,' muttered Owen.

'Do it again, Owen and Viv,' Josie sang out.

Owen and Vivienne both swung a look at Josie, to find her the very picture of innocence.

Owen chose 'movie' once more, provoking groans.

Vivienne had it in moments: '*The Quiet Man*.'

Owen's whole face lit up. Vivienne felt hers do the same.

He began to mime more rapidly.

'*Othello*,' she declared, without delay.

'Yes!' he cried, triumphant. 'No one *ever* gets that!'

Owen was facing Vivienne, playing to an audience of one. On it went between the pair, while the rest of the family watched in a dazed spell: *The Barefoot Contessa*, *The War of the Worlds*, *Kiss Me Deadly* . . .

A heady exhilaration swept over Vivienne, such that she hadn't experienced in many years. Her eyes shone with the exuberance of it, and *him*.

The first cushion hitting the side of her head felt, perhaps, like a mistake. About the second soft furnishing sailing into her face, there could be no doubt. Josie's brothers were pelting her with their couch cushions! Was *this* country hospitality?

Vivienne spun; mouth agape. *Do you realise you're throwing things at a* guest? The next cushion got her right in the gob, lipstick and all.

Josie, who might have enforced the most basic of manners among these sozzled farmers, was merely laughing, saying something about being 'one of us now'.

Vivienne was just reaching for a cushion to return fire, when the lounge door whacked open to admit Gabe, thus far absent from their games.

'What is it?' Josie said; instantly alert. 'The baby?'

'No,' Gabe said, looking past Josie, at Vivienne. 'It's Beryl. She's coming up the drive.'

Josie's grandmother was by all accounts a battleaxe. Vivienne didn't have it in her to meet, much less explain her whole story, to someone else's matriarch. She turned helplessly to Josie, but her friend was already two steps ahead:

'You'd better go hide, Viv, hurry!'

CHAPTER EIGHTEEN

UNTO THE BREACH

Josie straightened the flounced valance on her bed, double checked no feet could be seen poking out beneath, and rushed out to meet Grandy Beryl, coming up the farmhouse steps.

All the Monash siblings crammed the kitchen to greet her. Grandy hadn't been out to the farmhouse for over a decade.

'What are you doing here?' This from Gabe, standing in the circle of his family; face grim.

'I promised Maureen I would be here for all the births – and so I am. For her Reg.'

'Golly, thanks, Grandy,' Reg said, whiskey having leavened a shaky emotion in his voice. Many faces turned to regard him. Was Reg making a stand? No one ever made a stand, much less took a side.

Beryl was not waiting for permission. In she came, gripping at her walking stick. Beryl went around the group, pinching cheeks, unsmiling in her ministrations. When she reached Gabe, she stared until he stepped aside, allowing her to pass into the lounge. Nervous glances passed between the trailing siblings.

Josie hurried to pull a chair over for Beryl, carefully turning over the cushion with its lipstick imprint. Beryl remained standing, scrutinising

189

the room. Had she raised her nose to sniff the air next, Josie wouldn't have been surprised. When her grandmother's gaze circled towards the sleep-out, Josie could not prevent a tiny whimper.

Ernest and Reg, for so long trying to keep their faces straight between them, sprayed the room with rough laughter.

'They're full as bulls,' Josie muttered.

Beryl gave Josie an oddly assessing look. 'While we're waiting for the West girl to bring us good tidings—'

'*Daph*,' Reg interjected, with a protective quaver.

'—I'd like to see your play research, Josephine.'

'Not right now, Grandy. I've got such a mess spread everywhere. How about I grab my script instead?'

'I don't want your polished script, Josephine. I've come to see the material you worked from. I've heard all about your walls covered with Celeste Starr.'

Josie swung a dark look around the lounge – which one of them had been feeding Grandy information? At this juncture, Gabe left the room. Josie heard him filling the kettle in the next room. Was he abandoning her to Beryl?

Beryl was clucking, there was no doubt about it. Josie tried to keep the panic from her voice. 'Let me go grab a few things for you to look at, then.'

Beryl was having none of it. Josie followed her grandmother's straight back and netted hair down the hallway to the sleep-out.

The valance hung undisturbed, with no sign of the hidden blonde. Beryl walked slowly around the room, carefully studying each thumb-tacked page and photo, every set direction and costume note. Josie watched the slew of reactions on her grandmother's face – from condescension to contempt, and every dismissive shade in between.

Beryl finished, as Gabe had done, standing below Josie's picture of her mother. But where Gabe had softened into sorrow, Beryl's spine went stiffer still.

'And which of these ridiculous stories,' Beryl said, rounding on Josie, 'are you bringing to the Obsidian?'

Ridiculous?

Josie took her script from atop the dresser, and passed it to Beryl, saying, a little petulantly: 'It's a love story.'

Beryl sat down on the bed with a solid whump that did not quite cover the startled cry from beneath.

There was a single beat of curious silence, after which Beryl turned her eyes to the script. While Beryl's eyes were scanning through the lines, Josie's gaze flew to the valance. Was Vivienne *alive*? Josie wouldn't want to be squashed by Grandy – though she often felt she was.

Finally, Beryl looked up. 'Is *this* it?'

'Do you not like it? Obviously in a mere skim read it's impossible to really feel the story's aching, poignant heart. But you'll have to take my word for it: it is there. I'm proud of this script, and I especially love my ending, because—'

'You're waffling, dear.'

Josie watched in astonishment as Beryl heaved herself up and charged out of the room. Josie knelt to look under the valance. Vivienne, clutching the side of her head, waved her out after Beryl.

Beryl had gone straight to the kitchen; Monash brothers parting like the Red Sea before her. Josie arrived two skips behind her.

Beryl repeated her statement to Gabe, sitting at the kitchen table, with his saucer full of tea. 'Is *this* it?'

'That's Josephine's play, yes,' Gabe said, expressionless.

Josie winced at the paper clutched in Beryl's hand.

'You're just going to stand shamelessly by and watch Josephine produce this play?'

'I'm proud of Josephine. She's a gifted and courageous writer.' Gabe's voice was restrained, but Josie did not miss the slight tremble of his saucer, and the tiny spill of tea, as he returned the contents to his cup.

'Josephine's skills are not in question, her knowledge is.'

'Josephine has told a story she believes in, and one that befits the hopes of this town. I'm very grateful to her for that.'

'I *bet* you're grateful to Josephine!'

Why did they both throw her name at each other like that? Josie felt her hands rise in a uselessly placating motion, with no words to accompany it.

Beryl had countless measures of scorn to squander on their father. 'You're a coward, Gabriel Monash.'

'As you've said, many a time, *Beryl.*'

Well, at least now they were pelting each other's names.

'You *never* deserved to have her,' Beryl said.

'If you mean Maureen, perhaps not, though I always tried to be a loving husband and a good provider.' Gabe's voice had taken on the quality of cold steel. 'But if you're questioning my right to my own daughter – *yet again* – I have no qualms about telling you how very wrong you are and always were. At some point you have to accept you lost. Josephine is my daughter to raise, and not yours.'

Josie felt Owen's arm come around her shoulders. She knew he meant well, understood he'd always tried to be her grounding strength in this bitter tug of war that never seemed to end, still; at this moment, Owen was another constraint upon her.

Josie struggled out of his embrace. 'As the object of property ever in question, I'm asking both of you to stop. We've heard this a hundred times, and on the night that Reg becomes a father, none of us wants to rehash it. Right, Reg?'

Josie looked to her eldest brother. *Step in!* Reg's face stayed blank, but a choking sound came, from low in his throat. *Coward*, Josie countered with a bull's snorting.

But maybe he was right to baulk. Beryl turned her granddaughter's way. 'As for you, Josephine, perhaps you'd like to tell your father about the person you've got hidden under your bed?'

Kudos to Gabe: his teacup settled back in its saucer with barely a rattle. 'Josephine doesn't have anything she needs to tell me this evening.'

Josie heard Beryl's wily intrigue beginning anew. 'So. You already know about the person Josephine has in her bedroom. Well, you never fail to disappoint me, Gabriel.'

Beryl turned to the empty hallway. Heads swivelled to follow her glare. 'Young man,' she hollered. 'You've been given away! Come out and face the music.'

Young man? Josie couldn't prevent a yelp of laughter. 'You're completely mistaken, it's nothing like that.'

'Grandy,' Owen tried, in the caressing tones only a grandson could lavish on his grandmother. 'Josie has been secretly mentoring a friend for her play. It's meant to be surprise for Barrington. We don't want to ruin it . . .'

Josie's most honest brother was getting quite good at lying to save Vivienne. At some point, Josie would have to sort out the Vivienne George problem Owen was fast developing. Right now, though, she had to neutralise the Grandy Beryl predicament.

Beryl turned and barked a command down the hall. 'Come out, whoever you are! I'm here until that baby arrives, so you've got no way out.'

Gabe pushed his tea away with an appalled sigh. 'Must you always be so—'

He did not finish, for coming up the hallway, face pale, was Vivienne herself.

Josie stepped in front of Vivienne. 'Grandy, meet Viv. She's over from Malanda.'

Grandy stared hard at Vivienne, making no effort to disguise her appraisal. Vivienne stretched out a slim hand. 'I'm very pleased to meet you, Mrs Frances.'

Beryl discharged a disparaging puff of air. '*You're* not a Tablelands girl. You don't belong here for one second.'

'*Grandy!*' This cry seemed to come roundly.

Beryl shrugged. She was often mean, but rarely too far off the mark. 'You're a fish out of water, it's written all over you! You don't know who you are or where you're going.'

Josie watched Vivienne's hands fly behind her back, fingers flayed, scrabbling for something to grasp. She saw Owen's large hand go to be grasped.

Beryl, however, had discovered a new target of torment. She rounded on Gabe. '*You,*' she said. 'Up to your old tricks again, *aren't* you!'

Gabe rose from the table, his indignation a quiet blaze. 'Leave,' he said, reaching to open the door.

'Dad! You can't!' Another unified cry of protest.

'Leave,' he said again.

'I'm here for Maureen's Reg, and the baby,' Beryl said, not moving an inch.

Reg seemed to think it a good time to hotfoot it for the outhouse. Owen cracked his knuckles, trying to assemble the right words. But this was a mess for Josie to fix.

'Dad,' she said, coming to stand at his elbow. 'Please don't throw Grandy out. She's so rarely here, it would mean a lot to us kids, if we could share tonight with her. Besides, Grandy is going to behave—'

'I am not,' said Beryl.

'You will,' Josie said, 'if we're going to have any peace tonight.'

'Believe me, Josephine, there will be no peace for any of us until Gabriel Monash finally stands up and—'

'Get out,' said Gabe.

'Dad,' Josie implored; hand on his arm. 'Please don't do this. We've all had enough of this war between two people we love so very much.'

'Get out,' he repeated, not acknowledging Josie.

'No!' Josie cried. 'If you send Grandy away, I'll go too.'

The very moment she said it; the light of long-awaited glory seemed to come, rapturously, into Beryl's eyes. 'I mean it, Dad. This rift ends, here and now, or from this moment, it includes me too.'

There was a blessed pause, in which Josie dared to hope her father would see the sense and mercy in this or, at the very least, that he might retreat to his bedroom, leaving the kitchen to Beryl; the battle to another day. 'Please, Dad.' Her voice pleadingly small. 'If you could just forgive Grandy, if you would finally let this go . . .'

Gabe leaned down, parted her bangs, and placed a kiss on her forehead. 'It's your choice, Josephine. It will always be your choice.'

He straightened, and faced Beryl. 'Leave. I'm tired of your blackmail, and I won't have you in my house coercing my children.'

Josie noted three things: her grandmother's triumphant grin; Vivienne's distraught state; and how it was *her* shoulders Owen had an arm around now.

'Come on then, Josephine,' Beryl said, with a sharp double tap of her walking stick. 'We'll get home and have supper together, and probably hear the news from the Wests first to boot.'

'I'm not coming with you, Grandy.'

Beryl tsked. 'The first thing you need to understand about grand declarations is that they must be carried out, or you appear weak.'

Josie didn't dare look at Vivienne, who was entirely unaware she was holding a giant basket, into which Josie was about to place her every egg.

'I *am* leaving home tonight,' Josie said. 'But not with you. I'm going to stay with Viv. And hear this, both of you: I will not be coming back until you heal this division, once and for all.'

PART TWO

'The dramatic art would appear to be rather a feminine art; it contains in itself all the artifices which belong to the province of woman: the desire to please, facility to express emotions and hide defects, and the faculty of assimilation which is the real essence of woman.'
Sarah Bernhardt

CHAPTER NINETEEN

HELPMEET

Vivienne awoke in the seeping light of dawn, startled to realise she was not alone. She rolled onto her side to stare at the pretty, freckled face, slumbering in a nest of blankets alongside hers on the library floor. Bright-eyed and ever-so-pushy Josie Monash, invading *her* hideaway. What a turn of events!

Josie, it turned out, had little need or aptitude for sleep. The young women had lain wakeful most of the night, talking loudly over the tree groans, bat calls and, even more unsettling when it came, the sudden cessation of all forest noise. The last thing Vivienne remembered, before sleep had finally claimed her, was Josie's lament that the library of Sylvan Mist had turned out to be a damply unwelcoming place, smelling of unloved stories mouldering away. Vivienne couldn't have said it better herself.

She extricated herself slowly from her blankets, loath to disturb Josie. Vivienne was determined to take her morning lap, though Josie had made her *swear* last night she would not go to the lake. Vivienne felt no guilt at having kept two fingers firmly crossed behind her back. She wouldn't be out long; back even before Josie stirred.

Silently she eased past Josie's humble pile of belongings – her mystery novels, a knot of clothing, the framed photograph of her mother – and slipped from the library. There was no need to unbar the door. Vivienne had been too embarrassed at bedtime to drag all that furniture across in front of Josie.

Vivienne sped along the trail, wriggling her fingers against the chill. Like a movie set she had no charge over, the forest had changed again – this time, to macabre. A golden orb spider was shedding its exoskeleton, which hung, limp and tentacled; there were fungus-zombified insects on the climb; a forest dragon eyeing her from a lordly height.

As she walked, the big, boisterous Monash clan occupied her thoughts. There had been a secret at the heart of that familial drama and now that her initial distress had passed, Vivienne was *intrigued*.

The first half of Vivienne's swim was uneventful, despite a brisk wind turning the surface choppy. Turning back from the opposite bank, however, Vivienne could just make out Josie's figure, waiting on the amphitheatre steps. Evidently she'd been too frightened to stay alone in the lodge, perhaps planned to chastise Vivienne the moment she emerged from these oh-so-cursed waters.

Vivienne powered up into her favourite stroke – the Australian crawl. She smiled as she went, thinking of the clever things she might say in return to Josie's paranoid bossing. Mid-point on her return, Vivienne raised her head to check her progress; and took in a shocked gulp of water. That was not her petite friend waiting on the shore at all.

It was, unmistakably, a man.

Owen, come to check on the women? The shoulders weren't broad enough, and Owen would surely raise a friendly hand to identify himself. It might be her caretaker – but why would he come here? Her every instinct shrieked danger.

Vivienne trod water, trying in vain to keep her mind off the depths below. *I can stay afloat*, she reassured herself; *no matter how profound the drop.*

The figure on the shoreline showed no inclination to leave. Boldly he stood on the steps, with arms crossed and face fixed in her direction. *Waiting*, for her. Could this be her night watcher – he who jiggled doorknobs and propped ladders in the dead of night?

She could stay out here, treading water, and hope he tired of waiting. Or trust his intentions were honourable and meet him there on the shore? *No fear.* Anger pinched her gut. She knew her own damned way around and there was more than one way out of Lake Evelyn!

Vivienne launched out on a bolt of ire, and began to stroke hard for her turtle observation spot, further around the lake circumference. A quick glance, and she saw the watcher had begun to move too, following her direction.

Oh no, you don't!

Vivienne chopped harder through the water, her heart rate at a wild gallop. *She* had the advantage of knowing exactly where she planned to dock. Her arms and legs burned. Hungrily she sucked at the air, wasting no more time to scan the forest for her watcher. *Keep going*, her mind screamed to blot out the pain of exertion, *keep going!*

Vivienne was in the shallows now and fast approaching the horizontal, underwater forest. Turtles darted away as she chopped in. The underwater logs were slimy, impossible to gain purchase on. She scrambled along the sunken trees, fell between them; scraping knees and elbows. Finally, she met the steep bank, her nails digging in earth, gripping at root tentacles. Out of the water, she'd lost her weightless speed and grace. She hauled herself over the bank like a sack of stones.

There no sign of her watcher, but not a second to waste. Vivienne charged up the trail, wet hair flying in her face, tripping and sliding on snaking roots and muddy earth, stopping for nothing until she came hurtling into the lodge clearing.

She clutched at a tree, bent double, forcing air into her lungs on ragged gasps.

'*Viv?*'

Vivienne looked up, stomach heaving. Josie was sitting on the lowest step, tossing cut fruit to a bird with speckled breast and vibrant green wings. The sheer mundanity of this tableau made Vivienne's knees buckle out beneath her. Grimly she held to the tree.

'What is it?' Josie cried, instantly alert. 'What's wrong?' *Ready*, Vivienne knew, for all her suspicions about lake wraiths stalking girls to finally be confirmed.

She put a hand to her chest, trying to press in the oxygen. How could she possibly explain the watching stranger, and the terrifying sense of swimming-for-her-life, without enflaming Josie's already absurd fear of the lake? Vivienne couldn't do that to her friend.

'Nothing's . . . wrong,' she panted. 'Just rushing . . . to get back before you woke.'

'Should have run faster. You *promised* you wouldn't swim it anymore.'

Vivienne slumped on the step beside Josie, exhaustion falling over her like a net of lead. Rivulets ran down the back of her neck. 'What *are* you doing?'

'Feeding the catbird. I'm missing my calves, I had to feed *something*.'

'This sweet bird does all that feline screeching?' Vivienne considered the pawpaw Josie was throwing. 'Where did you get that?'

Josie wiped off her hands. 'A food delivery came while you were out.'

Vivienne paled. 'He didn't *see* you?'

'No, he woke me stomping around the porch, though.' Josie raised an eyebrow. 'Why should it matter?'

'He can't know you're *staying* here!'

'Don't see why not. It was only Niall, Sylvan's caretaker. I don't give a fig what *he* thinks, and you shouldn't either.'

'But my uncle hasn't organised for your board here yet, with Rudy. I'm sure it will be fine, Uncle Felix is always so terribly generous, but he didn't say anything about me being permitted any guests of my own. I should have liked to ask first. I don't want to disappoint him after everything he's done to help me get away from Mother . . .'

Josie frowned. 'I hope you don't mind me saying this . . .'

'Now I'm certain I will.'

'You're so oddly . . . biddable, with that uncle of yours.'

'He's taking care of me! Should I be intractable?'

'That depends, precisely, on how far his care takes you.'

It was Vivienne's turn to frown.

Josie pushed up to stand. 'Come on, I'll make us breakfast.'

Inside the lodge, Vivienne gaped. Josie had been moving furniture around, clearing off shelves. There were sheets and towels, even table-cloths, pegged to the louvres. '*What on earth* have you been up to?'

'For a start, I got rid of the blasted peacock feathers everywhere. We don't want the evil eye on us.'

'What have you done to the windows?'

'Oh, that,' Josie said, bustling around the kitchen. 'We're not living in an aquarium. We deserve privacy.'

'But where did you find all this?'

'Raided the linen press down in the laundry.'

'The laundry,' Vivienne repeated; rather stupidly, it felt. 'I've been hand-washing everything in the sink.'

Josie gave her a look faintly incredulous. 'There's a huge laundry downstairs, right next to that absurdly well-stocked cellar.'

Vivienne was beginning to feel quite the butt of a joke. 'Downstairs,' she echoed. 'Cellar?'

'Must have made a mighty fine air raid bunker down there during the war – just Rudy Meyer, his bathing beauties . . . and all that wine.' Josie was spooning something thick and steaming hot into two bowls. 'I've already put a wash on, but you'll need to hang it out.'

'And the clothesline?'

'Out back, on the way to Chimera Falls.' Josie handed her a bowl. 'Do you take sugar or honey on your semolina?'

Vivienne looked down at her plate. 'I don't eat . . . neither, thank you.'

Josie sat opposite Vivienne and picked up her spoon, beaming. '*Bon appetit!*'

'Indeed,' Vivienne said, raising her own spoon. 'Thank you. But you really didn't have to go to such effort for me.'

'*Effort*? I usually start by feeding calves, then make breakfast for four men, and pack their lunches too. Sometimes they'll come home for lunch. Cooking for one lodgemate is a breeze.'

Lodgemate.

Sunshine had invited herself into the lodge – permission be damned. Vivienne ought to bask, while ever it might be allowed to last. The question was: what could she possibly offer Josie in return for such a kindness as this?

'Now listen,' Josie was saying, 'you'll have to whip up your own dinner tonight. Got my theatre meeting; I'll be late home.'

'Should I save you some?'

'That'd be grand, thanks.'

Vivienne sat back in her chair and watched the tiny brunette spoon her porridge in rapidly. She barely let it touch the sides of her mouth, yet enjoyed it with a gusto Vivienne was unaccustomed to seeing in females. Vivienne found herself more flummoxed by this vignette of cohabitation than her earlier flight from danger.

'What's this?' Josie picked up a small bottle of medicine left on the table. 'Dr William's Pink Pills.' She glanced at Vivienne sharply. 'Surely not the ones for "*pale* people"?'

Vivienne's sudden hue did not throw Josie off. 'Geez, Viv! Forget this snake oil. You just need beef, sunshine and fresh country air. We'll fix you right up.'

Vivienne stepped politely over this bluntness. 'And will you be casting this evening?'

'Hope so, but I'm worried I'll be introducing my play to an empty Igloo. And while I like the sound of my own voice, I'd *prefer* to hear my script read by others.' As she spoke, Josie kept making a peculiar tapping gesture just below her clavicle. It was a superstitious motion – that much Vivienne could figure out – betraying nerves at odds with Josie's audaciousness.

'I wish I could come and watch. If not for all the—'

'People you'd have to meet. Yes, I know. Still, you *should* come.' Josie scraped her bowl clean. 'You've been a wonderful sounding board thus far; I wouldn't be nearly so proud of my play without your input.'

Vivienne hardly had a moment to accept this compliment before Josie was up and out of her chair, dumping her bowl in the sink. 'If you wouldn't mind washing that up, I have to fly.'

'Yes, you go, fly!'

Josie swung her handbag over shoulder, straightening the fuchsia dress she seemed to wear every day to town. 'Can't wait to tell you all about it! Then we should crack open one of those expensive bottles to celebrate. I might be late – but *don't worry* I'm coming back to keep you company.'

Josie charged out of the lodge, lobbing an air-blown kiss from the door. Vivienne, still sitting before an untouched bowl, listened to the old Ford grunting into action, and grumbling away. She looked back at her bowl of porridge, thoroughly bemused. *Lodgemate,* Josie had called Vivienne.

Upstairs now, the Bakelite began to ring.

Felix.

Vivienne tipped her head to the side, acknowledging its shrill insistence she leave this meal cooked by her eager, puppyish friend. *Should she obey?* Of course! Felix might be ringing to convey last instructions before he went abroad. She could ask his permission for Josie to stay right now, and have done with it.

Biddable, Josie had called her.

Vivienne shook her head. She scooped up a spoonful of semolina, savouring its smooth, warm texture on her tongue, while the call rang out.

The telephone promptly signalled its demand a second time.

Perhaps Felix was ringing to warn her that Geraldine was roaring up the range road this very minute – no gatekeeper a match against her – and bringing with her: Howie, the priest, a wedding band, and an army of men in white coats, just to be sure! The strident trilling became an ache in her back teeth: *Get up, run up, pick up!* She clenched down on it. *No,* Vivienne told herself; *I won't answer.*

A third time now the bell pealed.

And what if it was Mother herself, calling to say Vivienne was forgiven, that everyone had already forgotten? *Come home, darling, I've missed you.*

Vivienne dipped and lifted her spoon again, marvelling at how simply *good* it tasted – the porridge, and resistance both.

The telephone did not ring a fourth time.

After her porridge, Vivienne tracked the noisy agitation of a washing machine. In all her wanderings of the lodge, even in her methodical room by room erasure of Celeste Starr's image, the basement level had remained hidden behind a nondescript door at the rear, which she had, puzzlingly, never opened.

She descended the stairs to the laundry and cellar, the temperature feeling to drop with each step taken. At the foot of the staircase was a narrow vestibule, opening into two rooms. Vivienne felt herself to be on a dreamer's expedition; sluggish and surreal. For many years, she'd had a repetitive dream of this very thing: a dark, lonely house deep in a forest and, within it, a secret room she had somehow always known existed, yet long ago stopped visiting. Always, in this dream, Vivienne found herself wonderstruck at rediscovering her secret room, moreover; at having forgotten it in the first place.

Had she somehow foreknown this lodge? Vivienne braced against a prickling shiver.

She went dazedly into the laundry. The freshness of laundry flakes was unable to cover the pervasive damp, suffocatingly worse below. Vivienne didn't know much about washing machines – having relied on housekeepers to know it all – but since this machine was still loudly shaking, it was safe to assume she had time to kill.

She'd scope out the cellar, instead. One place she could show off some modest expertise, after several months cramming wine knowledge before her first, very planned encounter with Howard at the opera.

The cellar was a forbidding cavern, thickly shrouded with dust and cobwebs. Blowing warmth into her hands, Vivienne pulled on the light, then wandered around the room, drawing out bottles from the racks, wiping away grime to read labels. Most of these were European wines, very fine. Vivienne wondered if she were hoping, or dreading to find the familiar Woollcott family crest here.

Her throat closed painfully over. There it was: the coat of arms emblazoned on everything in Howard's mansion – even his pyjamas –

which had so nearly become the proprietary stamp on her life, too. Vivienne shoved the Shiraz back in, and whirled out of the cellar.

A few steps short of the stairway, she lurched to a stop. Beneath the stairs, just visible in the triangle of light, was another door. It was almost certainly a storeroom, but at this juncture there was no way Vivienne was leaving any more surprises. She stepped quickly forward to jiggle the knob, but though she twisted it so hard her engagement ring dug painfully into her flesh, her ingress was denied. She straightened, breathing hard, and ran her fingers up the door.

Near the top, she found not one but two deadbolts, much rusted.

Whatever lay beyond this door was long ago made secret – and meant to stay that way.

CHAPTER TWENTY

EYEBALLED

The whole day long, Josie had struggled to keep her focus on the excitement of the evening ahead, and off the heartbreak of the one previous.

It was impossible to keep her mind away from her calves, however, and though she knew her brothers would have stepped in to cover for her, Josie's guilt was undiminished. All day, she'd been followed around Barrington, by large, sadly blinking bovine eyes.

That gaze was trailing Josie still as she marched down Main Street with her scripts, freshly typed up by Barrington's Secretarial Class. The sun was setting over the town in long sashes of mauve and amber gold; the moon, near full, was already on the rise. Countless times today she had reached to pat her mother's locket, before remembering it lay on her father's bureau, overlooked when she had fled the farmhouse. Not hers to take in the first place. Compulsively, she traced the heart's absence.

The Igloo came into sight, a circle of familiar faces already gathered outside the front door. 'You are the director,' she told herself under her breath. 'This is *your* theatre group. You are a playwright. This is *your* play.'

Her heart quickened as she neared the assembled members, expecting any minute their faces to turn, revealing . . . what? Excitement? *Censure?*

The group, however, paid her no heed. They were peering over something, squawking and gesticulating. Josie frowned as she clipped closer. OK, so what was more interesting than the arrival of their theatre director? Josie elbowed her way into the circle to see.

On the Igloo's front step lay two balls of pale, pink flesh and twisted sinew, with a clouded blue lake floating in each centre.

Eyeballs.

As though the gentle, trusting calves' eyes, which had followed her the whole day, had been gouged out and cast at her feet. Revulsion climbed her throat.

No – these were not calves' eyes. They were bulls' eyes, like the ones they had been required to dissect in high school science.

Josie went on staring at the bulls' eyes, loath to look up and discover any variety of I-told-you-so in her actors' faces. Just how much outrage was her play going to draw this evening? Right this second, she didn't think she could stomach it.

Peggy West nudged one bull's eye aside with the toe of her red suede stiletto. 'Josie, it seems to me there's a malicious spirit against your play.'

There was that I-told-you-so.

Josie tugged up her handbag. 'Nonsense. Just some stupid young kid being a nuisance, looking for attention. But I won't have congealed eye tracked through my Igloo. Let's get this cleaned up before the crowd arrives.'

Crowd, indeed. Josie had her biggest turnout yet, with new members galore!

It should have been a validating triumph, but mostly, Josie was peeved about their progress this evening. The first read-through had taken forever, beset by interruptions, conjecture and, most maddening of all, suggested *improvements*.

'Just wait until we reach the end,' Josie repeated, ad nauseam. '*Then* we can discuss ideas.'

But they hadn't waited, and her stunning conclusion evoked more questions than it was meant to quash.

Opening up casting was proving even more contentious. Josie could have been flattered that so many members wanted to contribute to the success of her play, but she was too busy trying to head off an outright, transparent coup. Inexplicably, her motley bunch had come along convinced that community theatre should entail community consensus, and now her every casting choice was up for vigorous debate, followed by round circle vote. Josie couldn't understand this new modus operandi. Had they all met, without her, to establish a takeover?

Some of her actors had secured the parts she'd intended for them. Constable Jacobs was voted in as Barrington's formidable sergeant of the 1940s. *A promotion*, he'd exclaimed. And Peggy had been chosen for Celeste's glamourous fellow actress, Milly – blowing a perfect smoke ring in acceptance. Most fittingly, Athol had nabbed the role of gregarious and eccentric Rudy Meyer. *Thanks, Boss Lady*, Athol had effused; *Best role in a genius play!* (A bit of sycophancy was just what she needed tonight.)

Lamentably, several townsfolk had volunteered for the fictionalised versions of themselves. Josie thought she'd covered her tracks very well with name, physicality and occupation changes – but nooo, they'd rooted out their avatars anyway, right down to Elsie winning the part of 'Pearl-clutching Shopkeeper's Wife'. Yes, *even* Elsie, for all her yelling and protesting, had pushed her way into the play.

Most unpardonably of all, Niall had nominated his shopgirl Laura for Celeste Starr, citing Laura's long, dark hair, and 'natural sensuality'

as perfect for the role. Laura had been swiftly voted in by the company –
almost, if Josie wasn't imagining things, as though they'd been prepped
ahead to do so. Anyone else would have done over *Laura*, who had
beauty in spades, and the acting talent of a shovel, too.

Only left to cast was the romantic lead role of Zach. Josie had
planned that role for Ernest from the very beginning, had already
been coaching him for it. The fact he was the only one of her brothers to bother showing up tonight, only justified her nepotism. Ernest
deserved the starring role, and he sat up proudly in the front row
waiting to receive it.

So, of course that wasn't how it went.

With disbelief, Josie watched Ernest's initial triumph at being
announced for the role of Zach fall into resentment, as the wider group
loudly chanted their own choice: *Niall!* This time, they didn't even
bother to vote; it was a foregone conclusion. All too easy for Niall. Josie
had him figured out – he'd plainly been getting around town drumming up support for himself. If there *had* been a secret meeting, Niall
was the cunning one who'd convened it.

Sure enough, there was Niall standing, oh-so-humbly, to accept the
role, making motions to quell the rising cheer of approval, which only
intensified the more he hammed up false modesty. If the casement windows weren't so small, she'd defenestrate him!

Josie raised two fingers to each corner of her mouth, rolled back her
tongue and blew her loudest farm whistle. *Pffwhiiit!*

The rabble quieted, looking at her aghast. Whistling in a theatre was
bad luck, but frankly she didn't care if a batten fell on all their heads
tonight.

She crossed her arms. 'As your *director*, I say Ernest and Laura would
be more believable as love-struck duo.'

'We'd have better chemistry,' Ernest confirmed.

Curiously, Laura coloured at this. Laura had feelings for *Ernest*? But she was letting Niall suck on her neck behind shop doors! Josie made a mental note to revisit this incongruity.

'Laura and I *already* work well together,' Niall countered.

'Nope. I've already made up my mind. It's Ernest.'

The room exploded in dissent.

Niall, motioning for calm, was all snide humility: 'Everyone, listen; I know how upset you are to have your unanimous choice overruled, but Josie wants to get the final say.'

Of course she should have the final say; it was *her* play! Her mutinous cast, however, groaned in disagreement. A groan that dragged on and on.

Well, it was no freckle off her nose! They could try and swap as many roles as they wanted, suggest all the plot points they wished, but they couldn't sub out the controversial, curse-breaking venue, could they?

Josie smiled, confidence on the rise again. 'I'll have a final look at the cast list and decide who plays Zach before next week's meeting . . . which will be a site visit to the Obsidian. So, I'll see you all over at Lake Evelyn, Friday.'

Around the Igloo, nervous faces turned, one to another.

How's that coup working out for you, dear company?

At the meeting's conclusion, Josie wandered through the group congratulating her own picks, establishing expectations for the others, and ignoring Niall entirely. She waved the stragglers off at the door while Clarence and Ernest stacked chairs into the corner.

Rita gripped Josie's hand as she was leaving. 'I *need* to talk to you.'

Josie allowed herself to be towed from the door, into a piquant grove of citrus trees. 'I'm sorry you didn't find a role you liked, Rita . . .'

'It's not about your play – this is much more important!'

213

That sounded like something Josie could take offence to, but she hadn't the chance. Coming out of the door were Ernest and Clarence; all the Igloo's lights, bar the ghost light, switched off.

Clarence trotted off, while Ernest loitered with pointed sullenness beside the two women. Josie patted Rita's arm. 'I'll come and see you tomorrow. I have an unsuccessful auditionee to console.'

Josie and Ernest stood in silence until Rita had disappeared up Main Street. In the lime tree above, a striped rufous owl swivelled its large yellow eyes upon the siblings.

'Sorry, Ernest,' Josie started. 'I tried to get it for you.'

'Niall has been busy canvassing votes.'

'The whole thing tonight was a power play. I hope you're not too disappointed.'

Ernest pshawed. 'You'll write better characters, there'll be other plays. But, Jose – you can't let *Niall* have Zach.'

'What option do I have? If I kick up a stink, I'll need a convincing alternative. And it can't be my own brother.'

'No, it can't be me.' He slid his lucky cigar out of pocket, tapping it against his other hand. 'But it must be anyone else over Niall.'

'You've got to admit; he *can* act. And Zach was a good decade older than Celeste, so the age gap isn't an issue, either.'

Ernest tapped the cigar harder, looking away into the darkness. 'He's out to humiliate Laura.'

'*Humiliate* her? What do you mean?'

'It's not my business to tell, and it's not in Laura's nature to tell. And that prick *knows* it!' Ernest shoved the cigar back in his pocket, lips a hard line.

Josie held this guarded revelation up against the insights she had gathered of her own accord: a hand clutched over blooming love bite; Laura's stubborn reticence despite her courage to join a rowdy theatre company; her evasive gaze, never landing more than a moment or two on anyone. So, Laura wasn't a wallflower, but a wildflower under shade. *Wanting to be seen.*

'OK, I'm with you now,' Josie said, wondering how Ernest had come to be the trusted recipient of this information from a woman so unforthcoming as Laura. What *was* it with the Monash men and their damsels in distress? And why must they always foist said damsels upon Josie?

With a sudden, violent flapping, the rufous owl swooped from its branch upon a squeaking fawn-footed melomy below. The Monash siblings shared a shocked expletive, followed by a chuckle.

'You coming back home tonight?' Ernest asked.

Oh, it would be so easy to say yes. She still had the family car. They could go home together, right now – to where her father was, her necklace lay, her happiness resided. She could say *yes*, and put this whole ultimatum to rest. No one would think less of her for either running away from home, or her meek return to it.

'Come on,' Ernest cajoled. 'I'll make us a cuppa, then I'll let you beat me at Stratego.'

Josie could see it already: sweet tea and victory both.

'Besides,' he went on, 'you've got to come with us all tomorrow morning when Reg goes over to meet his daughter.'

'She had a girl, then.' What kind of prospective aunt forgot all about her first niece or nephew?

'Only a couple of hours ago. Daph's in a bad way, though. The little blighter didn't want to come out, no matter what they tried, so Daph was rushed off to the operating theatre—' Ernest made a hoicking sound, miming a slicing motion up from belly to neck.

Josie grimaced. 'Jeepers.' *Does sound like the daughter of a limpet, though.*

'Reg is pretty cut up himself. Owen's been trying to get him sober all arvo.'

Well, at least that explained where all her other brothers were. Fair enough . . . this time.

'Any names yet?'

Ernest didn't seem to want to answer this. Josie glared him down. Even in the dark garden, Josie could see Ernest bracing for an explosion. 'Oh, don't tell me! She took *my* name, didn't she? I told her Maureen was my future daughter's name! I *told* her!'

'It's just a name. You can still use it. But like Daph said; who knows if you'll ever have children. It would be a shame for Daph not to honour Mum, now that she's got the chance.'

'*Bulldust!* Daphne just saw another thing of mine she wanted.' She'd never forgive Daphne, or Reg for allowing it or, for that matter, anyone else who referred to the kid by name.

'*Anyway*,' Ernest said, 'you've got a brand-new niece, so you've got to come home. Daph is going to need help. She says it's a long recovery, and she can't take care of all us boys, as well as a baby.'

'Oh, *I see* . . . Josie should run home and take care of the whole *lot* of you!'

'We miss you, that's all.'

'I bet you miss me. Well, I don't care if you all think I'm selfish and heartless. I have too much pride to play the live-in nanny for Daphne West. She can rope in her own mother to help, or better yet – go live with Grandy. God knows that would fulfil all Grandy's prayers: a new Maureen Monash finally returned to her!'

Ernest took a long moment to digest this. 'You're really not coming home?'

'Really not.' Josie reached for her absent necklace, settling instead on her shoulder, to grip her handbag strap.

'I had a bad feeling about tonight,' Ernest said glumly. 'And it wasn't Zach I was worried about losing.'

'You're not losing me. But I want to focus full time on my theatre. And Grandy and Dad need to reconcile, once and for all. Most of all, I have Vivienne to take care of.'

'You'll never come home.'

Her eyes stung. 'I might not.'

Ernest reached into his pocket again. She'd expected him to take out his cigar, but he produced a white envelope instead.

'This came for you today. It's from Miles Henry. I didn't know you two were writing to each other.'

'We've exchanged a letter or two.'

Ernest held the letter out. 'I don't suppose this bodes well for your moving back home, either.'

'Guess it depends on what the letter says,' Josie answered; flippant tone belying the pounding in her ears. 'Come on, you should take the Ford back to the farm tonight. You can drop me off at my place on the way home.'

The letter was exchanged for car keys. Now that the envelope was in her hands – solid, smooth, and firmly sealed – Josie could scarcely breathe.

'Hey, Jose . . .' Ernest said quietly. 'You know you can't live in that haunted lodge forever, right?'

'Maybe not, but neither does it have to stay haunted forever, either.'

The lodge was all darkness as Josie waved Ernest off from the front porch. He reversed out of the narrow road, watching his rearview mirror; evidently unable to look at her. Josie's smile ached, but she did not drop it until the headlights arced out of sight.

In Ernest's wake, a profound blackness engulfed the clearing. A discordant cacophony of insect and amphibian noise – clicking, blaring, buzzing, ticking, trilling – swarmed to fill the silence left. There was a clawed scurrying down a tree trunk nearby. *Sugar glider*, Josie told herself sternly, but the back of her neck burned until she was safe behind the front door.

She hadn't realised how late the meeting had run – nearly midnight, according to the grandfather clock scolding her from the staircase. Vivienne had obviously given up waiting and gone to bed. In the kitchen, Josie found a rather fancy-looking French omelette, with an artistic leaf garnish and a sweet note entreating her to enjoy it. Josie wolfed it down, then dashed upstairs, clutching her letter.

In the last seconds before Josie reached the library, she screeched to a stop, struck suddenly paranoid. What if Vivienne *wasn't* in there? Worse; hadn't existed at all. Maybe Josie was all alone in this godforsaken lodge. And the spectre of Celeste Starr had dragged herself out of the lake once more, and waited for Josie now inside the library: opaque eyes unblinking, vines trailing from her etiolated neck, water pooling round chalk white feet . . .

For the first time since checking in to Vivienne's lodge, a frisson of terror ran through Josie's belly.

She took the final, creaking steps into the library, winded by dread.

Within, a Tiffany lamp glowed on the roll top desk; embers smouldered in the fireplace. There was a softly breathing shape curled up in a nest of blankets.

Thank God.

She crouched down beside Vivienne, waiting for her eyelids to stir. Set beside Vivienne was a large, brown paper-wrapped parcel. Josie tipped her head, considering it. Had Vivienne been trying to wait up for her?

Josie took her own blanket, and her mother's picture, and went to curl up in the oversized wingback chair by the fire's warmth, fast fading. She propped the frame up beside her, then turned to a study of Miles's letter.

The tree kangaroo was on the back of the envelope again, this time rendered in cartoonish fashion. The little fellow was chartering a boat – a Barrington belly tank model – across a wide expanse of water. Only it wasn't a *fellow*, there was a fringe and long lashes, however improbable, on the mammal.

The caricature was clear: Josie, traversing Lake Evelyn.

Josie laughed gustily. A hand flew to cover her mouth as Vivienne stirred within her pool of blankets. Josie peeled the flap open and drew out Miles's epistle . . .

Dear Milkmaid,

For days, I rattled my brain round my head, trying to guess how you were planning to eclipse me, from so far away . . .

Then Mum called, to convey the best news she'd heard in years: Josephine Monash, out to rewrite The Curse of Lake Evelyn!

So, you're going to outshine my most celebrated feat: escaping Barrington for the bright city nights and national stage. No one will take any notice of what I'm doing down here, while you're up there, breaking curses and reopening lakes.

Should have known that undaunted brunette riding to school with me on the back of Monty's milk truck, the smart-arsed Monash girl who routinely hid stink bugs down my collar, or got me with a burny bean . . .

Josie saw again, the beetle sliding down Miles's shirt, felt the shape of the burny bean, heated by friction on concrete, ready to brand her unsuspecting victim. Had she really been so *mean* to the boy of her dreams? She'd always aped the antics of her brothers, but with a bonhomie that could never be ascribed to malice.

. . . should have known that girl was capable of overshadowing me with one flourish of her writing hand!
  And so, it seems, she is.

Josie smiled, as though seeing Miles's roguish grin before her now, with that crinkling downturn of eyes.

If I may be so presumptuous to offer you a word of advice?
  Josie, it's your right, and you are right, to tell this story.
  Don't believe anyone who says you're out of your depth. You're a skilful director and a talented playwright, we all saw that in senior year. More than that; you lived through the worst of their propaganda about Lake Evelyn. We both did – the first generation of kids banned from the lake, no . . . purposely terrified of it.
  Do you recall, as the milk bus would go by the lake turn off, all those horror stories flying thick between us? What about that ditty someone made up about the Curse, and how I teased you with it?

Josie murmured quickly: 'Dark within the crater lake, lurks the Nightingale. Up she reaches from the deep, to grab your ponytail.'

Miles always gave a cheeky tweak on the end of her hair, as he delivered this rhyme. Remembering it anew, the same delighted indignation returned to her in a heated rush – Miles deserved every burny bean he ever got!

To be fair, though, you had told me I'd be the first boy taken by the Nightingale, because she wouldn't know the difference.

Oh, Josie had forgotten that comeback. She snorted; a hand drifting to tug, just once, on the end of her own ponytail.

I think you and I would both agree: we've surpassed that lousy curse.
I know you'll tell the next generation a much better story.
  Set that lovely lake and her ghoulish Nightingale free!

In defiance of childhood superstitions,

Miles

Josie folded her letter back into its envelope, and held it beneath her nose, inhaling greedily for some skerrick, even the smallest trace, of his old scent.

Sighing then smiling, she eased herself out of the wingback and crept over to Vivienne. Josie's mind having journeyed to childhood days, the flaxen-haired woman lying at her feet seemed more a stranger than ever.

She sank into her own nest of blankets, studying Vivienne. Her fair lids moved rapidly as a dream-reel played, a soft smile spreading across her face.

Josie was unable to suppress the chronic insomniac's stitch of envy. Everyone in the world it seemed slept easier than she.

And of what, could a missing heiress, marooned in a haunted eyrie, dream so happily?

CHAPTER TWENTY-ONE
BRIGHT YOUNG THINGS

Vivienne was coursing back to Sylvan along the forest trail, dripping wet, and marvelling at the morning rays shafting through the mist, like pylons keeping the canopy aloft. Her mind was too much on the excitement ahead – several times she nearly lost her head to hanging vines.

Vivienne had a gift for Josie. She'd ducked into Barrington yesterday, and found the perfect present for her writerly friend. The thought of Josie unwrapping it quickened her footsteps to a reckless pace. Narrowly avoiding yet another rainforest tripwire, Vivienne shivered with anticipation supreme.

Josie, however, wasn't anywhere to be found at the lodge.

After searching high and low, Vivienne slumped on the front step. She'd gone. Had Josie tired so quickly of Vivienne and her strange lodge?

A tuneful whistle, coming down the drive through the foggy soup, brought Vivienne to her feet. She gripped at the railing. Josie emerged, beaming brighter than any headlights might have done. Answering joy rose in Vivienne's breast.

'You came back!'

'You didn't think I'd leave you? I decided; if you're not giving up your morning swim for *me*, I'm not giving up my calves for *you*. I went and fed my babes.'

Josie plonked a pail of milk at Vivienne's feet. 'Nicked that from the dairy, too. Nothing beats warm milk. Get that into you for brekkie.'

Vivienne smiled. 'And how was your family today?' *Have you made up? Did you see* Owen?

'Managed to skirt the lot of them,' bragged Josie. 'I left a note on the kitchen table to set out my terms for rapprochement. And I claimed this from dad's bedside!' She pulled an ornate gold locket out of the front of her blouse, waving it around. 'It was Mum's. I've been waiting too many years for Dad to finally give it to me. Thought I'd better take it, before Daphne gets *her* bloody hands on it.'

Sentimental worth of the necklace aside, Vivienne could appreciate the value of the piece too. How did a simple farm wife come by such stunning jewellery?

As was her way, Josie was already steaming on to the next topic. 'I had to get my writing paper first thing, too.'

Vivienne followed Josie into the kitchen. 'Something important to write about?'

Josie was clanging out the saucepan to make porridge. 'I have to make a reply to the boy I spent most of my youth in love with.'

'I assume these feelings have survived into your old age?'

Vivienne watched the tide of colour rise over Josie's freckles amusedly.

'My attachment has been more of the nostalgic kind. We grew up together as children, but by senior year of high school we were only ever theatre club rivals. He hardly noticed I existed offstage, or the back of the milk truck.'

The latter part of this explanation made no sense to Vivienne. 'And yet you're ready to write him before nine o'clock in the morning, as a matter of urgency?'

Josie brought Vivienne up to speed on Miles's letters, while she stirred the pot of porridge with increasingly rapid turns.

'Is it possible to overwhip porridge?' interrupted Vivienne.

Josie laughed, removing thoroughly harassed semolina from the stovetop. 'So *anyway*, I intend to write to Miles first thing, and tell him he hasn't heard the half of my audacity. You'll *never* guess what I've been up to, I'll say. You're pretty proud of yourself for living in Sydney, but *I'm* living in Rudy Meyer's haunted lodge with a runaway society bride!' She broke off, seeing Vivienne's alarm. 'Geez, don't worry, Miles won't have a clue who you are.'

'I wouldn't be so sure,' Vivienne said slowly, 'Howie loves the theatre, and he's always in some nightclub or other after a show. If everyone really has been talking about me in Sydney . . .'

Josie snorted. 'Yes, I can just see your jilted fiancé marching up to Miles: "Happen to hear about a beautiful, blonde woman being anywhere in Australia?"'

How should Vivienne dispute that without revealing the true extent of her paranoia? Any connection to Sydney, no matter how vague, was a connection all the same. High society was a small society.

The women sat down together, bowls steaming.

'How was last night's meeting?'

Josie choked down a mouthful, fanning at the heat long after it had passed her gullet. 'It was a shocker! I mean, they loved my play – and well they should – I didn't know just how good it *is* until I heard it read aloud. Hell of a story. I had goosebumps all over. In fact, at one point when Athol was—'

Vivienne's mouth hitched up to one side. It was hard not to be taken in by Josie's rambling storytelling, and ironic, too, that she wrote in a style so concise.

Josie, evidently beginning to learn Vivienne's wry expression, paused to re-route. '*Anyhoo*, when we got to casting – it turned into a coup!'

Vivienne's mouth lifted even more askew. 'Against you?'

'They took it into their heads to elect their own parts, didn't they?'

'I'd have thought that's rather important, for an actor to have a say in their part?'

Josie tsked. 'They're welcome to say whatever they like, but I get the final word. But they went and chose Niall for my Zach. *Niall!*'

'Niall, *my* caretaker?'

'That's the one. He'd stacked the meeting with votes ahead of time. And then Niall nominated Laura for my Celeste.'

'Saint Laura the Silent?'

Josie tossed back her head. 'Yes! You remember everything I tell you, all my best lines – you're such good egg!'

Vivienne, crimsoning, turned to the task of filling her spoon.

'I don't want Laura *or* Niall,' Josie stewed. 'I've half a mind to rewrite the whole play, cutting out both their parts.'

'You might need a new plot, then.'

'If I have to rewrite a play in one week, the plot is irrelevant.'

Rewrite! Vivienne's gift was recalled to her with a great bolt of joy. 'Good gracious, I almost forgot!' She sprang to her feet, heedless of spoon's proper placement. 'I have a present for you!'

Vivienne stared in disbelief at Josie, with her head laid upon the table, sobbing convulsively. 'I didn't mean to make you cry, I really thought you'd be pleased. Indeed, it seemed to scream your name the moment

I saw it in the shop window. I *had* to get it for you, to repay you for all your kindness, since I've come here.'

Josie heaved out another wail.

Vivienne sagged in horror. Where had she gone wrong? The coral pink typewriter in Barrington's Old Curiosity Shop had seemed *made* for Josie Monash. Patiently, Vivienne waited for Josie to come to the end of her outpouring.

Josie raised a blotchy countenance to smile. 'I'm sorry. This is the most special gift anyone has ever given me. I didn't expect it, that's all, it was a bit overwhelming . . . sitting in Sylvan Mist, of all places, with a letter from *Miles Henry*, and unwrapping the present of my dreams.'

'You *do* like it!'

'Would you believe I've saved for this very typewriter, countless times. Already have a spot on my writing desk at home, cleared and waiting for her . . .' At this thought, Josie descended into snorting tears, her head pressed against the improbable pillow of the typewriter, arms around it.

Vivienne's hands rose, as if to pat Josie's head, then fell back to her side. Josie might be free with her expressions of affection, but Vivienne's barriers were lifelong; inbuilt.

'I'm glad I resisted the shop owner's bullying, then. Prim woman, with a helmet full of hairspray. She all but refused to let me buy the thing. Upped the price, tried to talk me into some hideous cheap vase instead. I practically had to prise her talons from your typewriter.'

Josie snivelled dramatically through laughter. 'Poor Rita! Probably why she wanted to talk to me last night, must have felt terrible for . . .' Josie paused. 'Wait, you went shopping in town yesterday, and *talked* to people!'

'I had a grand time. Your stores are . . . quaint. And since I haven't been permitted to spend a thing without Mother's approval, it was such a thrilling freedom.'

Josie fairly glowed. 'I'm glad you braved good old Barrington. I just *know* my town will love you and take you under its wing, while you're here.'

Josie's confidence in community spirit must be one of the few recommendations for backwater living, but Vivienne would believe in this mythical kinship when she experienced it for herself.

'Oh!' Once more Vivienne plonked down her spoon. 'I need to show you something *else* I found . . .'

'Well, that's just *rude.*' Josie hammered at the locked basement door with her torch. 'Fancy locking us out like this.'

'Does make me wonder what he's hiding in there.'

The idea seemed to entrance Josie. 'If we were in one of my delicious gothic romances, this door would be the entrance to a secret passage, leading somewhere dark and forbidding.' She mimed a shiver.

'Where?'

'I'm joking, Viv.'

'I hope so,' Vivienne said, having never enjoyed the kind of books Josie subsisted on. 'But where do secret passages normally go?'

'The most obvious place is our creepy old library, where we would find a revolving door. I'll show you.'

To the library they went, where Vivienne's bed sheets sat neatly folded, and Josie's lay in a tangled heap, with script kept under pillow.

'Usually, you do this . . .' Josie pulled a heavy-spined tome halfway out of its shelf. 'Then there's a grinding, mechanical sound, and the scraping back of old wood as the door swings round to reveal, let me think . . . an old skeleton, curled in foetal shape, her hand still outstretched, from clawing at the locked door!'

'*She?*'

'Celeste Starr, entombed in Sylvan Mist.'

'She who drowned?'

'Or maybe she inadvertently wandered into our secret passageway, got trapped, and has waited these many years to reveal her secret!'

'She wrote a suicide note before accidentally locking herself in?'

'If you're going to play devil's advocate, do it properly. *Obviously*, the letter was faked, after he turned the key.'

'*He* now?'

Josie tugged her heart locket back and forward along its chain. 'Let's say Rudy Meyer.'

'*The* Rudy Meyer murdered her?' Vivienne was falling entirely out of this conspiratorial spell.

Josie wasn't letting her go that easily. 'You said it: he was infatuated with her. The photos everywhere? His way of confessing.'

Vivienne was dubious. 'Rudy wants to be found out?'

'He can't bear what he's done to our town. The guilt eats him up!'

Vivienne pinched the bridge of her nose, sighing. 'Sometimes with you, Josie, I truly can't tell when you're being serious, or having a lark.'

'More serious it is, the bigger the lark.'

Yes, Vivienne thought Josie's flair for drama and play – her obsession with it – had much to do with warding off life's sorrows.

Vivienne crossed her arms, wanting to be frank. 'You're play-hunting for silly secret passages because you're really searching for . . . *what*?'

Josie's face fell. 'I want to find the poetry book from which Celeste drew her suicide note. I feel it would still be here, and I need that last quote. Thought we might have a poke around today for it.'

Vivienne motioned Josie on. 'All right. Turn your hidden levers.'

Within the hour, they had it.

Standing in a sea of antiquated books, Josie held aloft a fine, hardcover volume of *The Poetry of Oscar Wilde*. Her eyes were big. 'Imagine . . . Celeste might have used this *very* book.'

Vivienne plumped down on the wingback chair. 'I'm glad you found your needle in the haystack. I can't believe you can even make a library search entertaining. When you spin a story, Josie, it's hard not to get swept up in it.'

'Comes from having many brothers. All we did between farm chores was muck about. We missed school altogether during the war years, and it only gave us more time for play. But that's still learning, isn't it?'

Vivienne swallowed a lump. She'd never been allowed to miss a day of her fine education, and what had all that learning and finishing been for in the end? A gilded life, as a rich man's chattel.

'Anyway,' Josie ran on, 'I hope Reg's little girl will have lots of playmates to grow up with, too.'

'Your sister-in-law had a baby girl?'

'Aren't I the worst aunt?' Josie laughed. 'Haven't even told you the big news. I guess babies don't really interest me that much.'

'They interest me,' Vivienne said, feeling Josie's interest snap upon her. 'I've always longed rather desperately for children. Probably to make up for the siblings I missed out on, or so that I might mother a child the way I wish I'd been.' She said this matter-of-factly, but a wince betrayed her.

Josie tipped her head. 'So, in addition to Howard's staggering wealth and influence, and all your mother's dragooning, you also resisted your own desperate longing for children when you cast out thus alone?'

Vivienne boggled at Josie's reframing of her own actions.

Josie's eyes flashed understanding. She reached to pat Vivienne's hand. 'I'll keep showing you how strong you are, until you credit *yourself* for it.'

Tears rushed forth with a blinding heat. Vivienne rose, eyes a-swim, and went to stand at the roll top desk, putting her back to Josie. Her hand hovered above the telephone, wishing she had the courage to lift that handset from its cradle, put it to her ear, and *speak . . .*

You may never forgive me, Mother, but I'm beginning to forgive myself.

'Anyway,' Josie said, with a wicked grin. 'It's good that you're unencumbered by children. Because for the rest of today, we're going to raise spirits . . . *on the house*!'

Vivienne was in her bathers, seated in a bolt of sunshine within the pool of Chimera Falls. Her back was against the mossed rockery, she nursed a crystal goblet of wine against her knees, and she was comfortably, warmly, delightfully drunk.

Through the open windows of the lodge, drifted the warble of a gramophone. Spider webs of lustrous gold were strung from leaf to leaf, shimmering in the gentle, stirring breeze. From the murmurous overstorey came piping bird call, susurrations, a single branch squealing like an opening door.

Imagine *this* being called a winter! *Preposterous.*

Josie had left the water for their picnic blanket, and her typewriter, where she alternated between swooning over her pink beauty, and orating lines of her letter to Miles aloud – all while imbibing. Josie's inebriated writing was far less coherent than her usual, but more comical too. Vivienne's belly ached from laughter.

Their second bottle of wine stood neck deep in the pool, naturally refrigerated. They had left the bottles of Woollcott wine untouched – despite Josie's interest in tasting the 'finest wine in the country'. Unbelievably, in both cellar and kitchen, they had been unable to locate a corkscrew, and in their impatience had resorted to using a knife. Tiny pieces of cork floated in their bottle, a shocking desecration to Vivienne, yet she took an odd pleasure in each sliver plucked from her glass.

There was a glimmering ball of sunlight floating in her wine. Vivienne turned the goblet in her hand, splintering rainbows across the gold-sparkled pool. She tipped her head back to that ray of light. It was impossible to get enough sun on her skin in this forest deep.

'Tell me what you're up to in this epic epistle,' she said.

Josie cackled. 'I can't remember. Was I not reminding him of the cassowary dung we mistook for thylacine droppings, and how we carried it to school on a shovel for our science teacher to examine?'

'Actually, last I heard, you were espousing the benefits of hosiery for male actors.'

Josie rolled in a new page. 'Ah, that's right! But I was listing the benefits for Miles personally, not actors generally.'

'However, I believe you were diverted by your diagram.'

Josie reached for her sketch, smiling to herself. '*Indeed*. Miles is about to discover he's not the only one who can draw ironic cartoons.'

'It seems to me your cast is about to discover a rather *shocking* costume vision for the new play.'

'Tosh! I wouldn't mandate tights unless Miles Henry was in my play.'

Vivienne splayed her toes underwater, studying Josie. 'Why *isn't* he then?'

Josie slapped her thigh on a raucous laugh. 'Isn't that the million-dollar question!'

Vivienne swallowed a mouthful, not taking her eyes off Josie. 'Is it really so unanswerable a question? It seems, at least to me, you are sending silly pictures to a high school crush, instead of asking a professional and highly esteemed actor to fill a main role shortly to be vacated by an unsuitable man.'

Josie was no longer laughing. 'Can you imagine *me* begging Miles to come home and do a charity run for a community theatre?' Vivienne could hear Josie's valiant attempt to keep the question rhetorical.

'Can't imagine you *begging*, no.'

Taking umbrage, Josie turned back to her typewriter; striking out a few keys stroppily.

Vivienne savoured another swill of wine, waiting for the eruption she sensed was coming...

'Listen here! I'm not going to write to Miles and ask him to save my play for me! It doesn't need saving! I can make a success of myself and my debut production all on my own, thank you very much! Just because Niall won't do for Zach, doesn't mean I have no other choice but to call in our town's sole successful stage export to replace him! And the... the... hide of *you* thinking I can't find anyone else instead of Niall, like all we have are *creeps* in this town!'

'Yes, the hide of me.' Vivienne's cheek had puckered full into a dimple.

Josie's hands stroked the typewriter keys in concentric circles. 'It's especially rude of you to assume I'd automatically cast Miles even *if* he turned up in town for an audition.'

'It's especially rude that I assumed you would give away the audition date, time and location in your soon-to-be-posted letter.'

Josie wound in a sheet of paper. Her fingers came to settle on the keys, primed and ready. 'I suppose you're going to assume I'll enclose a copy of the script for him to learn, too.'

'I'd assume nothing less.'

Josie nodded, fingers beginning to clatter. 'Bestir yourself there, and top up my glass. I need to rewrite this letter.'

Vivienne grinned, drawing up the bottle from the sandy bottom. 'To the top and overspilling, my lady.'

The light had contracted to a gold, glinting orb sinking through the forest; shadows burgeoned heavily in the understorey. Playful birdsong had long since ceased. There was a chill in the air.

Vivienne stepped inelegantly from the pool into a towel stretched out by Josie. She seemed to slip sideways out of Josie's grasp, righting herself with a snorting laugh. Vivienne knew herself to be very drunk, and revelled in the disgracefulness of it. There had been no Mother here, to circumspectly cover Vivienne's glass with a hand when the waiter leaned over to pour.

'I do deserve to have fun,' she told Josie. 'I'm a person *too* – a person!'

Josie, no steadier on her feet, joined Vivienne in this refrain. 'You *are* a person, Viv. You shall have all the fun.'

'Another bottle?' Vivienne said hopefully.

'Already got it,' Josie cried, waving a full bottle aloft in triumph.

'You're a geeeenius.'

'No, I'm *egreeegious!*'

Vivienne leaned in close, gripping Josie's arm, whispering overloud. 'Do you want to do something really naughty with me?'

Josie seemed to think this a great caper. 'Lead me astray!'

'To the Obsidian,' Vivienne declared, wobbling down to retrieve the goblets lolling on the earth. 'We shall bless your new theatre!'

Josie's bleary eyes went wide. 'Oh yes, we can have a re-dresshearsal!'

'A *what*?'

'No, I meant: a fulldress-reversal, no that's not it! I don't know what I mean. Stupid words.'

'You are *scuppered*, Josie Monash.'

'Am not. I am undrinkable. I mean, unsinkable.'

Arms interlocked, Vivienne and Josie tottered off down the trail towards Lake Evelyn. The path did not seem pleased to carry the women, bucking them off like a bull. Here, they toppled into the underbrush; there, they clung to the lichened poles until the ground had stopped tossing beneath their bare feet. At each turn and tumble, laughter was effervescent between them.

They arrived at the amphitheatre as the last rays were scything low across the Tablelands. The lake had returned to the magma whence it came, reflecting a sky ablaze. Had Vivienne really swum this same body of water in thick fog this morning?

'From fog to fire,' she sighed. 'What a grand lady.'

Josie looked up, bemused, from the goblets brimful. 'Who?'

'You,' Vivienne said, endeared.

After clinking glasses for the umpteenth time that day, they claimed the best view of the lake from the centre row and sat, shoulders touching through their towels, to watch the show of glowing colour. Vivienne inclined her ear to an unheard opera. '*Götterdämmerung*,' she murmured. 'The Twilight of the Gods.'

'Goddesses,' Josie corrected.

Vivienne hummed an operatic crescendo. Josie, at first tittering, soon fell quiet. Her head dropped to Vivienne's shoulder. 'Gosh you have a lovely voice, Viv.'

'I spent long enough in voice training to be tolerable.'

'You *must* know you're a beautiful singer. I wonder if you're the first woman to sing here since Celeste.'

Vivienne sang on, hearing such improvement in herself. Perhaps having greenery all around truly was good for a voice.

Her soprano dwindled with the colour. Josie refilled their glasses as charcoal began to shade in the grooves and ripples of the sky, and the lake turned to a void of unfathomable blackness. A full and lustrous moon was rising behind the dark wall of rainforest. The bats were on the move.

Vivienne shivered in the rising chill, pulling her towel tighter. She guzzled her drink, then jumped to her feet on a sudden impulse. 'Let's test out your stage walk.'

Josie laughed with a vehement headshake. Vivienne held out her hand. 'Come on, hurry that down, come dance with me.'

Josie tossed back her wine, and took Vivienne's hand. The women took large leaps down each step, grass cold beneath their feet, to the floating walkway, suspended over the barrels.

Vivienne stepped boldly out onto the planks, but Josie pulled her hand free. 'I'm not going on that in the dark.'

Vivienne reached again for her hand. 'The theatre director is afraid of her own set!'

'I'm not afraid. But I wouldn't trust *my* brother's engineering, until it's been finished properly.'

'Fraidy-cat.'

Josie's hands went to her hips, refusing Vivienne's insistent reaching. 'Please hop off, Viv. Wait until we know for sure it's finished. We're in no state to be on the lake.'

Vivienne stepped further out, laughing. 'Look, it's holding up fine! You can't be squeamish about this, Josie.'

She twirled on bare feet; face tipped back to the light of the moon. A glamourous spectacle, she imagined herself to be. Josie flung a fretful plea from the bank. 'Please, Viv. You're blitzed, and so am I. Please come back.'

'Pretend I'm Celeste.'

'Viv, *please* – this isn't fun! I'm not play-acting anymore! Come down!'

'There has been no music in me, for so long. Let me dance . . .'

Indeed, Vivienne *was* dancing on the lake. The moon had risen full behind her, lighting a runway across the water, setting her platinum locks aglow, silhouetting her moving figure, so that she appeared to spin, magical and diminutive, like a music box ballerina upon the lake itself.

Vivienne was dancing.

And then she wasn't.

She was falling.

CHAPTER TWENTY-TWO

FALLEN STAR

One instant Vivienne was ghoulish spectre dancing over the volcanic crater; the next, a lightning-struck bough, splintered off.

Sobriety seemed to crash over Josie, even as the last guzzled alcohol hit her system. She staggered to the lake's edge, screaming. 'Viv! *Viv!* Come back!'

There was no sound, no movement on the surface of the lake; Vivienne had been subsumed, whole. Josie ran along the shoreline, hearing herself screech, not understanding a word of it. Panic drowning her on dry land.

The torch!

Josie stumbled up the steps away from the deathly quiet lake, reaching blindly for the torch, head reeling, stomach swelling up to empty itself. She tumbled back down the amphitheatre steps, arriving in the same instant as a great, gasping cry, jettisoning up from the black depths.

Josie fumbled with the torchlight, found her beam, threw it out over the water towards the new commotion.

Vivienne! *Alive.* On the surface, laughing and kicking.

'Come in,' Vivienne sang, floating on her back, hair shining like quartz in the moonlight. 'It's warmer in than out. Come swim with me.'

Josie stepped onto the walkway, relief running freely down her face. 'I thought you were drowning!'

'I was sinking like a stone,' Vivienne sighed, eyes caressing the moon. 'And for a moment, I just wanted to see how deep I could go.'

Josie began to shake. 'How could you do that to me?' She knelt down on the bridge, wrapped her arms around her legs, letting herself cry. Vivienne's laugh died away. She lapped over to the walkway. 'I am sorry, Josie, I didn't want to frighten you.'

Vivienne pulled herself up onto her forearms on the floating edge, directly in front of Josie, so that their foreheads were touching.

'I thought the Curse had taken you,' Josie wailed. 'Right in front of me swallowed you whole!' They stayed, head-to-head like this, for some time. Josie, sobbing; Vivienne, crooning apologies.

Josie's tears stopped abruptly. From beyond Vivienne's hanging figure, out upon the lake, came another sound. A great splash, there and quickly gone again, but now wide ripples rolled out towards them.

There was *something*, out there, disturbing the lake's placidity, and it could no longer be Vivienne. Dread pulsed through Josie's veins.

Do not think of her, do not do not do not . . .

Josie swung the torch up over Vivienne's head, tracing the rings back to their epicentre; praying wildly for a duck, an eel, a turtle – *anything* that might explain the disturbance; anything but Celeste Starr, resurfacing from the deep . . .

'*Josie*,' Vivienne lilted anew. 'You can trust me, it's perfectly safe in . . .'

There was another flurry, out beyond the pair. This time, Vivienne clocked the commotion, too. She looked back over her shoulder, squinting into the darkness.

Josie's hand clawed into Vivienne's arm. 'It's her! *She's here.*' Panic was near-strangulating. 'Get out, before she takes you!'

Vivienne resisted for one last moment as Josie wrenched at her arm, squalling.

A third splash decided it. Vivienne pulled herself onto the walkway in a single, smooth movement, to crouch beside Josie. 'It's just a bird,' Vivienne whispered. 'There's no one out there.'

To this, Josie did not respond. The torch shook in her hand, beam strobing the dark lake.

'Ducks,' Vivienne tried again, but her skin pressed, cold and quivering, against Josie's shoulder.

There! What it is *that?!*

Ripples ran out from a long, moving shape, glimpsed in a shutter-fast blink. Josie's light beam went, shaking and leaping, after it. She opened her mouth to shout, choking on her own words. '*Croooo—*' Her whole body had begun to shudder violently.

And there was Vivienne, swooping in, drawing her away from the water's edge, muttering soft, cajoling words. 'You're OK, Josie. *See?* There's nothing there. You're just very frightened. We're both OK – *look!*'

But Josie's eyes were hard kernels, squeezed shut, unable to block out the afterimage burn of an ancient horror . . .

Crocodile.

Josie had dragged Vivienne along with her on this morning's calf feeding. There was no way that she was leaving her stubborn friend unsupervised. She'd go swim again, Josie knew she would.

A lurid, salmon light ribbon stretched wide on the horizon as they stomped across frost-bitten paddocks to the Monash calves' shed. They conversed little, occasionally meeting eyes to exchange lamentations on aged wine's debilitating after-effects. All the while, Josie replayed a silent, jolting horror film reel, a memory becoming more surreal with each rerun . . .

Crocodile.

Though the women had quarrelled about the crocodile – or, from Vivienne's vehement position, *the lack thereof* – until late into the night, they did not speak of it again in the coral glow and clouded breath of this new morning.

A stonkered Vivienne dozed quietly in the corner of the shed throughout Josie's chores. Even slumbering, perhaps especially slumbering, Vivienne seemed determined to refute the prehistoric monster Josie had seen.

But *had* she seen it? There had been more bottles rolling on the grass than Josie actually remembered pilfering from that cellar. Perhaps she had been blind drunk in the truest sense? No. She had *definitely* seen it. Vivienne was just too stubborn to admit she ought not to have been swimming in that lake in the first place, and never should again.

After the milking, Vivienne insisted they pay Owen a visit next. Sly move, so far as Josie was concerned, for she knew exactly what her friend was planning – to charm Owen into siding with her on the crocodile dispute. But Josie *had* seen the crocodile, and Vivienne must be made to accept it.

Owen might be just the person to convince her.

Her brother's corrugated iron hut sat on top of the hillcrest, under the shade of an Atherton oak. Owen was bent over a timber cutting bench, large back to the women. There was a second home under construction, right beside his hut, with a foundation already laid. Taken aback, for a second Josie actually forgot the score she and Vivienne had come here to settle.

'You're building a proper house here,' she cried. 'Why didn't you tell me!'

Owen straightened from his hardwood beam, turning to the women with saw in hand.

Josie's hands flew to her hips. 'Are you *ever* moving home now?'

Owen grinned. 'Are *you*?'

Pointless answering that, Owen had eyes only for Vivienne. Josie fiddled with her fringe, letting them have their fill of each other. There was a strange hurt in being disregarded by her most beloved brother – a warm pleasure, too.

But enough was enough. 'I'm thir-sty,' she sang pointedly.

Owen motioned the women to sit at his crackling campfire kitchen, ringed by tree-stump seating. While they sat before the boiling billy, feeling sorry for themselves, Owen washed at the water tank, then prepared tea.

Josie took Owen's proffered tin mug so fast, tea sloshed over her fingers. *Blinkin heck* her head hurt!

'You won't *believe* what happened last night,' she began emphatically, tossing her friend right into it: 'Viv was swimming Lake Evelyn.'

Owen looked between the women. 'Of course I believe that. I've seen her swim it. She has a beautiful stroke.'

Vivienne hid flaming cheeks behind her mug, leaving Josie to her story.

'But have you seen her swim it after a solid day's wine tasting in Rudy Meyer's cellar?'

Brief concern creased Owen's brow, but he smiled. 'You've found a friend even more daring than you, Josie.'

'She's a terrible influence. Tried to make *me* swim it with her – and I was even drunker.'

This picture appeared to entertain her brother. '*Anyway*,' she said, 'I refrained from tempting the Curse, and lucky I did . . . because I saw a crocodile!'

Owen chuckled, draining his mug. 'Out of the jaws of death!'

Josie stomped her foot. 'A genuine crocodile. I *swear* it!'

Owen's eyes were even more lit with amusement. 'And was it a Tasmanian crocodile?'

She was firing up to deliver sibling invective, when Vivienne interposed. 'Josie really does believe she saw a crocodile.' Every syllable of this statement slowly and carefully enunciated.

Owen stopped smiling and put his mug down on the sawdust floor of his camp kitchen to rub his beard.

There were pointed looks flying to and fro over Josie's head. She'd give herself whiplash trying to follow them.

'So,' Owen allowed, at last, 'you saw a crocodile, Josie.'

'I get it,' Josie snapped. 'You're only going to take my word for it, because *Viv* warned you to indulge me. Well, there *is* a crocodile in that lake. I saw it, and Clarence Reece will back me up on it!'

Owen and Vivienne exchanged another volley of looks. Josie rolled her eyes heavenward.

Owen smiled. 'I guess someone should probably go check around the lake then for any signs of crocs lurking about. But *who*?'

Josie opened her mouth to rebuke the jest concealed in his tone. Once again Vivienne intervened, blinking as sweetly as Josie had ever seen her. 'If *you* wouldn't mind, Owen,' she said, 'I would certainly feel better to know there wasn't anything hanging about.'

'And if I find one?'

'Shoot it,' said Josie, deadpan.

'*Shoot* it?'

Josie crossed her arms. 'I can't have a crocodile turning up in Lake Evelyn right when I'm about to break the Curse! It will ruin everything!'

Owen looked, Josie had to give it to him, sympathetic. He watched her for a long moment. Josie stared so hard back her eyes watered.

241

Owen cracked his knuckles. 'All right. I'll keep an eye on the lake, then. For my own peace of mind . . .'

Josie shrugged. 'If it makes *you* feel better. Only, don't go making a big deal of it, people will think *we're* scared of the lake.'

'No, I wouldn't want to give anyone that idea.' The jest, this time, unconcealed.

Josie shot up, the day's plans unfurling rapidly ahead of her. 'Come on, Viv. We've got loads to do – letter to post, lead actor to fire.'

Vivienne turned to Owen, lips quirking sideways. 'Today, Josie's issuing a de-Niall.'

Owen laughed heartily, while Josie looked at him reproachfully. How was it that *Owen* managed to bring out Vivienne's sarcastic streak most easily?

Vivienne and Owen were sharing another gaze between themselves; a steady look that wholly excluded her. Too bad for them, Josie wasn't dawdling for any more *looking*. 'Let's go, no time to waste,' she said, hauling Vivienne up.

Owen stood. 'What more can I do to help?'

Her answer came with the twanging sting of a mousetrap. 'You can tell *Vivienne* she mustn't sneak out to swim the lake anymore – now that I've seen the crocodile.'

Owen tipped his head towards Vivienne. 'Will you stop?'

Vivienne smiled serenely. 'No.'

Josie knew full well that Owen's hand was back at his beard only to hide a traitorous grin. 'Sorry, Jose, I tried. Anything else I can do?'

'My floating stage was too wobbly when we tested it,' Josie snapped. 'Fixing *that* should take precedence over this unnecessary house.'

Owen gave a mock salute. 'Be careful today.'

'Of what?' Josie demanded.

But it was at Vivienne he glanced now. 'Smiling at a crocodile.'

Josie and Viv were flying into Barrington. The roadster accelerated up and over the many undulations, as though it might take off into the low-slung clouds, or was just now landing from orbit.

Josie's yodelling exhilaration was almost swallowed by the motor roar, and the wind which whipped long streams of dark hair across the wide laughing gash of her mouth. In the driver's seat, Vivienne's sunglasses were outsized only by her smile. Her hands gripped the wheel – lest she throw her arms into the air, roller-coaster fashion.

Every head on Main Street turned to watch the roadster come winging around the large central island, laughter billowing through the open windows.

A woman could get used to making this kind of entrance, Josie thought, as she swung out of the passenger seat.

The plan was this: Vivienne would dash the letter down to the post office, while Josie went to sack Niall. Shouldn't take more than ten minutes, Josie reckoned, even accounting for hubris. (Niall's.) Errands done; then the women would convene at the teahouse.

Only Laura, however, was behind the lolly counter at the Corner Store when Josie clipped through the front door. Laura offered to assist, without once looking Josie in the face. Why did shy people think avoidance of eye contact would save them? *I can still see you*, Josie wanted to say; *you're not invisible!*

'Is Niall in?'

'Mr Jeffries,' Laura called out, 'Josephine Monash here to see you.'

Niall hollered something indistinguishable from the back room. Laura's eyes flickered closed, for the length of a careful swallow. 'He'll be out in a moment,' she told Josie, returning to the slow folding of paper napkins.

Josie studied her sullen leading actress, boggling at how she could possibly have been railroaded into casting *Laura* for Celeste.

Or had she?

Josie stepped close to the counter; voice low. 'Laura, are you . . . OK?'

Another swallow, eyes aflutter. 'Yes, thank you.'

Josie glanced at the back room. Still no Niall in sight. 'I heard you've got the apartment upstairs now; it was certainly a stroke of luck Niall had that to rent. But it's a big step, isn't it, leaving home? I recently moved out too.'

Laura looked up in surprise. Blue eyes fixing briefly on Josie's, before dropping away.

'And my flatmate and I were actually just saying how we'd love to have you over for dinner. I've been meaning to catch up with you, about the play. Would you be free sometime this week?'

Laura nodded, quick but emphatic; moving smoothly clear as Niall appeared in the door frame.

Niall came forward with a cocksure smile. 'Checking in on your leads? Believe me, we've been getting in *lots* of rehearsal.'

Oily bastard. I'm about to show you . . .

Josie's smile spread from ear to ear, beatific with the blow she was about to impart. 'Well, temper your disappointment, Niall. The officially sanctioned cast list is up, and you're not on it.'

Behind Niall, Laura's eyes raised slowly to Josie's face, and stayed there.

Niall laughed. 'I'd like to see you try. I was unanimously voted in.'

'Vote stacking has no role in community theatre. As director, I have the final say, and I say you're not Zach.'

Niall stared at Josie, only the micro-squints of his pale blue eyes giving his rage away. 'You can't do that.'

'It's already done. I've got someone else for Zach.'

'Who!'

In her mind's eye, Josie was chasing Vivienne up Main Street. *Quickly, Viv – mail it!*

'That's a . . . surprise.'

'No one will dare accept it once they know you've robbed me of it.'

Josie shrugged. 'Think what you like – but you will not fill Zach's shoes on my stage.'

Shove that letter in there, Viv!

Niall cracked out a hard laugh. 'Just try and take it off me and *see* how far you get.'

'You're not to attend any more of my meetings, until you've come to grips with my decision.'

'I'll be there Friday.'

'If you turn up, you'll be made to leave.'

Niall came towards Josie on three, tall strides; so fast that she had no time for anything else than a half-gasp. In the very last moment before it seemed he would smash right into her, Niall halted. He leaned over her, moist breath blasting over her face heavy with mint and onion.

'Listen to me, *girly*. You don't run this town, or that theatre company. We'd get better reviews if we got rid of you all together. Might call yourself a little director, but every one of us in that group knows you're not worthy of the title. You're nothin' but a play-acting child, in over her head!'

Don't believe anyone who says you're out of your depth, Miles had written: *It's your right. You are right.*

'This is *exactly* why you don't get Zach, and why you never deserved it in the first place.' Her voice shook. 'You're no woman's romantic lead. You're a bully, and a creep.'

Josie turned to Niall's shop girl; gone deathly pale, all agape. Her eyes were glued on Josie's face.

'I'll send Ernest tonight to pick you up, Laura. We've much to discuss for the play.'

Laura's nod was small, but unmissable.

Josie thundered down Central Ave to the teahouse, head pounding in time with her footfalls.

'Have you seen a blonde woman come in?' Josie demanded of Rhonda at the counter. She couldn't seem to shake off her choking rage. 'Pretty, thin, wearing a scarf.'

Rhonda shrugged with infuriating indifference as Josie went slamming out the front door. Viv must been delayed at the post office.

Only she wasn't there, either. The postmistress said the fair stranger had long been and gone. Josie was nearly tripping over her feet as she charged back down Main Street, panic bubbling.

They hadn't missed each other between teahouse and post office – she checked that twice – Viv wasn't in the library bunker, or waiting at the car. Josie stood in the middle of the main road, one hand gripping at her heart locket, the other shielding her eyes from the noonday sunshine, sweeping a frantic glare.

Where are *you, Viv?*

'Josie!' An urgent command, hissed from the sidewalk. Rita Caracella, motioning Josie over with her spectacles. 'I need to show you something.'

'Not now, Rita, I'm busy. I've lost—'

'Your blonde friend. I know. Come with me, quickly.'

Josie followed Rita inside the Old Curiosity Shop, scanning the jumbled aisles for Viv, while Rita locked the door behind them. Rita had not yet filled the gap in the front window left by the missing typewriter – *Josie's* pink beauty – and the empty space gave her heart a strange, poignant thrill. For so long she'd coveted it, and now it was *hers*. All because of Vivienne George.

'Where *is* she?'

Rita drew near, more serious than Josie had ever seen her. 'I wanted to talk to you on Friday night.'

'Yes, about the beautiful outsider who had rolled into town and snapped up my promised typewriter.'

Rita tsked. 'Money is money, and it's all the same to me. *Better luck next time, Josephine*, that's what I told myself as I laid those notes in my till.' Josie knew that was a lie. She beamed, wanting to throw her arms around Rita.

Rita pretended not to notice. 'No, I want to talk to you about the woman herself.'

Josie's stiffened. 'She wishes to remain private, and she's got her reasons.'

Rita waved this away. 'I don't care why she's hiding out – one glance at her thumping great engagement ring told me enough. But I do care what she can do for Barrington while she is here.'

Josie frowned.

'Come.' Rita led Josie towards her back office. Rita had evidently been in the costumery section of her shop, every chest lay open. Clothing, wigs and trimmings were draped everywhere; the smell of mothballs nauseatingly thick. As a theatre director, it was hard to tear her eyes away from all that costume gold, but the closed curtain partition between this section and Rita's back room was stirring, two bare feet poking out beneath.

'Viv,' Josie called. 'You don't have to play whatever game this is.'

Vivienne's voice came, in cut-glass perfection, from behind the curtain. 'Please, let me make the grand reveal. Do go on, Rita.'

Grand reveal?

Rita gripped Josie's arm. 'When your friend first walked through my door that day, I got full body tingles. She's the very picture! Then she walked by my shop again this morning, and I had to act! I called her in, tried to explain everything, but she *already* knew every intimate detail of your play. Like a good sport, she's been letting me dress her up. I had just the outfit, and exactly the wig . . .'

Josie turned.

Vivienne's slender hand fumbled through the fabric, opening a gap.

'*Look*,' Rita declared. 'Here she is, come to life again.'

Through the curtains, arrayed in a marabou-trimmed, charmeuse dressing gown, with stardust crown and dark locks streaming, stepped Celeste Starr.

CHAPTER TWENTY-THREE
CROWN OF STARS

For the third time in so many days, Vivienne had made Josie cry.

She rushed forward, downy feathers stirring at wrists and ankles, to clutch Josie's hands. 'I meant no harm! It was only a little dressing up, but when I put it on, just like last night, I felt I really *was* Celeste.'

Josie howled harder. Vivienne looked for help from Rita, but the older woman kept back, watching the girls without emotion.

'I'll take it off,' Vivienne said, head beginning to ache with regret.

She turned away, reaching for the heavy crown.

Josie's hand shot out. 'No! Stay in costume.'

She waited while Josie trumpeted her nose loudly in a handkerchief. 'Now we've got that shock out of the road, let me look at you properly.'

Vivienne stood mannequin still in her confection of silver froth, while Josie walked slowly around her. 'The question is not whether you would make my dream Celeste, but *if* you are willing to take on this. Viv, would you be my Celeste?'

Vivienne had hoped this question was coming. Realised, too, she'd been yearning to hear it for weeks, without admitting it as anything more than wistful, wishful thinking.

In another life, I might have been an actress, and this could have been the role I was born to play.

Now that it had been asked of her, however, Vivienne could think only of the sheer outrageousness of it: Vivienne George, on an amateur theatre stage, playing a suicidal pin-up girl!

Then again; perhaps taking the role of Celeste was choosing a new life.

Vivienne stared at Josie, and the constellation of freckles become so dear. She reached to touch her glittering crown. 'I want that, very much.'

Josie whooped up and down. 'Oh Viv, *yes*! With your voice, and beauty, and vulnerability, you're going to knock their socks off!'

Vivienne flamed; terror rising up in the same swell as exhilaration. *I can choose another life!*

Josie turned to Rita. 'How can I ever thank you enough? First, you give me all your research on Celeste Starr, and now this amazing costume – it looks so real!'

Rita lifted a proud chin. 'It *is* real. It's Celeste's dressing gown, her swimmers, her crown.'

Vivienne George, wearing a dead woman's garments. *It is outrageous.*

Josie reached to stroke Vivienne's gown. 'How is that possible?'

'I paid top dollar for these things when Rudy sold off Celeste's possessions. Memorabilia like *this* is as rare as hen's teeth.'

Vivienne frowned. *Rudy* sold off Celeste's things? The same man who'd kept his lodge as a mausoleum to her memory? 'I'm surprised Rudy would have been willing to part with such things.'

'Well, he did,' Rita said stiffly. 'And I purchased them. So that's his loss, twice over.'

Josie had started into her beguiling nose-scrunch. 'Would you be willing to lend these to Vivienne, for our play?'

'Only,' Rita said, 'for Celeste's sake.'

Josie wasn't done asking for favours. She motioned towards the apparel across the room. 'What about the rest of this? Will you be my costumier? I can't think of anyone more suited for the role.'

'There'll be no disputing my decisions.'

'You'll have complete control of costumes and props.'

Rita gave a short nod. 'All right, I'll do it. But only for . . .'

'Celeste,' Josie and Vivienne finished, in laughing unison.

As the roadster was flying over the hills, back to Sylvan, Vivienne realised neither she nor Rita had confessed to Josie about the *other* person who had been in the Old Curiosity Shop, before Josie finally tracked them down. The person who'd convinced, nay ordered Vivienne to try on the costume in the first place. Who had declared her approval with a most vociferous tap of her walking stick, only then to disappear, straight backed, up Main Street once Rita went to find Josie.

Vivienne glanced at Josie in the passenger seat. With her face set to the open window, sun upon her closed lids, and hair whipping across her laughing mouth; Josie was the very picture of joyful oblivion.

What Josie didn't know, couldn't hurt ruin her gladness. There was no harm in keeping this between Vivienne and Rita, and Beryl too.

There were *many* people in Barrington invested in Celeste's story, Vivienne saw that now. And it was Vivienne's job, as conduit, to bring that tale to life.

Josie and Vivienne were sitting on the lodge stoop in the birdsong of sultry dusk, a bottle of Chianti already open between them, awaiting Laura's chauffeured arrival. Inside, Vivienne had spicy pumpkin soup simmering on the stove.

A patina of red volcanic soil lay over the parked roadster, and the sight of it gave Vivienne utmost pleasure. She wondered if there was a chance Owen might crash their dinner. It seemed unlikely – but she might well hope.

'How do you think Laura will take it?' Vivienne asked. Now that the elation of winning Celeste's role was ebbing, guilt was beginning to seep in.

Josie was playing distractedly with her gold locket. 'Everyone likes soup, she'll be fine.'

Vivienne nudged Josie. 'You know, in all the excitement at Rita's, we forgot all about the crocodile.'

'I *didn't* see a crocodile,' Josie replied calmly.

'That's great news,' Vivienne said, not missing a beat, 'because once Laura is sufficiently drunk tonight, I plan to take her for a midnight lap of the lake. We'll let the *crocodile* decide who tastes most like Celeste.'

'Celeste wasn't taken by a croc. If you're going to take ownership of the role, you have to believe the story.'

Something in this grated at Vivienne. 'You say "story" not . . . facts.'

Josie tousled her fringe, took a sip of Chianti before answering. 'As rich as my literary diet of Nancy Drew and Agatha Christie *was* growing up, I'm not a sleuth, I'm a playwright.'

'Dramatic licence, then?'

'Balance of probabilities.'

Vivienne put her glass to her lips, but did not drink. 'So, what happened to the other girls?'

'Celeste's fellow actresses? After Celeste died, Rudy closed the theatre. They all left, presumably moved on to new lives.'

'No – what happened to the other *local* girls?'

'The Curse took them.' Josie gave Vivienne an odd look. 'We've well and truly covered this ground.'

'Actually, you've told me next to nothing about the missing girls.'

'Because they aren't missing! Every one of them turned up drowned, in some fashion or other.'

Vivienne had turned fully to face Josie. 'You don't like to talk about it.'

'I'm traumatised by growing up with young women drowning all around me!'

'How many have there been?'

'Seven, including Celeste.'

'Seven drownings in only, what, fourteen years?'

'Correct.' *End of discussion*, said Josie's tone.

Vivienne was dogged. 'All suicides?'

'Not *all*.' Her look at Vivienne was almost pleading. 'You can't really want to hear the gruesome details.'

'I quite insist.'

Josie exhaled long and hard. 'The first girl was Valerie in 1946, only two years after Celeste. She was a *Floater*. That was what we called the ones who went missing for a while, only to . . . pop up some time later in the lake; the Floaters. After her, there was Barbara in 1948, but she left a note first. Martha drowned in 1949, she got trapped in the reeds, couldn't find her way out, drowned in full earshot of her friends. Glenda, in 1950, was another Floater. After that, Grandy campaigned to close the lake. In 1951, she got her way, and we were all banned from the place. For a while, it seemed like that had done the trick. But then there was another Floater: Loreen, in 1954. And the last girl, Denise in 1955, was out here swimming drunk with friends, in defiance of all advice and bloody common sense . . .'

Vivienne ignored this pointed dig. 'You know all their names and dates, off by heart. It must have been a living nightmare for a young woman growing up here . . .'

To this, Josie made no reply.

'But none of the girls was torn apart by a crocodile?'

Josie gave her a dry look. 'You are *not* swimming it until that croc is removed.'

'The crocodile you don't want anyone to know is there just yet?'

'Until my play is finished, that's all.' Josie narrowed her eyes at Vivienne. 'You must think I'm terribly selfish for deciding that.'

'No ... I think you're tremendously invested in this play, and redeeming Celeste's story.' Vivienne's voice and eyes were very gentle. 'It is awfully convenient though, Josie.'

'What is?'

'A *crocodile* showing up, to scare people away from swimming in Lake Evelyn, right when you're reopening the Obsidian.'

'You think I made it up to stop any more girls from swimming the lake.'

'Well, I drove the Range Road not too long ago, and I didn't pass any crocs coming up the mountain.'

Josie had taken a mental detour. Vivienne awaited her return patiently.

'*Imagine,*' Josie said, marshalling her most thrilling tone, 'the lake harbours a secret that someone wants to protect at all costs. Like a ... an underwater cave. Perhaps *that's* where Celeste was entombed. And whoever put her there, must *keep* Barrington out of the lake!'

'Might Celeste have been murdered?'

'Investigators didn't think so. And there was her suicide note, too.'

Vivienne thought of her watcher by the lake, her prowler outside the lodge. 'And what are the chances someone murdered some of your local girls?'

Josie gave a short laugh. 'What are the *chances*? This isn't a casino game. Again, the police investigated, and none of the deaths were found to be suspicious. They drowned, and that's it.'

'But *you* find at least some of them suspicious. If I were to hazard a guess; the so-called Floaters.'

Josie's face revealed internal conflict.

'You *do*!' Vivienne cried. 'You think someone else was involved in those drownings.'

Still Josie was not contradicting her, a full mental skirmish underway. Vivienne's thoughts dived rapidly to make sense of this, though she suspected Josie's thoughts ran faster than hers possibly could.

'I daresay,' Vivienne began lightly, 'that an audacious play, undermining a superstitious "curse", perhaps even making a mockery of it, certainly capitalising on it for community gain—'

Down the driveway came the rumble of the Monash Ford.

'—*that* kind of play,' Vivienne concluded, 'might be one way to rile up and possibly even *draw out* a local murderer . . .'

Headlights winked into the clearing. The Ford rattled to a stop. In the coupé utility, Ernest and Laura were turned to one another, talking animatedly, oblivious to the waiting women.

Josie was standing, ready to welcome their dinner guest. Though her eyes were set on the newcomer, her ear was tipped to Vivienne.

Vivienne pulled herself up alongside Josie. 'One might even regard *such* a play—' She was talking out the corner of her mouth, eyes on the handsome Monash brother opening the car door for the beautiful, raven-haired woman.

'—as a perfectly contrived and skilfully set *trap*.'

Josie went down the stairs, smiling.

Ernest, stomping up the front steps at the appointed hour to ferry their guest home again, came – he was later heard to remark – upon a witches' enclave, cauldron and all . . .

The three young women were gathered in a cackling circle, heads close together, round an ironstone tureen. Blanket wrapped, after their late-evening swim in Chimera Falls, where they had imbibed unrestrainedly of the lodge's finest wine, they were now enjoying the spoils of Vivienne's toiling over the hot stove: fragrantly mulled wine.

'I'm staying here,' Laura told Ernest. And though both Josie and Vivienne shared a look at this flouting of polite invitation, much less the invasion of their happy privacy, both women would later agree in hushed tones, across Laura's sleeping head, that the idea was one of their best. They'd always meant Laura to stay over, had intended her to move in, too.

It was with enthusiastic heckling they sent Earnest home again, passenger seat empty. Earnest reversed out, shaking his head.

So, there were three runaways sheltering now in Sylvan Mist.

Vivienne, the first to emerge from the lodge next morning, went to Lake Evelyn on unsteady feet. Her thoughts ran sluggishly over one another, as she replayed the astonishing evening previous.

The women had discovered themselves a most compatible trio over the course of their evening. St Laura the Silent turned out to possess a tongue easily loosened by copious goblets of wine; followed by the belly-clutching, conspiratorial laughter of women unconstrained. Laughter that had, in time, given way to Laura's sobbing in the well of Josie and Vivienne's shared embrace.

Out then had come a wretched tale.

In desperate want of a job and home after the death of her useless father, Laura had accepted Niall's oh-too-generous offer of the vacant flat above his shop – and a front counter job within it. For Laura, it had seemed like an answered prayer, at first. But she had been fending off Niall's advances ever since. He pestered her from dawn till dusk, and frequently the hours between. His favourite tactic: trapping her in corners from which she could not escape his lecherous molestations.

He took particular, perverse pleasure in being *caught* in these compromising situations.

'But the worst of it,' Laura said, 'even more dehumanising somehow than the groping and fondling and . . . other things, was when he tried to make me pose for filthy photographs.'

There was a sickened silence.

'It was like he saw me as piece of meat, to be laid out for him.' Her venom was no less deadly for being quiet. 'As though I existed solely for *his* consumption.'

'We'll never, ever let him near you again!' Josie cried, one fist slamming into its fellow.

Laura seemed to believe this, drawing nearer. Josie's bullish self-confidence was a brazier to warm cold spirit by.

'You'll live here with *us*!' Josie had declared, oblivious to Vivienne's silent dismay.

Vivienne had wanted to object that Laura was merely moving from Niall's flatlet, in the relative public safety of a main street, to a deserted lodge in the forest, instead. The very lodge Niall tended.

Would Niall come after Laura here? Did he pose a threat to *all* of them? And if word got back to Rudy, through his disgruntled caretaker, about the growing group of refugees in Sylvan Mist, might it put Vivienne's lodge stay at risk? She didn't want to be thrown out, not now that she was so invested. If only she had a way to talk to Uncle Felix, he would surely smooth everything over for them.

Vivienne groaned; these ruminations were driving a headache up the base of her skull. Mustn't get stuck in spiralling cogitations! She had to trust Josie's wisdom, according to which, Niall was thoroughly manageable.

Vivienne should have been grateful to have gained another lodgemate – safety in numbers, as Felix would say – but she knew the sanctuary they'd found together was naught but an illusion. Temporary accommodation, organised and paid for by another. And when Felix returned from abroad, to take Vivienne home, where would her friends go then? So busy and entertained had Vivienne been, she had managed to largely ignore the dread coiled at the pit of her being, hissing warningly: at some point, she *would* have to go home, she *did* have to face the music.

Reaching the amphitheatre, Vivienne found Josie's so-called 'ghost light' – a regular old hurricane lantern, so far as Vivienne could tell – extinguished. In the howling enjoyment of their evening with Laura, the women had forgotten to come down to the lake and refuel it.

Vivienne stepped into the shallows, cold encircling her ankles. Before her, the lake spread out in shimmering turquoise, wreathed with mist. Serene, and unremarkable. Nevertheless, as she stood here, feet numbing painfully, the memory of Josie's terror from two nights earlier, and that ghastly choking sound she'd made, sprang up most inconveniently . . .

Crooo–

It was complete nonsense, of course it was. Vivienne *knew* it was bunkum. There had been no crocodile that night, only a terrified young woman, traumatised to the point of self-delusion. Oh, Josie had been adamant though! Vivienne recalled their arguing with a cringe. Neither woman had grown up with a sister to bicker against, but they'd certainly made up for it together.

Vivienne would concede this: if it were easier for Josie to cry 'Crocodile!' than admit her own monstrous fears, then who was *Vivienne* to deprive her of the crutch? Let Josie have her figment, for now. That gutsy woman was out to break the superstition that had held her in its thrall for more than fourteen years.

Still; the blood did hammer at Vivienne's temples as she waded in. The chilly rings climbed higher on her calves, past her knees, to her thighs; becoming a single icy circle around her waist. She took tiny, gasping breaths, belly sucked in, wanting to submerge all at once and be done with the shock of cold.

Vivienne had reached the edge of the drop-off shelf. She swayed a little, dizzied by the profound darkness only a single footfall beyond. Was it at least *possible* a crocodile might lurk deep within this mountain lake? Josie swore there were sunken boats and army jeeps laid to rest upon the bottom of the crater – and you wouldn't have a clue from up here. Wouldn't be so hard, really, for a crocodile to hide here; to trail Vivienne underwater, learning her habits, readying to wrestle her unto the depths . . .

'What *tripe*,' Vivienne muttered.

She might wear Celeste Starr's crown, but she would never *believe* in her curse.

With a gasp of exhilaration, she dived out, into the deep.

CHAPTER TWENTY-FOUR

USURPER

Alone down at the Obsidian this Friday afternoon, with only an hour before the Barrington Theatre Company was due to arrive for rehearsal, Josie was faced with a bloodbath.

Her vandal had struck again. The amphitheatre steps splashed haphazardly with blood, as though someone had walked around tossing a bucket of offcuts, here, there – everywhere. Might as well have been a slaughterhouse floor, so shocking was that crimson stain. Josie had sent Vivienne and Laura tearing back to the lodge for a pail and scrubbing brush, and was now pacing her theatre, fulminating against stupid pranksters, and Curse-upholders alike. She should have anticipated her amphitheatre would be targeted next!

Josie looked again to the forest path, anxious to sight Laura and Vivienne speeding across the clearing before the rest of her company arrived on Athol's Chook Chaser, specially chartered. Josie wasn't scared by blood – cow's presumably, there seemed to be a theme going – but she refused to let *her* troupe be intimidated, made skittish, or otherwise induced to question Josie's leadership and endeavour.

Here was an emboldening thought: her play's saboteur was obviously convinced that, without interference, Josie might ultimately succeed in, and be vindicated by, her Curse-breaking objective.

And by golly she *would* . . .

Lake Evelyn glowed golden within its dusky forest circlet as Vivienne stood quietly alongside Josie on the stage of the Obsidian for the introductory spiel.

Josie was lying through her smiling teeth, and loving every creative word of it. Vivienne, she had explained, was a professional songstress from 'Down South', with years of acclaimed experience, kindly donating her time and talent to regional community theatre. To her own ears, it sounded plausible. To her eyes, this was plainly a theatre group in dissent. Both their lead actors lost in a week? They would not abide this! But what could they really *do* about it? Laura was here herself to affirm her replacement. Reluctantly, Josie came to the end of her spiel. Hands were already shooting into their air.

Elsie didn't wait to be called upon. 'What we all really want to discuss,' she yelled, 'is the other, *far* more shocking situation!'

Josie's eyes flew to the steps scrubbed clean in the nick of time, and still glistening with soap bubbles – nothing shocking to see there. She looked hastily to the lake – nope, crocodile conveniently hidden. Lastly, her eyes landed on Laura, standing beside the stage with guarded eyes, but a quiet new confidence. No one would be permitted to say a single word here about Laura's abrupt resignation from the Corner Shop, or the reasons for it.

'Shocking situation?' asked Josie. *Butter wouldn't melt.*

'Niall, chucked out of the company! He's our best actor!'

'Oh, *that*. Niall and I had personal differences.'

'Those being?'

'I personally wanted a different actor. I have recast the role.'

'Who *is it* then?' cried Elsie. 'We discussed this at length on the bus ride here, and there *is* no one else for Zach!'

'The consensus,' Peggy West interjected, with a sly breath of smoke, 'was that you've rigged it all for Ernest.'

Athol's head was bobbing mightily along. 'We don't mean to undermine you, boss. But you gave us that lecture the other day about not letting personal issues impede performance, and now you've gone and had a tiff with our lead star . . .'

She felt Vivienne slide closer. Oh, the kindness of her ever-present solidarity!

'I don't blame you all for having these questions,' Josie said. 'But you're just going to have to trust, there *is* a method to my madness. I have the *perfect* Zach for us. It isn't one of my brothers, or indeed anyone else in Barrington . . .'

How could she be *saying* these things? Was it really possible, even in her most far-fetched fantasies – of which she had many – that Miles Henry would want to make the long, costly, *improbable* journey home, just to audition for Josie Monash's small-town play?

Why shouldn't he?

Josie squared her shoulders. 'But you will have to wait until next week to meet him.'

'Next *week*!' Peggy's scarlet lips, parting in shock, made a perfect 'O'. 'How do we rehearse now without a Zach, for God's sake?'

Laura stepped forward. Three women stood together now at the front of the amphitheatre, facing the disgruntled company.

'*I'm* going to read Zach's part today,' Laura said. 'And if any of you have any further queries, you can wait to see me after today's rehearsal. As Josie's newly appointed stage manager, I'll be ensuring things run smoothly from here on.'

Josie swivelled to stare at Laura. *Stage manager? You crafty minx!*

Josie turned back to her theatre company, feeling taller than she had in years. 'You heard the woman. Got a problem, see my stage manager. Leave *me* to make the magic . . .'

Growing up, Josie had always dreamed of forming her own clandestine club, thwarted only in the persistent lack of interest shown by her brothers, instead having to tag along on their games and adventures.

But at last she had her own secret gang, and who was tagging along now?

It was the day of Zach's recasting, and Josie was in the Igloo, seated at her director's table; waiting. Laura sat beside her, a picture of self-composure, Vivienne paced the stage before them and, seated in Josie's private audience, was Owen, Ernest *and* Reg.

The Igloo's door was wide open to the mid-afternoon sunshine, but it was cold in the auditorium. Then again, perhaps Josie's periodic shivers were born not of the mild temperature, but thrumming nerves. Josie rubbed her goose-pimpled arms until the friction burned. Her toes tapped a mad dance.

This whole scheme was lunacy, and though she knew none of her friends or brothers would laugh at her expense, Josie dreaded the mortification ahead.

He wouldn't come.

He *couldn't* have come home to Barrington. The news would've been all over town, and then it wouldn't have taken much brainpower for her company to put it together: Miles Henry home, Josie's mystery actor due to be announced . . . *ta-da!*

No, he definitely hadn't come.

He must have opened her letter, laughed uproariously at her nerve, and binned it. He was probably sitting in his Sydney flat this very moment, looking to the clock, smirking about the pitiable farm girl expecting him up north.

But Miles *should* have come home to play Zach! He owed it to Barrington. How could he stand her up like this? He'd had enough time to telephone and refuse the request, hadn't he?

On the other hand, she'd been explicitly clear about the need for secrecy. Surely the only reason she hadn't caught wind of his return, was because he was following her instructions, to the letter. He hadn't laughed when he received her offer, he'd punched a fist in the air.

'Oh Josie, do *stop* that,' Vivienne called from the stage.

Josie broke dazedly from her conflict. 'What?'

'I can see your thoughts warring it out from all the way up here.'

Josie straightened her fringe – hand covering her face. Laura pushed a notebook and pen closer. 'Here, why don't you look over my notes.'

Josie took the notepad, dropping the pen straight down. Her hand went to worry at her locket. 'But what if he doesn't come?'

'He'll come,' Vivienne said.

'He wouldn't *dare* miss it,' appended Owen.

This settled, her secret society moved smoothly on to their plans for the rest of the afternoon. As though this audition were just a blip in their schedule, and not the most nerve-racking moment of Josie's whole year.

'After the milking,' Ernest said, 'we could all catch the flick down at the Regent?'

'What's showing?'

'*Silk Stockings*,' Owen said. 'Already seen it.'

'Why don't we have dinner at the milk bar?'

'I can't come,' Reg said. 'Daph needs me to help settle Maureen. The poor thing has to do it all on her own . . .'

264

It's her bloody baby, Josie opened her mouth to say, *who else should have to?* But the words slammed up against teeth clamping down.

Miles Henry stood in the door of the Igloo, script under arm, smiling his most incorrigible smile.

'The man of the hour arriveth,' Ernest cried, falling into silence at one striking look from Laura.

Josie half rose. Sat back down. Stood again. Her face burned; heart galloped.

Miles came into the Igloo, hazel eyes taking in the assembled group interestedly. He was older, shorter, and even more handsome than Josie remembered. Her font of lively words had run dry; she opened and closed her mouth like a fish.

'Have I come to the right place?' Miles said. 'I'm looking for . . .' He pretended to consult his letter. '*The Usurping of the Town Cur.*'

Josie flamed. Yep, she'd written that. It had sounded clever when both waterfall and wine were flowing.

Miles tapped the letter. 'Alternative title was, *The Greatest Show This Country Has Ever Seen.*'

'Geez,' put in Ernest, 'you don't undersell yourself do you, Jose?'

Why *should* she? But that was her cue, Josie stepped forward.

Miles's gaze settled upon her, enjoyment in his eyes. 'How are you, Milkmaid?'

Josie might have been wearing a chain-mail vest, so heavily did her nerves weigh upon her chest. But Josie had learned long ago: nerves meant it mattered. All she had to do was open her mouth, and trust the words *were* there.

'Welcome, Mr Henry,' Josie replied. 'Competition is tight for this role. I hope you haven't come all this way for nothing.'

His smiling eyes turned further down. In reply, her nose crinkled up.

Her brothers had risen, coming to shake Miles's hand. Miles chuckled with surprise when introduced to Josie's stage manager. 'Well well, if it isn't little Laura Adams!'

'It's just Laura, thank you,' she said coolly, gesturing to the stage. 'Let's get this underway. We've got plans for this evening.'

Josie turned to stare at Laura in astonishment. This meek and evasive girl had revealed a steely backbone.

'You bet,' Miles said, laying his script atop the piano. 'Where would you like me?'

'Centre stage, thank you.'

Miles turned smilingly towards the stage, taking the steps in easy bounds. Vivienne, hanging back at the curtains, looked to Josie and Laura for her own direction.

'First though,' Josie said, 'Let me introduce you to our Celeste . . .'

Miles had already taken notice of Vivienne and was heading in her direction, hand outstretched. He stopped, just short of shaking her hand, to exclaim: 'I'll be! You're Howie Woollcott's missing heiress!'

There was always a moment Josie marked when she helped her father fell a tree, just as the chainsaw finally sliced through, that a ragged break seemed to cut through time itself, in a breathless, lurching anticipation of the toppling crash. One instant, the tree growing tall against gravity's inexorable might; the next, succumbing.

Josie felt that standstill once more, as she watched Vivienne's mouth open, and her knees give way. Unlike a tree's felling, there was no cry of 'timber' or safe clearance taken. Josie ran towards Vivienne, and though she was too far away to ever make it, her arms were outstretched to catch her.

It was Miles who reached Vivienne, and caught her on his own knees, before her skull hit the stage. A dead faint.

Josie pounded up the stairs, came to her own knees beside Miles, crying out for Vivienne. Together, they worked to gently ease her down onto the stage floor. Miles, bundling up his jacket beneath her head; Josie, fanning her with a script.

'If you've killed my Celeste, look out.'

Miles had his fingers on her pulse. 'Just a faint,' he said, looking up at Josie. Their faces were mere inches apart, hands overlapping. Heat seemed to shimmer up from Josie's collar. She looked away, smoothing golden strands back from Vivienne's face.

Owen had come charging up the stairs after Josie, and eased himself in to replace Miles at Vivienne's right-hand side. 'Water,' he ordered Miles. 'Cold. From the supper room.'

Gently, he lifted Vivienne into his arms and carried her down to the rumpled old couch, normally reserved for senior audience members. Vivienne was making incoherent sounds against his chest.

Josie had trailed Owen, but stood back now indicating for the gathering group to stay behind her.

'Anaemia,' Ernest said, in aside. 'Get the woman a steak.' Laura delivered a deserved elbowing.

Miles set a glass of water next to Owen, who was kneeling beside the couch, oblivious to everyone. Miles came to stand beside Josie, with a mock sheepish look. Josie looked away, suppressing a highly inappropriate laugh. His ever-acting eyebrows were entirely to blame!

Vivienne resurfaced slowly, groggily, then fighting wildly, throwing her fists. 'Hey,' Owen said. '*Vivi.* It's just us, you're OK.'

Vivi? Josie frowned. This thing ever deepening between brother and best friend had the potential to leave the two people she dearly loved bereft. Josie didn't think she could bear to live alongside any more broken hearts.

Owen's face was lowering towards Vivienne's, as though in front of all of them, he was going to . . .

Josie pushed hurriedly forward. Vivienne's hand, reaching to cup Owen's jaw, fell away. 'Josie, tell me I just dreamed that.'

No, Josie could tell her no such thing – much as she wanted to.

Vivienne rolled upright and sat silently, while Miles pulled up a chair in front of her.

'Sorry about that,' he began. 'You just took me by surprise being *here*, when they've all been talking about you down there.'

Vivienne's face was hard. 'What are they saying?'

'That you took off . . .' Miles glanced briefly at Owen, standing by, arms firmly crossed. 'With a lover.'

The whole group seemed to grow indignant on Vivienne's behalf.

Miles raised a hand. 'That's not the worst of it. Others swear you're in a straitjacket somewhere, and with the way the Woollcotts are talking about your purported breakdown . . .'

'So, I'm either insane or duplicitous, couldn't just have changed my mind.'

'You asked what they're saying.'

Vivienne drew back her shoulders, lifted her graceful neck. 'Do you know Howard?'

'I know *of* him, who doesn't? I've chatted to him in a few clubs. When I can afford it, I have a penchant for his wine, too. But I'm no friend of your fiancé's. That's what you're asking, isn't it? Will I call in the runaway bride? This is a remarkable coincidence, our having a connection, but I won't compromise your privacy here.'

Josie found herself nodding vigorously. Her nodding froze, at Laura's interjection . . .

'You will, though.'

All heads turned to Laura. 'You *will* expose Vivienne to the gossip-mongers of her old life, if you take on this role.'

Josie saw the patently obvious now, wondered how she'd been so ignorant.

'With *your* profile,' Laura said, uncompromisingly, 'and the publicity Josie wants you to bring to our play – Vivienne will be in the papers, right alongside you as Celeste.'

Vivienne rose unsteadily to her feet. 'I can't be in your play, Josie. I don't want anyone to know where I am. I'm not ready to be found.'

Miles stood too. 'No, I'm the problem. It's me that will draw the media interest.'

'That's the point. You're my big drawcard, to bring Hugo in. But Vivienne *is* Celeste, she just *is*! What a nightmare . . .'

'Nightmare?' Reg interjected, having watched most of this bemusedly. 'To have your dream Celeste already, and your dream actor lined up for Zach? Reckon that's a nightmare most directors only wish they'd encounter.'

Vivienne looked miserable. 'I'll withdraw. You should have the Zach you want. I'm not even a real actress.'

'Please don't quit,' Josie said. 'We don't even know if Miles will be any good for the role.' She was dead serious, but also pleased to hear Miles chuckle behind her.

'And Laura refuses to take Celeste back.' This from Laura herself.

Josie gave a beleaguered sigh. 'What to *do*?'

From the doorway, the strident tapping of a walking stick. 'What a mountain you like to make out of your anthills, Josephine. I raised you better than this.'

The group turned.

Beryl Frances crossed the room with a majestic presence, eyes locked on her granddaughter.

Josie had never gone so long without seeing her Grandy. Behind the mask of irritation, she ached. 'Not now, Grandy. I'm busy.'

But her brothers were already heading, arms outstretched, to kiss their grandmother, close behind was Miles too. 'Mrs Frances, how lovely to see you again.'

Beryl proffered her cheek, still not taking her eyes off Josie.

Josie imagined the powdered, petal softness of that cheek under her own lips – and hardened. 'How did *you* find out about my audition?'

'Rosa was just in the teahouse telling everyone about her son being home. Took two seconds to figure out the rest.'

Miles groaned, mostly to himself.

Beryl turned to Miles. 'I suppose you think you're here to save Josephine's play. Riding in on your white steed, are you?'

It was Josie who answered. 'My play doesn't *need* saving. Miles saw an opportunity that couldn't be missed.'

From the corner of her eye, Josie watched Miles's grin crack open.

Beryl addressed Vivienne now. 'What about you? Happy to use Josephine as your buffer against the world, but not willing to confront a new future for yourself? She won't hide out with you forever.'

'*Grandy*,' Josie scolded, ignoring the chastised look on Vivienne's face. 'Vivienne isn't ready to be found.'

Grandy dismissed this with a headshake. 'She's not playing *herself*, child. In Rita's wig, with a stage name, who's going to know her for a missing heiress?'

How the devil did Grandy find out about Rita's costumery? Honestly, sometimes Josie thought her grandmother sent minions into the dark night to eavesdrop through every open window.

Vivienne was nodding keenly. 'I could easily take another name for the press.'

For the press. It would be *Josie's* headshot in the paper, not Vivienne's. Josie allowed herself a moment of fantasy; saw her name struck out in bold typeface above a wildly enthusiastic review.

She considered Vivienne, masticating her bottom lip. 'What name would we use?'

It was Grandy, ceasing with the closed-mouth clucking, who answered . . .

'Victoria Bird.'

CHAPTER TWENTY-FIVE

BIRD OF PARADISE

Josie had convened an after-audition, after-milking party back at the lodge to celebrate leads chosen, with a whirlwind four weeks to go. The pool of Chimera Falls was filled with bathers and bottles alike, high spirits and ebullient laughter seeming to raise the canopy itself.

The Monash siblings were dominating the celebrations, with Josie the garrulous ringleader. Josie had not dimmed or diminished one bit in the presence of her old high school crush. If anything, she'd gone bolder still. Much of the entertainment comprised sparring wit, or competing tall tales, informed by a colourful, country childhood.

Vivienne knew herself to be the outsider here, in every sense. Quietly she sat and sipped, trying to follow each volley of teasing reminiscence, watching for signs the repartee between Josie and Miles was anything more than long camaraderie and competitiveness. Vivienne longed to be a part of it all, but she could not get Beryl's words out of her head this night . . .

Confront a new future for yourself. She won't hide out with you forever.

Vivienne had felt herself too long manipulated by maternal manoeuvres to warm easily to Beryl Frances. The woman was overbearing, and had an uncanny ability to see things she ought not. In fairness to Beryl, her pushy interference seemed designed to embolden Josie, whereas Geraldine's cold detachment and affection withheld had been calculated to shrink unladylike vitality. *Only vulgar people honk like geese and hog attention.* Decorum, refinement, elegance, finesse – these had been inculcated in Vivienne, but how much richer might her life have been for loudly speaking her own mind and to hell with the consequences!

Vivienne gazed once more around the pool at this circle of country folk, so enjoying one another's rowdy company. In the midst of it, she was mealy-mouthed and self-conscious. No wonder they had called her dull. Vivienne sent a silent plea to her friend for attention, for inclusion. She watched it splash unheeded.

Confront a new future for yourself. She won't hide out with you forever.

Vivienne rose from the water, goblet clutched tight, and wrapped herself in a towel. There was something she had to do, while her limbs still glowed with this pleasant numbness. She felt Owen's eyes snap up to her, and stay on her as she walked towards the lodge.

In the library, Vivienne sat dripping in front of the roll top desk, and stared at the telephone, sick to her stomach. Josie's framed photograph of her mother sat on the desk, beside her pink typewriter. Vivienne stared at Maureen Monash, as she glugged back her glass of wine without decorum.

All Vivienne had to do was pick up the handset, and ask for connection to her mother. Simple as that.

False. Vivienne had craved connection, all her life, and only ever received it fleetingly. She closed her eyes, conjured up her mother's Arpège fragrance; imagined her cool, dry voice rustling down the line.

Then she wasn't imagining it: the handset was clutched hard against her cheek, and her mother's voice – clipped, guarded – was in her ear.

'Yes? Hello?'

'Mother, it's me.'

There was an indrawn breath on the other end of the line.

Say you missed me. Say you love *me.*

Her mother made no reply.

Vivienne's chest deflated; her lids squeezed shut. 'Are you still there?'

'I'm right here where you left me, Vivienne. *I* haven't gone anywhere, nowhere at all these last months. Thanks to the utter selfishness of my only daughter, I have become a social pariah.'

'I'm sorry—'

'*Sorry!* Are you! Well then, I'll let everyone know, and everything will be just *fine*. With that *sorry* of yours, we'll make our name good again, and wipe all our accounts clean.'

'What else do you expect me to say?'

'If *sorry* is all you've managed to come up with after so much time, what point is there asking you to finally explain yourself.'

'But I already explained why I couldn't marry Howard. I was wretchedly unhappy. You wouldn't hear of it—'

'I refused to indulge your reckless stupidity. Tried to make you see sense. But *no* – you decided to act like an ill-bred hoyden, and look how that turned out. You've ruined your life.'

How much easier her mother's eviscerating was to bear, with her face unseen.

'Maybe I haven't.' It was barely more than a whisper.

'Stop your mumbling.'

'I said: maybe I haven't ruined it.'

'You've certainly ruined your life. Mine, too. You can't redeem this kind of reputational damage.'

'But what has damaged my reputation most – my running away, or the way Howard and his family have been talking about me? Accusing me of insanity, and infidelity—'

'Would you prefer they all think you're a capricious twit who cares for no one's feelings but her own, and cares not at all for propriety?'

Never before had Vivienne realised how close were the words, propriety and *property* . . .

'You don't own me.'

'*Own* you? Don't be vulgar.'

'I am my own woman.'

An unnerving silence, conveying her mother's twisted countenance. But it couldn't touch her through the telephone – could it?

'I get to choose my own life.'

'What kind of life can you possibly imagine to have in – where did the telephonist say?' A scathing laugh. 'The back of beyond, without hope or expectation.'

'It's a lovely, quiet place, where I can gather my wits. Uncle Felix was very kind to find it for me, he was the only one willing to help me.'

'And Felix will answer to me when he returns from America. He's been in your ear again, hasn't he? Filling it with his nonsense. That's what's wrong with you!'

Vivienne gritted her teeth. 'I know you're bitterly disappointed in me, but please understand, I'm simply trying to direct my own life. And I'm not doing too bad a job of it. I've found friends – *real* friends – who care for me, call me brave, say I deserve happiness. That's not all, I've joined a local theatre company, and won the starring role. *Me*, singing and acting on stage! Does that shock you?'

'Why should it shock me? You owe your every accomplishment to me. All your singing lessons, and your elocution and deportment classes, not to mention the rest of it – *I* bankrolled the lot.'

'Then don't you wish you could see me on stage?' Girlish hope surged in her breast. 'But you can see me! Our opening night is the first Sunday of spring. Won't you come?'

'*All that way* for some two-bit theatre?'

'All this way for *me*.'

On the grand staircase, the grandfather clock had begun its sonorous tolling of the eighth hour. Even that dramatic peal could not cover the length of time it took for her mother to answer.

'I have too much on, Vivienne, it's impossible. You just get yourself back home, and hurry up about it. You need to set about making things right with everyone.'

White-hot frustration crawled up Vivienne's spine. *Enough of the endless crawling and contortion, trying to satisfy this unappeasable woman. Tell her!*

'I've had *enough*, Mother.'

She held her breath.

But from that faraway parlour came only the muffled sound of Geraldine speaking to someone else – likely their housekeeper, Anita – with a hand over the mouthpiece.

Louder, then. 'I've had *enough*!'

Geraldine's muting hand rustled away. 'No, it's nothing important,' her mother was saying to Anita, 'I can come and see to that directly.'

Geraldine spoke into the handset again. 'Good evening, then,' she told Vivienne in the feigned, dulcet tones of an acquaintance.

The connection severed.

Curlew cries had joined the cacophonous forest opera by the time Vivienne emerged once more from the lodge, dried and changed, and sobering fast. Great weariness, an enveloping sadness, had come over her in the wake of such tremendous crying.

Owen was sitting, waiting for her, on the bottom step. He looked up at her with no small measure of concern, but stood to accompany her back to Chimera Falls, without question. Only a single crack of his knuckles told her his thoughts were running in earnest.

Midway to the falls, where neither the light from the house could touch them, nor the rowdy group spy them, she stopped abruptly. Owen came to a standstill beside her. Vivienne turned to stare at his broad chest only inches away. For so long now, that chest had invited her head to rest upon it. Why else was it so wide and strong, and positioned at her precise head height?

She took a full step closer, so that her nose was nearly touching his shirt. Owen, simply stood. She did not raise her eyes as she nudged forward, pressing her face full into his warm chest. Owen's arms remained at his side, while she inhaled his scent of earth and oakmoss, face first. His steady breath fanned over her eyelids. Beside her cheek was the slow thud of his heart.

'*Vivi*,' he said at last, and she felt the full timbre of it from the throat above her head. She lifted her face to his, lips parting – but the sharp crack of a branch nearby, loud as a gunshot, made the pair leap apart, squinting into the darkness. Vivienne's heart, dragged so rudely from its pleasure, hammered painfully.

'Go to the others,' Owen said, waving her on. 'I'll have a look around.'

Vivienne fled for the oasis of noise and laughter. She did not dare look behind her.

By the pool, the group was closely gathered around a campfire, towel-wrapped, their chatter a warm tide, lapping languidly. She inserted herself into the space opened for her between Josie and Laura, and put her head to the former's shoulder, while her breathlessness abated. Josie patted Vivienne's head idly for some time, still regaling the group.

Owen arrived a while after her, with only the faintest shrug for Vivienne. She watched him take his seat across the circle. Though he was much further removed from her, the intimacy of his quiet gaze across the fire was now too much. She understood how she must look to him across this dazzling firelight: as soft and luminous as carnival glass. But did he also see how *love* – deep and tender – might shatter her?

She pulled her eyes away, and resolved not to look again.

At length Josie straightened, gently tipping Vivienne's head off, giving her an encouraging arm squeeze.

'All right, you lot – it's time for you to hear my Celeste sing.'

Vivienne looked at Josie, surprised, but found she didn't mind. Celeste belonged to Vivienne, she must show she had the pluck for it.

Vivienne lifted her chin and began to sing the ballad for Celeste's final walk along the shore of Lake Evelyn, 'The Song is Ended (but the Melody Lingers On)'. Shy at first, gathering poise and poignancy as she went, ending with a full-throated gusto, and a single tear running down her face. It was a consummate performance – she *felt* every word of it, and knew her audience did too.

There was a silence, a sigh indrawn, then Owen set the circle off in an applauding cheer. Vivienne swept the bead of emotion from her cheek and smiled, still keeping her eyes from Owen.

'Didn't I tell you?' Josie said proudly, pulling Vivienne tight to her with one arm. 'She's going to make this play the best Barrington has ever seen! She's my songbird.'

'Now that,' Miles said, 'is what I'd been meaning to ask you about, Josie. Why did you not include Wilde's "sad bird" line in Celeste's suicide note?'

"Honestly, I just haven't been able to turn it up,' Josie said. 'I knew she'd taken the line out of the "The Burden of Itys" but the poem wasn't in our copy of Wilde at home.'

'But what about the edition we found in Sylvan's library?' Vivienne said, astounded Josie had not returned to it yet.

Josie sat bolt upright, clapping her hands hard together. 'I comp-letely forgot about the lodge copy. Wait here, everyone!'

She tore back to the lodge, returning at a sprint minutes later with the book brandished on high. 'I've got it, I've got it, I've got it! Just *listen* to this—'

Standing before the crackling fire, breathless and radiant, Josie read . . .

"'Cease, cease, sad bird, thou dost the forest wrong, to vex its sylvan quiet with such wild impassioned song.'"

Heat suffused Vivienne. *Yes.* Delivered in a fine, silvered voice, carrying all her own pain and sorrow, the line would be . . . *tragic.*

Josie and Miles clearly shared this thought. Their eyes, flashing with fire, locked across the circle.

'That's it, Milkmaid. You just found the heart note of your masterpiece.'

Another week had passed, filled with planning and rehearsals, wine cellar raids, sundowners at Chimera Falls and late-night library floor talks.

All this activity and frivolity should have kept Vivienne's mind from rumination, but she *still* had not heard from Felix since he'd gone abroad. Frankly, it seemed rather cruel of him to just abandon her here, without so much as a word. She had so many things to tell him! Even a simple postcard – '*Thinking of you, my girl, won't be long now, don't fret*' – might have eased her gnawing disquietude. Several times, she'd picked up the telephone to call Geraldine, in the hope of gleaning news, but contrariness, and pride in her new self-sufficiency had made her slam that handset down again each time.

There were better ways to subdue persisting dread. Chiefly, through her daily lake swims, and Josie's heartening fortitude.

Josie seemed to think of everything. She had cancelled Niall's weekly food deliveries, so that their caretaker had no good reason for being out at the lodge. She'd invented a mostly believable story for her theatre group about Vivienne's newly acquired stage name, which was mostly believed. Lastly, she'd set the Monash brothers on regular surveillance of the lake and amphitheatre, to dissuade the vandal. *Should* they happen to sight a rogue crocodile while they were at it, Josie had stipulated they were to 'sink it'. Josie's unrepentant cheek remained a novel delight to Vivienne.

Returning from the lake this morning through a thicket of ferns, lurid-lit in a shaft of light, Vivienne came upon quite the strangest sight.

Upon a tree stump in the very centre of that light ray, danced an exotic bird, fanning out his velvet-black wings in swooshing cape-like fashion. A Phantom of the Opera, shrunk to doll-sized. His dark plumage shone iridescent purple as he circled out his cloak, on his chest sparkled a triangle of sequinned turquoise, with a wedge of the same at crown and tail feathers. With a bullfighter's proud intensity, his head flicked from side to side, shimmering breast puffed out, mouth gaping open to reveal saffron colouring.

Vivienne dropped quietly to her haunches, half hidden by the flanged buttress of a tulip oak; *wonderstruck.* The bird disregarded Vivienne with an imperiousness that carried well with his performance. Sighting a flash of brown nearby, she began to understand: the female of his species, watching on. He was displaying for her.

She could not bear to move and risk disturbing the pair. Just as her thigh muscles were burning beyond endurance, there came a recognisable whistle up the trail.

Her eyes grew large and soft in anticipation of the dark-bearded man who came around the corner moments later, whistling softly under his breath. His jerk of surprise at finding Vivienne crouched on the track amused her greatly.

She motioned him to her, with a single finger pressed against her lip. He crept forward in a spirit of boyishness which reminded her this was Josie's favourite playmate. The thought made her eyes grow softer still.

Owen knelt close beside her, and together they watched the bird dance in enraptured silence. After a time, the large shoulder pressing against hers took on a featuring role all of its own, and then she could concentrate on nothing else but how she might somehow get her head back onto Owen's broad, warm chest once more. Her breath, seemed to Vivienne, to fill the clearing.

She felt Owen turn to look at her. Her eyes remained fixed ahead, but all her awareness was on her cheek, heating under his regard. She could resist no more, and turned to meet his gaze.

She couldn't hold it. There was too much at stake between them now.

Her face crumpled with the sudden urge to cry. Owen's brow rutted with emotion. She shaded her eyes beneath her lashes and spun back to the bird, concentrating on breathing evenly; quietly.

She sensed his own struggle in the shift of his body away from hers.

'What *is* this bird?' she threw out, to prevent his leaving. She thought Owen would not be putting his chest in the vicinity of her seeking head again after this moment.

His voice was thick. 'The local aboriginal people call him "duwuduwu". Common name is Victoria's riflebird, after the Queen. A bird of paradise.'

Bird of paradise. That pleased her. The riflebird swept high his cape with dramatic flourish. 'Quite a show he puts on.'

'It's his mating dance.'

She shot a glance at Owen. 'What do you think the literal translation is?' She'd sought make light of the topic's awkwardness, but had overestimated her ability to carry the jesting tone.

Owen did not reply for a long time. She inclined her ear towards him, breath tight. Would he have a flippant comeback, or make no reply at all?

Finally, Owen answered; quietly, and with no trace of levity: 'Choose me.'

Vivienne turned to Owen.

Emotion was cut raw across his face. 'When you're ready, if I make you happy, please choose me.'

Panic seized Vivienne. 'I don't . . . know what I want.' Her throat had become chokingly tight. 'I don't think I'm . . . *capable* of the kind of happiness you mean.' The ring on her finger was heavy as lead, and sparkling traitorously. 'I've spent a lifetime overthinking all my choices, and I still wish I could go back in time and unmake every one.'

'But then you wouldn't be *here*, now.'

'I've become such a . . . wavering woman, always hovering above my own life.'

Owen's voice was deep and urgent. 'I'm offering you a solid place to land.'

A solid place to land. The words were a salve to her soul. But her mind went, inanely, to half-dried cowpats in a country paddock; this utterly foreign clime.

'Owen, I don't belong here. I'm only hiding, temporarily. I could never really live *here* with—' The last, cruel word snatched back in time. Even unuttered, she saw it hit his face . . . *you.*

There was a long beat, impossibly sad.

Vivienne felt her face screw up into ugly, quaking regret.

'Hey,' Owen said. '*Vivi*, it's OK.'

'I'm so sorry.' And she was; sorrier than she'd ever been. 'If you only knew how I . . .' But she couldn't bear Owen to know what he truly meant to her. The *untold want*, indeed.

He stood up, rubbing his beard, full of quiet dignity. 'I didn't plan to . . . I was just heading up to see Josie, I won't stay long.'

He turned away.

A cavernous desolation had opened in Vivienne's chest. 'Owen, *please* – wait.'

He looked back, face placid. She yearned for the raw look that had been hers, only moments ago. 'Do you believe in second chances?'

Owen didn't even stop to crack his knuckles, so readily did the answer spring from his lips. 'My father always taught us: God calls us out onto the water as many times as we need.'

CHAPTER TWENTY-SIX

STONEWALLED

With only a week to go until opening night, endless items to check off her to-do list, rehearsals in full swing, and sleep eluding her almost entirely, Josie was running on pure adrenaline. And when that wasn't sufficient, a liquid diet of coffee and cream. Countless times a day, she gave thanks for the two women shoring her up at every step.

Vivienne, with her steadfast belief in Josie, supporting her with dry wit, and a droll smile. And Laura, running a tight ship, indeed sometimes it felt the *whole* ship, whose firm purpose was the perfect complement to Josie's passion and energy.

How had two such friends fallen in Josie's lap at this most pivotal moment of her life? Providence itself could not have planned it better.

And nothing would stand in the way of *Nightingale Lake* . . .

There was someone standing in Josie's path right now, however.

She was alone in the driver's seat of the borrowed roadster, on her way up the dim forest road, and there he was . . .

Niall.

Smack bang in the middle of the dirt drive, blocking her exit. Josie resisted the urge to rev the engine and shoot forward – though she'd have liked very much to wipe that smug look off his face. Josie sorely lamented having turned down offers of company from Laura and Vivienne for her afternoon of errands.

When Niall refused to budge, Josie harrumphed and threw open her door. She leaned out of the roadster. 'I cancelled your deliveries, so you've got no reason to be lurking around here anymore.'

'What's your excuse, *girlie*? You're trespassing.'

'I am an invited visitor of the lodge guest.'

'You won't be once I let my employer know his property has been overrun by *squatters* . . .'

Josie laughed. 'Sure, go on: tell Rudy Meyer that his old amphitheatre dream is being revived. Complain that the Next Big Star is staying in his lodge.' Was she referring to Vivienne, or herself? Josie wanted to smirk.

But it was Niall who was smirking. She could have smacked him for it!

'Shows just how ignorant you are. Rudy Meyer won't ever hear about your production. Even if it *were* to go ahead—'

'Nothing can stop our show from going on!'

His smirk deepened. 'Even if it were to go ahead, Rudy couldn't care less. He doesn't have a thing to do with the lodge. Sylvan Mist is *mine* to oversee.'

'Vivienne's accommodation is *hers*, paid in full, to do with as she wishes.'

'That's what you think. But go on, make a bigger mess of Sylvan Mist, touch things you have no right to, keep stealing wine none of you can afford, and just *see* how pleased I'll be to keep you.'

You slimy, spying bastard.

'I'll report you for harassing a paying guest. Sneaking into the lodge while Viv's out, leaving your fingerprints all over the place. Rattling doorknobs in the middle of the night, trying to frighten her.'

285

'I'm the *caretaker*.'

'Not anymore. I'm taking care of the lodge and its guest.'

'You'd want to take care. Wouldn't want to find *yourself* on the chopping block next.'

Josie, about to duck her head into the car, straightened. *Taking blatant credit for the puerile cow pranks!* 'Are you *threatening* me?'

Niall had begun an advance towards the car.

Josie hurried into the driver's seat, slamming the door. She was not quick enough to wind up the window.

Josie looked straight ahead as Niall leant over the window, breath of minted onion invading her cabin. 'You might think you're in charge of that theatre company, but you'll never be the boss of my lodge.'

Josie turned to eyeball Niall back. 'You're nothing more than a glorified janitor here, but I certainly am running our theatre company. And without you, both lodge and company have never been better.'

'You'll find out who's really running what soon enough, you stupid girl.'

Josie revved the engine. 'The person who needs to start running is *you*.'

Niall's laugh was the last thing she heard as the window wound full up. But he *was* leaving – in a slow saunter.

'Sonofabitch,' Josie seethed after him. 'You meddle with my play again, and I'll destroy you.'

Too worked up to head directly into Barrington, Josie called by the farmhouse, instead. After her brush with Niall, she wanted – *needed* – to see her father. It had been weeks since she'd sat one on one with Gabe, sighting him only from a distance across the paddock, or dairy yard. He knew she was still coming to feed her calves, and might easily have met with her there, but did not. The longer their separation went on, the heavier weighed Josie's heart.

The property was quiet as Josie cruised up the sweeping, fir-lined drive, hoping against hope that Daphne would make no appearance. Josie parked far back, wincing as she eased the car door quietly closed. All she asked was for a few precious minutes alone with her father, like the good old days.

Tucking her locket under her neckline, Josie tiptoed towards the open kitchen door. She spied her father instantly, seated at the head of the table, with his back to the door and a pot of tea set before him. The last moment of repose before he headed back out into the paddock for the afternoon.

What luck! She'd sit down with her father now and tell him everything, all the ways she'd grown up, away from his eyes. Any awkwardness between them would be quickly subsumed by Josie's scintillating chatter, how she'd always covered for her father's sadness, and her own.

She was already taking a smiling step forward when, before her startled eyes, Gabe pushed his teacup away with a sudden jolt, spilling liquid across the farm table. He laid his head upon the table and in the cavern of his arms, began to weep.

Josie stalled, stricken, as she watched her father's back and shoulders shake. Never once had she seen him cry openly like this before, tears always kept to the privacy of his bedroom.

It could only be Josie's rebellion causing him such pain. She could, she *should* go to him this moment, wrap her arms around his shoulders and tuck her face into his neck.

I've come back, Pa. I won't do the play. I'm sorry I disappointed you, I won't ever go away again.

But she did not take a step forward. Gabe wept quietly on, while Josie stood there, unable, no, unwilling, to move. She did not agree to be reconciled to her father on the condition of surrender. And, she realised, he would never wish for it either.

Before her father's back had yet straightened, Josie turned on her heel and strode quickly back to the car. Driving back down the driveway, Josie kept her eyes from the rearview mirror. If her father were to appear in the kitchen door behind her, calling her back, Josie did not wish to see it.

At the foot of the drive, well beyond the gate, an apparition of dread stepped into her path, holding a small bundle against her chest.

Daphne.

Her sister-in-law came towards the driver's side, while Josie sighed between closed teeth, and wound down her window.

'Nobody told me you were coming by to see us,' Daphne said. 'I would have cooked luncheon, but how could I possibly prepare when I wasn't given any warning?'

Oh, for God's sake – this never-ending defensiveness!

'I didn't come to see you,' Josie said, producing no smile. 'I was checking something quickly, now I'm off again. Don't trouble yourself.'

Daphne looked equally put out now, at not being put upon.

Josie glanced around. 'What are you doing all the way down here, anyway?'

On cue, there came a snuffling noise from the bundle at Daphne's chest and then, with the stridency of an alarm, a baby's outraged squall.

Daphne's face broke into despair. She turned away from the car, bobbing up and down frantically on the spot.

A stroke of sympathy for Daphne – an alarming new feeling – gave Josie pause. 'Unhappy little mite then?'

Daphne rolled her eyes to the heavens, bouncing from foot to foot. 'All day and all night, she never shuts up!'

Maybe Maureen Monash resembled her aunt in one regard, then. Josie stifled a smile.

'And I've been so ill with mastitis.'

Josie grimaced. She'd seen more than her fair share of cows with mastitis. *Poor Daph.*

'The doctor said it's because I don't get enough rest. But, how *can* I? No one wants to help me; everyone cares more about *your* play than me. Even the cows get more attention – and what do *they* have to do all day? They don't even have to feed their own babies.'

Here was where Josie's sympathy stopped short. Had Daph never heard the plaintive bellow of a cow searching the farm for her calf removed?

'And you're out for a wander?'

'It's the only thing that works. We're going broke buying gripe water – and it doesn't seem to stop her griping at all!'

Josie's cheeks bulged against laughter. Daphne looked properly affronted.

'I don't know if Dad told you, but I was exactly the same as a baby.'

Daphne looked no less indignant, but her eyes betrayed interest.

'*Really,*' Josie said. 'If you think I make a lot of noise now, you should have heard me then. Dad had to walk me round the paddocks at all hours of the night to shush me up. The only way my mum got any rest when she was well, or peace and quiet once she was sick. After she died, Dad kept walking with me, even though I should have outgrown it years earlier. He'd walk me halfway round the lake every night.'

'I didn't know.' Rare softness came into Daphne's face.

'Oh yes, I've always been terrible. Dad just did what he could to cope. Then Grandy used Dad's night walks as one of her many justifications for taking us kids off him. Said it wasn't right for a man to leave his other children alone at night like that, even though the boys were asleep anyway. Claimed he was reckless and irresponsible . . .'

At this, Josie had a sudden recollection: hopping off the milk bus after school, to the sight of her father on his red tractor, hurtling down the hillcrest – eyes glazed, speed unchecked . . . hands off the wheel.

Josie blinked this image away. 'I digress. Point is, you've got another mouthy Monash girl on your hands.'

Daphne was frowning, but her lips moved to smile. Josie felt her own lips do the same. 'I'd promise you she'll grow out of it in time but, well, you know . . .'

Daphne laughed. *Laughed!* 'And does Father Monash still walk you around the lake at night?'

Josie grinned back. 'No, I retrace the insomniac's path around my own loud mind.'

'Oh, OK,' Daphne said, this wit apparently sailing straight over her head. 'I thought maybe that's where your father goes sometimes late at night.'

No one ever accused Daphne of having a sense of humour, Josie told herself; though it did not negate the guilt . . .

Ask her if Dad is suffering. Ask her how often he cries on the kitchen table. Ask her if she's looking after him properly in your stead!

Josie would rather throw herself on the barbed wire fence running alongside than ask Daphne any such thing.

Thankfully, from within the blanket mound, a caterwauling began anew. Josie gave Daphne a sympathetic, yet unarguably parting look. 'Got to go, but hey – if you're ever out walking in our neck of the woods, you're welcome to drop in for a visit at Sylvan Mist.' Josie was regretting saying that before she'd even wrapped up. Would she never learn to shut her mouth?

As though for effect, the newest Monash daughter rent apart the quiet country air with an almighty screech.

Josie smiled, beginning to like tiny Maureen.

There were soldiers on Main Street once more.

Out of Rita's Old Curiosity Shop came the young men, and some not so young, in a jocular, khaki stream. At the pub and milk bar, patrons craned and jostled to watch this procession, elbows nudging into sides, proud comments lobbed into the main street.

Josie, parking at the library bunker just as her cast of soldiers were leaving, sighed to watch them walk by. Rita had not been underselling her ability to 'get her hands on whatever Josie might need'. Rita had clothed an army, just in time for final dress rehearsals. And sending them down Main Street like this, with the whole town abuzz, was a brilliant advertisement, even better than the show posters pasted up around town. Those last few unsold tickets had surely just gone.

Josie made straight for Rita's shop. As she was cutting across the road, the door of the Old Curiosity Shop opened, and one last soldier, in a captain's uniform, stepped out onto the sidewalk, eyes curving at the sight of her.

Miles.

Her clipping pace slowed to a tremulous plod as Miles came towards her. It was impossible to look away from the handsome, tawny-haired soldier advancing.

They came together on the sidewalk outside the teahouse. Tea-swillers, just settling back into their seats after the earlier commotion, stood again to watch the pair. Was hamming up cow-eyes at Miles Henry supposed to be part of Josie Monash's promotion, too?

'What do you think?' asked Miles. 'Am I fit for you to send off into battle?'

'No way,' Josie blurted. 'I wouldn't let you anywhere near my army.'

Miles's confident smile faltered momentarily.

Oh cripes. Josie's toes clenched hard in her Mary Janes. 'You look . . . fine. For the role, I mean. But seeing you, like this, makes me glad we live in this generation, and not our fathers', that's all.'

Miles nodded. 'OK, that wasn't too bad a note. I took that quite well.'

Josie released a laugh; toes unclenching.

Miles nodded over Josie's shoulder at the roadster. 'Is the whole gang in town?'

'Just me.' She watched Miles's face for any sign of disappointment. It was only natural, she warned herself, that a man of Miles's status and worldliness would be attracted to a woman as beautiful and sophisticated as Viv. And most onscreen duos as passionate as Zach and Celeste were proving to be, must feel some echo of attraction offstage too – surely?

But Miles's amiable grin did not shift. 'Are you busy? I'd love to buy you a drink.'

Josie's tummy took a precipitous drop. They hadn't had a moment alone, or separate from the production, since he had arrived back in town. 'I guess I could go a milkshake. It's my turn to cook tonight – so it doesn't matter if my dinner's spoiled.'

Miles cocked a brow. 'I was hoping you'd share something a bit stronger with me.'

'Oh,' Josie said, unable to produce anything else. She was ready to throttle the recalcitrant words hiding themselves from her.

Walking at the captain's side to the pub, Josie hoped the warm afternoon was excuse enough for the high flush of her cheeks. The curtains at the front of the Purple House rustled just enough to let Josie know she was not only under watch by Grandy, but she was to *know* she had been seen.

In the quiet pub garden, they claimed a picnic table under the leopard tree, beside a historic volcanic rock wall, climbed by hot pink bougainvillea. Josie looked around, making shallow remarks on the prettiness of the vine, while Miles kept his eyes on her face. Finally, sick of her uncharacteristic shyness, Josie raised her brown eyes and planted them directly on his face. If she had to die of discomfiture, she'd do it for boldness, not coyness.

'Sharing a beer with Zach Miller is excellent publicity for my play,' she said. 'Thank you.'

She was rewarded with a broad grin, big, movie-star teeth revealed in full. 'You don't have to thank *me*, Josie. You don't know how honoured I—'

But the barmaid had arrived at their table with their beers. Josie glowered at the woman who had interposed herself between Josie Monash and a compliment.

Their barmaid left, and Josie looked to Miles expectantly. Miles took a hearty swill, seemingly unaware there were few things so infuriating in life as those who did not finish their sentences.

Miles sighed in satisfaction, thumping down his glass. 'Not a bad drop.' He seemed to become aware of Josie's anticipation, and smiled. 'I have to say, I don't know how I'll ever go back to playing Hamlet in my fetching stockings after this role.'

Josie gave a great snort, beer rushing up her nose.

Did he just say what I think he said?

While she coughed to clear her shock, Miles's grin went wily.

Yep. He said exactly that.

'How do you know about the stocking joke?' she demanded. There was no point denying it.

Miles took another calm sip. 'You're a shocking artist, Josie Monash.'

Her mind ran frantically to account for the error. Had she accidentally folded one of her sordid drawings into the envelope?

Josie shrugged. 'My talents lie in other areas.'

'As do mine,' Miles said, considering his glass with mock seriousness. 'Apparently.'

Josie was going to crack her teeth cringing this hard. She must have typed his letter onto the paper with her pencil sketch on back. That's what you got for typing under the influence of expensive, aged wine. *Wait until Viv hears about this!*

Josie lifted her chin. 'Just thank your lucky stars Rita took over my costume direction then.'

Miles smoothed the metal pips on his epaulettes, the Australian Rising Sun badges on his lapels. 'She must have outranked you.'

'Outplayed me, I suspect, though I can't quite figure out how or why.' The heat on Josie's neck began to recede. No time to stay embarrassed when there was intrigue to entertain. 'I have been unable to shake the feeling I am a pawn in a much larger strategy.'

Miles looked entirely unsurprised.

'I'm not blinkered,' Josie rushed to clarify. 'Grandy talked me into the idea of retelling Celeste's story, which almost certainly means she's scoring points, somehow. But it isn't just Grandy. There's others, invested in my play for their own reasons . . .'

Miles bent his head closer, with a quick glance around the garden. 'I was under the impression *Nightingale Lake* was Josie Monash's break-out production, originally conceived to exact revenge on a hoity-toity theatre critic, but really designed to rectify a cruel superstition, once and for all.'

Josie tsked. 'That's not an impression, that's what I *told* you my play is.'

'And yet,' Miles said, voice dropping lower, 'I arrive home to Barry, and find you've got a cast full of schemers, with a secret ringleader. And I'm sorry to say, Josie – it isn't you.'

'Don't be sorry,' Josie laughed. 'Whatever mischief those malcontents are up to, I would never lead it.'

'Who *is* then?'

'If I had to guess, it's Niall. The man's a pervert. He's been thwarted in both his latest obsession, and his lead-role ambitions, and now he wants to take my play down with him.'

Miles threw a dark look in the direction of the Corner Shop. 'He tried it once on my mother, when they were at school together.'

'*No!*'

'The way she tells it, in those days he went after *any* woman young and naive enough to be left alone with him.'

'That *bastard* hasn't changed at all.'

'But Mum says women talked behind closed doors back then, warned each other about young Niall. It got so that at no woman would be caught on her own by him, none would dance with him, much less ever marry him. Even when the war came, and so many fathers and husbands were gone, women kept right out of Niall's way.'

Rage lit Josie's tone. '*Nobody* warned poor Laura! Why are we still letting such a man live amongst us? Why the *hell* hasn't he been tarred, feathered and run out of town?'

Miles nodded hard. 'I suppose most people put him down as a sort of repulsive Lothario best ignored and mostly harmless, if you knew how to avoid him.'

'Doesn't excuse it one bit.'

'My concern,' Miles said carefully, 'is that as Niall grew older, he found ... other ways, and better places for catching women alone.' Miles pushed his beer aside so that he might lean closer over the table. 'Have you never wondered why Niall applied for that caretaker job, right after Rudy Meyer left the Tablelands?'

Josie leaned forward, gasping. 'It's given him the perfect excuse for loitering about around that lake!'

'Consider this,' said Miles. 'Until they finally stopped us swimming there, he had ample access to bathers and picnickers.'

'If it hadn't been for the Curse, many more of us might have been caught out there alone with him!'

'Precisely.'

Josie had become acutely aware of how close Miles's face was. If she'd truly believed he felt anything for her more than platonic camaraderie, her eyes might have dipped, right now, to stare at his full, beautiful lips.

Too late, just did.

Heated colour flooded the freckled apples of Josie's cheeks. She leaned back, looking anywhere else but at his lips, behind which she sensed a rascally smile. Her stomach was a revolt of nerves and conflicting urges.

Josie pushed her beer to sit, sweating, alongside Miles's glass. She cleared her throat officiously. 'Let's be very serious about this. What are we saying here?'

'I'm loath to actually say it.'

'I will, then. We suspect the town pest of murder. Bit laughable, isn't it?'

'Not so laughable as the idea of a lake turned serial killer.'

Josie wrinkled her nose. 'Pity me, trying to sleep in that lodge now, thinking of him skulking around in the forest, watching us.'

He chuckled. 'Lucky you're not burdened with an overactive imagination, then.'

'You're one to talk. Look at Miles Henry, sitting around playing "detective" with Josie Monash.'

Miles eyes dropped, at this juncture, to her breasts.

Josie wouldn't have blamed him one bit – her bosom was as perky and pointed as she, and deserved as much attention – but she was forced to correct herself: his eyes had in fact dropped to her fingers, compulsively worrying her locket along its chain. Josie's hand stilled. She waited for Miles's eyes to lift again to her face. Every second longer his eyes remained in such close vicinity of perky pointedness worthy of attention, her breath stayed trapped in her ribs.

When Miles finally looked up, it was without guilt – seemingly unaware he'd nearly caused Josie to suffocate. Indeed, his mind seemed to be somewhere else entirely.

'Talking about overactive imaginations,' she said, mostly for her own benefit, 'Viv and I found a locked door in Sylvan Mist's basement. We've been speculating it's a secret entrance to the lodge. I'd already been meaning to bust it open, but now I'm determined! Mr Caretaker deserves it . . .' Josie proceeded to lay out the points of Niall's petty vandalism in revenge for his ousting. 'My theory,' she concluded, 'is that Niall wants to protect either the lodge or lake, maybe both, from public scrutiny, and he foolishly thinks a few cow parts are going scare us all off. Had he kept the role of Zach he'd contrived to steal, I think Niall would have been sabotaging the production from within, too.'

She watched, fascinated, as private conflict played out over Miles's expressive features. With a concern that could not be laughed off, he said: 'Please be careful out there, Josie.'

Josie thought better than to reveal she'd already been warned by Niall himself to *be careful*. 'We are. I've hung privacy curtains, we lock everything down and the three of us try and stick together.'

'Maybe your trio could share a house in town, when the play wraps up.'

'Laura and I are already talking about it.'

'Not Viv too?'

Josie forced breeziness. 'I'm not sure what Viv will do next. Says she'll have to go back home to Sydney eventually, and face the music.'

'She should say *good riddance* to the lot of them. Howard Woollcott is a hypocrite, and a pig.'

Josie's eyebrow shot up. 'Explain yourself!'

'He's never seen without a beautiful woman or three on his arm, and neither his engagement nor his fiancée's disappearance have put a dint in his habits.'

'A philanderer?'

'His legend precedes him. Has two love children – that I've heard of.'

'*No!*'

'Yep.'

'But Viv has no idea!'

'I'm going to guess she's been sheltered from a lot of life?'

'Shockingly so, for a city woman. Her mother's an ice-breathing dragon – think that has a lot to do with it.'

'I haven't told you the worst of it.'

Josie planted her upper teeth firmly in her bottom lip.

Miles took a breath. 'So, the story goes: Vivienne George went around to Howard's Rose Bay mansion on the eve of their wedding to break it all off, but he wasn't home—'

Josie gestured him on impatiently. 'I already know this.'

'Did you know it was because he was spending the night with the mistress he'd been keeping in a Potts Point penthouse.'

'That *prick*!'

'Indeed.'

Indignation furrowed Josie's brow as the enormity of this revelation was realised. 'So, the Sydney society columns were full of *Viv's* shocking behaviour in leaving her groom stranded at the altar – meanwhile, Howard was in another woman's bed on the morning of his own wedding?'

'Everyone's talking about it.'

Josie's teeth clenched furiously. 'That makes the Woollcotts' carry-on about Viv losing her mind even more heinous. He *deserved* to be humiliated!'

Miles did not object. 'Vivienne should be counting her lucky stars she got out in time. Howard's also been telling people she ran off with a lover.'

'She has *not*,' Josie spat, thinking of her brother's stoic quiet over recent days, the anguish lurking in Viv's soft eyes.

Miles shrugged. 'She could, if she wanted.'

'In time, I hope she will.' Josie smiled. 'If it was me, I would take a lover just to spite him.'

'Do you often take lovers out of spite?' Miles's delivery was deadpan.

'I've never found a good enough reason to take any lover.' Whatever the liberal lifestyle Miles was accustomed to, however urbane he might have become, he should be reminded: he was back in Barrington now, and she was Josie Monash.

Miles smiled. 'In time, I hope you will.'

Josie choked on a laugh; beer rushed back up her nose. She coughed, and coughed.

'Do you need a pat?' Miles asked, the very picture of innocence.

Josie washed down her embarrassment with a large swig. 'Tell me about Sydney. Is it everything we dreamed it would be?'

Miles's boyish grin returned. 'It's *everything*.'

'Damn. I was worried you'd say that.'

Miles cocked his head. 'It's strange, my being down there living out *your* dream, when you were always the more talented one. I've been expecting you to turn up at any moment and upstage me.' The old taunting line from her autograph book.

Josie looked away to the volcanic stone, the bounteous bougainvillea, eyes burning. 'You're a man. It was easier for you to go.'

'I don't think the Josie Monash I grew up with would ever have let her sex stand in the way.'

'I didn't,' Josie said, tears rushing to blur stone and blooms together. She turned her face further away, blinking frantically.

Miles's hand came to rest firmly on Josie's. Her eyelashes, glugged together, were no longer any use in clearing her tears. Josie turned back, to stare at Miles's hand covering her small hand so completely.

He spoke softly. 'Why *did* you stay then?'

When she didn't answer, he gave her hand a small squeeze. There was an answering squeeze, low in her belly.

It was hard to speak, what with a heart pounding in her ears, but she tried. 'Why would I give up a happy place in my family of men, and my theatre group, my calves, my Grandy, and everyone else I love here in Barry?'

'What could be worth more than all that?'

My childhood dreams of writing and directing for the stage! She shrugged. 'It doesn't really matter, because I couldn't leave my father all alone.'

Miles tipped his head, trying to catch her eyes. Sighing, Josie lifted her face to his. With their hands still pressed together, Josie found herself one giant throb of emotion.

Miles smiled lopsidedly, far more like the boy she had collected thylacine poop with, than the dashing theatre star he had grown into. 'He wouldn't have been *alone*. There's too many of you Monash kids.'

'I promised, as a girl, I would never, ever leave him.' Josie's reasoning was feeble, even to her own ears. She was glad when Miles had the clear mind to dispute her.

'But every girl has to leave her father someday. And every father has to let go of his girl.'

Josie saw again: her father, weeping face down on the kitchen table.

'Maybe,' Josie said. 'But I didn't want to!'

His hand tightened around hers. 'Didn't – or *don't*?' His expression was more earnest than she could bear.

'Please,' she said, drawing her hand out of his, holding it to her breast. 'Don't question me on this. Dad needs me, and I walked out on him!' Josie leapt up from the table. 'Thank you for the drink. Thank you for helping me make this play a success. That's all you have to do, OK? Help me bring Celeste's story to life, help me break the Curse. That's all you're here for.'

Miles stood, with a brief, wordless nod, as Josie swept out of the pub garden.

CHAPTER TWENTY-SEVEN

SPEAKING IN TONGUES

In all her lake swims over the last month, Vivienne had seen no sign of Josie's crocodile, or her own watcher, much less Barrington's lake wraith. She *had* spied gigantic jungle pythons sunning themselves on the bulrushes, eels battling in the shallows, platypuses cavorting at dawn and dusk. To think she shared her lake with so many strange and marvellous creatures! Perhaps, after their show was done and the Curse deemed broken, tourists and townsfolk alike would return to play here.

They were so *close* now . . .

The Obsidian had risen again from ruins: the diving platform reconstructed; signage repaired; cark park reclaimed; amenities shed re-plumbed; and Owen's floating stage walk was a masterpiece revealed. Laura had repurposed army canvas tents going up now for the cast and crew, and at this evening's rehearsal, her newly procured spotlights would be used for the first time.

All of Barrington was abuzz with preshow excitement, *Nightingale Lake* proving the hottest ticket in years. Vivienne glowed to hear Josie's name on everyone's lips, wherever she went in town – and she did go freely about Barrington these days. True to Josie's word, the community had opened its arms to the 'city actress' named Victoria Bird.

Guilt plagued Vivienne that she should be thanked so incessantly for 'donating her stardom to amateur theatre' when she knew *herself* to be the charity case in receipt of lavish kindness. Oddly, Vivienne received more praise for 'what she was doing for Josie' than for Barrington's big play itself. She couldn't profess to understand precisely what they thought she *was* doing for Josie. It was quite the other way around. Josie had given Vivienne a reason to stay, and a new future to imagine.

Playing Celeste Starr with all her heart and whatever talent she possessed, was the best way she knew to repay Josie.

It appeared there was only one person still standing in objection to *Nightingale Lake*: their mystery vandal. Or, *non*-mystery vandal, according to Josie, since she was convinced it was Niall depositing the macabre mementos.

Two mornings earlier, it had been a grotesquely large cow's tongue, left on the lodge front stoop. The three women had discovered it together as they were leaving to help Josie with her calves. There it lay; a pink, livid thing, bulging.

There could be no doubt about its intended meaning.

In her revulsion, Vivienne had struggled to find words to soften this insult for Josie. Though Laura had hurried to clear away the tongue, with just the right words offered, the courageous Josie had looked, at least for one moment, *afraid*.

It was *that* look which sent Vivienne across the Monash farm-land this morning in want of Owen's help, despite the continuing schism between them. Whoever was trying to intimidate Josie, they were creeping, ever closer, from Igloo to lodge. And since Josie would never deign to ask for brotherly protection, Vivienne would request it for her.

Light sun-showers had swept over the Tablelands all morning, and over the gully at the foot of Owen's hill lay a mere of rainbow mist.

With her mind already on the man living on top of this hill, she was unprepared to encounter Mr Monash at the bottom of it.

Gabe Monash sat on a large boulder within a grove of melaleuca trees, in what appeared to be a dried-up billabong. His back was to her, head bowed. There was a mouth organ in his hands. Was he playing? Praying? *Crying?* This was, undoubtedly, the most private of moments.

No sooner had Vivienne begun her mortified retreat, an incriminating branch cracked underfoot. Gabe's face swung towards her, with so hopeful an expression, quickly dashed. He'd wanted her to be Josie, hadn't he?

'Mr Monash,' she said. 'Forgive me. I was on my way to see Owen.'

Gabe was already on his feet, unfurling a wide-brimmed hat. 'Please, don't mind me.' He stood aside with taciturn dignity, motioning her through.

She stepped gingerly across the dry creek bed, cringing with every crackle of leaf and twig. She was disturbing something sacred here, she just knew it. Her learned reflex was to hurry by, feigning polite indifference, but this was the man who'd raised the irrepressible Josie Monash. *Speak*, she told herself: *speak!*

She paused. 'Josie does miss you – most fervently.'

Gabe nodded.

'But you are doing the right thing, letting her go out into the world. Josie is capable of so much . . .' She fumbled here for the right word.

'Magic,' Gabe supplied quietly.

'Thank you. And if you *let* her leave and go make a life for *herself*, she'll come back to you again one day – more fulfilled than she could ever have been, if she had just stayed here.'

Gabe pulled his hat onto his head, pocketed his mouth organ, dark eyes expressing a hurt she could not quite account for having caused. 'Thank you,' he said. 'I'll try that. Good day.'

She went on up the hill, cringing.

Owen was nowhere to be found at his tin shed. The billy was empty over a wetted-out campfire. Evidently the man didn't sit around waiting for errant blondes to show up on his sawdust step.

Vivienne wandered around the foundation of Owen's build, trying to imagine where he had planned to set each room. Was he making it large enough for a jolly, wide-hipped country wife who would give him many children? Vivienne *hated* the woman already.

At the front of Owen's future home, she gazed out over the verdant folds of crushed velvet to Lake Evelyn. She treasured the thought that Owen had been watching over her hiding place from his hilltop hut.

If Vivienne was the woman of the house, she would *insist* on so many windows, they would never be without a view of Lake Evelyn. She saw hardwood walls rising up around her, heard tiny voices at play, imagined she could feel Owen come up close behind her, his breath hot on the nape of her neck. Vivienne's shoulders raised, a shiver bursting up her spine.

But Owen came up the very hill before her.

He stopped, taken aback. She did not miss how his broad chest expanded, then contracted.

'Goldilocks better not have eaten all my porridge,' he said.

Are you sorry you didn't find Goldilocks sleeping in your bed?

'I didn't break any of your chairs, either.'

She knew instantly, from Owen's rising hue, that his mind had gone first to beds over chairs, too. Vivienne flushed to the roots of her hair, unable to think of anything else *but* a bed shared with this large man.

'Tea?' Owen said mildly.

'No, thank you.' She cleared her throat. 'I've actually come to ask a favour – for Josie's sake.'

'Give me a moment.' He shucked off his boots at the front door of his hut, ducking his head as he went within.

Vivienne followed Owen inside. His abode was clean and homely, with only a mattress on the floor, a single table and chair, and a hand-crafted cupboard. The hut smelt, rich and enticing, of Owen's oakmoss signature. Her nostrils flared subtly, as she imbibed this scent.

Owen had only come inside to change – Vivienne realised this a second too late, as Owen peeled his shirt off, muscles rippling. She spun away, face ablaze. It wasn't her head any longer she wanted to lay against that broad chest; rather her own naked breasts. She imagined how it might feel to kneel astride his hips, hands splayed over his strong torso, and slowly—

Oh God.

She fumbled with the books on Owen's table, as he pulled a clean shirt on in her peripheral vision.

'All done,' Owen said. Amusement lit his eyes as she risked three darting glances, before looking at him in full.

'So,' he said, motioning for her to claim his single seat. 'How may I help Josie?'

Vivienne declined to sit. Her eyes went over Owen's shoulder to his mattress She cleared her throat, again. 'The cow-chopper has struck again. This time with a tongue left out for Josie to find on the lodge front step.'

Owen considered this. 'Josie surely isn't intimidated by a cow's tongue? Dad often has a tongue in the fridge for special Sunday lunches. It's quite the delicacy, round these parts.'

She managed to conceal a gag at the thought of a cow's tongue laid out on a plate. Chalk it up to another irreconcilable difference between the world she'd known, and the one he represented. Reminded anew of this crevasse between their lives, her throat ached – joining body parts already aching in his presence, and the intimacy of this small space.

'Owen, I don't think anything in the world, much less cow parts, could put Josie off this close to her grand opening. But it's the *meaning* of the thing.'

'Yes, I hear you.'

'She's had another run in with Niall, told him off, and he told her to be "careful", said she'd soon find out who was really "running" the show. It could very well just be bluster from the man but—'

'You're not taking the risk! I'll go see the prick, and sort him out.'

Vivienne exhaled. 'Josie will be relieved.'

'Josie will be peeved. I've wanted to sort him out myself for ages, but she's determined to look after herself – and everyone else too.' There was nothing critical in his tone, only an abiding understanding of his sister.

'You don't have to tell me. She's taken both Laura and I under her wing, all while redeeming her theatre company's reputation, and a haunted amphitheatre too.'

Owen nodded. 'I did warn you about Josie.'

'And now I need to warn you. What she's really trying to do here, with this play, have you guessed it by now?'

'Knowing Josie's taste in books . . . I've suspected she's out to solve a mystery.'

'Force a reveal, more like. And you must be able to figure out why?'

'Accolade would be the obvious motivator for my sister.'

'Close, but no.' She smiled. 'Solving this "curse" is the last thing Josie thinks she needs to do, before she can finally leave. Josie says she's breaking the curse for Barrington, but really, it's for her. She wants to grow up.'

Owen took one closed fist in the other hand, considering this. She waited for the cathartic pop of knuckles.

There it was. 'So, Josie's putting away her childish things.'

She nodded.

'In that case, I've found something to help her.'

He reached for the books beneath her hands. Her hands quivered as his fingers slid by hers. She hoped Owen had noticed her newly bare ring finger and, if not, how she might draw it to his attention. She wondered if Josie had told him about Howard's philandering, too.

'Would you give this back to Josie? It's Sylvan's copy of Wilde's poetry.'

'She's already seen it. It's how she found the last line of poetry from Celeste's suicide note.'

'Indeed. I nabbed the book to compare to our Monash copy.' He handed her the second book. 'Show her both together.'

Vivienne looked at him, bewildered. 'But she already *knows* "The Burden of Itys" wasn't in your old family copy. They're different editions. She said so.'

'They're the same edition, Vivi.' He opened the Monash copy to reveal, barely visible in the centre spine, the thinnest stub of missing pages. 'The poem was torn out of ours, years ago.'

CHAPTER TWENTY-EIGHT
THE DARK ROOM

The Monash brothers swore: leave Josie alone in a blank, empty room, and she'd invent enough drama to entertain herself for days. Josie had never denied this. She simply pointed to the 'leave Josie alone' part of this equation.

It was the morning before her big debut and Josie had been left alone at Sylvan Mist, and to her own devices for too long. Laura was down at the amphitheatre meeting with the stage crew, Viv had claimed she was going out for a walk, but was obviously sneaking off to see Owen, so what else was Josie to do but pry somewhere, in something?

She had been searching outside the back of the lodge for a hidden entrance; the mythical tunnel into the basement's locked room. Josie knew the idea was pure fancy, but that locked door provoked her beyond reasonable ire. It was the insult of being denied access, moreover, the *indignity* of Niall telling *her* to be careful. If that man had a secret way into their safe haven, they would be bloody stupid not to check! Doors could be replaced, but friends could not.

There was nothing else for it.

Josie stalked down to the basement with the axe she had nabbed from the farm, after her last run-in with Niall. Viv had refused to let Josie bring back a shotgun.

She considered the door before her, she did not consider waiting for the other women. With time and patience, she might have taken the door off at its hinges, but if she just could splinter the wood around the internal lock instead . . .

Josie raised the axe without effort. She'd been helping chop wood since she was a girl, had wrestled much bigger brothers all her life, could proudly lug a milk can. Her arms were strong and sure.

She threw every ounce of her rage at Niall, at Hugo Bernard, at mothers taken too soon or controlling too long – into that first thunderous chop. As it happened, she had many more ounces of rage to expend on the next dozen chunks, too. Josie seemed to feel every axe fall, not just in her arms and abdominal muscles, but in her teeth, which were clenched like a vice.

Pulling her axe out for what felt like the fiftieth time, Josie found a breach beside the doorknob. The axe clattered to the floor. She dropped to her knees, shoving her hand through, minding no splinters, reaching for the lock. The door opened.

She tucked her torch under an arm, picked up her axe as a precaution, and stepped inside a tiny, dark room, no bigger than a water closet.

Six feet in front of her, was a second door.

'For pity's sake!' Josie was already raising the axe, when the thought occurred that she might try the knob first.

It opened easily. Josie stepped inside; an acrid chemical smell rushing to envelop her. She squeezed her nostrils shut with one hand, and pulled the hanging cord for the light. Josie blinked, taking in shelves and benches, large glass bottles and silver trays, strange equipment akin to a salon hairdryer, a thin wire extending across the room, and a long, velvet settee covered in large print rolls.

The whole space resembled something between a laboratory and a kitchen. A terrible-smelling room for cooking *something* up.

But it was, thankfully, just a room. Not a hidden entrance to the lodge.

Dimly now, from the floor above, Josie heard voices on the stoop. Laura and Viv returning. Hurriedly, she went to greet them, preparing her story: *I was just walking around with my axe and I accidentally fell into the locked door, whoopsie.*

By the time she met her friends at the foot of the grand staircase, she was ready to confess the truth. *Since I'm squatting here, I thought I'd ruin the place.*

'We've each got something to show you,' Vivienne said. Neither Viv nor Laura looked happy with their news.

Vivienne was holding a bundle of peach-coloured fabric, and some books. Empty-handed Laura bore an expression of outrage far more compelling.

'What is it?' Josie demanded first of her stage manager.

'We've just been at the Obsidian. The vandal – *Niall* – has struck again.'

Josie had gone quite puce with anger.

'Don't worry, it'll be his last trick,' Vivienne hastened to add. 'Owen *insists* on putting a stop to Niall's troublemaking.'

Josie blew a scornful raspberry. 'As if we need his help.' But if Owen was so disposed, perhaps she wouldn't prevent him. 'What part of the beast this time?'

Vivienne and Laura shared a look. 'It wasn't fresh cuts,' Laura answered. 'There was a stuffed dummy, set up in the middle of our stage.

Josie was having trouble taking this in. 'Like a . . . scarecrow?'

'A ghoulish one, made to look like Celeste, with long hair, a crown made of sticks and a dressing gown. And she, or rather *it*, was wrapped in lawyer vine, with a noose around her neck.'

'It was an effigy,' Vivienne muttered. 'But that isn't the worst of it.' She plonked her poetry books aside, and unfurled the material in her hands. 'The dummy was wearing *this*.' A beautiful peignoir was revealed, heavily stained with dirt, leaves, and substances unknown.

Josie prodded it gingerly. 'Well, it looks expensive, but it isn't Celeste's gown.'

Vivienne gave her a dry look. 'I know it's soiled, but you really don't recognise the style?'

Josie looked again. Vivienne had a matching negligee. 'It's yours! You think he snuck in here and stole it?'

'No. I laid this peignoir down on the shores of Lake Evelyn the first week I arrived, when I struck out for a swim. He must have stolen it then! Niall has been watching me swim for months.'

Josie could not supress a full body shudder. 'It makes me sick to my stomach.'

'It's even viler than that,' Laura said. '*I* recognised that gown too, the moment I saw it.'

Josie turned to Laura in shock. Laura nodded, face pinched. 'Niall gave this dressing gown to me. I never wore it – shoved it straightaway in a drawer. Thought it was hideous – sorry, Viv. But it turned up again on the day he'd planned that . . . photo shoot for me. I walked into my flat, and there he was waiting for me with camera and a backdrop set up, music playing, and that gown laid out on the bed. His hand was already down the front of his pants . . . on himself. I'll never be able to get out of my head how *excited* he looked. His face was . . . that grin . . . it was demonic.'

'*He's vermin.*' Josie put a hand on Laura's arm, and did not know if it was to steady Laura, or herself.

She glanced rapidly between her friends. 'I should be thankful we've finally got proof that revolting, despicable man has been behind all this, but it's terrifying to think he was sending a message to both of you.'

'I'm less terrified than infuriated,' Laura said. 'We'll report him to Constable Jacobs now, and the whole town will be done with him.'

'You'd think,' Josie said darkly. 'But as I've learned, he's been at his lecherous behaviour for years, and no one has strung him up yet.'

Laura's beautiful eyes flashed fire. 'That was our mothers' generation! This is ours. We won't let them cover for him this time around. It's *my* secret to reveal.'

Vivienne balled up the peignoir. 'I suggest we see Constable Jacobs pronto, lest I am overcome by the urge to incinerate this. What good luck solving this mystery on the cusp of our debut.'

Josie cleared her throat. 'You're not the only ones who have been solving mysteries today.'

'Uh-oh. I know that look by now,' Vivienne said. 'What have you been up to in our absence?'

'Now, Viv, don't be cross. It's nothing we can't fix.'

Vivienne observed the high pull of Josie's sweat-matted ponytail, her sleeves rolled up, the torch tucked into her waistband. 'You look like someone who's been destroying property.'

'I found our secret passageway!'

Down in the basement, her friends stepped warily past the shattered door, torches sweeping around. Vivienne turned a dry look on Josie as she stepped over the axe.

'It's like a tomb in here,' Laura said, gripping her nose. 'You can still smell the embalming chemicals.'

Vivienne snorted. 'That's just stop bath. This is a photography darkroom.'

'*Genius!*' cried Josie. 'Viv, you are the gift that keeps on giving.'

'Not at all. If you know anyone with a keen interest in photography, it's easy to tell what this room is. It's here in the basement for minimal light, and the antechamber is to protect the dark room. See, these are his developing trays, and that line is where he would hang the photographs to dry.'

'He?' Josie was watching Vivienne carefully.

Vivienne turned, surprised. 'It's obvious, surely? Rudy Meyer was producing his photographs of Celeste down here, most for his personal obsession – but you told me Niall was also selling French photographs under the counter of the Corner Shop during the war.'

She struggled to unfurl a large roll, revealing a French Riviera backdrop of improbable hues. 'Look, here's one of the backdrops he used. I remember seeing the end result hanging in the master bedroom when I first moved in.' She raised a hand. 'Hang on, let me show you.'

Vivienne disappeared upstairs, returning to offer up an armful of photo frames. Carefully she prised open a frame, turning the photo around to reveal a black and white image of Celeste. Proffering the image to Josie, Vivienne began pulling boxes off a high shelf, evidently searching for more to illustrate her point.

In the meantime, Josie stared at this photograph, throat tight. Celeste, covering her bare breasts with two crossed hands, was sitting before a faux vista of the French Riviera. She wore nothing but a gold chain and diaphanous wrap, long hair tumbling around her. Her head tilted to the side with a sultry look of invitation.

Josie thought she'd seen all the pictures of Celeste there were to see. Presented with a new image, Celeste sprang to life again. Josie heard her bright laughter, saw her large eyes full of mischief, watched her cross the room on the balls of her feet with that odd, sprightly walk she had.

How the hell did Josie think she'd divined *that*? It certainly wasn't how she'd written Celeste for the play. Just how many of these back-to-front images were in Sylvan Mist? Josie had been so taken up with her plans, she hadn't thought to ask for them.

'Viv, let's turn her around in all these frames! We'll hang them up for our opening night celebrations.'

Vivienne wasn't listening. She stood unnaturally still at one of the boxes, back against the other women.

'Viv?'

Vivienne turned; face drawn hideously back, as though to cry or scream. 'There are more photographs of Celeste in here.'

Josie was already taking an eager step forward. Vivienne motioned her back. 'You don't want to see these.'

'Of course I do . . .'

'They're *dreadfully—*' she cast a pained look at Laura '—exploitative.'

Josie wasn't letting that stop her. She reached in for a handful of images. Her breath wedged painfully in her chest as the image of a naked, shackled, splayed Celeste Starr imprinted itself upon her brain.

She'd never seen or imagined such a thing in all her days.

Hastily, Josie flicked this image to the bottom of her pile. '*Oh no,*' she cried, as Celeste was revealed in a pose more degrading than the first: mouth gagged, eyes wide with terror, parts of her anatomy revealed that Josie had never been confronted by before. The next image repeated its blow to mind's eye; soul's innocence. And the one after that, and after that too. No matter how quickly Josie shuffled through the images, there was no escape for Celeste from her bondage.

'It's not only Celeste, here.' Vivienne had pulled another trunk down from a higher shelf.

Josie reached in, flicking through photographs of another young, raven-haired woman. She looked vaguely familiar, as people often did in rural districts, but no name or family resemblance sprang to mind.

'*Dear God*,' she breathed. 'That means he did it to more than one woman! But who is she?'

'And who will *they* be?' Vivienne said, nodding towards the highest shelf, where sat another half-dozen boxes, dust-coated.

The women regarded these boxes in sombre silence, no one showing the slightest inclination to investigate further. A prickling heat climbed the nape of Josie's neck. Might she know some of the women in those archived collections? Had any of *Barrington's* girls come down to Rudy's lair?

Laura who had been standing by Josie's side all this time, began to sob convulsively. Josie drew Laura against her side, squeezing tight. 'Niall will never have the chance. We'll never let him near you again.'

'*Hell is empty*,' Vivienne whispered. '*All the devils are here.*'

For several, suspended minutes, no one said another word, each woman needing time to feel the weight and safety of their clothing upon them, the free movement of their limbs and mouths.

Vivienne broke the pall of horror. 'Rudy Meyer was running a filthy photography operation out of this basement.'

Josie nodded darkly. 'And Niall either knew about it at the time, or discovered it later in his role as caretaker. He's been protecting or otherwise ... profiting himself from this disgusting room ever since. He probably comes down here and—' She broke off. 'I'll have him drawn and quartered; I swear it!'

'No wonder Celeste killed herself!' This fierce cry from Laura. 'If I knew such images of me existed for men to see and use, I'd want to drown myself too!'

'Don't!' Josie yelped, a moment too late. 'Please don't say that. I understand, but I can't stand to hear you *say* it.'

Laura turned a defiant look upon her, tears glistening on her lashes. 'I won't take it back. If that were *me* in those pictures, I couldn't live with myself, and I don't blame Celeste for not wanting to, either.'

'Nobody blames Celeste,' Josie said, pulling Laura into a cuddle. 'None of us do!'

'The whole town blames her!' Laura cried, struggling out of Josie's embrace. 'These last fourteen years, they haven't *stopped* blaming her for cursing the stupid lake! That poor woman, she just wanted to put an end to it all, she thought she had no way out of her nightmare, no escape, no one to help her or believe her.'

Vivienne, alone of the three women stood in silent thought, lips pursing sideways. Josie watched the dimple in Vivienne's cheek disappear and resurface, disappear and resurface. 'What is it, Viv? What are you thinking?'

Vivienne shook her head. 'I'm not there yet, give me a bit. Something about all this isn't . . . right.'

'Everything about this is *wrong*,' Josie fired back. 'But we're going to make it right, this Friday night. We're giving Celeste back the dignity she deserved, and a happy ending to boot – our star-crossed lovers finally reunited on Eternity's shore.'

'That's part of what's bothering me. Why did Celeste not tell *Zach* what was happening here at Sylvan Mist, why did he not step in?'

Josie gave her a look. 'I don't want to spoil the play for you, Viv, but he is very much dead by intermission. Rudy got her while she was laid low with grief, *obviously*.'

'The only thing that seems obvious to *me*,' Vivienne said, 'is that we have to see Constable Jacobs as soon as possible – right now, in fact. All of this is crucial evidence.'

'Not until after the play.'

Vivienne was scandalised. 'I thought you were out to expose secrets, not cover more up. First you're asking your brothers to shoot a crocodile before anyone sees it, then you're madly hosing off cow gore so no one knows about it, and *now* you're going to stay quiet about a sexual assault operation run by an international celebrity?'

'*Crocodile?*' Laura repeated dazedly.

'Long story,' Josie said, patting Laura on the shoulder.

She raised her chin at Vivienne, bullishly. '*Nothing* will stand in the way of my play. Nothing! Tomorrow, we break the Curse, then *all* will be revealed.'

CHAPTER TWENTY-NINE

LOCKET

Vivienne was alone on the top floor, still wrestling with her fury. Hours after the darkroom horrors had been revealed, and Josie's cover-up strategy affirmed, her agitation and sense of powerlessness had not abated.

She'd been trying to soothe her anxiety with the task of removing Celeste, once and for all, from each picture frame around the lodge. Sylvan Mist should never again keep that beautiful woman interred!

She wanted the truth set free, too. Had Laura not been sticking so close to Josie all afternoon, Vivienne thought she might have held Josie to the point: *exactly* what are you playing at here?

She really had no right to question Josie's tactical concealment, when she herself had been raised to dissemble first, and reveal true feelings and motives only as a last resort. But Josie was the boldest, bravest woman Vivienne had ever met. There could never be any going back to ladylike quiet, to the hell of politesse, now that she knew there was a Josephine Monash speaking bravely in the world.

That was it! She must say that very thing to Josie. She charged downstairs, ready to make her case, and make it loudly.

In the library, Josie was bickering merrily with Laura on the precise folding of the show programs. Vivienne stood a moment, side-tracked by the female camaraderie, finding herself in a marvel at just how much this lodge and all its occupants had changed. Whatever happened after their show was finished, wherever Vivienne might end up next, she had known now the love of a sister, and the protection of a true friend.

She felt, welling up within her, a most uncharacteristic urge to initiate affection. Smilingly, she went towards her friend. Josie, becoming aware of Vivienne's presence, looked up with an abstracted grin; hand reaching, to tug her heart locket along its chain.

Heart locket.

Vivienne stopped on a dime, face paling, smile stalling; now falling away completely . . .

Heart. Locket.

Josie gave her an odd look. 'You all right?' Her hand had gone still on her gilded heart. Vivienne could not take her eyes off it.

'Oi,' Josie said, trying to catch Vivienne's eyes. 'What is it?'

Vivienne shook her head, pulse cantering away.

Laura was looking up now, a groove of consternation forming between her brows. Josie set aside her show program, beginning to stand. 'Viv, you look like you've seen a ghost. What's *wrong*? What have you got there?'

Vivienne gawped down at the pile of photographs in her hands, seeing it, at last seeing it . . .

Heart locket.

Her fingers opened. The photographs slipped to the library floor, sliding out.

Vivienne turned, and fled the lodge.

On Main Street, the roadster came to a jerking stop outside the Purple House. Vivienne slammed her car door closed, hurled open the garden gate, strode determinedly through the Orchid House.

'Mrs Frances!' she cried out, stomping over the tiny pond bridge.

Inside the formal lounge room, the sound of low radio murmuring could be heard. The *Blue Hills* radio serial, if she wasn't mistaken. Her own mother listened to it, religiously.

Fine then, she'd disturb the conniving old bat in the middle of her show!

She was almost through the lounge, when she spied the photograph of Maureen Monash on top of the pianola. She took the image in hand, staring hard.

Though she'd never seen Maureen's face, Vivienne would have known Josie's mother anywhere. They had identical open-mouthed laughs and kittenish faces. Maureen Monash's belly was high and full – and probably about the last place Josie Monash was ever inaudible.

There was Owen, too, just a small boy on Maureen's hip, beardless and sweet. Vivienne put a finger to his face. Though there was no suggestion of the broad-chested woodcutter here, his dark, placid eyes were just the same. A soft, endearing boy. Would his own sons be so handsome? In her mind's eye, a small dark-haired boy with a wryly quirked smile was running across the paddock, with arms outstretched for *her*.

She plonked the photograph back on the pianola, not bothering to wipe away her stroking fingerprints. Her very last question had been answered with this picture.

Further into the house she went, calling for Josie's grandmother. The radio was on in an elegant and finely furnished dining room, but there was no sign of Beryl Frances. How peculiar that Josie had willingly given up both the trappings of a well-off life – at least by small town standards – and the bull-headed devotion of her grandmother, for a life in that ramshackle farmhouse among the hills, and cows, and men. To think Josie had never moved back to live with her grandmother, though she might easily have used proximity to her theatre company as an excuse.

She turned on her heel. Beryl clearly wasn't here. But Vivienne had a fair idea where she might be. She went swiftly down Main Street, grappling with the anger she meant to discharge.

The welcome sign on Rita's Old Curiosity Shop door was turned to CLOSED. *At this hour? Hardly.*

She flung open the door, and marched inside. Animated female voices came from the rear of the shop; Beryl Frances's voice chief among them.

Ducking beneath hanging spools of vintage artefacts, Vivienne held herself to this vow: *Speak! Do not let them get away with this lie a single day longer.*

The group of women was seated in Rita's back room, beyond the red curtain partition. Beryl was visible, front and centre. Before she'd yet entered the rear section, Vivienne rushed to speak. Her stomach contracted against her own audacity. 'How *dare* you!'

Beryl's eyes flew to check beyond Vivienne.

'No, Josie's not with me, but you've been caught all the same!'

She stepped closer, taking in more faces: Rita Caracella, Elsie Reece and Peggy West. All her life, Barrington's motherless daughter, had looked to *these* women for supplementary female guidance and wisdom. She'd been betrayed by the lot of them.

'How *dare* you!' Vivienne said again – louder, beginning to feel exhilarated by the sheer novelty of having a ground, at last, to stand.

There was a deepening hush.

Vivienne set her wrath on Beryl. 'I know the truth! And I've figured out *your* part in it, Mrs Frances. But I had no idea you'd spun so many others into your manipulations. How could you send that courageous, talented woman off to write that story, all the while concealing your part in it? How could you *do* this to her?'

Beryl was making that awful clucking noise of hers. Vivienne despised the sound of it, which seemed to represent at this moment every scheming sin against her dearest friend.

'When were you finally going to tell her? When were you going to set her and this whole town free of your odious lie?'

'Not *her* lie, Vivienne.' A familiar male voice, from beyond the curtain.

Vivienne took another step, peering around.

Miles Henry, seated in this circle of traitors, with a notebook resting on his crossed knees. He did not even try and look guilty to have been caught here.

Shock came, like a noxious odour, making her eyes and throat burn. What had Miles to do with this? Had he known all along too, or was that nefarious old shrew just now entangling him in her plot?

Miles raised his hands against Vivienne's look of searing condemnation. 'I'm only two steps ahead of you figuring it out, Viv. I came to Mrs Frances in quite the same state as you.'

'Maybe you *did*—' Vivienne's voice broke. 'But now you're sitting in their midst!'

Beryl pushed to her feet, ramrod straight; imperious as Vivienne was indignant. 'Don't just stand there squalling. If you want to help Josephine too, then get in here, and shut the curtain.'

PART THREE

'Act well your part; there all the honour lies.'
Alexander Pope

CHAPTER THIRTY

A WALK IN MILES'S SHOES

On the morrow, *Nightingale Lake* would premiere. But right now, in Sylvan Mist, it was the dead of night and Josie Monash could find no rest.

Up and down the grand staircase she went in the fusty darkness, thumping her unlit torch from palm to palm, as her mind sprinted from one dead end to another.

Something is wrong with my play.

It was a familiar refrain for the eve of opening night: the terror that there was *something* most vital forgotten, or that the full dress rehearsal hadn't gone badly enough to ensure the play would. Opening night nerves were as predictable as closing night tears. Normally, she'd remind herself this flood of sweat from clammy palms and the suffocating corsetry of fear simply proved how much the theatre *mattered*.

But this time was different.

This time, she *knew* there was something wrong with her play. A catastrophe looming that would expose her for the amateur hack she was before all her family, all of Barrington, in front of Miles Henry, and Mr Hugo Bernard, too. It should have been elation with which she received Mr Bernard's last-minute acceptance to her opening night invitation, not *this* unbridled terror.

Several times now, Josie had stormed the stairs to the library, and her slumbering friends, ready to shake them both awake. Why should she suffer this dark night of the soul alone? Both those traitors had drifted off so easily, despite all Josie's efforts to keep them awake with talking, and the odd poke or two.

Vivienne's present indifference to Josie's insomnia was especially cruel on top of her absence all the long and busy afternoon. First Vivienne had bolted so dramatically from the library, then she'd slipped back into Sylvan Mist just before bedtime, without apology or explanation, strong in the face of Josie's interrogations. Vivienne had offered only Owen's name in defence of her truancy: 'We had to sort some things out together.'

Josie had narrowed her eyes suspiciously at *that*. It didn't ring true. Vivienne and Owen were past due for their dénouement – but Vivienne did not look like a one who'd been rolling ecstatically in the Monash hay shed all afternoon.

Josie growled, sleep's refusal to heel was *infuriating*.

When she couldn't sleep in girlhood – and truth be told, beyond girlhood – Josie would holler out from her bedroom until she heard Gabe's slow, dependable gait up the long hallway to the sleep-out, creaking each noisy floorboard in all the right places.

'I'm here, Chickadee,' he would say, and if the moon was falling brightly enough, she might make out his weary, but no less loving face.

'Did you call out for me?' she would ask – their familiar charade – and he'd give her exactly the lie she wanted: 'I did. Just needed to know you were here.'

It wasn't much for Josie to ask: not to be left behind by those entering another realm still closed to her, be it dreamland or the grave itself.

Josie's eyes filmed. She never would be so near her father again. At least, not in the way of an unmarried, spinster daughter. Now that she'd had a taste of life, with all its fears and freedoms, outside that crooked little farmhouse, she could never return to the spoiled queendom too long taken for granted. It didn't matter that Daph was still living there, or that she'd arrived in the first place. Well before the Monash party of five was intruded upon, it had been time for Josie to leave home. Even the tug of war between Grandy and Gabe had since ceased to matter, too.

The only pull now was from the world out beyond Barrington.

Josie climbed the stairs again, slowly now, weariness at last taking a slumping hold. There was no point staying awake to fret and stew. Whatever was wrong with her play, it was surely nothing that couldn't be remedied by courage, and creative prowess.

Tomorrow, the Curse would break, and Josie would be free.

Josie must have slept, for Vivienne was shaking her awake in a library bright with daylight. Heck, she'd *over*slept! Groggily, she stared up at Vivienne, trying to make out the words forming on her lips.

'—waiting at the door for you.'

Josie pushed up, wiping a line of drool, to scowl. 'What did the bastard leave this time?' What could be *worse* than a tongue? There might be one cut obscener . . .

Vivienne was drawing Josie's blanket away. Goosebumps sprang up along Josie's legs in the morning chill. Josie looked longingly back at her pillow. Somehow, now that this momentous day was finally here, she wished it . . . wasn't.

But Vivienne was even dragging her pillow away too. 'Quickly,' she said. 'He's downstairs.'

Josie scowled harder. 'I can't *believe* he'd show himself here today! I'm going to destroy him!'

Vivienne looked appalled. 'You did hear me say it's *Miles* at the door?'

'Obviously not,' Josie muttered, jumping to her feet, looking around for a hairbrush to tame her bird's nest.

'Here.' Vivienne handed over Josie's favourite dress. 'I ironed this for you.'

'But *you* hate ironing,' Josie said, taking the fuchsia dress. 'And you didn't use a pressing cloth, I'm going to re-iron this. Miles will have to wait.'

'No! He can't. Put it on.'

Reluctantly, Josie pulled the dress over her head, glowering at Vivienne.

Vivienne had produced a brush, and was hurriedly dragging it through Josie's fringe and the lengths falling softly over her shoulders. Hanging loose, Josie's hair only *invited* people not to take her seriously – she never wore it down. Vivienne was having none of Josie's objections; brusquely she pushed Josie towards the door.

Josie allowed herself to be propelled only so far as the staircase, before she rounded on her friend. 'What the hell, Viv? I hate surprises! I insist you tell me.'

Vivienne's dove-grey eyes were full of empathy, but the set of her face was unrelenting. The sonorous chiming of the grandfather clock curtailed any weakening of Vivienne's resolve. 'You really have to go, right now. They're . . . he's waiting.'

Miles was on the front step in his old farm boy clothes, with morning-soft countenance and mussed hair. Josie's cheeks were almost as pink as her dress as she was pushed unceremoniously onto the porch. Vivienne pulled the door shut behind Josie, and a second later, the lock was pulled.

Josie swung a scathing look upon the door. When she turned back to Miles, she found him grinning, eyes almost disappearing into their own downturn.

'I haven't had breakfast, much less a cuppa tea. If you're not here to report my theatre closed due to plague or fire – watch out.'

Miles removed a wax-paper wrapped parcel from under his arm. 'Breakfast for the lady.' Peeking out of the paper, were two golden croissants.

Josie's hand shot out. 'Please say they're your mum's.'

'She'd have my head if I brought you *anyone else's* pastries. Will you take a walk with me?'

'Wa walfh?' Josie said, around a mouthful of butter soft pastry. Miles was halfway down the stairs.

Fine, she'd walk with him so long as this heavenly croissant lasted, but at the rate she was scoffing . . .

Josie had expected Miles to lead her towards the lake – a path that had become increasingly well worn in recent weeks – but he seemed to be taking her towards the road instead. Good thing she had the croissant to keep her mouth busy, because Josie counted at least ten things she might have said, and quickly regretted. She cast a suspicious gaze at her fellow walker, enjoying his own croissant so heartily. Yes, Miles had planned this too well.

By the time they emerged into farmland steeped in swirling mist, Josie was licking her fingers clean, ready to dominate the conversation. Miles ushered her towards a gate in the Monash property line. 'This way. I want to show you something.'

'Be careful,' Josie said, as he reached for the fence. 'We've electrified it.'

Miles whipped his hand back sharply. Josie guffawed. 'You should see your face.'

Miles put his hand firmly on the fence, giving her a sardonic look. Josie went along quite happily now; this prank having remedied some of the imbalance.

Down the hill they went, kicking up dew. Josie was pleased Miles could match her pace, when so few people could.

'Do you remember this route?' Miles said, stopping mid-way.

'Sure. We took this exact way home off the milk bus together.' Josie was pleased as a teacher's pet with this answer. But Miles was looking around, apparently waiting for someone or something else to appear.

Josie followed his gaze, frowning. 'If I recall correctly,' she said, 'we used to get dive-bombed by nesting plovers here.'

Miles was suppressing a grin – she could tell from the mischievous sparkle in his eyes. 'Run,' he said, looking over her head. 'Now.'

Screeching, wheeling across the paddock behind Josie, came the first plover.

Josie tore away from Miles, hands over her head, racing for the creek line at hill's bottom. The first bird swooped low over her head, accurate as a bomber. Josie shrieked, picking up speed towards the creek, concealed by remnant rainforest. Miles came pounding down the hill after her, hollering – or was it laughing? Josie sensed the second bird diving in. She bent her head lower, screaming a curse – not sure if it was at Miles, or his dastardly birds.

Finally, she'd reached the shelter of trees. When Miles joined Josie under the canopy, she let spray with a volley of outrage.

Miles grinned. 'That's more like it.'

'*What?*' she demanded; once she had grip of her dignity once more.

'That's the Josie Monash I know.'

'Swearing like a farmer?' She smoothed her wind-tousled fringe back to centre.

'Your brothers don't swear.' No, they didn't either. Josie had always been the lippiest of the lot. 'I was referring to the girl who sacrificed me to the plovers most afternoons.'

Josie gave an outraged laugh. 'This is revenge is it?'

Miles stepped closer. 'No, this is a history lesson.'

Josie squared her shoulders. 'I beat you in History, too. There's not much you could teach *me*.'

Miles shrugged, moving on towards the creek, shimmering around its rocky course. 'You can remind me about this place, then.'

Josie followed Miles along the shallow creek, leaping from mossy rock to rock, stomach jolting when a rock proved too slippery. 'I imagine you're referring to our yabbying competitions.'

'Of which I won most.'

'That's fair. But as I recall, you declared yabbies were small fry, dreamed of catching a big red claw in Lake Evelyn one day.'

'Still do.' He looked at Josie under an arched brow. 'Do you remember the platypus that used to live just down there, around the bend?'

They were nearing a deeper curve in the watercourse, where rare blushwood fruit floated on a pool of shadowed indigo.

'Mr Beauman, you mean.'

'I believe it *your* idea to name that poor platypus after the headmaster.'

'Both Mr Beaumans were venomous, with a face like a duck.'

'And both of *us* shared the scandal, when some dolt at Barrington High exposed the joke.'

'Shared the cuts too. That sanctimonious prick caned us out of hurt pride.'

They were heading away from the creek now, and up the other side of the gully. Josie cast a quick look up under her fringe at Miles. He was sure of step, with a man's broad bone structure and bristled chin. But if she squinted, like this, his dark-lashed eyes were every bit the same; and full of boyish charm.

Josie was beginning to understand. Wherever this walk would end up, they must first tour the highlights of their growing up together.

But *why*?

She had no more time to indulge romantic sensibilities – for now, they had reached the Battlefield. So named, for the line of cannonball trees planted along the lane to McGinty's farm. Clustered up the trunk of these trees grew large, woody shelled fruit shaped like cannonballs. In the years after the war, many a battle had been re-enacted here by farm kids.

Miles turned to Josie now with a hand held to his forehead, and a look that needed to explanation.

'I'm sorry!' she cried. 'I *said* I was sorry a thousand times that day. I even came around to your house with a handwritten letter of apology.'

'"Dear Miles",' he intoned. '"Next time, duck."'

Josie stood, arms akimbo. 'As punishment, I had to cover Owen's chores for a solid week! I resented you for making such a big deal out of it.'

'I was concussed by Strong Arm Josie. Your brothers carried me home by my hands and ankles.'

'And I *cried* all the way home by myself! I thought I'd killed you, I couldn't bear it! I always thought I'd end up one day marr—' Josie forced a cough.

'You'd end up *what*?' Miles asked seriously, hand coming away from his old wound.

'Making a *martyr* of you,' she answered, with an insouciant toss of head.

'OK,' Miles said, lightly. 'Shall we continue then?' He walked ahead, waving her on. Josie followed after, lobbing a scowl at the back of his head.

Scoundrel.

They were heading, in a roundabout way, back to Lake Evelyn. Was *this* all their walk through the annals of childhood rivalry was meant to achieve – a reminder of Josie's brazen, tomboy ways; a past impossible to rewrite?

Smarting, Josie quickened her pace to come alongside Miles. 'Did you bring me out here to show me, before the biggest moment of my life, that I'll still always be the smart-mouthed Monash girl from over the hill?'

Miles stopped. 'Is that what you think this is, Josie?' No longer did he look roguish. In his hazel eyes there was a quiet plea for patience. The hardest virtue of all. But she would *try* . . .

'You're losing your audience,' she snapped. 'Get to it.'

Miles squeezed out a half-smile. She'd seen Miles carry that expression before both exams and musicals. So, he was nervous.

Companionably, they went on towards the jungle-enclosed lake. Josie's forehead pinched and leapt, trying to contain her own mounting nerves. She was terrified and delighted, but didn't know which was most excruciating.

Miles was leading her through an overgrown pathway to the lake, which could be glimpsed, glowing turquoise, through the jungle. Giant, dew-wet elephant ears slapped at their limbs and faces as they pushed in.

They were on the opposite side of the amphitheatre and lodge here. A place Josie hadn't visited once since the Curse had . . . emerged. In fact, Josie barely remembered coming to this side of the lake at all.

'In here,' Miles said, with the confidence of long familiarity. They were threading through trees close together, with no track distinguishable. At the bottom of a muddy slope to lake's edge, they came to a colossal tree overtaken by a strangler fig. The thriving fig had sent roots down into the water and long branches spreading out. The result was a secret cavern, festooned in staghorn ferns and hanging vine, all aglitter

AVERIL KENNY

with dappled light and sun-sparkled water lapping quietly in. Beyond the hollow, a haze of sunshine.

Josie walked around this wonder; eyes wide. 'So, *this* is your secret lair.'

Miles smiled, but his nerves were now plain to see. 'Discovered this place when I was nine. Came here all the time, when I couldn't round up any Monash kids to play with. I named it the Boathouse.'

'The Boathouse,' Josie repeated approvingly. 'Did you *have* a boat?'

'A little dory. I was too scared to take it right out on the lake, in case some tatterdemalion wraith clambered out of the water into my boat with me.'

'I don't see what *you* were frightened of. She was only after us girls.'

'I was mostly frightened of my mother, if she ever found out.' Miles tipped his head. 'You said "was" – past tense. Does that mean . . .'

'You don't have to rub it in' Josie tossed her ponytail. 'I'm embarrassed I believed in it so long.'

Miles did not grin as she'd expected him to. 'It's not your fault you were fed a pack of . . .' he paused '. . . a very convincing legend.'

'An overactive imagination made me more susceptible to it than most.'

'To be fair,' Miles replied, 'we theatre folk are notoriously superstitious.'

'Because we work in another realm, inhabited by whimsy.'

'Perhaps. But you and I *both* know we saw a thylacine that day.'

'I've come to think it was probably just a quoll.'

'I trust *my* eyes.'

I trust your eyes too.

The spirit of camaraderie had dissipated. There was an unrelenting seriousness to Miles, a sense of something scripted, and unstoppable.

Josie levelled her gaze on Miles. 'What's all this about? You take me away from my show preparations mere hours before my big debut for a walk down memory farm-lane, and our every childhood superstition. What's the point?'

Her hand seized on her locket; she ran the gold heart up and down, waiting for her answer. Miles's eyes were on the necklace however, and something like hurt – no, pain – knitted his brows together. Pain for who? *Her?*

Her mind had dashed away to find a new theory, she proffered it somewhat foolishly: 'Vivienne wanted me out of the lodge, and Laura wanted me away from the theatre – and your job is to keep me occupied. Why are my lead stars and stage manager conspiring against me?'

'To help you finish what you've started, to expose the Curse . . . for what it really is.'

Josie crossed her arms. 'Tell me everything, or take me back to my theatre.'

'Josie, I haven't been entirely honest with you.'

'Evidently,' she replied, rolling every syllable out.

'I'm not referring to just – today.'

'Oh, so there's a whole *pattern* of dishonesty now.'

He gave her a brow-furrowing look of supressed amusement. 'You're not going to make this easy for me, then.'

'Why should I?'

Miles was peering up into the Boathouse roof. Josie followed his eyes. What now?

He looked back at her, the roguish glint returned to his eyes. 'My role was only to keep you busy—'

'You mean babysit me while the coup is on.'

A conceding chuckle. 'But I've brought you *here*, for reasons of my own.'

Josie was in all kinds of knots – irritation, trepidation, frustration – and now the morass had grown to include a breathless hope she thought herself far too old for.

'Will you come up the tree with me? I'd like to show you something.'

'Up there?' Josie indicated her best dress. 'In this?'

'A dress never stopped you before.'

'Didn't care about you seeing my unmentionables then.'

'But you care about me seeing them now.' Only his lips twitched.

Josie tousled her fringe, insouciant. 'You go up first – and stay above me.'

'I won't look.' Miles waded, thigh deep, into the water, to a lower bough. 'Start climbing on this one.' He pulled himself up onto the giant bough. It didn't even move under his weight.

'Nobody said anything about going in the lake,' she called after him.

He grinned. 'Thought you didn't believe in cursed waters anymore?'

Josie glared, wading in.

Carefully, she copied his path, from bough to bough, letting him stay one above her. 'We're not *actually* meant to break our legs today,' she huffed.

Miles had come to a seated position now, surrounded by staghorn ferns; waiting for her, but taking care not to watch her.

Josie plopped down beside him. 'Out with it, then.' But her eyes were taken from Miles's face to the view beyond. Lake Evelyn was a vivid, glimmering emerald. 'Oh, she's too beautiful for this stinking curse.'

'She is,' he agreed.

Her eyes flicked back, to find Miles's gaze set sincerely upon her.

'Josie, I haven't been entirely honest with you.' Again, Josie read the painstaking rehearsal behind this line. Her belly flip-flopped.

'About?'

'When I first wrote you, it wasn't only because I wanted to congratulate you on earning the wrath of Mr Bernard. I had desired *any* excuse to write you, for some time.'

She'd intuited as much, hadn't she? Then called it wishful thinking.

'And when you wrote of your play and plans for reopening the Obsidian, I was *desperate* to be part of it. I'd have volunteered for any role in Josie's Monash's debut, would've felt privileged just to be in your fly crew.'

Josie mocked up indignation. 'Yet you let me think that you were doing *me* a favour in *my* desperate need!'

'Have I though?' His tone was earnest.

No, he had not. On the contrary, Miles had come the very instant she insinuated he might audition, and he'd never mentioned any cost or inconvenience to himself.

'Why,' Josie rushed to ask, 'were you so desperate to be involved in my play?' The last conjecture to nullify. 'Because you knew it was going to be so controversial? That would be the Miles Henry I knew. Wherever mischief was to be found, there you were.'

'No.' His eyes and voice both took on velvety warmth. 'Wherever *Josie* was to be found, there I was.'

'What are you saying?'

Miles lifted her hand from where it anchored her to the bough, and placed it several inches further along the branch. Josie's eyes did not leave his.

'I'm saying the same thing I've been scratching into trees since I was thirteen.'

Miles gently parted her fingers, took her index finger and pressed it into the wood. Beneath her flesh lay the scar of carved letters. Miles led her finger along each letter, his eyes staying on hers.

She mouthed the words as they were spelled out . . .

Miles Henry
loves
Josephine Monash

Josie's breath ran short, felt like it might run out entirely. Her eyes filled.

'*Nobody*,' he said, 'has a laugh like yours, Josie Monash.'

'You like my *laugh*?' Josie thought the next snorting sound she made might convince him otherwise.

Through a blur, she watched Miles take up her hand and press it to his heart 'I love the woman who puts such vivacity into the world.'

She couldn't seem to take it in. 'But . . . all through school you never treated me as anything more than a theatre club rival . . . you moved away without giving me any sign.'

'Because you scared the *dickens* out of me. No boy was good enough for you. Your many large brothers indicated as much, and you out and out declared it. I knew I'd only have one chance to try out for your heart, and I was petrified to blow it. It's been the worst kind of stage fright I've ever known.'

'I don't believe you.'

'Didn't you read what I wrote in your autograph book?'

Read it? Memorised it! '"*I'll look for you upstage, Daydreaming Milkmaid.*" I thought it an infuriating taunt: you hogging centre stage, and me left behind. But then I was so taken by the idea you'd look for me at all . . .'

There was such warmth and admiration in his eyes. 'I was saying: I'd turn away from *any* audience for you.'

Of all the promises he might have made her, he chose this.

340

Miles pulled her arm firmer against his body. Josie went after her lost limb.

So many years she'd tormented this boy, and herself over him, but she'd never been so close as this. She could make out the capillaries in his eyes, fine stubble on his philtrum. Her eyes went from his eyes to lips, and back again; quite unable to breathe through the wanting of his kiss. She found she did not very much like romantic suspense, after all . . .

'There's only one girl who's ever knocked me out,' Miles said, his lips hovering stubbornly above hers.

'If you don't kiss me right now,' Josie said, between her teeth, 'I'll knock you *out* of this tree.'

Miles was unrelenting. 'First, she clocked me with her notorious strong arm. Then she wiped me out with her wit and pluck and unbeatable talent. Most recently, she stunned me with glimpses of her pink undergarments.'

'You're incorrigible.'

Josie took her hand from his, and pulled his face to hers.

CHAPTER THIRTY-ONE
ELEVENTH HOUR

Vivienne and Owen were waiting on Sylvan Mist's front steps, eyes trained on the forest path opening through which Miles and Josie were due to re-emerge at any moment. Around them, the forest was preternaturally hushed; not even cicada song transgressing on this expectant lull. Miles was keeping Josie out far longer than he'd been instructed, and Vivienne was giddy with anticipation on her friend's behalf.

Not *all* the giddiness was for Josie's sake, though. Sitting so close to Owen, with only their elbows touching, was a dizzying strain upon her nerves. But while she was acutely, miserably aware of each elbow brush-by, Owen seemed all placidity and calm indifference.

It wasn't fair.

Vivienne had rejected *Owen*, intimated his means were beneath her, wounded *him* – yet she was the one supressing long-suffering sighs.

Owen tipped back his head to regard the canopy, which lay still and heavy over them. 'I don't know how I'm going to break it to Josie—'

'You're not supposed to break *anything* to her! Your role is only to escort her over to him.'

Owen smiled. 'I meant, break it to Josie about the weather.'

She looked around the clearing. Every sunray piercing through seemed cranked to maximum. It was the hottest she'd felt since arriving on the mountain. 'What's wrong with this glorious day?'

'We're in for a humdinger of a storm tonight. And I don't mean your soon to be thunderous director.'

'There's only one kind of hailing Josie will permit this evening.'

At Owen's hearty laugh, she indulged an inward smile, allowing her elbow to fall against his again. 'Once she's here, you'll need to move quickly. Laura wants her back down at the lodge by one o'clock to go through the changes.'

Owen's elbow nudged hers back. 'And if Josie calls the whole play off?'

'What, miss her chance to blow this whole story open for critical acclaim? I put more stock in your sister's ego than that.'

'Imagine the size of her head after tonight. She'll be impossible to live with.'

'After *Nightingale*'s success, neither of us will be living with her.'

Owen turned to her and for the first time in weeks she caught a glimpse of raw feeling behind the stoic ease. 'Where will *you* be living?'

She shrugged, her elbow drawing away from his. 'This has been a nice interlude, but it's time to confront my own future. Josie has her brilliant destiny to pursue off this mountain. Laura is planning to take on the Barrington Theatre Company, after Josie leaves. Tonight's the start of many wonderful things . . .'

Owen nursed his knuckles solemnly. 'And the end, too.'

It was certainly the end of this moment together. Josie was flying up the path, with Miles two steps behind. Vivienne and Owen stood together.

'How nice of you finally to resurface,' Vivienne said.

'Apologies,' Miles said, eyes twinkling. 'We took the scenic route.'

The scenic route had apparently left both Josie and Miles with inflamed lips.

Josie stopped abruptly at the sight of Owen. 'Oh, not *you* too.'

'Me too,' Owen said, going forward to meet his sister. 'Come on, Josie-Posie. There's someone you need to see.'

Miles joined Vivienne on the step, as Owen and Josie went up the drive together – their contrasting height and stature making them an odd pair as they disappeared into deeper shadows.

She looked to Miles. 'What did she say?'

Miles had not stopped looking after Josie, though she had truly gone from sight. 'She threatened to knock me out of my tree, unless I kissed her.'

Vivienne glowed. 'That sounds like a line only our Josie could write.'

Miles finally looked away from the path, brow troubled. 'I wish I could go with her for the revelation.'

But Vivienne knew: some conversations must be faced alone.

CHAPTER THIRTY-TWO

PERIPETIA

Owen walked Josie to the Monash property. Josie went in uncharacteristic silence. She did not even open her mouth to curse the thunderheads billowing up over the far distant ranges. Josie trusted: whatever lay ahead, her sagacious big brother thought it as necessary to face as her best friend did.

Still; she could not help the sense of heart-sickened betrayal.

At the top of the dairy hillcrest, Owen halted and turned to her. Josie knew then exactly who waited for her at the bottom of the hill. She swallowed compulsively, gripping Owen's arm. 'Do I *have* to talk to him?'

Owen drew her against his side. 'You have to know the whole truth, Josie. I told you, months back, I thought all this was somehow about you. You're meant to set things right. *You* are.'

Gabriel Monash, tall and dignified, was waiting under the shade of melaleuca trees, at the Hiding Billabong.

'Chickadee,' he said as she drew near.

'Don't call me that. It's a baby name, and I'm a grown woman.'

Gabe motioned to a boulder opposite his. 'Will you sit with me?'

She did not. 'You had something to do with it, didn't you?'

He tipped his head patiently, with that old invitation: *go on*.

'With Celeste. You had something to do with her death, didn't you? You've been letting me humiliate myself, making lies pretty to impress some idiot critic. But all the while, *you've* been keeping the truth from me! You had a hand in her death. And Grandy knows it, doesn't she? That's what the great big dirty secret hanging over our heads has been this last fourteen years. You're a *murderer*, and Grandy knows it!' Josie came up gasping for air.

Was she really saying these things to the man she loved and trusted more than any other?

Gabe sighed – a great tsunami of outbreath. 'Is that what you believe?'

'I gathered all the clues these last months, and pieced my evidence together in *front* of you. I wrote the play in plain sight. I showed you how much *Nightingale Lake* meant to me, what it would cost me to be made a fool. I gave you and Grandy that ultimatum *together* . . . and after all that, still you refused to step up and set things right.'

'Oh, Josephine—'

Sorrow wrenched across her brow, like a pull through stockings. 'Why didn't you stop me?'

'I've been a coward too many years, afraid so long to lose you and your brothers; I didn't know *how* to tell the truth.'

'You, who modelled integrity to me my whole life.'

'I enabled a lie, let the whole town carry it on, and made you all to live in it. A lie that might have cost innocent lives. On that count, I might as *well* be, as you say, a murderer.'

Enough.

Josie sat on the boulder opposite Gabe. She gripped her gold heart locket in both hands and yanked, hard. The chain, worn and weakened from years of friction, snapped like a thread. She held the broken necklace up, fist tight around the chain.

'Tell me why you kept a drowned woman's necklace on your bedside table for fourteen years.'

Gabe reached to take the locket, cradling the ornate gold heart in his palm.

'I *know* it's Celeste's locket,' Josie said. 'I've seen it now, in her photographs at Sylvan Mist – so don't you dare tell me one more time it's my *mother's* locket.'

'I never claimed it was your mother's locket.'

Josie opened her mouth to dispute this, before biting closed. No, he hadn't. It had simply lain on his bedside table all these years – and Josie had done the claiming.

Anger swept up her chest again. 'You never corrected my thinking it was hers!'

'I wasn't supposed to know you wore it. That was your secret. You had it back on my dresser before I returned from the milking each evening.'

'You knew I cherished it as a connection to my mother, and my few memories of her. *Why* did you let me wear the dead actress's necklace?'

At this, Gabe winced.

'Tell me the truth, or watch me walk away forever.'

The handsome planes of his face seemed to spasm, sag, and then regather. 'I failed your mother's last request. On her deathbed, she *knew* you were too young to ever remember her. She made me swear: *don't let her forget me.*'

'Don't talk about my mother, get to Celeste!'

'The story starts with you, Josephine. If you want the truth, you must have it in full.'

Josie's nails drove hard into her palms.

Gabe leaned forward, steepling his fingers. 'Your mother fell ill before you were even born. Maureen was determined to hold it in check long enough to deliver you safely. But after that, she could hold it back no longer. By the time you were two years old, Maureen was so ravaged, they were talking weeks left, not months. She slipped away – I won't say quietly, *or* obediently – in her own bed, before another fortnight was gone.'

Josie pulsed with pain. It had been many years since last she heard this tale; perhaps not since girlhood.

'After Maureen passed, I did the best I could. But with four young children and a farm to run, my best wasn't good enough. That's where *they* stepped in.'

'*Who?*'

'All of them – every person in Barrington, it felt. Under your grandmother's direction, they had a whole production line running on our account. Meals delivered morning, noon and night, washing and cleaning done for us, volunteer mothers to care for you while I worked.

'Everyone loved Maureen Monash, and in her stead, Barrington adopted you as their own orphaned babe. Elsie Reece came just to soak your nappies. Rita Caracella brought you funny old toys and books – and stayed to read to you. Athol Harford would take you and the boys out for drives on his bus. I couldn't ever seem to get Rosa Henry out of my kitchen – though Rosa had her own wee boy, tagging along.'

Tears stung to imagine Grandy commanding her legion of volunteers, and a tiny Miles Henry trailing her around the farmhouse. To think how many people in this town had watched over her life without her ever knowing it.

'Then the war came, and life changed drastically for us on the Tablelands. They were hard years. So many families struggling, or separated. Too much need, everywhere. And there I was, busy producing milk to feed an army. I tried to manage for you children as best I could on my own. If things had been different, if not for my children, and the farm being so essential, I'd have gone to fight . . .'

Josie dismissed this impatiently. She'd never condoned her father's sense of inadequacy for being spared enlistment.

But today, Gabe was pressing harder. 'You see, if I'd been off in Europe or New Guinea somewhere, I wouldn't have been here when Rudy Meyer opened that theatre. And I would never have gotten involved.'

'Involved in *what*?'

Gabe's eyes closed for a moment's reprieve. 'You were a terrible sleeper, Josephine, right from birth. Cried half the night, like you never wanted to let go of the day. It was unfair on Maureen. She couldn't walk the hall with you, when she was so poorly, and it was a terrible thing for her to listen to you. So, I would walk you round the farm, in my arms – for hours on end.

'I walked you every night until Maureen died, and . . . after, I kept on walking with you. Up the hillcrest, past the dairy, over the paddocks, along the lake road, down to the very shoreline. We'd sway together, watching the lights of the amphitheatre, listening to those raucous Sylvan Mist parties, sometimes we'd spot the crocodile.'

'The *what*?'

'The freshwater crocodile that's been in Lake Evelyn for years. The same one you've seen.'

As if she would be made to feel guilty *now*, for inveracity.

'We might have walked the lake this way years more, but then Beryl came and took you all away to live with her.'

This part of the story Josie knew all too well; those thin justifications for removal. Josie pictured the four of them in the back of Beryl's car, with faces pressed to the back window; their father a small figure, left behind.

Gabe's head dipped low; he gripped his temples. 'Without you all, I had nothing but milking and misery. I worked all day, and walked all night. The missing weight of your tiny body was unbearable. I walked around Lake Evelyn every night, as lights of the Obsidian danced across the lake.'

Josie's throat had gone bone dry. She could sense the revelation coming now, saw it forming, wanted to be led, every step of the way to meet it.

'Then, one night, as I was heading home again at the end of my lake circuit, I came upon a lady in the lake.'

'The lady *of* the lake,' Josie corrected.

'She wasn't *of* the lake then. She was late of Adelaide, in fact; come to the Tablelands to perform at Rudy Meyer's amphitheatre. A beautiful actress, much talked of in town, frequently photographed in the paper, and a favourite pin-up girl for the soldiers. But that evening, she was most certainly *in* the lake – struggling amongst the bulrushes. You would recognise what she wore from your own costume direction . . .'

Josie's whisper was trance-like. 'Her hand-woven suit of stones and lawyer vine.'

Gabe had gone very still, seeming to stare right through Josie, to that evening, long ago.

Josie's voice was a tremulous thread. '*Tell me* you didn't stand there and watch her drown herself.'

Gabe's eyes snapped back to hers, and this present hour. 'I wrestled her from the reeds, dragged her back to shore, and lay there on the ground holding her as she beat her fists against me with a desolate fury that would never be quite spent enough.'

He saved *her?*

Gabe bowed his head, wouldn't look at her. 'When she was all wrung out of tears, weak and floppy as a rag doll, then I picked her up, and carried her home.'

Josie squinted at her father, straining to see the truth in this. 'Why would you do *that*?'

'I had no choice. She swore she'd throw herself back in there the moment I left. I told her I would sit with her all night – I had as little use for sleep as she. But she was adamant she would go into that lake. If not that night, the next. What else *could* I do?'

'Walk her back to the lodge. Tell one of her friends, or Rudy Meyer himself! She was their responsibility to care for, not yours.'

Gabe made a barking sound of disagreement. 'She was never going back to that lodge. Not ever. To her mind, there was only one way to escape the horrors of Sylvan Mist.'

But Josie already knew some of this, didn't she?

'She consented to come with me back to the farmhouse only after my-hand-on-heart promise I would never say she'd been there, and never stop her from leaving again.'

'Celeste Starr was in *my* house?'

'She was in *your* bedroom. She collapsed from exhaustion, not long after I brought her in. I fed her a warm tea and put her in your empty room. Then I sat at the kitchen table and tried to wrap my head around what to do next.

'I rose, unslept, and did the milking – and as I came back from the dairy, I told myself: she'll be gone again. Like an apparition. But there she was, sitting at the dining table, in your mother's chair, waiting for me. I made her breakfast, she ate it without speaking, then went back to sleep for the day. I made her dinner, she ate it without speaking, and went back to sleep. I thought she'd slip out during the second night, as she'd sworn to do. But there she was again the next morning, at the table, in your mother's place.'

There was a concrete block in Josie's throat.

The hidden watercourse running beneath the surface of her life; divined.

'By this time, news had broken in town of her disappearance. We were somewhat secluded from it, initially. It was only when old Charlie came by with the milk truck that I heard she was listed as missing from Sylvan Mist, presumed drowned.'

'*Presumed* drowned? But she'd already left the note, *telling* them she was going to do it.'

'No.' A heavy sigh. 'I slipped back and planted the note a few days later, to make sure they – *he* – believed she was dead. Buying her some time. I was worried they'd bring in the Aboriginal tracker they often used to find soldiers lost during jungle training. She'd have been quickly found.'

'You helped Celeste Starr *fake* her own death?'

'Yes.'

'*Why?*'

'After hearing what he did to her, and seeing how traumatised she was, I would have helped her write *any* note to be free of him.'

'So, you took some lines of poetry from your copy of Wilde, and faked a suicide letter.' Josie gave him a hard glare. 'And you can stop being vague about what he did. I've seen the photographs for myself. He was dehumanising her.'

Gabe shook his head in slow wonder. 'I've raised a sleuth.'

'The natural consequence of having secrets hidden from me my whole life. It makes one suspicious of everything.'

Gabe was unabashed. 'It wasn't *my* secret to tell, Josephine. I would never have put her in any danger by sharing it. I'd given her my word *never* to betray her secret, or location.'

'Because he'd come after her?'

'He'd sworn he would never give her up. And she believed she'd never escape her shame and self-loathing. The existence of those photographs, his threats of exposure, it was a hellish torment to her. He vowed: if she ever left him, he'd *finish* her . . .'

'But how long did you possibly think you could keep her hidden?'

'We didn't think that far ahead, at least not in the beginning. I just wanted to keep her hidden from harm. While ever they were waiting for a corpse to come bobbing up, she was safe to stay with me. There was no rush for her to move on. I was all alone. Beryl was still keeping you children away from me, and I was desperately lonely.'

'Didn't we come and visit you?'

Pain crossed his face like a cloud shadow. 'Rarely. Beryl would let you come back with me after Sunday services. The only time I had alone with my own children, then she'd be back, in short order, to collect you all.'

'Where was Celeste when we came to visit?'

'She would wait in the old Monash cottage, until you'd gone. She didn't want to intrude.'

Josie slapped a hand on her thigh. "The wraith the boys saw! The one they've talked about for years. That was *Celeste*?'

'She didn't mean to frighten the boys. Celeste never wanted to harm or hurt a soul.'

It was the first time he'd said her name aloud. There was an odd tenderness on it that made her heart hurt. Josie was not yet ready to touch this. 'And so, everyone in Barrington just believed she'd killed herself?'

'You're asking *me*, Madam Playwright?'

Josie had been gnawing at the inside of her cheek, becoming aware of a painful lump. 'I'm asking if *he* believed it, if the police believed it.'

'Investigations were properly done. Her fellow actresses all testified to her bleak mental state, her drinking. There was the note found, in her own handwriting, and the suit which later resurfaced, in part. The range road gatekeepers were questioned, and being wartime there were roadblocks, checking travellers' passes. There was no evidence she'd gone down the mountain. She ceased to exist.

'Without her, there was no Nightingale of Lake Evelyn, no enthusiasm for the shows. Rudy closed the amphitheatre not long after she disappeared, and the lodge shortly thereafter.'

'You were hiding Celeste, while they were closing theatres because of her?'

'If playing dead might save her life, and if it wasn't hurting anyone else – why shouldn't I?'

Josie served her father a censorious look. 'Six lives have been lost because of Celeste's playing-dead game.'

Gabe didn't flinch. 'It was no game, and she should bear no blame.'

Josie would have to be crueller, then. 'What about you, who planted the note and hid her while they were scouring the lake and forest, then kept a lie going for fourteen years. You started the Curse of Lake Evelyn.'

He bowed his head again. 'And now you sound like Beryl.'

This was the deep, dark divide at the heart of their family: Celeste.

'*Grandy* guessed she hadn't killed herself.'

'Beryl guessed nothing. She believed the actress had drowned, along with everyone else in Barrington. And whatever Beryl claims now, she'd never have doubted the official story, if she hadn't come nosing around here one day, and walked in on us . . .'

'I'm surprised you couldn't convert Grandy to Celeste's defence. She would never throw another woman to the wolves. Could she not understand why you were providing sanctuary for Celeste?'

Gabe scratched the back of his head, colouring. 'Beryl came upon us here . . . living like man and wife. Celeste had moved out of your bedroom, and into mine.'

Josie blinked away the mental image, face carefully blank.

'After that discovery, Beryl didn't give two hoots why Celeste had faked her death.' Josie marked again the tenderness on Celeste's name – protectiveness too. It was a betrayal of her mother, this she understood, but there was something that made instinctive sense about *her* handsome, dignified father finding love again with the beautiful and tragic Celeste Starr. Josie wondered at how none of them had thought of it before.

'So,' Josie recapped, 'Grandy came out here and found another woman living, *loving* in her daughter's place, while *she* was taking care of the children. Not just any woman, but the one who first scandalised Barrington with her skimpy showgirl outfits, and then plunged the whole town into tragedy with her faked drowning.' Even rushed and raw as this summary was, Josie knew it was far more salacious a story than the one she had actually written . . .

Damn.

'That's how Beryl saw it, yes. She demanded I give Celeste in to the authorities, or she'd do it for me. You have to understand how hurt Beryl was. She claimed I'd been carrying on with Celeste while your mother was still sick. Wouldn't believe we'd been drawn together as a natural consequence of trauma and loneliness shared.'

'Grandy *contributed* to your loneliness, by keeping us children from you.'

'In my defence, I said things similar. And then *Beryl* said I would have you children back again over her dead body.'

'But she *did* give us back. What happened?'

Gabe's smile was achingly sad. '*You*, Josephine. You begged Beryl to go home. After she'd discovered Celeste and I, Beryl stopped bringing

355

you children out on Sundays, and it was breaking your heart. You kept telling her: *Papa needs me.*'

Josie would not cry, she would *not*!

'You were so young, so homesick. Beryl might have despised me, but she would have given her own life for *you*, Josephine.'

Yes, Josie had always known this.

'Unable to bear your heartache and pleading, Beryl agreed for me to have you back for a little while. Just you, and on one condition—'

'Celeste.'

'She was not to have a thing to do with you. Not to see you, talk to you, or be in the same house as you. I agreed. I wanted you back, Chickadee. I needed my little girl.'

'So, what, I came home, and Celeste left?'

'No. I lied to your grandmother. Celeste stayed on with me. And for a few weeks, it was just the three of us . . .'

'I *remember* her.' The words were out before the realisation was even fully won. 'I remember Celeste!' Josie's mind was spinning like a windmill under cyclonic gale. 'She played games with me, and taught me funny dances! She had an airy sort of laugh, and this funny, sprightly way of walking on the balls of her feet. She sang to me. That's right – she would sing to me, and it was so beautiful. But, why haven't I remembered her before now?'

Gabe's eyes were beseeching. 'You've always remembered Celeste. When you were younger, you talked about her all the time to your brothers.'

'No, I've only ever talked about . . .'

'Maureen,' Gabe answered, in the same instant Josie said: '*My mother.*'

Father and daughter stared at each other. Grief seemed to draw his face towards the ground. Incredulity contorted hers. 'My memories of my mother – they're really Celeste Starr?'

356

Gabe reached for her hand. Josie snapped it out of his reach, swallowing at a painful lump.

'You were far too young to ever remember anything of Maureen, or having a mother at all. And you were still too young to understand properly *who* Celeste was, or why she had appeared.'

'But I was hungry enough for a mother's love to pretend Celeste was my own for a while.'

'You've always had such a gift for make-believe. You met Celeste, and decided there and then she was yours. I hope you can forgive me; for letting a motherless girl have something so precious.'

It was Josie now who reached across the divide, taking his hand. 'You hoped she might *become* my mother.'

Gabe bent his head to stare at her small hand gripping his sun-coarsened one. 'She might have never left us – if Beryl had *allowed* her to stay. Maybe I could have hidden her here with us forever.'

'You couldn't have. You would have been found out eventually. She was too recognisable.'

'And Beryl knew it, even when I wouldn't admit it to myself. Sometimes, I think she gave Celeste and I those precious few weeks as a gift, before the inevitable.'

That didn't sound like a benevolence Grandy would entertain, but if it helped, let him think it.

'When our time was up, Beryl came out to the farm, and gave me an ultimatum.'

'Your children – or Celeste.'

'She said I could live on with Celeste, but she would report us. Or, I could send Celeste safely away, and have all my children back.'

'You couldn't have left the Tablelands with us kids, and started a new life with Celeste?'

'Beryl wasn't going to lose you kids like that. And I couldn't leave my farm. The only life I've ever known, or wanted.'

'Why did you not go to the sergeant and confess about the faked death – tell him all about the photographs, and the things he made her do?'

'Nothing on earth would have moved Celeste on that count. As far as she was concerned, Celeste Starr *had* died in that lake – and no one was bringing her back. No matter how much she loved me, she was more frightened of him.'

'Oh, *Papa.*'

He was weeping now, openly. 'You were my *children*. I couldn't live without you. Maureen might have forgiven me for finding love again, but she would never have forgiven me for robbing my children of their father, *or* grandmother.

'In the end, it was Celeste who decided it. She understood what it would cost me to choose her over my children. So, finally, when Beryl came over here again, harassing me to make a decision, Celeste stood up and . . .' He choked off.

Josie's vision went unfocused, seeing her bedroom wall, the image she had looked upon every night before sleep. She finished the story for her father . . .

'Celeste said it was time for her to leave, without further delay. You knew you had no right to hold on to her, so you *let* her go. Knowing Grandy, I imagine she must have come prepared that day with funds and a whole escape plan for Celeste, to make *sure* there would be no turning back.

'You followed Celeste down to our front gate to say goodbye, but no further. She stood there, for one last moment, turned towards the distant hills; a future unknown. She looked so vulnerable standing there, her whole body stooped with sorrow and regret, but this time, you didn't step in to stop her—' Josie considered her father in pale wonder. 'I'm not making this up, am I? I really do remember her . . . this. Where *was* I?'

'Just a little way off. Beryl was with you, holding your hand.'

'Holding me back, more like. Grandy took that photo too, didn't she? Probably gave it to you sometime later, in a victor's magnanimous gesture.'

'No, she gave the photo to *you*.' Tears coursed down Gabe's face. 'Don't you see? Beryl and I both let you keep what little remained of Celeste, for yourself.'

Josie reached to wipe his cheeks. 'You got us kids, but lost love. You've grieved double. Protected Celeste's secret, gave her freedom, yet sustained a lie ever after.'

'And then,' Gabe sighed, 'the girls of Barrington started drowning in Celeste's stead.'

In her compassion for her father, Josie had forgotten the second act of this tragic story. The copycats, coincidences, poor swimmers, and pure bad luck which, together, had contrived to make a curse.

The Curse she had set out to break this very evening . . .

'Oh my God – my play!' Josie shot up from her rock, panting with panic. 'My whole play is a *lie*. I can't present this steaming cowpat to my audience – to Hugo Bernard!'

And why must her father just *sit* there, unperturbed? Had he considered for a moment the impossibility of these last-minute revelations? 'It's too late, my play is ruined!'

'I've taken too long, but it isn't too late,' her father said.

'I can't force Miles and Viv, two people I love so much, to stand up there and portray something so untruthful. The Zach–Celeste, died-for-love tragedy is absolute nonsense.'

'The Zach–Celeste element might not be the entire story, but it's the one Celeste had wanted told of her life – not the dark reality of Sylvan Mist.'

'How do *you* know what story Celeste wanted of her life?'

'Because, years later, *Celeste* wrote that story serialised in the *Worldly Woman*, under the Victoria Bird pseudonym. She sent me a copy of the finished work, one of the few times she reached out, after leaving. Celeste hoped the story might help us . . .'

'Help who?'

'Barrington. By then, three girls had drowned. Celeste felt a harrowing responsibility.'

As she should have! Shouldn't she? Josie didn't know what to think anymore 'But she still didn't come forward – even though she was safely away?'

'She said she'd never be safe from that man. Didn't think he'd bought her suicide, feared he was on her trail, that it was only a matter of time.'

Josie's head reared back, with a painful jolt. 'But after he closed up the lodge and amphitheatre, Rudy Meyer moved back to *Europe*. He's been there ever since. I know this for certain, it came up in my research. He's still living there now. Celeste has always been safe here in Australia.'

Gabe was thrown. '*Rudy Meyer* wasn't the man exploiting Celeste. Rudy adored Celeste. She was his star.'

A hidden door trundled open; the secret passage came into view. Josie pumped a triumphant fist in the air. '*Niall!* I knew it – that bastard was selling her pin-up cards, of course he was making the perverted images too. And he's been obsessively guarding that lodge ever since.'

Gabe frowned. 'Whatever Niall's latter obsession with Celeste, he didn't get near her during the war. The man terrorising Celeste, was a friend of Rudy's, come to stay in the lodge during the war. A photographer. With all the servicemen in town, he quickly seized on the opportunity to produce pin-up cards. At first, relatively tame images, the kind popular in the day. Something to lift spirits, trade for cigarettes and the like.

'Celeste was initially keen on the idea, thought it would advance her stardom, as much as it promoted the Obsidian. But never could she have foreseen what would come of those sessions in that man's studio...'

Josie couldn't seem to absorb anything more: her mind beginning to fatigue. 'Who was he then?'

Gabe looked equally deflated. 'I can't tell you; Celeste refused to say his name. In part to protect me, from my own rage. I'd have killed him with my bare hands, if I could have tracked him down.'

Josie shook her head, slumping. 'Are you *sure* it wasn't Niall?' She wasn't able to keep the disappointment from her voice.

'Do you think I would let him live among us?'

No, not from that look on her father's face.

'Tell me about this other fellow, then ...' Her heart wasn't in it, though. How she yearned to definitively expose Niall for all his lying and harassing and stalking!

'He was bit of a playboy. Rudy's starlets fell over one another wanting to model for him. Celeste was just as excited for her pin-up modelling. Before she first unrobed for him, there was never any hint of his darker nature ...'

Josie made a most unladylike noise. 'Sometimes there's lots of hints about a man's nature, great big obvious ones that a whole town knows about, and still those perverts get away with it for generations.'

But no more! Josie would go to Constable Jacobs herself and make a report about Niall, straight after this evening's curse-breaking.

Because she had to go through with the play, didn't she? Her father had just rearranged the story of her childhood, confessed his duplicitous part in a fourteen-year lie, and made a mockery of her play, but still; her show *must* go on ...

CHAPTER THIRTY-THREE
THE GOING ON

'I have to go back to the lodge, right now, this instant, and change my *scène à faire*. Celeste has to *live*!' Josie clapped her hand over her mouth, dragged it away again in astonishment. 'That's how the Curse gets broken. *She lives!*'

'She lives with *dignity*. Celeste's trauma stays strictly between you and I.'

Josie wasn't letting that go without a fight. 'At the very least, I need some sinister phantom lurking in shadow, to represent her fear and brokenness in that lodge. Ironically, Niall would have been the just the right person to play it.'

Gabe shook his head, adamant. 'That is Celeste's secret.'

Josie chewed her lip, thinking out possible ways around this edict.

'*Fine,*' she conceded. 'But I have to go ahead with it tonight. If I postpone, I'll lose Hugo Bernard, and hope of a national review. But there's no time for a third act rewrite! I'll have to ask my actors to ad-lib, and most of them are terrible at it. Laura is going to have a fit! I'm throwing the whole plan in on her.'

Her father's silence was, as ever, a space held open for her.

'The biggest conundrum is: who am I going to get to play *you*? There's no one worthy left!' Josie knew she was spinning her wheels like a tractor in mud, but that didn't quite account for her father's odd expression . . .

'If you won't ask me,' he said, 'I won't push in on you.'

Josie's laugh was an incredulous squall, abruptly shuttered away. 'You can't be serious.'

Gabe smiled. 'On the contrary, I'm rarely anything but.'

'But you've never acted in your life!'

'I've been acting every day for the last fourteen years of it. And give me some credit, I would be playing . . . me.'

'What would possess you to do this for me?'

'Aside from making amends to the town who held my family together when my wife died? I want to do it for you, Josie – to set you free.'

'*Free?* Of what?'

'Me.'

Josie shook her head, but he was having none of it. 'Me, and your brothers, and the farm, your calves, in fact the whole town.' Gabe got up and came to kneel in front of her. He took her hand, opened it and gently placed the heart locket back in her palm. 'We don't *need* you here anymore, Chickadee. It's time to fly the coop.'

She dipped her forehead to his, letting her tears plop, large and fast, on the leaf litter between them.

'I *can't* leave you.'

'That's why I'm kicking you out.'

Josie burbled out a laugh-sob. 'But where would I go?'

'Certainly not to your grandmother's. Beryl won't have you either. Neither of us will be happy until you get off this mountain.'

Josie drew back, to stare at him. 'You've talked to Grandy about – doing this?'

Gabe parted her fringe. She did not rush to tousle it back, knowing in a few moments he would drop a kiss, right there.

'This truth-telling was your grandmother's idea in the first place. Beryl has been manipulating you and I into place for months now.' There was no animosity in her father's words. 'She's waiting for you, this instant, at Sylvan Mist, along with the rest of your company. All they know is the ending has to change, and they need their director to tell them why.'

Josie rocketed to her feet, heart throttling into gear. 'I've got to get over there, I have to save my show!'

Six hours to show time

Laura, acting as lookout, came storming into the lodge and the large circle of theatre company members. 'They're *here*!'

Vivienne's prompt. She stood, with a glance at Owen, sitting beside her. Owen raised his hands in a mime of praying-for-mercy. She tucked away a tender smile, and went to greet her friend.

Josie came barrelling up the stairs, with a look of premeditated murder. Seeing Vivienne, she stopped and tempered her indignant fury, at least for one squeezing cuddle.

'Viv, promise me it's going to work. Tell me Grandy hasn't stolen *all* my thunder.'

Vivienne's cheek dimpled. 'You were born with un-stealable thunder, Josie Monash.'

Josie jerked her thumb towards the lodge 'What does my company know so far?'

'They know Celeste lived, because your father saved her. They know he provided shelter and prevented her from carrying out her threat, but they don't know anything else about . . .' She paused as Gabe Monash came quietly up onto the stoop. 'Mr Monash, welcome.'

Josie looked between Vivienne and Gabe. Her eyes narrowed speculatively, then widened in delight. 'Yes, you two will be perfect.'

Vivienne absorbed her friend's dishevelled fringe, her red-rimmed eyes, and face still mottled. 'Are you very angry at me?'

'Not a bit. I saw the second you figured it out in the library yesterday. I know you weren't part of her machinations.'

Vivienne exhaled sheer relief.

Miles emerged onto the porch. 'What's taking so long?' He didn't seem any part nervous now, though Vivienne had seen him sweating it out for over an hour.

Josie and Miles stepped up close. 'Dad just kicked me out of home,' said Josie. 'I'm a vagrant.'

'You'll have to busk for your supper. Where will you set up?'

There was teasing affection in both their voices.

'Josie can stay on with me,' Vivienne put in, droll as you please. 'Really, I insist.' She was ignored. One side of her lip hitched up. Owen would have appreciated her sarcasm.

'Perhaps,' Miles said, turning to Gabe, 'I might come and see you after the play?'

Gabe laughed. 'If you intend to be worthy of my daughter, you'd best learn quick – she'll only give herself away.'

Laura bustled onto the porch, hands on hips. It was too crowded out here by far. 'Josie, the whole cast is ready and awaiting your direction. They're getting anxious.'

Josie spun to Laura, reverting to professionalism in that single revolution. 'Can we do this?'

'I've been working on it flat out. I think we can. If you like some of the fixes I've come up with, I believe we'll pull this off. It may even be better than—' Laura gulped back the last word, guiltily.

But Josie let rip a crow: '"Better than" is exactly what I want to hear!'

Josie led the charge inside. Vivienne marvelled at how every rapt face in the lobby lifted to greet Josie; eyes lit with admiration. It was, collectively, how a parent would look at a beloved child coming into a room, or ought to. Josie Monash *was* this town's daughter. No wonder not a single theatre group member had walked when Beryl Frances stood before them an hour ago and announced the play's imminent unravelling.

Josie was stepping up before that straight-backed elderly woman holding court over the large circle of townsfolk. Eye to eye they stood; vivid purple dress facing off against livid fuchsia.

'You *stole* my show,' Josie cracked out.

'You reopened my lake,' countered Beryl.

'You only sought its closure to cover for Dad's lie.'

'And you forced it open again for your own acclaim.'

'Well look at my "acclaim" now – in ruins!'

'Don't be melodramatic, Josephine, it doesn't suit you. You set out to break the Curse of Lake Evelyn, and here you are.'

Josie and Beryl eyeballed one another for a protracted moment.

Vivienne dared a glance at Owen, who was rubbing his beard pensively, then at Laura, drumming her pencil against a notepad, next to Miles, poised and ready to serve, and last at Gabe Monash, arms crossed in quiet dignity. Around the circle of townsfolk her eyes went, all these people she had begun to care so much for: Elsie and Clarence Reece of the Newsagency; Peggy West, smoke-fragranced flower seller; Athol Harford, loquacious bus driver; Rita Caracella, accumulator extraordinaire; the town constable, the butcher, the baker; *hell,* there was probably a candlestick maker among them too. Such a cast of characters this town had! Long after Josie's play was done, Vivienne knew she wanted to stay and be and live among them, too.

There was a sudden movement between the women. Vivienne's eyes flew back in time to see Josie throwing her arms around her grandmother for a ferocious cuddle. The old woman absorbed the power of this embrace steadily, her arms rising up to grip Josie just as fervently back.

Throats cleared around the circle, faces averted. Vivienne imagined that every pair of eyes burned and watered like her own.

Josie drew back, with a last squeeze of her grandmother's soft shoulders. 'Right then,' she declared, turning to her theatre group. 'This is going to be the most challenging production any of us have ever been part of. I'm changing our entire third act, and I'm asking you all to perform it with next to no rehearsal. But I didn't train you all so long in improvisation for nothing. There are no guarantees we'll pull it off, but we're going to give it every-bloody-thing we've got . . .'

CHAPTER THIRTY-FOUR
NIGHTINGALE LAKE

Thirty-five minutes to show time

In the gloaming, Josie stood at the top of the Obsidian, scanning her rapidly filling theatre for Mr Hugo Bernard's pinstripe suit and silver head.

The anticipatory buzz of the seating audience, louder than the school orchestra onstage, normally would send a thrill, hot and pimpled, all over her. This evening, however, her heart was frostbitten by fear.

It was too perfect an evening to be afraid. The theatre gods had delivered her the most dramatic of sunsets – empurpled clouds slashed with scarlet, and the first shimmering pinholes of starlight. The glassy surface of Lake Evelyn had mirrored this cinematic display, eliciting audible sighs from the audience members streaming down the granite steps, in pearls and heels, dinner jackets and polished shoes.

Josie could not have commissioned a more magnificent theatre backdrop. Theatre-goers would go home raving about the beauty, majesty and uniqueness of the Obsidian. All of Barrington had turned out for Opening Night, and many faces from nearby towns beside. Her most esteemed theatre critic had arrived early, made himself known to the young ushers, and claimed his prime seat in the front row.

There he was, taking out his reading glasses, smoothing the evening's program across his knee. Smoke rose from his pipe, as he studied his booklet. Josie's hand clenched hard around the same copy in her own hand. Between her teeth, she issued a sneer: 'Not so scared of our lake now are we, Mr Buffoon?'

Josie had refused to provide the play to Mr Bernard ahead of time, as he'd requested when booking, and hadn't *that* been a propitious call! In the best-case scenario, if her motley cast and crew somehow managed to carry off the whole shebang, Mr Bernard wouldn't have a clue what had transpired backstage today.

Everything was riding on best-case scenarios this evening.

The weather holding out, the full house, the light and sound checks going off without a hitch, the audience's obvious and expressed excitement; these were all diverting successes so far, but nothing could ease the frigid cold grip of fear upon her breast.

The hours just passed had been the most frantic of her life. Josie had worked like mad to write her father into the story, to bring Celeste back to life – without divulging the deepest scar at story's heart. Her group, to their absolute credit, had said *yes* to everything. How often had she instructed them on accepting ideas, offers, notes and direction as it was given? And now here they were, on the biggest night of her life, saying *yes*, and saving her show.

The only exception had been Constable Jacobs. Once the changes were explained in full, he stood up and excused himself from the play, forthwith. 'You're now alleging that a young woman faked her own death, after an unspecified offence against her, and that your father helped to cover it up!'

Josie gave an irritated sigh. 'I'm not claiming Celeste has hurt anyone, fled debts, or breached any contracts. I'm simply depicting a scenario in which she lived, and there never was a curse made upon our lake.'

'If this story ends up being anything more than your wild imagination, you should come and make a proper report, Josephine. And until such time—'

'Believe *me*,' Laura cut in. 'I'll be making a report very soon, about a perverted man, who's been harassing, stalking and molesting Barrington women for decades.'

Peggy West raised a hand. 'I'd like to make a similar report.'

'As will I,' chimed in Elsie Reece.

In the stunned silence that followed, Josie motioned Constable Jacobs towards the door. 'You'd better go start sharpening your pencils, Mike, you're going to be busy. I'll write your character out.'

A splutter came from across the circle. 'N–now . . . hang on, let's not be too hasty to kill off the sergeant.'

Josie spun. *Stage-fright-stricken* Clarence?

'I know the part well enough by now. I could play the sergeant.'

Josie considered her old friend's quaking resolve. *I'm so proud, I could kiss you!* Aloud she said: 'Done. Everyone, say hello to our new sergeant.'

There had been no more shock resignations, only hard work and all hands on deck. Could they have done more? Could they ever! Just *think* what she should have achieved with more time – she could weep for the misfortune of it. Had her father come forward sooner, had her grandmother schemed more quickly, had *she* solved the puzzle earlier; Josie might have written the play of her lifetime.

Within the row of army tents serving as backstage area, was the whirling urgency and joyful panic of pre-show jitters, misplaced accessories and warm-up exercises running over each other.

Vivienne, in her stardust crown and gossamer gown, was sure this excitement behind the scenes must be palpable to the audience too.

An enchantment seeping straight through the canvas. She stood in the midst of the commotion, as servicemen and bathing-suited beauties alike swept by her, and breathed deeply of her blessing: to be part of the theatre world, with infinite roles to create or choose from; none of which were prescribed by a mother, husband, or society itself.

Her hand went to the hard, circular lump, hidden in the ruched lining of Celeste's swimsuit. Josie had ordered Vivienne's ring be kept far away from her theatre, declaring real jewellery bad luck on stage. But Vivienne had a plan: when her debut was done, she would pitch that ring into Lake Evelyn itself.

Athol Harford came bounding up to her elbow, radiating big energy. Vivienne smiled to see how dapper he looked out of his epaulettes and long socks, and into Rudy Meyer's fine tweed suit. 'Ready to break some hearts, our Nightingale? Nervous?'

She wasn't, not one bit. This joy, surging through her veins and lungs, seemed like it might give her lift into the sky itself. After so many years of caution and smallness, rumination and silence, tonight she was taking that stage and letting her voice be heard.

I will not go back to that songless life.

Laura's strident call came from the tent flaps. 'Ladies and gentlemen of the Barrington Theatre Company. This is your ten-minute call.'

Athol dashed away, chanting about Peter's peck of pickled peppers.

There was someone else standing in the tent opening now, Vivienne could feel his eyes on her, without even turning. She savoured the blood rush to her cheeks; the heat of his tender regard. Slowly, she spun to meet Owen's gaze.

Flurried activity flowed around her, elbows jostled, noise rushed by, but there was a thread of stillness between and bonding them. She stood, and was beheld, and gazed back.

Then he came towards her.

She squirmed with the pleasure of his approach. He stopped in front of her, and she observed the widening of his pupils, flare of his nostrils, deep in-breath as he took her fully in. '*Vivi*. You look . . .' He gave a helpless shrug.

Her smile was wry as ever. 'Like a woman glad she doesn't have to drown herself tonight, after all.'

'Just so.'

Her eyes ran from his brown eyes to beard, and the lips pink and soft within that coarse hair.

Laura buzzed by; tutting. 'If you're not in my cast, you shouldn't be in my tent.'

'Sorry,' Owen said. 'I just wanted to wish Vivi good luck.' He glanced guiltily at Laura, but their stage manager was powering away, missing this faux pas.

Vivienne had not taken her eyes off Owen's face. 'I've had nothing *but* good luck since coming up this mountain.'

Owen nodded – but she wanted to be much, much clearer. 'And meeting you.'

She didn't have time to savour his slow smile unfolding, for a tiny brunette in a fuchsia dress had come barrelling into her.

'Thank God!' Josie cried, clutching Vivienne's arm with two hands. 'I wanted to say goodbye, before you went over the top.'

Vivienne laughed, taking Josie's hands in hers. 'I'm going to make you proud; I promise.'

'And I, you.'

The women embraced. Vivienne squeezed her eyes closed, feeling her false lashes kiss her cheeks.

They drew apart.

'Any last words?' Josie said, and Vivienne did not miss the hopeful tail of this request.

Vivienne thought hard. It had to be good, had to elicit the gusty warmth of Josie's laugh, and the full timbre of Owen's. She reached to straighten Josie's fringe, let her fingers run gently through it; scanning her catalogue of favourite movies. Then, she had it, from *All About Eve* . . .

'"Fasten your seat belts",' she quoted. '"It's going to be a bumpy night."'

With Laura making the five-minute call, and Rita the last-minute fluffs and tucks of Vivienne's costumery, Josie went to find her father.

Gabe, dressed as himself, was sitting quietly in a corner of the backstage tent, studying his script. Swamped by fondness and gratitude, Josie stepped up before him. He deserved one last out, if he needed it.

'Chickadee?'

'I want you to know, you don't *have* to go on tonight—'

Her father snapped the script shut. 'Thank goodness. I'm going home for tea.'

For a millisecond – but even that was too long for Josie's pride – he had her. She tsked. 'I want you to know, if there's any backlash in town, any at all, I'll have your back.'

Gabe smiled. 'Thank you, Josephine.'

Miles was passing by. Her impossibly handsome captain! Josie put out her hand to Miles, and they shared a fleeting hand squeeze. There would be so many nights backstage with this man, and she couldn't wait to live them all.

Josie was smiling giddily, as she turned back to her father.

Gabe took something out of his top pocket. 'I was wondering if it might be all right for me to play this tonight?' His harmonica. 'I know it's late notice, but I didn't know I was truly ready, until this moment.'

Josie cleared a wedge of emotion from her throat. 'When were you thinking?'

'In the final scene, when I'm walking the lake, looking to the stars . . .' He lifted his chin. 'After Celeste has disappeared, to freedom.'

'What do you want to play?'

'I was thinking: 'La Vie en Rose'. It was one of Celeste's favourites.'

Josie spun this across her imagined stage, *loving* what she saw. 'That's perfect. I'll see you out there, Dad.'

The lights had dimmed, the overture begun. Vivienne stood, just offstage, ready to make her entrance. The wall of rainforest had deepened into profound blackness, stars rolled across the sky, the inky lake lapped quietly against the floating stage walk upon which she would first appear as Nightingale singing under spotlight.

Vivienne strained to differentiate faces in the darkened audience. She didn't know these folk well enough to pick out familiar silhouettes by hairstyle, height or shape. At least, not yet. Out in that audience, somewhere, sat Owen. Tonight, she would be performing to *him*. And if she truly embodied Celeste this evening, every member of this audience should feel as she intended Owen to . . .

Enraptured.

There was one other person missing from this audience tonight. Was it really so absurd to hope her mother might have come, after all? It was, Vivienne knew, completely absurd. Nonetheless, her eyes swept the highest reaches and rows of the audience stubbornly for the one silhouette she would recognise anywhere, even after many months and miles apart. She saw only winking cigarette lights, amongst a nebulous mass.

But wait . . .

There! A single figure slipping in at the back of the Obsidian. Vivienne could just make out the usher's dim torch, dashing to intercept this latecomer. Too tall to be Mother, but for tonight, Vivienne could play pretend: that *was* Mother, and she'd come all this way to see her daughter perform. A second usher's torch had joined the first, obviously some conferring going on. Had Mother had forgotten her ticket, or her reading glasses? Perhaps another audience member had taken her seat.

The overture, swollen full, was beginning to recede. Vivienne was mere moments away from taking the stage, this was certainly no time to be distracted by a kerfuffle unfolding at the rear. Yet, her eyes could not seem to stay away. A third torch had joined the circle, limbs could be seen, gesticulating.

Still the woman had not been seated. Now a silhouette Vivienne definitely recognised – wide and short, with ramrod straight posture – had joined this disturbance. Vivienne's gut contracted. *Seat her! For Heaven's sake, we're beginning – Mother will miss my entrance!*

The overture was diminishing. Laura was at her side, hand on Vivienne's elbow, nudging. 'It's time. Out you go.'

It *was* time. Vivienne's hand fluttered at her throat, feeling vocal power swelling up. She drew back her shoulders, lifted her chin, and exhaled long and soft.

'No turning back.'

She stepped out.

Josie had positioned herself in shadows to watch Hugo Bernard's reaction in real time. If there was a hideous review to follow, she wanted to see it in his face here and now; suspense be damned. If *Nightingale* was set to fail in a flurry of shuffles and awkward coughs, she would not shy from it. Josie had been wrung out by surprises this day: love reciprocated, a childhood retold, her play's ending rewritten, her own future just beginning. If *Nightingale* stank, Josie wanted the truth tonight, and she promised herself she could handle it.

Josie could not, however, drag her eyes off her earnest troupe play-ing in the balmy air, under a net of stars, bright-lit against the ancient void of the volcanic lake. They were divine theatre, sprung to life. Her motley crew of amateur thespians was giving it everything they had, leaving nothing behind. The classical training of Vivienne's voice and comportment, together with Miles's flawless professionalism, imbued the whole play with a first-class elegance.

Pride inflated Josie's heart bursting full. Her hands came together in a pose of prayer just below her chin; her smile threatened to crack her face open. Josie had abandoned all interest in Hugo Bernard's face. For how could he *not* be feeling the same enchantment as she? So captivated was Josie, she did not even mark the transition from well-written and rehearsed lines to hastily learned alteration.

Suddenly, there was Celeste, lowering herself into the lake in her dreadful suit of braided lawyer vine – and a lone farmer was walking along the shore towards her, head bowed.

The collective gasp rising from the Obsidian, like a billowing plume, wrenched Josie back from her ensorcellment.

As Gabe Monash drew ever closer to the figure sinking deep, the shared gasp became a discombobulated silence. *What was Gabriel Monash doing at the scene of Celeste's suicide? Had he seen her death?*

But Gabe wasn't merely *seeing* her, Gabe was running towards her into the water now, shouting, arms outstretched for their drowning Nightingale.

The story they all knew by heart, the legend they had all played some part in propagating, was changing before their eyes. The audience strained off their stone seats: mouths agape.

Gabe was with the Nightingale in the lake, wrestling her back from the very edge of that dark abyss. And though Josie knew exactly how this scene ended, her heart pounded against her ribcage.

Save her! Her fingers were sunk deep into her palms. *Don't let her go down! Save her!* Josie knew her audience was feeling that struggle just as powerfully as she.

'*Holy moly,*' she breathed. It was the most powerful thing she had ever created on stage. It was what every playwright in their right mind dreamed of creating. No longer merely a play, not just a scene acted out, but life and death, hope and despair grappling for ascendancy.

Slowly, agonisingly slowly, but surely, life was winning. The battle came closer to the shore. Gabe stood tall, lifting Celeste into his arms, carrying her towards the shore. Water lilies parted around them, feathered gown trailed in the water, her head lolled back, hair tumbling long over his arms.

He lay with her on the floating walkway, cradling her as gently as a babe, as she sobbed out her defeat. Then he was drawing her out of those weighted vines, and casting them into the lake. At last, he was picking her up, carrying her home.

This, Josie told herself, *is magic.* An exaltation that trebled as the story rolled out its stunning twist: Celeste lived, and loved Gabriel Monash – who kept her ever from returning to the lake as she had forsworn. All the while, the audience sat in disbelieving silence.

Finally, Celeste was bidding farewell to her saviour, and dancing off into an unknown future – free, and full of life. Josie felt the change in her amphitheatre, from disbelief to elation. *Joy* ran through the audience, a warm current in cold waters.

At last, Gabe was left to complete the story. He traversed the floating walkway, eyes upon the stars above. Lifted his harmonica and began to play 'La Vie en Rose'. From somewhere beyond the reeds, rose Vivienne's voice.

It was the perfect finale – haunting, longing, redemptive. Gabe's simple harmonica rendition was more powerful than anything Josie had conceived. Her father's repentance, and his recompense. Josie raised her hands to wet cheeks. Once Gabe's harmonica trailed off, the lights would dim – then would come rapturous applause. This had been the performance of all their lives.

Gradually the lights began to fade, before the song had yet ended. Josie stood, ready to front the theatre, anticipating a standing ovation the moment it ceased.

From somewhere at the back of the audience, a commotion had arisen. A woman's voice, calling out. Josie shook it away, with no more significance than a wet-season mosquito. But there was movement now, too. Down the aisle came a figure. Perhaps someone returning from the amenities shed? The figure came closer and closer to the stage. Josie frowned, panic growing, raising her hand, wanting to swat the disturbance away.

The figure had reached the edge of the stage now. *Who* was *it? Why wasn't Laura running interreference?*

The lights fell, and at last the rapturous, standing, soaring applause erupted. Josie was on her feet moving towards the stage, soul singing with triumph.

In the darkness, the thunderous applause went on with the rolling tempo of a rainstorm. '*Encore,*' they hollered. '*Encore!*'

For the remainder of her life, Josie knew she would remember and cherish this hue and cry; the sense of perfect completion.

Then, that lone female figure ascended Josie's stage.

There was an emphatic *chunk*, as a single spotlight arced across the lake and over the forest, a meteorite shooting heavenward into the star-dressed sky. Down again fell the light, coming to rest upon the stranger standing on the floating stage, twelve feet from Gabriel.

A beautiful woman, dressed in an azure blue travelling suit, with raven hair neatly pinned back in chignon. The circle of light stayed on her, but she did not turn to acknowledge it, or the audience.

Josie swung wildly to the stage crew, a hand above her eyes, squinting. She could just make out Miles, behind the light stand, and knew instinctively that he was as surprised by this as she, yet had the temerity and professionalism to run with it.

Josie turned back to the stage just as the woman's hands came away from her head, releasing a silver barrette. Long, raven hair tumbled down her back.

The stage-lit pair stood, two lengths apart, and beheld one another.

'*Celeste . . .*' he uttered; part stupefaction, part joy.

'Gabe,' she answered – in a voice pure, rich and clear, and not heard on these shores for over fourteen years.

The Nightingale of Lake Evelyn, back from the dead.

The spotlight chunked off.

CHAPTER THIRTY-FIVE

SHOWSTOPPER

The audience was in uproar as they were herded back up the stairs, demanding more, more – *more*! The ushers were insistent, driving the hullabaloo towards the entry level and lighted car park.

The stage left behind lay still in darkness, and eerie quiet. Gabe and Celeste remained locked in an immovable muteness, eyes only for each other. The rest of the cast members crowded before the proscenium, in a stunned silence. Except for one.

Beryl, moving against the tide of theatre-leavers, had joined the cast at lake's edge. The company parted, as she barrelled up to the stage. All eyes turned to the unsinkable matriarch of Barrington . . .

'This,' she said, 'is how you break a curse.'

And Josie knew then that finding Celeste had been Beryl's own doing. How long had she held that ace up her sleeve – weeks? Or years?

The hectic swell of show-goers had begun to dissipate.

In the velvet blackness, the voices of Gabe Monash and Celeste Starr were heard; smooth and full of sorrow. Every ear of the Barrington Theatre Company harkened. *This show,* was for them . . .

'You came back.'

'Too late to save the other girls.'

'None of those deaths can be blamed on you—'

'And yet my lie has haunted this place.'

'Our lie. And tonight, we set ourselves free.'

'You did all this for . . . me?'

'No, I didn't.'

'I did,' Josie said, stepping onto the floating walkway. 'This is my play. And it wasn't for you, it was for my *town*.'

There was a whistle of approval from the gathered company, a ripple of light clapping.

Celeste faced Josie. Her voice was gentle, wistful. 'You're a young lady now. I never thought I'd get to see it.'

Josie trembled, head to toe. *This* was the 'mother' she had bade goodnight to every night of her remembered life. '*You mightn't have been mine for long, but how I loved you.*' Josie had worn this woman's necklace, close to her own heart, and derived courage and spirit from its talismanic powers.

Josie fumbled into her pocket, and drew out the broken locket. She stared at it a moment, then stepped forward, with hand outstretched to Celeste.

'Here,' Josie said. 'You left this.' Her grim tone revealed something of her old despair, the abandonment not grown out of.

Celeste took the locket, turning it over and over in her fingers, sorrow searing across her features.

Laura, arriving back from crowd shepherding, seemed the only person to understand this was strictly a private performance.

She broke the spell with a burst of strident clapping. 'All right, nosy parkers, the Monash family will be retiring for the evening to work all this out.'

Will we? Josie looked around, bewilderedly. *How?*

'And the rest of you,' Laura ordered, 'go bask in your glory now at the Grand with everyone else in Barrington. Soak it up, because you've bloody well earned it!'

The Barrington Theatre Company let loose a resounding cheer.

Vivienne sat on the floating stage walk, alone at the darkened amphitheatre, holding a stardust crown in her hands.

The cast and crew had long since gone. Laura, Ernest and Miles had taken off to join the celebrations at the Grand, promising to rendezvous with her at the Monash farm for further celebrations. Later, she would go to the farmhouse, but just now Vivienne wanted to linger on – still in costume, bare toes and caribou feathers trailing in the water – replaying every moment of this most astonishing eve.

The first flash of lightning was an annoyance; like lights coming up in a picture theatre before the credits rolled. The stupendous crack of thunder, which followed, seemed to shake the stage walk itself. She scrambled up, clutching tight her crown. The first heavy drops skittered across the surface of the lake like a hundred pebbles skipping.

She dashed up the stone steps, hunching as lightning flash strobed the amphitheatre. In the last second before darkness swallowed the scene, a waiting figure was illuminated at the top of the steps.

Vivienne jerked to a stop, with a rush of cold fear. 'Hello . . . ?' The clap of thunder covered her cry.

After the flood of lightning, blackness seemed to swamp the world.

'Hello!' she called again. 'Who is it? Please!'

'Don't be afraid, Vivi.'

'Owen!' The sheer relief of him, made her light-headed. Her crown had left painful imprints inside slackening hands. 'What are you doing here?'

'Josie sent me over to get you. She doesn't want you out here alone. I think she doesn't want to be alone there.'

She smiled. 'There have been so many people everywhere today, I don't mind a bit of peace and quiet.'

The heavens split anew; lightning forked across the sky. In the thunder crack following close behind, they shared an ironic smile.

'Besides that, only the Monash family were invited back,' Vivienne said.

'Josie said you'd use that as an excuse and to tell you, here I quote: "You're part of the family now."'

'Am I just?'

'The sister Josie always wanted.'

'There you go,' she said provokingly. 'That makes me *your* sister, too.'

'Well, I wouldn't say that . . .'

Her want was a flame-tipped arrow. Her courage, incendiary. *Did she dare? Did she ever . . .*

'I daresay Josie must be rather occupied right now, squeezing secrets out of her Nightingale. Perhaps she isn't likely to miss you and I, for a while yet . . .'

'Will she not?'

'I had a thought you and I might go and watch the storm, from your place.'

'*My* place?'

'Or rather, as I want to christen it – *Vivienne's Landing.*'

'You want to name my house?'

Her eyes shone in the dark. 'I said, I want to *christen* it.'

The big bob of his Adam's apple was audible.

She put a hand to the broad chest rising and falling unevenly before her, spreading out her fingers to feel all his warmth and strength, and desire. No, not all of it – yet.

When he managed to speak, his hoarseness sent heat spiralling through her centre. 'I love you, Vivi.'

'Owen . . .' She could hardly deliver her pun for the throb overtaking her. 'I udderly love you.'

In the little farmhouse, there were just three once more around the Monash family table: Gabe, Josie, Celeste.

Reg and Daphne, and squalling Maureen, had gone to spend the night at Grandy Beryl's, under the guise of freeing up room for the guest. Daphne had departed with a suitcase as oversized as her victory smile. Josie could not help the pettiness which flared: *she thinks she's escaping* us?

The hours had run past midnight, talk truncated only by thunder's cymbal crashing. Fourteen years of lies and longing, love and loss would not be untangled in a night. And how many times could two people say sorry in one night? Someone was going to have to draw the line soon.

Since Josie had sent Owen to collect Vivienne, she had certainly become the third wheel. There were things left patently unsaid between Gabe and Celeste, and Josie had begun to feel herself an overgrown child, up past her bedtime. Welcome overstayed.

She tried not to stare rudely at Celeste-made-flesh, carefully apportioning out her stolen glances. In the stark light of the kitchen bulb, Celeste's facial lines, first greys and sun blemishes were revealed. That Celeste Starr had not only lived, but gone on to age, like any ordinary woman, was perhaps the most surreal revelation of this whole evening.

A car roared up the drive. Josie sprang to her feet, eager to embrace Vivienne. It was Ernest and Laura who came carousing through the kitchen door, arm in arm, eyes glazed and overbright.

'Where's *Viv*?'

Ernest and Laura shared a volley of laughter.

'Last we saw,' said Ernest, 'Viv was helping Owen round up a lost cow.'

Josie crossed her arms. 'You take me for an idiot?'

'Trust us,' Laura said. 'They were going flat out up the hill to Owen's after *something* . . .' The pair went off, guffawing, to locate the cooking sherry. The night's revelry was not finished yet by half.

Josie went gratefully to encroach on Laura and Ernest's company instead, leaving her father and Celeste alone at the table. The younger set claimed the lounge for a desultory game of cards.

From the kitchen came low, urgent talk. A sudden cry of emotion, and a chair scraping hurriedly back. Silence.

In the lounge, the young trio slid a smile, one to another.

Ernest had taken out his lucky cigar, to tap against his palm. He stopped, and considered the cigar in his hand, then rose to light it.

'Really?' Josie said. 'After all this time?'

'If ever there was a night for it, Jose.'

Josie nodded, stretching out her hand for the cigar. Laura's hand reached next. Ernest's lucky cigar went around this circle, the reverence of the shared ritual interrupted only by rolling thunder, and inelegant bouts of coughing.

The kitchen beyond was soundless – perhaps empty.

Laura leaned in, with a sotto voce whisper: 'Should we go back to Sylvan to wait for Vivienne?'

'Not going out in *that*,' Josie said. 'We'll catch our death.' She refused another toke of the cigar. 'Right now, I need you to tell me what they were all saying down at the Grand tonight. I can't wait for tomorrow's paper! I want to know everything you heard, and please don't spare me a single flattering word.'

Laura's face was rapturous. 'Oh Josie, you've never heard such praise—'

Rain throttled the hut's tin roof, lightning threw the tiny shelter into stark relief, thunder shook the hill on which it stood, but *Vivienne's*

Landing withstood it all. The storm could not disturb, within those humble walls, the woman anchored strong and sinking deep; rising high and sinking deeper; drawing ragged breath, and now singing scales entirely new . . .

Outside Sylvan Mist, a rain-wet figure stood at the foot of the stairs, watching the balconies above, the windows without a gleam. Around the lodge, the forest bucked and shivered, whined and cracked under wind's assault.

He eased open the car door quietly, and considered the interior. From the passenger seat footwell, he picked up a wedding gift, still wrapped in heavy brocade paper, the gift's square edges piercing through. There was a small, dusty footprint right in the centre of it.

Lightning flared over the canopy, briefly illuminating the man as he climbed the stoop – heavy, careful.

At the door he paused, key in hand, listening. No alarm was raised. He placed the key deftly, and turned the knob. The door opened with a reluctant squeal.

He did not fumble for the light switch. With easy stealth he navigated between the furniture, and climbed the stairs, avoiding each creaking step precisely. The library doors were open, and he went straight in.

He stood, considering the shadowed mounds, side by side, in the middle of the floor. A strobe burst of lightning threw the room into flickering exposure. Before him, lay three messy, makeshift cots of blankets and pillows – empty.

He turned abruptly, ascending the stairs for the master bedroom. Empty. Methodically now he went from room to room, finding no one. Finally, he descended the stairs to the basement level, and tugged on the light.

He walked around the wine cellar, looking at the many empty bottles stacked together. Whirling sharply, he went to stand before the twice-deadlocked door, nearly fractured off its hinges, with an axe still propped alongside.

Into the darkroom he went then, breathing very slowly; very, very loudly, to see what she had touched . . .

CHAPTER THIRTY-SIX
THE HOST

Vivienne woke before dawn to find the cocooning warmth of limbs around her naked body withdrawing.

'I've got to do the milking,' Owen whispered, his warm breath across her neck springing up goose pimples. She suspected all she had to do was whimper longingly, and he'd never make it up to the dairy.

Vivienne stretched languorously in the darkness, breathing in the tang of sweat and sex mingled with sawdust, oakmoss. She listened to Owen crack his knuckles, then pull on his clothes and boots. He knelt beside the mattress to kiss her forehead and she lifted her lips instead, careful to show restraint despite the lush invitation her body was already preparing.

Cows, she reminded herself sternly as his mouth showed no similar restraint. *Lots and lots of cows waiting*.

Owen heaved himself up and away with an unwilling groan. 'I've never resented farming more in my whole life.'

'And I've never been *happier*, in all of mine.'

Owen was back on his knees in an instant, crushing her to him. Vivienne's arms opened with a wild, cleaving hunger.

The cows were going to have to wait, after all . . .

After Owen had dragged himself out of the hut, Vivienne went looking for Celeste's swimsuit and peignoir. Her fingers spread out over the ruched swimsuit lining, finding the hidden space empty. At some point during the play, as easily as a leaf snagged and brushed aside, she had lost a diamond.

She went across the sodden paddocks, under a sky dense with mammatus clouds, glowing eerily. The storm's night work was stark to see: a tree splintered apart; at her feet, the wide imprint of a lightning strike, currents fanning out over the grass like capillaries.

In damp air, her skin tingled in all the places reddened by beard-friction. Going up and over another hillock, she was recalled to the rhythmic undulation of her body astride his, and the rolling volume of her own pleasure, shouted into the storm.

Vivienne nearly doubled straight back to Owen. Head's resolve alone carried her on through the rainforest, down the drive to Sylvan Mist. First, to change out of Celeste's costume, then cook a celebratory breakfast for her friends. She wondered if Laura and Josie had been out already to get the paper, or if they would all go into town together.

Anticipation thrilled her to the bone.

Josie and Laura, having slept the night on the Monash lounge-room floor, were up with Ernest in time for the milking. The world was condensed to roiling mist and pouched clouds.

'We feed the calves,' Josie declared, 'then straight into town for the papers.'

In the calves' shed, the women shared the bucket feeding, talking animatedly of what astonishing acclaim the paper might hold for the Barrington Theatre Company, for the Obsidian, for Josie.

The look they exchanged to spy Owen cutting up the paddock, red faced, abominably late and still tucking his shirt in, was full merriment.

'We won't ask Vivienne to come into town then,' Laura said.

'Let her rest,' Josie agreed. 'We'll meet her back at the lodge.'

There was a strange car parked outside Sylvan Mist, right behind Vivienne's roadster. She stared at it, not knowing anyone who drove a car like it. Unless it was Celeste's? Perhaps she'd come over to share in the reviews. A small crowd was probably already gathered inside, hunched over the newspapers, back-slapping begun. How very like Josie, not to even wait for Vivienne . . .

She went quickly up the front stairs, smiling, ears pricked for Josie's most jubilant laughter.

The front door was half ajar, but the room beyond lay still in silent gloom and shadow. No one appeared to even be awake, much less reading anything. The cloying damp rushed to greet her, noxious as ever, but there was something new behind it; something . . . familiar.

She stood a moment, letting her eyes adjust to the dim light, listening for Josie and Laura, in the library above. Nothing. The pair had evidently gone to Barrington for the papers – but it didn't explain the car.

Vivienne reached back for the light switch, and flicked it on. Light went meekly forth to interrupt the shadows. Her eyes darted around the lobby level, searching.

A yelp ripped from her throat. Her hand flew to her chest, to prevent her heart hurtling out of her ribcage.

Sitting in the leather couch near the stairs, just sitting there, staring at her all the while, was Uncle Felix.

At least she thought it was him, for he seemed more like a wax statue than anything. Unmoving, unblinking.

'Uncle Felix!' She panned for even a glint of the joy she'd expected to feel at his arrival; drawing up only dismay. 'I'm sorry I wasn't here when you arrived. Did you just get in, or . . . ?'

He did not reply, but his eyes moved, indeed his whole head – gaze sliding from her face, slowly down her figure, to her bare feet, feather brushed. Vivienne glanced down at herself, scantily clad in Celeste's costume. She drew her dressing gown firmer together at the waist, blushing furiously.

'You'll have to forgive me – looking like this. It's a costume. I was actually in a show last night, it was our opening night, and I was out late – celebrating. You see, I've joined the local theatre company, and I've been making some friends here—'

Felix cut across her, pouting. 'Aren't you *coming* to give your dear old uncle a kiss, my girl?'

She'd prefer not to, actually. The thought of leaning in close to Felix right now, when her every pore exuded the scent she and Owen had created together, was frankly repulsive.

Felix did not move from his couch. She took a few steps forward, before stopping in surprise. Spread out over his lap was a copy of last night's show program: with Vivienne's face front and centre on the cover page, as sultry Nightingale.

'Oh, look – you found one of our programs! That saves *me* explaining the whole wonderful story of our play. Isn't it marvellous? Tell me you think it's marvellous!'

Her uncle was disposed to do no such thing. He was boggling at her again, eyes roving. 'You look just like her,' he said, in a voice strangely squeezed.

Her? Of course – Celeste. How imperceptive she had been! It was only logical Felix would have known Celeste – he'd stayed here himself during the war. How daft to just think of that connection.

Vivienne went forward more boldly now, bending to kiss her uncle on the cheek, stepping quickly out of reach as she felt his arms rising to embrace her. He stank of red wine, and the sour odour of long-distance travel. She saw now the empty bottle – *bottles* – on the side table.

'Why did you not call, to say you were on the way?' Hard as she tried, she couldn't bring a natural lilt to her voice.

Equally though, Felix's tone and expression were devoid of his usual flippancy – indeed, had gone very serious indeed. 'I wanted to surprise my girl. After all this time, so lost and lonely up here, I expected she would be *hanging out* to see me. Come running to meet me and throw her arms around me, thanking me for not forgetting her . . .'

Vivienne swallowed distaste. Months ago, she'd have done that very thing.

'Instead,' he said, 'I arrive to find the lodge in an appalling state: uninvited guests, expensive wine taken, priceless pictures desecrated. Things touched, that should never have been *touched*—'

A shiver galloped up Vivienne's spine. *What is he saying?*

'And my niece herself, just plain . . . missing. Where were you last night, Vivienne?'

'The play,' she blurted. 'I told you.'

'Yes, the play. About our Nightingale.' He patted the program on his lap. 'Our little drowned songbird.'

'But that's just it,' she cried. 'Celeste didn't drown. She lived! In fact, she—'

'Got away, didn't she?' His face was victorious.

It wasn't a victory Vivienne felt she was invited to share in. She made her own face very calm, and flat. 'You must be pleased, having known her, to hear that.'

'And I have my very own niece to thank, for bringing my Nightingale back to me.'

'It wasn't only me,' she said, lightly. 'We all solved the mystery, together.'

Felix smiled. There was nothing playful or warm in it. 'But tell me, Vivienne. Why didn't you open my gift?' His eyes dropped to the space between his thigh, and the side of the armchair. Vivienne followed his gaze to the red brocade covered gift, wedged in.

'Come and open it for me.'

'It wouldn't be right,' she said. 'All the wedding gifts should be given back.'

'And here I am. Give it to me.'

She had become so frustrated by his oblique manner and tone, and this disconcerting stand-off. In fact, she was growing frightened. No longer did she feel herself the playfully indulged niece, rather the *toyed with* . . .

'No thank you,' she said; quiet, but firm.

'I insist.' He wasn't just insisting, he was pulling the gift out, tossing it to her.

Vivienne lunged forward to catch it, with a shocked expulsion of air. Inside the parcel, a pane of glass reverberated.

'Open it,' he commanded, as she was yet straightening.

She held the gift steadily in her hands, knowing full well what it contained: the bridal portrait he had taken. She tore a strip across the face of the photograph, then a second, and a third. Slowly her face and form were revealed. She could not help the audibly indrawn breath, for he had captured her, truly, as the beautiful bride she might have been.

'It's lovely,' she said obediently. 'Thank you very much.'

But she didn't like it – did she? Not at all. There was something quite wrong about this portrait. What? The inviting look cast over bare shoulder? It was coquettish for a society bride, she saw that now, though admittedly she had been desensitised in recent days by the images found in that dark room. Was it the removal of her bolero jacket for this image that bothered her? She remembered the cajoling persistence with which Felix had pursued the removal of that bolero, how enthusiastically he had flashed away, yet how abruptly he had excused himself from the studio and—

French Riviera.

Vivienne's expression did not alter from polite admiration. But around the gilded edges of the frame, her nails dug in so hard, she expected the glass to shatter . . .

French Riviera.

The backdrop Felix had used for her wedding portrait – that pastel-hued, impossibly glamorous vista of the French Riviera was the very same backdrop used in so many of Celeste's photographs, both the tame images above ground, and the sadistic captures below.

Celeste's photographer.

Slowly she raised her gaze from the portrait, to find Felix's eyes locked on hers. He was grinning.

Her eyes dropped back to the portrait, breath changing in an instant, to the short, shallow pant of the hunted. The prey.

Uncle Felix is the man who drove Celeste to the lake.

The earth tilted away beneath her feet.

Run.

She raised her eyes once more.

Felix was beginning to stand, the show program tipping from lap to floor.

Run!

Vivienne flung the photo frame, like a flying disc, at her uncle's head. Even as she spun to flee, she registered the *thunk* of its impact, splintering glass, a high-pitched howl of rage.

She tore across the lobby floor towards the green rectangle glow of the open door, with a baying hound in pursuit.

Laura and Josie were speeding toward Barrington in the Monash family Ford. Josie's mouth was running harder than the motor.

'So, after we pick up the papers, I'm putting my foot to the metal and we're flying straight back to Sylvan Mist, to open it with Viv.'

'Your foot's already through the floor,' Laura said, knuckles white on the open window.

Josie laughed. 'Should see me driving Viv's car; I launch off these hills like Sputnik!'

'And if she's not at the lodge?'

'She'll be there. She's not going to sit around Owen's stinking hut all day. We can keep Viv with us at Sylvan at least until my brother has finished building that house for her.'

'But you'll soon be heading out of Barrington, chasing your fame and fortune. Then I'll be homeless again.'

The colourful buntings and hanging flowers of Main Street flashed by.

'I'm sure you could stay on in the lodge for a while longer.'

Laura grimaced. 'I couldn't handle a single night alone in that place. I'm not as brave as Viv. And I could *never* afford Mr Brinsley's exorbitant accommodation fees.'

Josie shot her a sharp look. 'Who did you say?'

'Sylvan's owner.'

The Ford slowed; Josie was scanning for a parking space. 'What do you mean by Sylvan's *owner*?'

Laura looked at her askance. 'Surely you know Rudy Meyer sold the lodge on? Years back. Some other chap owns it now.'

Josie harrumphed. 'So, all this time Barrington thought it still had a connection to Rudy Meyer, and he'd long since sold out. Why didn't you tell me?'

'It just didn't occur to me. It will always be *Rudy's* lodge to us.'

'Have you met this new owner?'

'No. I was forever taking his calls for Niall, though. He's ... a strange man.'

Josie swerved into a fortuitous parking spot, directly outside the Newsagency. She tore the keys from ignition. 'Strange, how?'

There was a pause as the women climbed out of the Ford and slammed shut the doors. Laura spoke across the utility's roof. 'I mean, charismatic as all get out, lays the flirting on full thickness, but it was a strange, swamping sort of charm. I could never escape the feeling he was having a sly joke at my expense. He couldn't have been aware I was Niall's plaything, and yet I always felt Mr Brinsley knew *exactly* what he was interrupting, when he called. Like he *enjoyed* it ...'

Josie frowned, put her hands to her head, reeling with déjà vu.

No, not déjà vu ... dread.

Loud rapping sounded on glass. Elsie Reece, at the Newsagency window, waving a newspaper; exultant.

CHAPTER THIRTY-SEVEN
SAVING GRACE

Laura was trying to read aloud portions from Hugo Bernard's review as the girls bumped and jolted over the hills towards home, but the newspaper pages flapped at in her face from the airstream.

Josie squealed, making a shushing motion. '*Not yet!* We have to read it with Viv!'

Laura laughed, trying to straighten the newspaper. 'Aren't we going up to the Henry's farm to collect Miles first? We promised him we'd share it with him.'

Despite how much Josie longed to watch Miles's face as he read their review, to witness first-hand his pride and admiration in her – the pull to Sylvan Mist, and the sister of her heart, was inexorable.

'Vivienne awaits,' Josie declared.

But Vivienne was not waiting at Sylvan Mist.

Laura and Josie stared, bewilderered, at the unfamiliar car parked in the driveway, behind the roadster.

'What the devil?' Josie said. The women went hurriedly up the steps.

The front door gaped wide open – something Vivienne was always too cautious to allow. 'Viv?' Josie called, trying to stay on top of rising alarm. 'Viv, are you here? *Vivienne!*'

The lobby reeked of red wine. At the foot of the stairs, was a single Samsonite train case, unopened. Not Vivienne's. A man's jacket had been thrown over it.

'Hello!' Laura hollered up the staircase, with a hand gripping the bannister. 'Who's here?'

Not far from the train case lay a large, gilt-framed portrait, surrounded by strips of red wrapping paper, discarded ribbon, shattered glass.

Josie recognised this wrapping from the wedding gift which had languished on the floor of the roadster these many months. The one Vivienne had refused to open against all Josie's badgering.

So why had Vivienne unwrapped it today? Why had she *broken* it?

Josie knelt to picked up the portrait, gently swiping glass away. It was Vivienne, in a wedding gown of finest white lace and tulle: with princess seams; a piped, nipped waist; and a scalloped sweetheart neckline. Her modest bolero jacket had been removed. She was half turned away, as though caught just leaving; a startled glance cast over bare shoulder.

Viv was indisputably beautiful and alluring here. But there was something disturbing about this picture of her dear friend, something Josie couldn't quite place her finger on. Was it the pose? Photographers seemed to favour it; Celeste's pin-up portraits were often done this way.

Celeste's portraits.

Josie looked again. That was it – the background! Vivienne, too, had been photographed against that now familiar, faux backdrop of the French Riviera.

Josie whirled on Laura and knew, from the large, blue hollows of her eyes, she was thinking the same terrible thought . . .

'*The photographer*—'

At the bottom of the stoop, Vivienne had made a split-second decision to take the mist-shrouded track to the lake on foot.

She had to trust she held the advantage this way: she'd grown so strong in all her lake swims and walks; she knew the pathway like the back of her hand, having traversed it in rain, mist and dark; she was thirty years younger than Felix *and* had soberness on her side.

She had not, however, reckoned on the power of his rage – which had blown him out of the lodge after her, roaring obscene things.

Her hammering footfalls and the sound of her own pant could not shield her from the hatred he spewed, or the relentless crash of his pursuit. Sticks cracked up as she sprinted, biting the back of her calves. She slipped on mud, stumbled over roots, took countless vines and branches to the face and torso, but somehow managed to stay upright; to *keep going*. She did not even sweat – goose pimples spread, ice-cold, over her limbs. Desperately she tried to swallow fluids into the parched folds of her throat.

Though she was still keeping just ahead of his sight, she could hear him to be *gaining* on her.

If she could get to the lake ahead of him, she could certainly *outswim* him. This thought impelled the last bolt of adrenaline needed. Passing through the fig tree tunnel, into a realm even more thickly sunk in mist, Vivienne veered off the path, weaving between trees, towards her turtle lakeview.

Behind her, she heard Felix go charging by, following the lake path. She did not pause to see if he might redirect. She had reached the water's edge. It would be difficult to see far ahead in the fog, but it was the very cover she needed.

She scrambled in between the slimy underwater logs, kicking hard now, out into the mist-cloaked deep.

Josie yanked up the label on the travelling trunk, forcing her eyes to focus through a blinding haze of panic.

'Felix Brinsley.'

Josie turned the label over and back again, shook her head, stared harder. It made no sense. Wasn't *Felix* the name of Viv's uncle?

'*Mr Brinsley?*' Laura's voice, climbing to a shrill pitch. 'What's *he* doing here unannounced?'

Josie looked between Laura and label, her eyes widening to the point of pain. Why hadn't she made the connection earlier? How had she been so sluggish and self-centred – so *stupid*? Josie shook out the jacket, hands trembling so violently she could hardly feel for the pockets.

'What are you doing!' Laura cried. 'What are you looking for?'

Josie didn't know what she was searching for, only that when found, it would answer *everything*.

A brown cowhide wallet tumbled out. Josie snatched it up, flung it open. She snapped through his pictures, seeing all the trappings of a well-to-do life: a yacht, expensive cars, trips to London, Paris, Rome. And, hidden behind all these, three images of Vivienne George.

The first: pretty and virginal in a private girls' school uniform, smiling primly at the camera. Next, caught unawares in her tennis whites, long legs bare beneath a skirt whipped up in a breeze, head thrown back in laughter. Last, and most well thumbed of all: Vivienne in her swimming costume, atop a diving board, with her arched back to the camera, ignorant of the lens focused on her pert derriere, as her arms lifted to dive.

Laura's shriek of recognition confirmed what she was staring at, but Josie mind had already spun off.

She heard again her own voice chiding Vivienne: '*You're so oddly . . . biddable, to that uncle of yours.*' She recalled Niall's taunt on the long forest driveway: '*Rudy Meyer won't ever hear about your production . . . he doesn't have a thing to do with this lodge anymore . . .*'

Josie looked up at Laura, the flesh inside her cheeks crushed painfully between her teeth. 'Felix Brinsley,' she said, 'is Vivienne's uncle. *He* owns Sylvan Mist – unbeknownst to her. He's been keeping her in his lodge, lonely and isolated, far away from everyone. Biding his time until he could finally be alone with her and . . . fulfil his most depraved urges. Don't you *see*? The man who exploited, abused and harassed Celeste to the cusp of her own death has preserved Sylvan Mist as his private mausoleum to perversity, and he's come here again, after his own niece.'

With the jungle wholly hidden by mist, it was impossible to know when Vivienne had reached the centre of the volcanic lake – much less which way she was swimming. Adrenaline, and an alternate entry point, had bamboozled her sense of direction. For all she knew, she might be swimming in circles, at the shoreline itself.

Vivienne stopped to tread water, head low, straining for the sound of another swimmer, or shouting from the bank.

She was still wearing her dressing gown – the diaphanous material become a dead, dragging weight. She struggled out of the sleeves, which clung like seaweed. The gown was jettisoned before she was even aware of opening her fingers.

There was a sudden flurry, ten yards ahead. She yelped, kicking backwards, fear surging. The noise became a recognisable slap of wings. Just a flock of ducks, landing on the lake. *Bloody things!*

But ducks also meant she was far nearer the shore than she'd imagined – and, if she weren't mistaken, not too far from the Obsidian.

And was it her imagination, or had the fog begun to dissipate?

It was certainly dispersing, visibility lengthening out even as she watched. Her gut contracted. She could not just wait here for him to spot her or come out to her!

Silently as she might, Vivienne began to paddle forward again, eyes seeming to watch in every direction at once, her jaw aching with tension held.

Vivienne knew she was on the home stretch now – perhaps only twenty yards from shore. Through the grey soup, she could start to make out the diving platform. Conquest, just beyond her reach, allowed Vivienne to feel as though she were powered by a motor. No longer did silence rate over speed. She had to *get out*, before the veiling safety of this fog lifted entirely! Her arms cut through the water with robust grace; every muscle of her body finely honed for this.

Just ahead, she could make out the sandy shelf. Around her, she felt the jellyfish tentacles of the water lilies. In only a few more strokes, she would be able to touch again.

When she hit the obstacle suddenly looming up before her, Vivienne's first thought was that she had rammed into the Obsidian's floating walkway . . .

But then a hand, large and strong, came smashing down on her head.

In Sylvan Mist, Laura recoiled bodily from Josie's summation, head shaking.

Josie launched to her feet, heartbeat ricocheting. 'We have to *stop* him!'

'But how we will find them?'

'Isn't it *obvious*? They've left the cars, so where else could they go? He must have taken her to the lake – he'll drown her!'

Laura's headshake had gone violent.

Josie gripped her by the shoulders. 'Run upstairs! Call for help! Start with the farm, then the constable – call *everyone*!'

'But where are *you* going?'

'Got to get to the lake!' Josie was already hurtling off towards the roadster, swiping keys from the top of the piano.

Laura took the stairs to the library two at a time, bellowing.

Vivienne flailed and kicked and thrashed against the arms pushing her down, holding her under. Her lungs screamed for air; her limbs wrestled for freedom. This hunger for breath, for life, was more painful and powerful than anything she'd ever known. Vivienne was tearing out her own hair in her desperation to lever his hands off her skull.

Keep going, keep going, keep going!

She could not die here, when she had so much to *live* for.

One of his hands slipped, tangling in the streaming web of her hair. Vivienne yanked the hand to her gaping mouth, sinking her teeth into his skin, tearing at his flesh.

He jerked back his arm. Her head shot up for a gasping, shuddering breath that did not seem to draw past her mouth. Her lungs screamed, still, for oxygen.

Above the surface, his fury was a rushing torrent, almost unintelligible. Decades of thwarted rage and perverse hunger spewing out of him.

He was grappling for her face again. She sucked frantically at the air, kicking away, flapping and smacking at the water to confuse his grasping hands.

After her, he came – eyes bulging, hands outstretched. Water flooded her open-mouthed shriek as he forced her, choking and sobbing, down again.

The roadster chunked to a stop on the very edge of the amphitheatre itself – Josie flung herself from the car, hands flying to shield her eyes against the light scorching across Lake Evelyn, burning through the mist. In the shallows, was a two-headed creature in a violent death roll. Reeds shook in water churned up dark; the floating walkway juddered upon the waves.

Josie tried to run, but she couldn't seem to command her feet – heavy as stone, to which no blood did flow. Paralysing terror had taken her lungs and throat too. Her mouth moved soundlessly. *Viv – make him stop! Please, Viv!*

In the lake, the beast had come apart. Vivienne's head shot up, Felix reared back. Now Vivienne was chopping away, managing to put a foot between them, then two, *three*.

Felix launched out after her, caterwauling.

They were in the emerald deep now – and the roles had suddenly reversed. It was Vivienne clinging around Felix's neck like a millstone, dragging his head under, hers clear of the water.

In the distance, Josie heard familiar car horns blaring up the road to Lake Evelyn. With a jolt, the fetters round her ankles released, lurching her forward.

I will not let the Curse take my dearest friend!

Josie tore down the amphitheatre steps, small legs having spent a lifetime going faster than a woman ought to. Her lungs vented with a warrior's full-throated howl. She charged in far as the edge of the drop off shelf. There she stood, and screamed.

Out in the deep, Vivienne's weight was beginning to take its toll around Felix's neck. His head bobbed barely above water, no longer breaking high enough for breath. His limbs, slackening. Only the crown of his head was visible above the surface.

All the movement now, belonged to Vivienne. She was seizing her chance, kicking away from him, landing one last *thud*, back-paddling towards the shore.

Josie's screams reeled her in.

When Vivienne was within a few yards, Josie threw herself out, guiding her back to the shallows. Vivienne tried to stand there, but the battle had outdone her. Josie caught her, groaning with the effort of keeping them both upright. It was an arduous stagger from the lake, Vivienne slipping lower, and lower.

Reaching the Obsidian's stage, Vivienne could stand no longer, even supported. She was a dead weight, crumpling. Josie sank to her knees beside her.

At the distant car park level, vehicles were skidding in, horns still blaring out.

Josie cradled Vivienne's head as she heaved, weakly. Her eyes were closed; skin, deathly white.

Through a sheen of tears, Josie looked up to see beloved faces, hurtling down the steps towards the women. Owen, sprinting at the lead; Gabe close on his heels. Behind, with blankets piled in arms, ran Laura and Celeste.

She raised a hand to beckon, but her fingers couldn't seem to unfurl. Her fist hung in the air for a moment, then went down.

Vivienne felt herself swaddled up and lifted high, but her eyes were so heavy, *too heavy* to open and look at the man carrying her back up the stairs, swiftly, carefully, his voice a tether: '*Stay with me Vivi, stay with me—*'

Her head pressed once to that broad chest, trying to draw in oak-moss, but it was *too tiring* to breathe anymore. Her neck tipped back over his arms, head lolling.

She had gone full limp. Voices seemed to come from afar; there was a white, warm glow, all-suffusing. She was falling again, falling and falling, and there didn't seem to be a bottom at all.

PART FOUR

'Long, long afterward, in an oak
I found the arrow, still unbroke;
And the song, from beginning to end,
I found again in the heart of a friend.'

Longfellow

CHAPTER THIRTY-EIGHT
CURTAIN CALL

Barrington Downs, 1963

Vivienne was soaring up into an oyster shell sky.

Now rushing down again, wind whooshing, houndstooth scarf billowing. From the radio swelled the crescendo of *'When the Stars Begin to Fall'*. A cheer rocketed from her mouth as the roadster bounced over a tiny creek bridge, accelerating again up the next hill.

She was on her way into town for Barrington's Christmas Eve pantomime at the Igloo, an original production, written and directed by Laura Monash. Vivienne had won the starring role, for the third year running. But this might be her last performance, at least for a while . . .

In the passenger seat, sat her husband of four years. Searing sunshine was on her right cheek and Owen's gaze, turned to savour her unbridled pleasure, was ever warm upon her left. His hand rested on her thigh but, from time to time, would wander to the modest thickening of her belly – meeting her hand, straying from the wheel.

She'd come so near to death, but soon would brim full of life.

At the homestead left behind, Owen's fine cut of beef marinated alongside Vivienne's plum pudding, silver coin embedded, for the Monash Christmas lunch tomorrow. As usual, it would be a crowded, chaotic affair, finished off with a fiercely competitive games session.

Vivienne and Owen dominated charades at every gathering, and none could unseat them.

There was only one Monash family member who rarely made Christmas, or indeed the long expedition back to Barrington; her theatre career now taking her far and wide across the country, even the globe itself. Family gatherings were never quite the same with that Josie-shaped hole always in the midst of them, and Vivienne sometimes felt herself a poor substitute for Barrington's brightest daughter.

How long had it been since Josie and Miles last came north? More than eighteen months, surely. It felt like forever. Josie's last letter had been full of exuberant bragging: the dynamic duo would be working together in Melbourne for at least another six months – in Her Majesty's Theatre, no less. *'Everyone wants a piece of me, these days!'*

Vivienne had learned not to elevate her hopes too much when Josie spoke of possible upcoming breaks in theatre schedules. In truth, Josie did not often raise the prospect.

It was silly, really; but Vivienne would have given *anything* to have seen Josie again before stepping into her most daunting role yet – as mother. She'd never have put that pressure on Josie, though, not even hinted as much. The unspoken Monash family rule: no one give Josie cause to think she was needed or necessary up here, when the world deserved her so much out there.

The roadster was passing the turn off to Lake Evelyn, with its new signs agleam. Tourist cabins, just built, could be glimpsed through the forest wall. It would be packed on the lake this summer, with canoes and swim clubs and water-skiers abounding. The lone freshwater crocodile recently discovered in Lake Evelyn had proved a quirky and harmless tourist attraction, since dubbed 'Monster'. Vivienne would always think of him as *'Josie's* crocodile', however, and she smiled to recall her friend's badly acted graciousness at being finally vindicated.

But as Vivienne's thoughts veered towards Lake Evelyn, her smile evaporated. Even after five years, she had never forced herself to revisit the lake. Perhaps one day she would go down to those waters again. For now, it remained the place where she had drowned a demon. And though police had determined there was no case to prosecute, she still had her own private sentence to live out.

Vivienne had yet to reconcile these two Felix Brinsleys: the closest man to a father she'd ever known, and the sexual deviant, the murderer, who had hunted her round a jungle lake. In the end, the girl he'd groomed the longest and saved for last, was his undoing.

As too, was his artistic vanity. Perhaps, if Felix Brinsley had not so lauded his own photographic skills, he might have destroyed the comprehensive documentation of his sadism. But he had been unable to let go of his vile trophies.

And when investigators went down to the dark room, they found, in carefully preserved boxes, all the evidence of his penchant for darkhaired beauties, beginning with Celeste Starr. Among the many boxes archived in Felix's dark room, three girls of Barrington were found, girls heretofore called Floaters: Valerie Rose, Glenda West, and Loreen Larson. Not every Barrington girl drowned in Lake Evelyn had come under Sylvan Mist's spell, but these three had been caught in a web expertly strung.

His modus operandi, Vivienne knew, must have been flattery sublime, a swamping charm. How many times had she imagined it? The young woman walking alongside the lake, the handsome stranger photographing birds on the water. Him standing to greet her, eyes large with admiration. How long had his polite small talk lasted before he came in boasting of having taken Celeste Starr's photographs, of knowing how to spot a star-in-the-making? She could hear his silky opening ploy . . .

I have to ask; do you have any idea how much you resemble the beautiful Nightingale of Lake Evelyn? No? How peculiar. Well, perhaps they don't want you taking it too much to your head, getting ideas about stardom – small town folks can be funny like that. But, you could do it, you know – model, I mean. You have just the face for it, the perfect figure . . .

Yes, Vivienne knew his inveigling all too well.

Starry-eyed each girl must have gone, back to Sylvan Mist with the gregarious Felix, to view his photographs of Celeste, and marvel at her beauty and allure. To imagine themselves something like her. A glass or two of bracing wine while taking Felix's tour might have set a young lady's shyness at ease, and hastened her agreement to go down with him, in the end, to his darkroom.

What came next didn't bear thinking about – though some days, it was all Vivienne did think about.

Felix Brinsley had not been alone in this perversity. For nearly thirteen years, Niall Jeffries had been employed to maintain Felix's hunting lodge, the pair having found a *common interest* during the war. Niall had turned out to be a very useful employee. He'd spied on Felix's guests, warded off local trespassers, and concealed that darkroom, with full knowledge of its contents. A partnership benefiting two monsters.

But there had been some justice served. The joint coronial inquest of 1959, undertaken after vociferous public outcry, had recommended police lay charges against Niall Jeffries as an accessory after the fact, in the murders of Valerie, Glenda, and Loreen. A dark resolution, for *three* of the six girls drowned in Lake Evelyn.

The community of Barrington had worked tirelessly to put those cursed years behind them: converting the amphitheatre to a picnic seating area, building a new teahouse to overlook the emerald lake; razing Sylvan Mist to the ground.

Barrington's heart, however, must go on mending.

The roadster was rounding the corner into Main Street: cottage fronts hung with wreaths, coloured bulbs strung up around the milk bar and Grand Hotel, the potted ferns outside the community library tinsel-glittered under summer heat. The Corner Shop, since converted to a Trading Store, hardly warranted a second glance. Niall would keep his sordid role in Barrington's history forever, but he'd left no legacy on Main.

They flew past the Purple House. Daphne was at the front gate, apron on, both hands at her hips, hollering at four small girls with identical French braids, chalk drawing on the path outside. The girls leapt up, rejoicing at the sight of Aunty Viv and Uncle Owen's approach, dissolving just as quickly into tears, as the car throttled by, without so much as a window roll-down. Daphne scowled after their tail lights.

Vivienne swung into the car park reserved for members of the Barrington Theatre Company – with a coach parking bay set aside for the Chook Chaser. The Igloo, freshly painted inside and out, was spilling out with pre-show preparations. The insufferable humidity within would be eased only by the sun's sinking, and fans at full shudder.

Laura Monash, lying in wait at the door, swooped on Vivienne. In their embrace, Vivienne could feel Laura fairly twanging with tension.

How lucky Vivienne counted herself to have Laura for her director, and as a new sister-in-law, too. But they had formed their own sisterhood long before Laura finally said yes to Ernest Monash.

'It's going to go down like a *bomb* tonight,' Laura declared. Vivienne knew very well that Laura said this to reassure herself, more than anyone else.

'Like a bomb,' Vivienne repeated serenely. 'There'll be nothing left of the place when we're done.'

Laura nodded hard. 'OK, good. Thank you.' She squeezed Vivienne's hand tight enough to crush bones. 'Everyone's waiting for you out back, hurry – *go!*'

Owen leaned to Vivienne's ear, a large hand spreading over her lower back. Breath and beard tickled at her neck. 'Good luck, Voyager,' he whispered. Their secret protection against superstition.

Bolstered she went, to find the rest of her company. Her *playmates*.

The Green Room was a cauldron of nerves and vocalisations, bubbling over. Vivienne threw herself into the mix.

An oboe was giving the note for the turning. Behind the curtain, ready to take the stage for her opening number, Vivienne was in a black and gold flapper dress, with ebony fringe stirring at her knees, glossy feathers fluttering at her crown. Rita had outdone herself as usual, perfectly invoking the Roaring Twenties with her exquisite costumery.

Theatre magic thrummed through Vivienne; every cell of her body *bewitched*. But before she would let that ephemeral power sweep her out onto the stage and into the light, there was one last rite to perform.

She closed her eyes, allowing herself a moment of yearning. '*Mother*,' she breathed: 'See how happy I am. Hear how strong I am.'

Her mother was the one person Vivienne held no hope of spying in her audience. Geraldine George had gone swiftly abroad when her brother's name hit the national headlines, and had stayed there ever since.

Vivienne pitied her mother, not herself.

She has missed the best and bravest years of my life. And going forward, into better years still, I shall no longer keep a ghost's seat reserved in my heart . . .

The conductor sounded three baton taps.

The tuning was done, and her spotlight awaited.

The show was over, the auditorium and supper room cleaned up and swept out; everyone else long gone.

Vivienne wandered slowly down through the theatre, extinguishing each light in turn. Overhead, the corrugated iron creaked as it cooled. The raucous after-party at the Grand, reached this inner sanctum only faintly.

Of all the show rituals Vivienne had claimed for herself, this was her favourite: being the very last member to leave the theatre. Owen would wait outside for her tonight, as long as she might need. She cherished this last moment, when all the people had finally gone, and she was free to take a quiet, proud reflection on her own performance. Her lifelong habit of overthinking and rumination had evolved into a practice far more mature, and edifying.

This evening's performance had been splendid, among her finest, but it could never hold a candle to her Nightingale. Roles like that came along once in a lifetime – if you were lucky.

Approaching the front door, she stopped before the feature wall of Josie's many, many reviews, mailed up to Barrington for framing and display. Vivienne knew every word by heart, so often did she pause beneath those sassy headshots, nursing the ache of Josie-sickness that never went away.

She reached for the final light switch.

Time to lock up, then home for a malted milk before bed.

In the car park, there was a dark figure, standing by the bonnet of her roadster. A petite shape, with an A-line silhouette, and a swishing ponytail.

Vivienne would have known it *anywhere*.

'You came back!'

There was a gust of laughter, carrying pure sunshine. '*Surprise*, Viv.'

A hot torrent hit her eyes. 'But you said you couldn't make it up north . . . you're playing in Her Majesty's Theatre—'

'You didn't think I'd leave it to my brother to plan the greatest baby shower Barrington has ever seen?'

Standing back behind Josie, Owen chuckled.

Josie held out a posy of orchids. 'I stole these for you, from Grandy's.'

Tears beaded large along Vivienne's lashes. Her cheeks quivered with the smile breaking wide. 'Do you *know* how much I've *missed* you?'

Josie's voice shook as she came barrelling towards her. 'I think I can imagine . . .'

Vivienne flung wide her arms, with all the radiance of the evening star.

ACKNOWLEDGMENTS

The Girls of Lake Evelyn centres around the fictional town of Barrington, set on the real Atherton Tablelands – an area of astonishing natural beauty, fascinating history, and close-knit, enduring communities. Of particular note, the Atherton Tablelands was an important base of military operations during World War II. My own grandfather, an Australian soldier who served in Papua New Guinea, spent time in this region during the war.

As a girl, I was blessed to enjoy countless hours on my father's tour coaches, as he guided visitors around Far North Queensland. One of my favourite tours to take with Dad was the Atherton Tablelands journey, encompassing the rolling green hills, waterfalls, quaint teahouses and majestic lakes of this stunning area. As Dad's coach toiled up the many, *many* corners of the Gillies Range Road, he would try to keep his passengers' minds off their travel sickness with wonderful commentary, full of history, nature facts, quirky local tales and, of course, dad jokes. While Dad was spinning his yarns, I'd have my face pressed to the window, making up my own stories. The sense of wonder instilled in my writer's heart by these adventures cannot be overstated. I have long desired to write a novel capturing, even in some small way, the beauty of the Atherton Tablelands.

In dreaming up *The Girls of Lake Evelyn*, I was incredibly thankful for the knowledge and expertise of the Eacham Historical Society, and the wealth of information shared in their many publications and resources. My novel, however, is purely a work of imagination, and any factual or historical errors are entirely my own, to serve the story.

Lake Evelyn is based on the volcanic crater lakes of the area – Lake Eacham (Yidyam), Lake Barrine (Barany) and Lake Euramo (Ngimun). These sublime lakes are most significant in the cultural history of the Ngadjon-Jii people, the Aboriginal Traditional Owners. A Ngadjon myth explains the origin of these crater lakes, ten thousand years ago.

While no eerie Nightingale's curse hangs over any of the crater lakes, there certainly *is* a crocodile in Lake Eacham.

Embarking on a second book to a deadline, in the midst of a pandemic, with four children learning at home, and the fear of 'second book syndrome' hanging over my head was an intimidating undertaking, to say the least. That I *made* it is owed to the incredible people who supported me through everything . . .

My extraordinary agent, mentor, and friend, Selwa Anthony, with her warm counsel, brilliant ideas and the laser-like ability to spot any characters or plot points I don't truly believe in. After initially going off track, my story found its beating heart again because Selwa guided me back to it.

Tegan Morrison, my most wonderful publisher, thank you for steering me through the publication of my first and second novels. Your finesse, attention to detail, gracious heart and encouraging spirit made this two-book journey an absolute joy!

The vibrant, fabulous team at Echo Publishing – Benny Agius, Juliet Rogers, Rosie Outred, Emily Banyard and Lizzie Hayes – thank you for looking after me, and my books, with such wonderful care, expertise and enthusiasm. Likewise, I am forever grateful to all at Bonnier Books

UK – especially my editor, Claire Johnson-Creek, and my copyeditor, Sandra Ferguson – for bringing the shining best out in my books!

My beloved Mummsy, thank you for reading each raw chapter of my manuscript as I churned them out, and for so patiently starting over again with me at the beginning, when it came to that. Aleta, my gorgeous sister, thank you for letting me steal your stunning middle name for my Nightingale. My brother, Rowan, thank you for joining the police service for the sole purpose of my being able to pepper you with policing questions during novel research. Any erroneous depiction of police work is probably my own . . . but it's pretty obvious I was set up by a dastardly sibling.

My Bossiest Beta Reader™, the frank and funny Kate DiGiuseppe, I cannot thank you enough for your emboldening support over countless exchanges. You reduce my writerly neuroticism by *at least* 27%! I'm sorry I couldn't name a Kate after you this time, but I did slip a Milly cameo in there.

To Wendy Kenny, thank you for so generously sharing your written memories of growing up in Far North Queensland in the fifties and sixties. It's been my privilege to incorporate some little nods to your amazing memory and entertaining tales.

I want to send a trillion thankyous to my beautiful readers, and the passionate librarians and booksellers who have so bigheartedly embraced *Those Hamilton Sisters*. Your moving responses have meant *everything* to me! Thank you for the many emails and messages, shout-outs and social media posts, and all the lovely photos of my debut novel out in the wild. At times, it can feel quite isolating for an author living in a far-flung regional area – particularly with border closures and lockdowns – but through your pictures and letters, you've helped me to travel right around the country, and the world, meeting avid booklovers.

Although I can never thank them in this world, I have honoured four remarkable grandparents in this novel: Amelia Frances and George Dixon, in the purple house on Monash Street; and Robert Henry and Eula Beryl, in the rambling farmhouse set in rolling hills of green. This novel includes so many tributes to my farm girl, small-town childhood, and my story's heart belongs to the grandest of grandies!

Finally, and most importantly, I want to thank the five people who've had to *live* with me over the last two years: Liam, Dash, Aurora, Eleanor and Teddy. Thank you, Team Kenny, for your unconditional love and unshakable faith in me. Liam, I treasure the memory of seeing you, on holidays at *our* 'Bonnie Doon', unable to tear yourself away from my manuscript, while everyone else was whooping it up in the pool. I have the courage to release this second novel into the world because you couldn't put it down . . .

If you enjoyed *The Girls of Lake Eveyln*, why not try
the author's debut . . .

Those Hamilton Sisters

**A warm, captivating and irresistible story of love, family, secrets
and finding your place in the world.**

Esther Hamilton had a reputation in the small Queensland town of
Noah Vale. That was until she ran away, twenty years ago, under a
cloud of shame. It is now 1955 and following her death, her daughters, the Hamilton sisters, have come to make the town their home.

Sonnet, at twenty years old, has never set foot in Noah Vale, but has
been the talk of the town for decades. Fable is a budding artist and
lovelier even than her heartbreaking mother. And Plum is just a little
girl who has been taken away from the only home she has ever known.

As the years pass the girls settle into their new life. But suspicion and
judgement follow them wherever they go. In a small town where everyone knows each other, it can be hard to escape the past . . .

Available now, read on for a sneak peek . . .

CHAPTER 1
TO NOAH VALE
1955

The Sunday train which snaked into Noah Vale that verdant, midwinter afternoon brought with it fire, sending an inferno of small-town gossip roaring up the valley.

Olive Emerson, a sprightly middle-aged figure on the crowded platform, shot off one last fretful prayer as the train jerked to a stop, then wandered slowly along its length, scanning each carriage for the first glimpse of her nieces – three newly orphaned girls come home to their outcast mother's birthplace.

And here they were. The fifth carriage was set to burn, flaming with redheads: the first, richest red, hauled back in an austere bun; the second, flowing strawberry flames striated with gold; and lastly, the burnished auburn curls of a clinging three-year-old. Olive marvelled at how Esther's radiant colouring had filtered down through her daughters. Each girl carried that wild, red streak in her own way – enough of their tragically beautiful mother to bless or curse, accordingly.

Superstitious fool, Olive rebuked herself. She'd vowed to wipe the slate clean with her nieces – a mercy Esther was never afforded.

Olive's eyes fixed on the carriage window, imploring the girls to acknowledge her before the murmuring crowd. She was acutely conscious of her assumed status here as rescuing aunt, when, in truth, she was naught but a stranger to these girls.

Olive had *heard* the voices down Main Street dripping with scorn over the latest Hamilton tragedy: the long-ostracised daughter of Noah Vale finally getting her comeuppance, and Esther's bastards coming home in repentance for her.

Even after all these years, Olive could not stomach what had happened to her kinfolk. The Hamiltons had been a founding family of this insular rural valley and, for generations, bastions of respectability in church, school and farming life. No one would have predicted it – least of all themselves.

Malcolm and Lois Hamilton, coming late to parenthood, had raised two girls who would take vastly different paths in life. Olive, the eldest, had finished school at fourteen, married a nice local boy and settled into her expected place. Though Olive and Gavin Emerson had produced no children of their own, they'd always given back to the community, and tried to be a light to others. Side by side, their shop shingles proudly hung: EMERSON'S HARDWARE, and EMERSON'S FASHION AND FABRICS.

Then there was Esther.

A change-of-life baby, born more than a decade after Olive, Esther had been an aspiring writer, with a bright intellect and astonishing beauty. The most promising debutante to have ever graced the stage of Noah Vale School! Or so they once had said. Esther Hamilton was only remembered now as a ruinous Jezebel.

The Hamiltons had lived with that shame chafing their infamous family pride for nearly two decades. But Lois and Malcolm had both passed away in recent years, unreconciled with a daughter who'd proven herself, time and time again, a woman of ill repute.

For twenty years, Olive had borne the comparisons between the Hamilton sisters, suffered their estrangement, and prayed unceasingly for little Essie to be brought to her senses and home to the family fold. But pride on one side, and shame on the other, had proven insurmountable on both counts.

Of the Hamiltons, only Olive had sustained tenuous contact with Esther. Odd letters and birthday cards, occasional phone calls, all attempted gently, through indirect routes. Mostly they went unanswered, or took so circuitous a journey back, they were hardly relevant anymore. But what more could Olive have done?

The question haunted her.

The Hamiltons' last contact with Esther, eight years ago, had been to inform her of Lois's funeral arrangements. What daughter *wouldn't* come home for her mother's funeral? Well, Olive knew now: the one who was telephoned for the first time in twelve years by her gruff-voiced father and expressly forbidden to attend, lest she bring shame on an honourable woman's memory. There was no question of Esther coming home for her father's funeral a few short years later.

Banished Esther had stayed, until her own wretched end three months ago – in a red Hillman Minx skidding across a wet, lonely road, with Japanese maples raining down. Drunk, as far as Olive could determine. What an ignoble ending for the girl who'd seemed likely to outshine them all.

Olive winced as the foot worrying at her calf began to cramp. She hadn't even received news of her sister's death until two months ago. There she was going about her quiet, orderly life for weeks with no idea her baby sister had been wiped from the face of the earth.

And here, now, were Olive's homeless, fatherless, friendless nieces: Sonnet, Fable and little Novella Plum, whom they apparently called Plum.

Unease prickled beneath Olive's collar. Perhaps she should have been more forthright on the phone with Esther's girls about their mother's history in Noah. It had been on the tip of her tongue, burning. But how *did* one initiate such delicate topics with grieving girls? And what right did Olive think she had to tell them anything?

No, they would have to take it one step at a time, together.

Finally, her eldest niece turned to the train window. Her weary gaze swept over Olive, taking in the sea of peering faces. Olive raised a shaky hand. Sonnet's eyes settled on her with an unsmiling nod before she turned away to snap shut Plum's tiny suitcase.

Olive wondered if she had time to swallow an aspirin before the girls disembarked.

First was Sonnet, new legal guardian, who, twenty years earlier, had caused her mother's belly to swell beneath her school uniform. Sonnet had never stepped foot in Noah Vale, yet she'd been the talk of the town for decades. Olive shivered. Unlike her willowy mother – all curves and slender limbs – Sonnet was tall and toned, matching a queenly athleticism to her mother's generous bosom. The severe hairstyle did nothing to flatter her strong features, but she was undeniably striking with her sharp green eyes.

Following close in Sonnet's wake was Plum. Olive's heart squeezed at the sight of the chubby girl cleaving to her sister's hand. To her chest, she clutched a comfort bear. Ringlets framed aubergine eyes, a heart-shaped face and full cheeks.

Twelve-year-old Fable was last to step down from the train, and when she did, Olive's lungs faltered on a disbelieving breath.

It was Esther in the doe eyes and full lips. Esther in the long, spilling mane, Esther in the slender limbs, and Esther plastered all over those fine features. Only the hair was different. And while Esther's eyes had shone vixen green, Fable's were a sunlit amber floating in a pool of violet shadows.

This young girl was lovelier than even her heartbreaking mother had been.

Four Hamilton women stood in silent regard of one another. All around them, curious eyes and ears strained; whispers crackled.

Blood of my blood, Olive thought, scouring her nieces for traces of herself.

She stepped forward to embrace the girls, and was rebuffed. Sonnet bore a frown that would intimidate the best of women. Fable, poker-faced, glanced rapidly between sister and new aunt. Plum quaked against Sonnet's skirt, reaching and mewling to be carried.

This was no place for intimate first meetings.

'After all these years, you've finally come to Noah Vale!' Olive said. 'I can't tell you how glad I am to have you here.'

She extended a hand to Sonnet. Instead of taking it, Sonnet leaned forward in tight-lipped appeal. 'Can we go straight to your car? This is too much. The girls are exhausted.'

Olive reached for the first of three shabby suitcases. 'Follow me!'

Sonnet heaved the last suitcase into the back of the Holden, then hurried an escaping red tress back into her bun. Olive straightened the smallest bag. Both women stared at the suitcases for a strained moment.

'Okay, then,' Olive said, slamming the boot. 'Let's get you girls home. I've got lovely chicken soup on the stove.'

Sonnet dallied, hand on boot.

Olive paused. 'Sonnet?'

'We'll go directly to the cottage.'

Olive made for the car door. 'Oh no, it's late. Gav and I will take you over in the morning. First thing.'

'We want to move in immediately,' Sonnet said, with eyes fastened on two small redheads through the back window.

'Goodness, we haven't prepared the cottage. It's not fit for living in – the electricity hasn't even been restored yet.'

'Not a problem.'

'No, dear, it needs plenty of work first,' Olive said. 'Gav was going to look at all that for you.'

Sonnet's jaw jutted. It was an expression Olive suspected she would come to know – and resign herself to.

'I told you on the phone, we intend to move straight in. I won't camp out in a stranger's home.'

Olive's forehead puckered. 'But we only want to take care of—'

'I've been caring for my sisters since they were born, and exclusively since our mother's passing. We don't need *taking care of.*'

Oh yes, Olive could only imagine how it must have been, living perpetually in flight – switching cities, homes and friends at their mother's whim. How could this young woman be anything but fiercely independent?

Olive was torn. Pursue, or let them be? 'I fear you'll be disappointed, dear. The cottage is run-down and infested with pests – gecko poo everywhere! Rainforest rats, too.'

'It'll be fine for us.'

'But it's hardly proper for young girls to be living all on their own. We've plenty of room at the main house. You'll hardly know we're there—'

'It's not up for ruddy discussion,' Sonnet snapped, 'I outlined my plans specifically before we left Canberra.'

'Yes, I recall. But, by golly, you must want a break? You've had so much to bear. Surely we could help shoulder your burdens?'

But she'd pressed too hard. Sonnet was about to blow her top.

'As you wish, then, to the cottage we'll go. I'll let you see for *yourself* the condition it's in.'

'You've arrived at our mildest time of year,' Olive intoned as the car began a steep ascent from the station. 'Winter in the tropics is paradise: picnics and swimming every day. We love life away from the big smoke. And we're a close-knit community.'

In the passenger seat, Sonnet sat in taut silence.

'Noah Vale is an old sugar town. You'd have seen our mill as you came into the valley. Cane all round these parts, but we can also boast of our tobacco, mango and banana plantations. Lots of historic properties.'

They emerged on a wide curve. Below, within a steep bowl of mountain ranges, on top of a rolling patchwork quilt, lay Noah Vale.

'*This* is our town.'

Late-afternoon sunlight, having loitered all day behind blanketing rain, broke forth at the mountain rim now, sweeping golden beams across the misty vale. It was a technicolour scene; overblown hues slickly accentuated by rain.

Olive cast a glance at the back seat and saw Fable's lips part wide. Plum, straining to see, was so bug-eyed as to be comical. Only Sonnet remained rigid, unreadable.

They began the descent into Noah Vale: past a tractor idling in a freshly tilled field, with egrets strolling the red rows; along an avenue of vermilioned mango trees; and onto a bridge spanning a wide, shrouded creek gorge.

'Serpentine Creek,' Olive said, nodding below. 'Winds right through the middle of the valley.'

'*Oh*,' Fable breathed, rousing from her slumberous enchantment. 'Sonny, it's *Mama's* creek! Remember? How she always talked about her Serpentine Spells . . .'

Olive tsked. 'What nonsense. Esther barely looked up from her books to notice the creek existed! And if she loved the creek so much, then why did . . .' Seeing Fable's face shuttering up, Olive halted. Tension infused the air.

Olive momentarily removed her hand from the steering wheel, to touch the foil of tablets in her skirt pocket. She'd make a cuppa for the girls once they arrived at Heartwood, and take a couple of aspirins then.

'Well, never mind,' Olive muttered. 'You'll be close to the creek at the cottage, so you'll see for yourself: it's just an ordinary, non-magical watercourse. At least until the wet season – then we have our own raging river!'

Plum's small face pressed worriedly against the window.

'The bridge into Noah floods over each year. All our bridges do in the Wet, cutting us off from the outside world. Wettest region of Australia, we can go weeks without a ray of sunshine. Practically need an ark!'

They were entering Main Street now. Impeccable art deco buildings with pretty, rustic facades lined the street front. Veritable institutions presided proudly: the Post Office, the Canecutter's Hotel, the Paragon Cafe – all respectably closed on a Sunday afternoon.

'There are our shops,' Olive said, slowing the car to a mere putter, as they passed the adjacent stores.

Olive admired her shop-window mannequins, garbed in modest, ladylike dresses for the occasion of her nieces' grand arrival. 'Not quite what you're seeing in winter fashion down south, I imagine, but we don't really *do* winter here.'

Seeing the wrinkle between Sonnet's eyes, Olive added, 'I'll be glad to have young women to inspire me now. My largest demographic is our middle-aged ladies, and I lose many debutantes each year to the big department stores in Cairns. I've got plenty of work for you girls in my shop . . . if you're interested.'

Sensing Sonnet bristling, she pressed her foot on the accelerator, leaving behind, for now, her dream of graceful nieces swanning between clothing racks, sprinkling youth and vivacity all about.

Main Street forked out around a large park, fronted with a wrought-iron gate. The giant trees within, their branches spreading so widely they might have roofed a house, seemed to pique Sonnet's interest.

Olive quickly resumed her tour guiding. 'Rain trees. They've been in Noah Vale since we were settled. In winter, our church – you see, just over there – hosts a Sugar Festival in the park, to kick off the cane-crushing season. Every family in town has a table. There are rides and stalls – you girls will love it!'

She'd lost Sonnet, however, to glazed indifference at the first mention of 'our church'.

They wound over another hillock, blanketed in banana crops, passing a school on the crest. Fable wound down the window.

'Is this my school?' she asked, eyes combing old timber buildings and the banyan trees spilling their long tendrils.

'Yes, primary and high are both together here. You'll be the fourth generation of Hamiltons to step over the threshold of Noah Vale School . . .' Olive paled, the rest of her story unuttered. . .

But the last Hamilton here was howled off the school grounds.

The journey continued where the proud commentary did not, as Queenslander homesteads spread out between farmland. The valley narrowed and deepened; looming mountains, implausibly green, enclosing them. Through one last grove of rainforest and there, proudly overlooking flowering cane, was the Hamiltons' colonial-style plantation house.

'This,' Olive said grandly, 'is Heartwood.'

Olive heard Sonnet's intake of breath as she clapped eyes on the sweeping veranda and hanging ferns, white shutters open to the bending pawpaws, coconut palms standing sentry around, and showy tropical gardens bursting against the white wood.

'It *is* nice,' offered Sonnet. 'I can see why you're keen to host us.'

'Gav and I inherited this home from your grandparents. The very land I was born on. It was a working cane farm back then, but most of the cane I roamed as a young girl is now farmed by the Hulls on one side of us, and the Lagorios on the other.'

The Holden pulled to a stop.

'And now,' said Olive, 'we make the short trek to your new residence.'

A golden retriever bounded over the grass towards the newcomers. Plum screamed, throwing herself onto Sonnet.

Olive tutted as the dog gambolled around them. 'Oh, never mind Zephyr, he's friendly.'

Plum wailed while Sonnet bobbed a hip to hush the crying. 'Olive, Plum's terrified of dogs!'

'Oh dear,' Olive said, with more peevishness than intended. 'Zeph adores everyone, so don't take his enthusiasm too personally. Down, boy, down!'

Zephyr sat with a grin and Olive shrugged. 'She'll get used to him quickly enough.'

'Or maybe we'll have to steer clear of his house.'

Zephyr was promptly removed to the veranda. His gaze followed the Hamilton sisters longingly as they girded themselves with suitcases.

Bypassing the main house, they climbed an orchard hill filled with exotic fruit trees. Fable reached out to touch a swollen fruit with reptilian skin.

'My custard apples,' Olive began. 'And wait till you try . . .'

But Sonnet wasn't stopping for anything now.

Atop the hill, they gazed over a flood-plain paddock stretching to a thick remnant ribbon of rainforest-shrouded creek. Nestled at the base of the slope was a ramshackle wooden cottage encircled by trees and a garden choked with allamanda shrubs, molasses grass and climbing mandevilla. In the falling darkness, the cottage was a beacon of homeliness against lush, dark forest.

Fable sighed.

'The cottage is Edwardian era, built by your grandparents,' Olive explained as they trotted, with increasing momentum, down the hill. 'I lived in the cottage myself during my early married life, and after me, it was always promised to your mother. Even after she . . . left Noah Vale, it was still hers. We've used it as a guest house, and more recently as a storage shed. But now, it's yours.'

As the younger girls streaked off ahead, Olive stopped. Sonnet turned questioningly.

Olive sighed, long and hard.

'Here,' she said, pressing her key into Sonnet's hand. 'You go ahead, make yourselves at home. I wish you'd believe me – it's really quite unliveable. But at least there are clean sheets on the beds, hurricane lanterns, and on the bench you'll find sugar bananas, fresh bread and passionfruit curd for your supper. I had suspected you'd insist on staying here tonight. You are your mother's daughter, after all. It will be rough for you, but if it's what you really want . . . ?'

Sonnet was a horse, already bolting.

Fable was first to step through the rickety gate and under the rotting arbour. She paused to admire the crumbling gables and attic windows winking in the last golden light; lifted her nose to receive the scent of gardenias blooming in the wild overgrowth; tiptoed over frangipani blossoms scattered on the stone pathway; and, hearing the creek song, felt her pulse beat double. Here was more beauty than she'd ever beheld in her young life. Here, her broken heart could heal.

Sonnet, striding up the stairs, picked at the peeling clapboard paint as she entered the fusty darkness, and began her inspection with a mental spring cleaning – obliterating years of dirt by force of imagination. She scoured the claw-foot tub in a mould-acrid bathroom, swept cobwebs from the exposed beams, chased dust bunnies down the long central hallway, banished clutter from the window seat in the sunroom, excavated furniture from debris, and scrubbed grime from the front bay window. She traced a finger along a grimy bookcase, counting spaces for each book she might one day display, and nodded approval at a simple, albeit cluttered kitchen. She finished her inspection with a sigh, as if after physical work. In all, she saw potential for a real home at last.

CHAPTER 2

HEARTWOOD

The greasy sizzle of eggs, announced by an insistent rainforest dove call, brought Sonnet, stomach clenching, to consciousness. Her eyes panned the attic bedroom, waiting for any of it to make sense: faded chintz curtains at the dormer windows letting in warm light; lumpy, left-sliding bed; vintage tallboy and dresser buried in bric-a-brac; and, in an imposing wardrobe, floral dresses and beaded gowns hung like limp, grandmotherly wraiths. Sonnet was home.

But without Mama, how could it ever truly be home?

'*Saudade*,' Sonnet whispered into the musty air – one of her favourite words from her collection, and lately a lifeline. Nothing else came close to describing this new existence: *the presence of absence*.

Now she had an aunt, and endless work ahead of her. Sonnet cringed to recall the tension of the previous afternoon. She hoped she hadn't put Olive offside already, but the woman was persistent as hell. Something about Olive's earnestness had immediately irked her. Though to be fair, many things annoyed Sonnet about many people. She should wait to see exactly what Olive had to offer them before she wrote her off completely.

Surveying the mess around her, Sonnet felt a spasm of panic in her gut, remembering the tiny, neat rental they'd left behind in Canberra as something like a castle. That flat had housed them longer than any other – three whole years – and was the only home Plum had ever known. There, for the first time, life had been stable, even bright; as if a shadow had fallen away from all of their lives.

Sonnet had spent her senior year at a single high school, a miracle itself, graduating with excellence. Not that there was much point in academic overachievement, or secret dreams of attending university. Straight out of school, Sonnet had eschewed higher learning to join Mama in her dressmaking work. It was the least Sonnet could do to help support the girls, and she'd suspected it was her destiny since the first stitch Mama insisted she sew in girlhood. Fable, nearing adolescence, had been thriving too – cherishing the new private art classes Mama scraped every last dollar together to afford. Plum, meanwhile, had been lovingly cared for by Esther's new friend, Maria, who lived across the hallway.

Plum had always known a different version of Esther Hamilton from the one Fable and Sonnet were born to. That dimpled darling had heralded such change in their mother, it could scarcely be believed. With Plum's arrival, Mama had finally seemed ... well, you could never say *content*, but something like settled. Sonnet supposed much of it owed to Esther's close friendship with mother-of-five and devout Christian, Maria. Despite Sonnet's distrust of religiosity, she conceded to Maria's calming effect on their mother. Life had been conventional, even banal. Almost forgotten were the days when Mama would uproot their lives without notice, desperate to outrun something, or someone.

Had Mama managed to stay ahead of her demons in recent years? Sonnet wanted to believe so. There had been less of the chaos and calamity of earlier years. No more of the month-long periods tiptoeing past the door as Mama tried to sleep her way out of hell. And none of those mystery lovers, experienced only in fragments – a sonorous voice on the telephone, a familiar scent on Mama's skin, the shadow passing their window in the wee hours. There had been more of Mama's buoyant, creative episodes, her literature quoting, that folksy alto drifting through the flat. Mama had still dripped with turquoise, incense and allure, but there had been maturation, at last.

Normality and predictability, after all, had always been hard won with their quixotic mama: vivacious and ferociously loving one moment, the very next blankly distant and overwrought. No one else seemed to have a mother as young and beautiful – or as sad. Esther was the girl play-acting a mother's role, and forgetting her lines. She who dragged them out to art galleries and literary festivals at late hours, though it always ended in tears – her own – yet avoided the school gate, school parents, schoolwork, even the mere mention of school itself. Esther would happily live in domestic squalor for months on end, and then embark on manic cleaning enterprises as if she expected any moment to entertain royalty. Perpetually tired, Mama could rarely muster the will after a long shift to make lunches, serve supper, or indeed provide nutrition at all. Her 'nerves', Mama described as constantly 'afire'. Sonnet might have corrected: *No, Mama, burning out.*

That was where Sonnet had always stepped in, wasn't it? She'd tried her hardest to lighten Mama's burdens. Sonnet: cook and cleaning lady; clothes mender; grout scrubber; school-bag packer; grocery shopper. Sonnet had realised at a young age what sort of girls they were – poor and fatherless, the kind to pity. Shrewdly, she'd learned to decode the prying aid of neighbours, and the recruiting charity of churchy do-gooders. Each claiming concern for the 'safety' of young girls left alone while their mother worked long days and nights to support them, with no father to guarantee moral decency – or rent, paid in full, and on time. Sonnet had learned, like Mama, to reject such charity with scathing pride. She'd embraced the lesson Esther had imparted in word and deed: 'We don't need anyone else; we Hamilton girls will always have each other.'

Until death came romping in and, suddenly, we didn't.

Plum seemed to suffer most, keening for weeks on end for the mother who would never, this time, come home. Plum had spent her infancy attached to Esther whenever she wasn't working. She was carried constantly, loved desperately and slept curled around Esther's breast.

But Plum had also adapted most quickly, scrambling for what she needed from Sonnet. She slept in Sonnet's bed by night, and clung tenaciously to her by day. All her pain was visible, treatable.

It was Fable, unnervingly serene since Mama's death, who kept Sonnet frozen awake at night. Fable was a smooth, mirroring pond of unfathomable depths; hidden waters always unplumbed. Mama always had a special way of reaching Fable there. But would Sonnet? Wailing and railing Sonnet might have soothed, but inner turmoil would go unchecked. And long had Sonnet vexed over Fable's propensity for secret worlds that could not be guessed at or entered into.

Fable Winter had arrived at a heartbreaking time for Esther, abandoned by another mysterious lover, who, in his absence, managed to fill their lives entirely. Fable's absconding father stole away with him most of Esther, too. The petite baby girl with the dark violet eyes, who rushed into the world one August morning, was placed into the arms of a hollowed-out mother. Sonnet was only eight at the time, but well she remembered the heavy-hearted mother who drifted from room to room with her bundle of strawberry-gold held near, yet so far. She had insisted Mama should 'send back' the baby who'd brought such sadness with her.

Fable seemed to know, from the moment she was born, that she ought not to make a fuss; rather, to soothe herself and be thankful for the smallest ministrations. Where Sonnet before her had been fractious and demanding – still *was*, she could admit – Fable was an obliging, placid child. She was also the sole recipient of Mama's creative passions; an avid writer, and a precociously talented artist. Yet while Esther's literary endeavours were frenetic and dispirited, Fable's artistic heart was sweet, steady and dreamy.

Or had been.

Frighteningly, Fable hadn't touched brush or pencil since the day Mama had died. The stillness and cleanliness of Fable's hands terrified Sonnet. It was for Fable, more than anyone, Sonnet had brought them here. Fable, heading into the tumultuous last years of girlhood, needed stability, quietude, security – all of which Noah Vale offered. From Sonnet's research, this valley sounded like an idyllic Eden.

In bittersweet irony, Mama's passing had presented the girls with a new station in life. Two unexpected treasures arose from Esther's carefully structured will: a cottage of their own and a generous fund for the girls – an inheritance Esther apparently had been too proud to spend on herself. Enough to set them up independently, in a real home, within walking distance of an aunt, who, by their mother's vague testimony, had a 'good heart'.

Too right Sonnet had jumped at this opportunity! Whatever the reasons Mama had come to despise her family and community, they were not Sonnet's. Mama was fond of saying, 'small towns breed small minds', and she'd avoided ever stepping foot outside a city again. But as the daughter of an unwed mother, even a seasoned city-dweller, Sonnet knew all too well: conservatism reigned *everywhere*.

How much worse could a small town really be?

Sonnet was pinning a nomadic lifetime of hopes on this move north; a clean slate and brand-new life for the Hamilton sisters. She had it all mapped out: do up the old cottage, ease the girls into the local school, get herself work, save like the dickens, and send the girls off to join the ranks of aspiring modern women at university.

Then it would finally be Sonnet's turn, too.

That, after all, was the one personal thing this regional move had cost Sonnet, at least in the short term: the tertiary education she'd long coveted. Sonnet had no intention of fulfilling the prescribed housewife's role; counting children instead of accomplishments.

But there was no way she could leave her sisters now. They needed her, as they always had. Sonnet's brilliant career would have to wait – but not forever.

No one was promised forever.

Her gaze went to the urn set gingerly last night on a grimy shelf, releasing Mama from her crude travel arrangements – the socks and undergarments that had protected her from bumps.

You'll be free soon, Mama.

It was a priority to choose where her ashes should be spread. Their mercurial mama would never be at rest in a ceramic urn.

Plates clattered, jarring Sonnet from her ruminations. She swung legs out of a bed conspicuously empty of the smallest Hamilton, and headed down creaking stairs to investigate.